Alpha Lover

by

Brenda Sparks

The Alpha Council Chronicles
Book 3

Alpha Lover

Cover Art by *Rae Monet, Inc. Design*

The Wild Rose Press, Inc.
PO Box 708
Adams Basin, NY 14410-0708
Visit us at www.thewildrosepress.com

Publishing History
First Black Rose Edition, 2016
Print ISBN 978-1-5092-1243-9
Digital ISBN 978-1-5092-1244-6

The Alpha Council Chronicles, Book 3
Published in the United States of America

Dedication

To my beloved heartmate, Don,
who is Nicholai personified.
Your quiet strength keeps me grounded.

Acknowledgments

First and foremost, my deep appreciation goes out to my readers, who mean so much to me!

Much gratitude to Lisa Rayns and DW whose insights and feedback were invaluable to me while writing this story.

And last, but most certainly not least, I owe my sincere gratitude to my fabulous editor, Callie Lynn Wolfe, cover artist Rae Monet, and the wonderful staff at The Wild Rose Press for helping me share the Alphas with the world.

She had only a second to realize Nicholai stood in the doorway before Desmond's powerful thighs brought him to the door in a single bound.

He grabbed Nicholai's shirt with one hand, his other made a fist that landed squarely on Nicholai's jaw.

Nicholai's head snapped back. Shock took his face. With a mighty push, Nicholai threw Desmond backward across the room into one of the flowery couches. It moved under his weight, crashed into the end table, and the Tiffany lamp tumbled to the floor.

Julie's eyes went wide. The two men became a blur of motion, bodies flying apart, then back together. She had to concentrate to make out the shapes of hard forms in the powerful whirlwind.

Connor pulled, lunging at the whirling mass. His deep growls and barks added to the chaos as the two males swirled around the living room. They spun around the room like a tornado, moving so fast Juliette's eyes did not register their kicks and punches. However, she heard bones crunch and the slap of skin while the two exchanged blows.

The furniture that exploded when the blurry mass neared evidenced the fierceness of their battle. Julie watched one piece of furniture after the next burst into pieces. First her delicate coffee table, next the end table where the Tiffany lamp had been, then the rocking chair. When the mass moved toward the antique credenza, Juliette screamed.

Her beautiful roses sprayed about the room. Red petals floated slowly to the floor in surreal contrast.

Praise for Brenda Sparks

"Ms. Sparks takes you on a journey that'll have you turning pages just to find out what happens."

~Rhea Regale

~*~

"Brenda Sparks shines…In all, it was a great book and has me wanting more from the *Alpha Council Chronicles*!"

~DW Adler

Chapter 1

Ba-dum. Ba-DUM! BA-DUM!

The steady beating of the hearts around him called to the beast deep within. Anticipation of thick blood sliding down his throat sent his hunger into overdrive, created a need so great it would not be ignored. Nicholai Peterhof's fangs lengthened.

It had been too long since he'd partaken of the life-sustaining substance. Tonight the craving gripped him with its painful talons and demanded fresh, warm blood.

Nicholai sat as still as the empty chair across from him. The clank of dishes in the kitchen, the conversations of the patrons, the clinking of ice in the glass when the bartender poured a gentleman another round, all assaulted his sensitive hearing. Banging. Clattering. Yakking. Never ending noise that grated on his nerves. But it was the steady drumming sound that drew his attention.

Ba-dum! BA-DUM! BA-DUM!

An image of the local blood bank teased his mind.

Nicholai shook the image from his head. *No, I can't. There is a shortage as it is.*

I need a distraction, he thought.

The Alpha's gaze skimmed over the newly redecorated restaurant décor. The rich burnt-orange paint on the walls complemented the fine tablecloths.

1

Dark mahogany chairs, padded with burgundy velvet, matched the linen on the tables. The lighting set the dining area in a soft, angelic glow, but even the romantic ambiance didn't provide enough distraction.

Nicholai sat at his private table in a dark corner of the restaurant, forked another bite of food, and wished like hell it was another kind of sustenance. His body cried out in protest when the food hit his stomach. He needed blood, not food.

An attractive waitress sauntered up to the table, pad and pencil in hand. "Is there anything else you desire, Mr. Peterhof?" she asked in Russian.

Her eyes indicated the type of "else" she intended. Oh, there was something else, but he had a rule against feeding from locals. Most of the villagers in this small town were his friends or business associates, and he experienced guilt when he fed from them, then erased their memory.

Nicholai forced down the last morsel off his plate and patted his lips with the cloth napkin from his lap before placing it on the table. "I think you've given me enough for tonight," he replied coyly in their native language.

"Was it good?" she asked. "Did you like it?"

As much as I could. "Tell Chef he outdid himself."

The server nodded and walked away. Desperate for a diversion from the pounding hunger, Nicholai's eyes traveled down her back to her hips. They swayed seductively back and forth as she maneuvered expertly between the chairs, then stopped in front of two giggling women.

His gaze rested on the pulsing vein beneath the skin on the neck of the woman his waitress addressed.

He tuned his hearing to their conversation. Their Russian sounded child-like when they tried to explain to the waitress they wanted a refill on their drinks.

Once the waitress left, the women reverted back to English. Curiosity made him listen unabashedly as the women discussed their vacation.

"I can't believe we are in Yaroslavia," the beautiful brunette commented with a big smile. "I'm so glad Moscow and Saint Petersburg are close enough it only takes a few hours by car to get from one to the next. We'll be able to see a lot if we hop from city to city."

"That's why they are called the Golden Ring." Her skinny, blonde companion chuckled. "I want to bring lots of souvenirs back from our vacation to show my students and make my history class come alive for them."

So they are here on holiday. Based on their accents, Nicholai presumed the blonde to be British and the brunette to be American. *Perfect!*

Their animated voices grew louder when their discussion continued.

The blonde leaned forward. "I'm just glad my husband agreed it was safe to go as long as I went with someone."

The brunette grabbed her friend's hand. "I don't mind tagging along. After all, there's no reason for me not to go."

"You're such a good friend." Blondie embraced her in a hug. "I'll never be able to thank you enough!"

"You don't have to thank me. I'm sure this trip will be fun...For both of us," she added as an afterthought.

Nicholai noticed the disingenuous grin on the brunette's face.

"I know this trip is taking you from all the important things you could be doing over the holiday. How will you live without watching TV, grading papers, and going to bed early?" Sarcasm dripped from Blondie's voice, but her friend took it in stride.

"Don't be snarky," the brunette teased. "I sometimes go shopping or rent a movie to shake things up."

"Oh my. Forgive me. Here I thought *I* had an exciting life. I didn't realize you were living large." The pair chuckled at the good-natured ribbing.

"I realize, compared to trotting off around the world, my life might seem boring."

"Boring, no—Safe. Predictable. Mundane—"

The brunette's gaze left her friend and landed on the family of four sitting beside them. A young mother fed a baby its bottle while the father assisted their older child by cutting his sandwich.

The brunette's eyes clouded, and a sad smile tugged at the side of her mouth as if the scene triggered an unhappy memory.

The blonde pulled her from the melancholy moment by saying, "I can't wait to visit the Kremlin and St. Petersburg Square."

"I'm looking forward to seeing the sights too, but the only sight I need to see right now is the bathroom."

With a giggle, the women stood together and went into the darkened hallway that led to the bathrooms and his office. Exactly the opportunity Nicholai needed, as if the Fates themselves were giving the cosmic okay to sate his hunger.

His muscular body rose in one graceful, fluid movement, and he headed through the hallway behind them. His office, located at the end of the long corridor, provided the perfect place to wait for the ladies to emerge from the restroom. He smoothed his black cashmere sweater and crossed his arms over his wide chest. Nicholai leaned against the doorjamb and waited for the right moment to pounce.

Turning his preternatural senses toward the bathroom, he sensed only the two women within. The fragrance from the fresh flower arrangement on the marble vanity inside mingled with the scents of the women in the air.

One of them commented on the romantic blue and white paisley wallpaper and then the water turned on.

They should be coming out any time now. Nicholai's muscles tightened in expectation. He closed his eyes and imagined the two women primping in front of the mirror. The brunette combing her fingers through her shoulder-length hair as her blonde friend cleaned her hands.

"Oh Penny, I'm so happy you talked me into coming with you."

The flowing water became silent.

"I'm so glad you agreed to come with me. When Frank refused to come to Russia, I didn't believe I'd get to go," the one woman commented.

"I realize how much the trip means to you," her friend replied.

Paper towels shuffled, and Nicholai's stomach growled in anticipation.

"I love this little restaurant. The food is to die for," one of the women cooed, pulling the door open to hold it for her friend.

As the pair stepped into the hallway, Nicholai

swooped in.

"Hello, ladies," he greeted in English. "Allow me to introduce myself, I am Nicholai Peterhof. I am the owner of this fine establishment." His thick, Russian accent rolled his R's. Nicholai flashed his sexiest grin, the one that could melt a woman's heart. "I hope you enjoyed the cuisine. I searched the world over to find the right chef."

The blonde looked up and smiled into his eyes. "You own this place?"

"Yes. I do."

"We love it. It is so charming, and the food is absolutely delicious."

"Yeah, to die for," her friend reiterated.

Nicholai pursed his lips in a smirk at the brunette's choice of words. "I am glad you find the food so tempting. When I hired the chef, I discovered his specialties were all served cold. That is what inspired the name for this restaurant."

"*Kholodnaya Plecha*," the British blonde supplied the name, "which I believe translates to The Cold Shoulder."

"You are correct." Tired of the cat-and-mouse game, Nicholai looked deeply into the blonde's eyes, caught her in his hypnotic gaze.

"Come," he commanded. "I have something I'd like to show you."

"Of course," she agreed amicably.

The brunette's body tensed. "Where are we going?"

He turned the strength of his stare on her, capturing her honey-colored eyes. "It's all right," he soothed. "You can trust me, come with me."

She nodded her head in acquiescense. Nicholai gently guided the women down the hall and through the open door to his office. He followed behind, closing and locking the door with a thought.

"Sit down, ladies." He gestured toward the yellow tapestry, upholstered couch against one wall.

They obeyed, unable to resist. Nicholai sat between the two, his knees falling open so his thighs touched theirs.

He took the blonde into his arms, looked deep into her eyes, and made sure she was completely under his mental compulsion. The pounding of her pulse rumbled in his ears. The steady rhythm beat under her flesh. His hunger begged him to take a few tiny sips. *Not too much*, he reminded himself. Only enough to sustain him until the blood bank replenished his supply.

His lips rested reverently on her neck, and his fangs sank just deep enough to allow the flow of her blood into his mouth. He mentally fed her the pleasure he experienced as he drank in her life force. A low moan escaped her red lips. She lay pliant in his arms, her head rolled back to one side.

The other woman remained motionless beside him, completely in his thrall. His gaze flitted between the two as he worked to control them simultaneously. It was difficult to influence both, but centuries of practice had honed his mental skills.

A rapid beat pulled his attention. He quickly recognized the sound. Like galloping horses, a tiny heartbeat came from the woman in his arms. The distraction of keeping them both under control must have been why he initially missed the extra heartbeat in the room.

Nicholai berated himself for not realizing she was pregnant and immediately stopped drawing from her neck. After licking the small wounds closed, he let out a string of curses in his native language, and returned the blonde to an upright position, reverently laying her head against the back of the couch. He placed an ear on her stomach. The baby's heartbeat sounded strong and reassured him he had not done any harm to the unborn child or the mother. Both were alive and well.

His hunger still burned in his stomach, gnawed at him like a bear eating its prey. Nicholai wiped the memory of himself from the pregnant woman's mind and commanded her to sleep before he turned to the woman on his left.

He gathered her in his arms and gently pushed deeper into her mind. He cupped the back of her head in one large hand and pulled it to the side to expose the soft spot where her neck met her shoulder.

You will feel nothing but pleasure, he sent into her mind, then sank his fangs into her neck. Nicholai remained in her mind to assure himself she experienced only bliss.

A tidal wave of pleasure coursed through her body. She convulsed slightly as the power of the bite took her soaring. He tightened his grip, drawing her life blood into him.

When the first swallow flowed down his throat, it tasted unlike anything he experienced before. Like lilac and honey, it warmed him to the core, making his body come alive in a way no blood had ever done. His vision swam. His body reacted like an adolescent, becoming hard and achy with desire.

Mine! The thought came unbridled. He'd never

8

experienced anything so sweet. Holding her in his arms felt right. His body quaked. Realization smacked him in the face and snapped his head back.

She's my heartmate! The idea came to him on a wave of passion that coursed through his body. He became completely lost in the sensation.

Nicholai smiled, and a little red liquid escaped from his mouth. The ticklish sensation on his lips brought him back to the here and now. The blood trail from the two small bite marks he'd made drew his gaze. He quickly licked the wounds closed and adjusted her, bringing her onto his lap so he cradled her fully in his arms.

My heartmate. After hundreds of years, I finally found her. The person who is the other half of my soul. The one person who can make me complete.

She'd been chosen by fate as his beloved long, long ago. He looked at the enticing brunette, and an overwhelming urge to protect her overtook him.

The realization he held his heartmate shattered his concentration. Both women blinked as they surfaced from the depths of his thrall.

The woman in his arms looked up, her eyes widening. She squirmed against his solid embrace, bringing his attention back to what he had been doing. Nicholai gave himself a mental shake and refocused his thoughts. His mind reached out again and merged with the two women, but it was difficult to regain control of both simultaneously, for Nicholai's mind wouldn't cooperate. Instead, it wanted to focus solely on his heartmate. He realized his only course would be to handle one at a time.

Holding steady the woman in his arms, he kept her

to him, and turned his attention to the woman beside them. *You will go back out to the table. You will sit down and wait for your friend to join you. She is still in the bathroom. Eat and remember nothing of your time with me,* he instructed, putting a mental compulsion behind the command.

As if in a daze, the pregnant woman stood, silently crossed the room, and closed the door behind her when she left.

Nicholai gazed back into his heartmate's frightened eyes and loosened his grip. She braced her hand against his muscular chest and pushed.

"Who are you?" she demanded. "How did I get here? Where is Penny going?"

He easily slipped into her mind. *Shhhh,* he conveyed, sending her a wave of reassurance. *It's okay. You are fine. You are safe with me. I would never let anything happen to you. Calm yourself.*

She stilled in his arms. Combing his fingers through her hair, he brought a strand to his nose and inhaled her essence. She smelled of sweet lilacs. *You're safe, my sweet.*

Removing all evidence of his bite with the healing properties in his saliva, he carefully licked the blood trail from her neck. Nicholai leaned his forehead against his mate's and held her a little tighter, allowing himself to revel again at the thought of finding his one true love, the woman meant to be his for eternity. The earth seemed to shift under them, and he knew his world had forever changed.

His breath came in quick gasps, his heart thundered as if he'd finished a hundred-mile marathon. His physical reaction to the woman astounded him. He worked to calm his response, taking deep, soothing breaths in an attempt to center himself.

Nicholai noted her features, memorizing them, locked them in the deep recesses of his mind. He ran his fingers through her brown hair and over the roundness of her face. Full-figured by today's human standards, each of her curves pleased him. He lost himself in the beauty of her face. Her pink, rosy cheeks stood out against her pale complexion. Savoring the softness of her skin, he ran the back of his hand down one of those cheeks. He wanted to remain there forever, holding her in his arms but knew her friend would be suspicious if he did not allow her to return to their table soon.

Unable to let her go just yet, his mind raced. A thousand questions pinged around his mind. *What is your name? Where are you staying? What is your favorite food? Favorite color? Favorite flower?*

He'd settle for her name for now. "Tell me your name," he commanded.

"Julie."

Nicholai straightened. *Julie,* he thought. *Now I have a name to go with that beautiful face. Julie. My heartmate's name is Julie. It's perfect, just like her.*

He struggled to come up with a plausible way to get to know her. A plan took shape, a little devious, but still. A mischievous grin tugged at his top lip.

Reluctantly, he gave her a command to forget him. *Go back to your friend and do not remember our time together. Go to your table, sit down, and enjoy the rest of your meal. But you are jet-lagged. You want to go to your hotel right after you finish your meal.*

She blinked several times and rose to oblige his command. When she walked through the door, his instincts roared at him, demanded he scoop her up in his arms and take her to his home. Reining in the urge, Nicholai eased back and laid his head on the couch.

He needed to devise a way to win her love, make her want to be his forever. They belonged together. He knew it, the Fates ordained it, but she was human and had no concept of a heartmate, so he would have to woo her.

Nicholai had other friends who'd recently found their human heartmates as well. He remembered their struggles to win their loves—it would not be an easy path.

He needed a well-thought out plan, and luckily, one formed in his mind.

Nicholai followed his heartmate silently into the hall and stood motionless in the shadows, observing the woman make her way across the restaurant. In a dazed state, she went to her table and sat across from the blonde.

"Took you long enough, girl," her friend quipped with a smile.

"Sorry," she muttered absentmindedly before wagging her head as if to shake out the fuzzies.

"I am jet-lagged, Penny. Let's pay our bill and go back to our hotel. I'd like to rest."

Her friend nodded in agreement. "Yeah, sounds like a plan. I'm kinda tired, too."

Julie beckoned the waitress over with a wave of her hand. After paying their bill, the duo left under Nicholai's watchful gaze. His lean, athletic body shimmered, dissolved, became a fine mist streaming through the restaurant and out into the night air behind the women.

Chapter 2

Nicholai learned centuries ago how to conceal himself from those around him. To the rest of the world, he did not exist unless he chose to reveal himself. The special talent set him apart from other vampires.

Most learned to dematerialize, disappear from one place, and instantly materialize somewhere else, or manipulate the thoughts of those around them to conceal themselves, but Nicholai had discovered how to hold his particles together at the molecular level in an invisible mist. He used the power now to ghost along the street behind the women and follow them to their hotel.

Arm in arm, they came to a quaint little inn, at the end of the street. The interior, dark with only a few sconces on the walls providing light, welcomed the women inside. They both waved to the portly woman behind the desk who greeted them with a wide smile and a wiggle of her fingers.

Nicholai trailed behind them while they ascended the stairs. Penny stopped in front of one of the doors and fumbled through her purse. "I thought I had the keys."

Julie opened her handbag and dug inside. "Penelope Jones, what am I going to do with you? Here they are."

Julie pulled two room keys from her purse and handed the one with tag number 203 to her friend.

Penny unlocked the door, but before she disappeared behind the wooden portal, she stopped and took one last look at Julie. "So, we're in for the night, right? You don't want to go do anything else?"

"No." Julie shook her head, tousling her brunette locks. "I'm too tired. I just want to take a long, hot bath and crash. We'll get up first thing in the morning and do some sightseeing."

Penny's face lit up. "And I know just the place."

"Oh, where?" Julie's eyes widen with curiosity.

"Not gonna tell ya. It's a surprise. You'll have to wait until morning."

"All right. Very well. Sleep tight, Penny."

"You too, Jules," Penny called out, then stepped over the threshold and closed the door behind her.

Nicholai followed Julie into her room. She slid the chain into the lock, shucked off her shoes, and tossed the key onto the dresser. His heartmate turned and looked toward Nicholai, almost as if she knew he was there. If he didn't know better, he would have sworn she sensed his presence. This woman piqued his curiosity more each minute.

Julie grabbed a flannel gown and headed into the bathroom. Honor kept him from following. Nicholai remained in the bedroom. The room, small but homey, contained a full-size bed with a red and gold quilt. Matching red drapes hung to the floor, framing a window covered by a white sheer.

From the next room, Julie ran the water for her bath, and he heard the telltale splish-splash when she lowered herself into the tub.

Physically exhausted from keeping himself insubstantial, his concern of not being able to cloak his presence again warred with the desire to see to her safety. He wanted…no, needed to care for his heartmate, see to her protection, but with a heavy sigh, he realized locking the deadbolt was the best he could do for now, for he didn't dare stay the night.

He materialized by the door to her room and turned the deadbolt. He cast one last wistful glance in the direction of the bath and, by mere thought, dematerialized to his office.

Once in the chair behind his oak desk, Nicholai grabbed a stack of papers that required his perusal. Concentration eluded him. He read through the first paragraph and then the second, but the words blurred and Julie's image flooded his mind. His hair flowed around his neck when he shook his head and tried once again to absorb the words on the page. The scribbles held no significance.

Realizing the effort as futile, Nicholai gave up and placed his head in his hands.

He'd found his heartmate at long last. When her blood fed his cells, her very essence stirred inside him. It wrapped around Nicholai's heart in a gentle embrace which he knew would never let go. He sensed his Julie. She was a part of him now, forever his. He couldn't lose her. His heart wouldn't survive it.

Nicholai's body tingled. The hairs on the nape of his neck stood at attention. He sent his preternatural senses out taking in the sounds, smells, and sights of the night, seeking the trouble that put him on alert.

Nothing. Panic gripped his heart until it struggled to beat. *It must be Julie!*

His next thought took him to her side, leaving only a wisp of black smoke behind.

Chapter 3

Muscles tense, ready to pounce at the first hint of danger, Nicholai's body solidified inside Julie's room. His gaze flew to his beloved where she lay on the bed, unharmed. Her furrowed brows gave the only indication she suffered any distress as she slept. He forced a deep breath that filled his lungs with her delicious scent. He took in the rest of the tiny room with a sweeping glance, searching for anything out of the ordinary. He noted nothing but a small dresser from which clothes tumbled out onto the floor.

As he glanced down on the beautiful face of his love, Nicholai's heart clenched, threatened to stop altogether. Distress rolled from her in waves. Nicholai faded back into the shadows and watched his heartmate sleep, determined to be here should she need comfort from what was obviously a bad dream. Dawn approached. He should be in the safety of his home to avoid the deadly rays of the sun, but he could not tear himself away from his mate.

Julie's face twisted in pain. She thrashed wildly. Arms and legs flailed in a mock battle. Nicholai rushed to her side and pushed into her mind, determined to sooth her, but to his great shock, a mental wall blocked him. He concentrated harder, gave a vigorous push against the mental barrier. Determination fueled his effort, but success eluded him. Julie's strong emotions held him helpless to do more than watch the nightmare take his heartmate, her mind and body. Julie continued to writhe. Her head whipped from side to side as little moans of "no" escaped her.

When a scream pushed through her lips, his patience snapped. He could not just stand by and do nothing. Kneeling beside her, Nicholai pinned her arms above her head with one of his hands. Next, he gently cupped her chin in his free hand, stilling her head. He turned Julie's face away from him and exposed her delicate neck. As her legs continued to kick, he lowered his mouth to her creamy flesh. Nicholai ran his tongue down until he found the place where her pulse beat the strongest. He sank his fangs into the soft skin and drank. The sweet nectar of life flowed over his tongue, created ecstasy so intense it curled his toes and spilled out into his Julie.

Nicholai drew small sips from her vein until Julie's legs gradually stilled. The passion curled in their bodies simultaneously as he suckled at the neck of his heartmate. It tightened, coiled like a cat ready to strike. Right before it overwhelmed his common sense, he stopped drinking, pulled away, and licked the small wounds closed.

He intended to form a mindlink by drinking her blood, but the process was only half complete. Nicholai released his hold on Julie. She lay beside him calm, her body once again still, but the expression on her face indicated something still troubled her mind.

He bit into his wrist, and tiny beads of his blood pooled on his skin. He placed his wrist over Julie's open mouth, then rubbed her neck, triggering a reflexive swallowing action. When Julie's mouth closed around his flesh and took what he offered, a moan pushed through Nicholai's lips.

He knew the exact moment the blood exchange created the link. With a mental snap, the private line of communication only the two of them shared fell into place. Julie stirred as her consciousness began clawing its way to the surface. Using the link, Nicholai again tried to slip into Julie's mind. This time no barrier kept him out.

He soothed her mind back into a state of deep sleep, allowing her subconscious to once again take control. But this time he was determined to keep the nightmare away. Keep her safe, happy.

With the mental barrier gone, Nicholai easily saw into her dream.

A brown pickup truck sideswiped a black SUV, sending it careening over the embankment. Julie ran to the side of the road, watched the car tumble down. Dirt and debris spewed like a bully kicking sand on the beach. She screamed and dropped to her knees with one arm outstretched as if to pluck the occupants from the vehicle.

"Nooooooo!" she screamed.

Julie's grief and terror swamped his mind. Unwilling to allow her mental anguish, Nicholai helped her subconscious change the dreamscape.

The crumpled SUV disappeared and a beautiful meadow replaced the highway. The sun beat down on Julie's skin. It warmed her from the inside out.

Nicholai knew his blood gave her the sensation, but he allowed her mind to work its magical interpretation.

Julie found herself dressed in medieval garb with her ample cleavage spilling out from the tight bodice.

Long sleeves draped from her wrists as she turned circles beside an inviting pond. The cloth, golden and heavy, shimmered in the sun.

Veiled by the surrounding forest, Nicholai observed Julie spin with her arms outstretched. She reveled in the warmth of the sun until dizziness overtook her and she fell onto her bottom, giggling.

The sound of Julie's laughter raced down Nicholai's spine, leaving tiny footprints of happiness in its wake. He smiled at his heartmate when she brushed a stray curl from her face and stared longingly at the pond. The cool water appeared inviting, and under the warmth of the sun, it only took her a second to make up her mind.

"If ever there was a day to go skinny-dipping, this is it," Julie said.

A wide, sheepish grin took Nicholai's face.

Chapter 4

Julie stripped her heavy clothing with haste and dove headlong into the welcoming pool of water. When she surfaced, she brushed the water from her eyes and glanced up to discover a man had joined her. Correction, a very beautiful man with shaggy, raven hair that hung loosely about his face. He wore a knight's armor, complete with a coat-of-arms painted on the chest plate. As he looked down on her, his amber eyes appeared older than their years. They did not match the smooth, youthful face with a smile that melted her soul.

The knight knelt on one knee beside the pond. "I see you are out taking a swim, milady."

"Yes. It is such a hot day. I thought I'd cool off." Julie swam toward the middle of the pond so the dream knight would not be able to see her naked body.

"May I join you? It's been a long, hot journey, and I too could use a cool dip." With the tip of one gloved finger in the water, the knight sent a sequence of ripples toward Julie.

Julie desperately wished she'd dreamt a bathing suit. Even in her dream world, she was self-conscious about her less than perfect forty-year-old body. She knew she was overweight with too-straight hair and a nose a little too long for her face. Julie was about to say no when her dream knight rose and started taking off his armor. Apparently, he had no intention of waiting for her reply.

"I- I don't know your name," Julie sputtered when her mind refused to work, too distracted by the sight before her.

The man slowly removed each piece of armor, exposing a bit of flesh with each subtraction. His muscles shifted with each graceful movement, drawing her attention first to his arms, then his handsome chest, next to his thick thighs and finally to the codpiece. With the last piece of mail finally removed, he exposed himself fully to her appreciative view.

"My name is Nicholai." A sexy grin took his face, but it didn't hold her attention for long.

Julie's eyes roamed his physique. He stood tall, his shoulders broad. A powerful, thick chest narrowed to slim hips. The muscles on his flat stomach divided into ridges, which led to the thick black curly hair that nestled his most impressive male part.

Julie blushed and glanced away as he dove into the water. She'd never seen such a perfect male specimen. As if chiseled from stone by a great artist, his body was an absolute contrast to her own soft curves.

Nicholai surfaced beside her and brushed his hair away from his face with one hand. His eyes sparkled as he looked upon her and smiled. "I hope you don't mind, but I couldn't resist."

"I know what you mean. The water is inviting."

"It is not the water I could not resist, my dear. I could not resist you." With that he reached for her and pulled her against his hard body. Julie opened her mouth to protest his statement, not believing for a second a man like him found her irresistible, but before

she said a word, his mouth covered hers.

His skillful tongue slipped into her mouth when her lips parted with a gasp. His kiss, light but thorough, made a sinuous warmth spread through her. She gave herself over to the sensation. Her inhibitions took flight as she decided to go where this dream took her. Determined to shut off the self-critical part of her mind, she allowed him to support her full weight as he swam the two of them to the shore. He picked her up as if she weighed no more than a child and carried her to a blanket that suddenly appeared.

When he laid her upon the soft blanket, the grass crushed beneath her body. She wished for darkness, so she could make love to him without worrying about her body. When the thought crossed her mind, clouds turned the sky to pitch.

Nicholai drew back slightly. "Why did it get dark?"

"I just thought it would be nicer in the dark." Julie brought her hand to her kiss-swollen lips unsure where the dream headed.

Suddenly the sun returned, bathing the lovers in its warm light. "I want to see your face as I ravish you. I want to see the passion in your eyes when you come for me. We will make love in the light, so I can see each and every lovely...sexy...inch of your magnificent body." Nicholai punctuated each adjective with a kiss on her neck.

Julie's head lolled back when Nicholai continued to assault her senses with his ministrations. Since this was a dream, she decided to live with the light.

Besides, I want to see his magnificent body as much as he wants to see mine, *she thought as*

Nicholai's lips started a path down her body.

A low moan pushed from her lips. Heat curled in her tummy, and her legs wiggled of their own volition.

Nicholai kissed his way to her stomach and took the weight of her breasts in each hand. She arched into his touch as he kneaded them gently, teasing her nipples into hard peaks with his thumbs. He followed his kissing trail back up and sucked one of the peaks into his mouth. His tongue swirled the pink pebble while his freed hand made its way to the juncture between her thighs.

There he teased her sensitive nub with his thumb as his fingers slid in and out of the silky folds nestled beneath. Pleasure built quickly within. Fostered by Nicholai's skillful touch, it rose until Julie screamed her release. Side to side her head turned while she gripped the blanket with both hands.

Nicholai watched, as he said he would, while she came for him for the first time. Julie's eyes focused on his, while the last waves rippled through her body. Nicholai looked down on her with intense hunger. Her breaths puffed heavily with the weight of her ecstasy.

A look of male satisfaction was wiped away by something darker. "I must go for now, my dear," Nicholai informed her.

"Why?" she cried, hoping she didn't sound as desperate as she felt. Her body ached with need. She frantically wanted him buried inside her.

Nicholai ran the back of one hand gently over her cheek. "Our time for tonight has come to an end, but I will return again."

His comment confused her. It was daytime in the dream. What did he mean by "our time for tonight"?

"Please stay with me a little longer. You didn't get to...I mean I'm the only one who..."

Nicholai smiled, seemingly pleased she cared about his pleasure. "Giving you pleasure, gives me pleasure. I live to see to your needs, milady." He tipped his head in a salute.

"Will I see you again?"

"Oh, yes. We shall meet again, soon. The approaching dawn is forcing me to leave, but nothing in the world could keep me from seeing you again."

Julie closed her eyes to the dream world and wished her dream man was real.

Her eyes fluttered open. In the dim light of the rising sun, she thought she saw a wisp of smoke. She rubbed her eyes, and it disappeared, much like the knight had.

Her knight in shining armor.

How amazing he'd been. Her mind had done her proud coming up with him. Of course, no such man existed in real life, but oh, to think of the dreams she would have, with her knight as the star. Her heavy eyes drifted shut, and Julie hoped sleep might take her back into Sir Nicholai's arms.

Chapter 5

Nicholai paced the floor of his bedchamber and let out a series of foul curses. He berated himself for the shared dream. With Julie radiating so much emotional pain, he only meant to slip into the dream to steer it in a positive track. He'd intended to ease her suffering and perhaps gather a bit of information about his beloved, but instead he'd lost self-control and the direction he allowed the dream to take shamed him. At any time, he could have changed its course, but he allowed his lust for his heartmate to rule. As a result, he had only learned about her body, not her soul.

But at least she wasn't in pain anymore. A smirk crossed his lips. Yeah, definitely not in pain, not after the way he pleasured her.

His cock, still hard from the excitement created by the shared dream, throbbed with each beat of his heart. He pounded his fist into the opposite hand in frustration, not from being denied his own release, but because once in the dream, his desire took on a life of its own. He found his lust rose to consume him and take control.

Nicholai removed his clothes with a little more force than necessary and balled up his shirt before he chucked it across the room. It hit the wall and dropped to the floor. He followed suit with his pants, which pooled into a heap on top of his shirt.

The frustrated vampire made his way to the bathroom and turned the faucet full force to the left. A cold shower was exactly what he needed. Hoping to force the need from his body, he turned each of the six heads in the large shower so they cascaded on him. The frigid water shocked his system into submission. But still, he could not tear his thoughts away from his heartmate and the passion that flowed between them.

He closed his eyes, then leaned his forehead against one wall as the shower heads pounded their icy fists onto his lower back. When images from the dream pushed into his mind, Nicholai took a deep breath. Needing a distraction, the Alpha washed his hair and body thoroughly, attempting to scrub away his lustful thoughts.

It worked. *Thank the Fates.*

Once his libido died down, he exited the shower and grabbed a towel. He wrapped it around his waist, then moved to the double vanity. After pulling a comb through his hair, he eyed his reflection in the mirror. *I need a way to win Julie, and sexual encounters in a dream world are not the way to do it.*

He needed a plan, but daylight had come. It pulled at him, begging him to rest. After patting down with the towel, he climbed in between the cotton sheets on his bed. Nicholai interlaced his fingers behind his head, closed his eyes, and tried to sleep, but his mind would not cooperate. Images of Julie haunted him like an ethereal muse. They urged him to create a plan to win his love.

He plucked the remote from the nightstand and pushed a button. Tchaikovsky, his favorite composer, played through the stereo speakers. As "Waltz of the

Flowers" serenaded him, Nicholai tried once again to sleep. His mind fought to devise a plan of action. He concentrated on the soft music, trying to quiet his turbulent thoughts, but sleep eluded him as he lay in his massive bed. His eyes flew open, and he forced them closed again.

He tossed and turned, battered his pillow in a futile effort to make it comfortable. After several fretful hours, he gave up on sleep and decided to replay his plan to win Julie in his mind.

Chapter 6

After sleeping late and having a leisurely breakfast at the inn, Julie and Penny toured the Kremlin. Julie stared in awe when they approached Moscow's Cathedral of the Annunciation.

In stark contrast to the white building, sunlight softly burnished the gilded domes of the cathedral with light and shadow. The white and gold reminded Julie of the angel costumes she had made the girls one Halloween. Tears pushed into her eyes at the memory of those little angels.

"Give me the camera," Julie commanded. "You get to be the model for this shot."

With Penny in front of the church, Julie let the camera hide the escaped tear running down her left cheek. She steeled herself against the memories that tried to flood her mind.

"That's enough," announced Penny when Julie kept clicking the shutter. "Let's move on. I want to make a true panoramic walking picture tour for my students."

"You mean like a virtual tour?" Julie handed the camera to Penny.

"Exactly." A wide smile lit Penny's face. "Why do you think I've been snapping pictures all day?"

"Then we'd better hurry, if you want to see the whole Kremlin today."

For hours, they walked inside the Kremlin. The pair went through Lenin's Mausoleum, admired the Broken Bell statue that had never rung, and strolled past a green oxidized cannon that had never fired. Penny took pictures of everything allowed.

As afternoon fell toward evening, they stopped in front of a green tank with a large red star painted on the side. Penny positioned Julie next to the vehicle. The thick cashmere scarf wrapped around her neck and the black trench coat she wore were not enough against the frigid December air. Even with the wool lining in the coat, she shivered when the wind whipped around her. She forced herself to remain still and smile when Penny stood across from her, camera in hand.

"You get into the picture this time." Julie motioned for her friend to switch places with her.

"No, my students don't want to see me," Penny protested with a shake of her head.

"They don't want to see me either," insisted Julie.

"I want to be able to prove you were here. Now smile." Penny lifted the digital camera in front of her face as Jules squinted against the sun. "Say Vladimir Putin is scootin'," called Penny, then she waited for Julie to flash her smile before she clicked the camera button.

Julie walked around the tank, admiring the grandeur of it. They appeared much smaller in pictures. Four of them lined up stoically as if ready to defend the Kremlin from a military onslaught.

She went around the front and regarded the barrel mounted on the turret. The distraction caused her to run headlong into a woman whose blonde hair hung down well past her waist.

"Oh, excuse me," Julie attempted to say in Russian.

With its wide eyes and flared nostrils, the woman's startled face said more than words could have.

Penny jogged up to join her. "She meant excuse me, not squeeze me," corrected Penny, speaking Russian much better than Julie had.

"*Da*," the woman replied tersely. She gave Julie a sideways glare as she passed, and a snarl pulled at one corner of her mouth.

"Sorry," Julie called out in English. "How do you say 'sorry' in Russian?" she asked her friend.

"Pra-stEE-te," informed Penny.

"*Prostite*," called Julie back over her shoulder toward the woman. "Dang, did you notice the way she looked at me?"

"Well, Jules, you did ask the woman to squeeze you." Penny laughed. "I might be a little upset too if you had run me over, then asked me to squeeze you."

"She looked like I disgusted her."

Penny wrinkled her nose. "Maybe you smell bad."

Julie slapped at her friend's biceps, and the two women laughed.

"Look, never mind. Don't worry about it. It's over and done with. Listen, I'm getting hungry again. Do you want to go to the GUM and get something to eat?"

"Thought you'd never ask!"

Julie had waited all day to go to the GUM, and it didn't disappoint with its three parallel arcades centered around a fountain. Light flooded through the building's glass roof to illuminate the souvenir stands, foreign stores, and designer boutiques that filled the space. Being Moscow's State Department Store, the GUM was the largest mall in Moscow. Christmas lights hung from the ceiling, and Christmas trees lined the walkways, adding to the ambiance.

Tray in hand, Julie turned around from her place in line and watched Penny sit at a round table under a red umbrella. The tables were arranged on a bridge that spanned the walkway three floors below. It afforded them a wide view of the Christmas shoppers milling about. With its elegant interior, the place appeared more like a palace than a shopping center.

Penny pulled the red pompom hat from her head. When her fine hair stuck straight out from the static, she smoothed it down, then glanced up and smiled as Julie meandered up to the table.

"Here you go, fresh off the grill." Julie placed the tray in front of Penny and sat across from her friend. "It's nice to relax for a while after all the sightseeing."

"I believe we walked about a hundred miles today." Penny crossed her legs and stabbed her rigatoni.

"Just think, Penny, we still have an evening of shopping ahead of us." Anticipation made Julie's smile reach her eyes.

She loved shopping, and the GUM had been at the top of her must-see list for the trip. It didn't matter how many miles they had already walked today; when it came to shopping, Julie had the energy to go.

"This place is so big. I'm not sure we can see it all before closing time tonight."

Julie nodded in agreement and took a bite of the lasagna she had ordered from the Bosco Café. The food tasted delicious and not what she'd expected. Eating gourmet Italian food in the Russian Kremlin made her smile at the contrast.

"What's got you so happy?" Penny popped another

bite of rigatoni into her mouth.

"Good food and a night full of shopping ahead of me. What's not to be happy about?"

"Only you would be looking forward to more walking."

"Think of it as more shopping, not more walking," offered Julie.

Unease crept over her skin, making goose pimples dot her flesh. Apprehension blanketed her, unsettled her. She glanced over each shoulder, took in her surroundings, but everything seemed in order.

A couple hugged by a Christmas tree. A mother tugged the arm of her child who obviously didn't want to leave the toy store. An older gentleman sat down at the table beside theirs. He smiled and gave a little nod in her direction when he noticed her looking.

Julie forced a tight smile. Though she did not see anything amiss, Julie couldn't shake the notion of being watched.

Chapter 7

After a quick shower, Nicholai carefully chose his attire. He picked a dark blue sweater and jeans. He took a moment to glance at his reflection in the mirror, liking what he saw. Suddenly, he realized how silly it was to be concerned about how he looked. If everything went according to plan tonight, Julie would not know he had been in her room, let alone see him. He shook his head at his reflection. *I'm acting like a fool.* He assumed that tended to happened to a male when he found his heartmate. After all, both Stephan and Marcus did ridiculous things once they'd found their mates. Nicholai chuckled. It must be a typical reaction for a male—to lose all common sense when thinking of his woman.

He descended the stairs to the first floor of his home and grabbed the peacoat from the closet. He shrugged into the dark jacket, wrapped it tightly around his lean body, and checked the time on his watch. Well after midnight, he should find Julie sleeping soundly in her hotel room.

He sent his senses out into the night to make sure he did not detect any unrest. Sensing nothing unusual, Nicholai cinched the belt around his waist. With the ease of centuries of practice, he scattered his particles to the wind and reformed in the hotel room of his beloved.

He stood next to her bed, expecting to find her

beautiful face framed by a pillow. The bed, still made with the quilt tucked beneath the pillows, appeared pristine and quite empty.

Where is she? It's midnight. Panic crept up his spine like the stinging tentacles of a giant jellyfish. It prickled his skin. He fought down the wave of dread threatening to consume him. Surely if something had happened to her, he'd know. He would have experienced it as he had the previous night when her nightmare gripped her hard with fear.

He took a deep, calming breath and tried to figure out where she might be at this late hour. Did she or her friend mention something yesterday about their plans for this evening?

As Nicholai replayed their conversation from the day before, he heard female voices in the hallway and tuned his preternatural hearing toward the door.

"Penny, that was the best! I had a fun time. What a great surprise. Thank you for taking me to Red Square today."

"Of course. I'm sorry we got back so late."

"Oh, that's okay," assured Julie.

The hell it is, thought Nicholai. *My heartmate should not be out this late, in a foreign country no less, alone and unprotected. Does the woman have no common sense?*

"But I am definitely tired," Julie continued.

"Yeah, me too, but we sure had an enjoyable day."

"All right, I'll see ya in the morning." With that, a key slipped into the lock, and the deadbolt turned. His body dissolved into an invisible mist. Hovering above the bed, he watched his mate enter. The sight of his mate made his heart sing.

Julie closed the door and slid the chain lock into place after bringing the deadbolt home to rest. He stayed insubstantial while she got ready for bed, brushed her teeth, and crawled between the sheets.

He waited, watched the rise and fall of her breasts beneath the sheets with each breath, reveling in the knowledge he would soon be treated to this sight every night—once she agreed to be his. Her breaths became longer, smoother. Her eyes flickered back and forth behind her lids, indicating she dreamed.

Nicholai materialized silently alongside the bed and ran the back of his hand down her cheek. He needed to be with her, beside her, the draw unlike anything he'd ever experienced.

He intended to slip into her dream and gather information about his love—that was all. But the tempting sight of her lying on the bed stirred his desire.

No male could resist the pull of his female. The need to lie down next to her was too strong to fight, he placated himself by deciding to remain on top of the red and gold quilt to make sure things didn't become too tempting.

When the mattress sagged under his muscular weight, Julie instinctively rolled toward him. She snuggled against his chest. He automatically wrapped one arm around her waist and hugged her to him in a gentle embrace, careful not to wake her. He inhaled her lilac scent.

A sense of peace and tranquility moved through him as he held the other half of his soul. Lying next to her, holding her, made him complete. It seemed so right. When she moved against him, the sinuous slide of her leg against his made his libido stand up and take notice. He closed his eyes and slipped into her dream.

****

Jara paced the cave. Her Amazonian frame created long strides that quickly ate up the space. A corona of blue light glowed around her as her energy gathered into her hand. She tossed the energy ball onto the torch sitting in a sconce on the granite wall. When she tossed a second ball into the fireplace, the kindle ignited, and a fiery glow bathed the room.

Her brother, the King of the Demons, was a wimp. Oh, he hadn't always been that way. Nope, he used to be a strong male. With the build of a warrior, his six-foot ten-inch frame boasted muscles so thick he'd put most body builders to shame. He could have any woman he wanted, and he wanted *her.*

"Elizabeth." Jara spat the name of her brother's mate and gathered her golden locks over one shoulder.

Great Spirit, how she despised the half-breed. Half-human, half-demon, she brought turmoil into their home. Her red eyes glowed in anger just thinking about how much Varrick obsessed over that woman.

The sound of a phone jarred her from her internal tirade, and she plucked the thing from the nightstand.

"Hello," she answered, knowing who it would be.

"Hello, dear sister."

"Lovazia, my darling. How are you?"

"I've been better."

Jara folded her gown around her legs and sat gracefully on the padded chair in front of the fire. "I'm sure, sweetheart. It's never easy to lose a mate. Alcid was a great demon. Powerful. Always treated you well."

A tired sigh sounded through the phone. "He was a

good mate. If those damned bloodsuckers hadn't ambushed him—"

"Do you know for sure vampires killed him?" Jara interrupted. "I mean, we all grew up hearing the stories, but very few actually claim to have seen a bloodsucker."

"His head was ripped from his body, Jara. All the blood drained." Jara heard a catch in Lovazia's voice. "And I'll never forget the smell. Great Spirit, the stench of vampire is unforgettable."

"I imagine." Jara crossed her legs and decided a change of subject was in order. "So tell me what has been happening in your life."

"I bumped into a vampire yesterday."

"You what?" Jara stood.

"I literally bumped into a vampire."

"Wha…where…how do you know it was a bloodsucker?" Concern for her sister made Jara pace the room.

"The smell. I knew the minute I bumped into her. Oh, she played it off. Made it seem like she'd accidentally bumped into me, but I knew better."

"What do you mean, you knew better?" Jara worried her bottom lip between her teeth.

"The stink of vampire rolled off her in waves. It curled my nose."

Jara's fingers curled into her palm. "Tell me you didn't confront her."

"No. I followed her though. She and her friend went shopping in the GUM, like they were just a couple of normal people."

"Maybe they *were* just a couple of normal people?" Jara's tone rose with hope as she pushed her fingers through her long, wavy locks.

"No. The bloodsucker has to die. They all deserve to die for what they did to Alcid."

Her younger sister had taken after their mother's side of the family. Her light frame and skinny physique didn't lend itself to winning a fight, even if the demon could morph into most any animal she wanted.

"Sister dear, don't do anything stupid. You should run. Hide. Don't go looking for trouble."

"Trouble found me, Jara. I'll do what I have to do. Gotta go. Bye."

The phone went dead. Dread coursed through Jara's veins. Her sister was halfway across the world in Russia. She must inform Varrick. He'd know what to do.

Chapter 8

Nicholai glanced at the surroundings in the dreamscape. Many youngsters milled about. Lockers covered one of the hallway walls, and a series of green doors lined the opposite wall. At the end of the hall, a small woman stood with her back to him. Her brunette hair swayed on her shoulders when she crossed her arms over her midriff. She appeared to be keeping guard.

It only took him a second to recognize the brunette. As the realization dawned, Julie turned around. He quickly scooted back against the wall, hiding himself in a break between the rows of lockers.

The banner strung across the hallway read,
Go Bulldogs!

Boys in varsity jackets walked, hand in hand, with girls in green and white cheerleading uniforms. A bell rang, and children scattered like seagulls on a beach running from the waves.

Pulled by a stunning voice streaming into the hall, Nicholai strolled through the hallway to where he had last seen his beloved. The beautiful aria pulled at his soul. It drew him toward one of the nondescript green doors.

He peeked through the tiny window in the door and found Julie singing. Her arms were outstretched, head held high. His gaze swept the faces of her students.

They appeared completely enthralled by her voice.

Having been to the opera many times, he'd heard hundreds of singers, but none compared to the way his heartmate sounded to him. Julie's range versatility astounded Nicholai as her voice rose three octaves in beautiful succession. The notes of her bel canto *floated on the air. The virtuoso runs and trills that demanded real flexibility and range of voice flowed easily from her lips.*

The beauty of her voice brought a tear to Nicholai's eye. Julie dreamt about singing in a secondary school. Was she performing for the students? Or was she a teacher here?

His mate stopped, lowered her hands, and grabbed the sheet music from the stand in front of her. "Okay, ladies, that's the correct pitch for the soprano part. Did you notice how the fifth flowed into the minor seventh?" She paused, allowing the students to nod. "All right, we will try again. Let's take it from the bridge."

Julie flipped through the sheet music until she found the measure she wanted.

"Are you ready?" Julie lifted her arms in a conductive stance.

"One. Two. Three. Four." She counted off the rhythm and swept her arms down to indicate the down beat, directing them.

The students sang in perfect harmony. The smile that crossed Julie's face took Nicholai's breath away. He'd never seen anyone more beautiful. The sheer bliss she displayed while listening to her students perform amazed him. Tingles worked through his body. She looked truly stunning, and her voice...Angelic was not strong enough a term.

Nicholai appreciated the talent his heartmate displayed and found it an aphrodisiac.

Maybe coming to her again in a dream wasn't such a good idea, *he thought.* It is too easy to change the course of the dream and allow my lust to rule.

Calm down, *he reprimanded himself.* You're only here to get information, nothing more. This time stay focused, do not let your lust carry you away.

With a swoop of her hand, she ended the aria.

One of the boys in the front of the room, a small boy with lots of freckles and short red hair, raised his hand. "Hey, Ms. Saint-John?"

Saint-John, *Nicholai repeated to himself.* Now I have a last name to go with the first. This might have been a good idea after all.

"Yes, Robbie," she replied.

"Can you tell me again what time we have to be at the theater for our performance?"

"I put it in the note you took home yesterday." Julie huffed an exasperated sigh. *"You must be there at six o'clock sharp. The show starts at seven, and you need to be there early enough to have time to get into your costumes." She turned her attention to the rest of the class. "Remember you have to come already dressed in your black pants or skirts and white tuxedo shirts. I'll have your green bow ties and cummerbunds. That goes for all of you. Make sure you are on time. Understand?"*

"Yes, Ms. Saint-John," Robbie and the rest of the students called out in unison.

Being a shadow in her mind, Nicholai sensed the students in front of her were indeed her real students.

She taught at a school with a bulldog for a mascot and green and white as the school colors.

Another piece of the puzzle. Finding out more about my heartmate may be easier than I had anticipated, *he thought.*

When an inspired thought crossed his mind, a roguish grin spread across his face. I know just how to find out more information about Julie.

He opened the door and stepped into the classroom.

Julie turned, and recognition widened her eyes. She cleared her throat. "Uh, may I help you?"

"Yes, you may. I need you to accompany me to my office," Nicholai replied.

"Where is your office?"

"I believe you know where the principal's office is, Ms. Saint-John. Please come with me. I have something I need to discuss with you."

Julie nodded, then turned back to her class. "Class, will you excuse me for a minute? It seems I'm being summoned to the principal's office."

"Ooohhh," sang Robbie. "Hope you're not in too much trouble."

When Julie opened her mouth to reprimand the child, Nicholai stepped further into the room and pinned the boy with his glare. "I can assure you your teacher is not in any trouble at all. But you will be, young man, if you disrespect her again."

He turned on his heels and opened the door, holding it for Julie as she walked through.

Nicholai took her arm in his to escort her down the green and white halls to the office. He shortened his gait, so her smaller legs easily kept pace. The hallway morphed into an office as they walked along.

"Please, sit down." He gestured to one of the two chairs situated in front of a large mahogany desk.

Julie obeyed, sitting quietly. She smoothed out her flowery dress, then folded her hands in her lap while Nicholai sat in the leather chair behind the desk.

"What did you wish to see me about?" Julie tugged her lower lip between her teeth. The nervous gesture made his desire stir.

"I have some good news." Nicholai leaned forward and rested his clasped hands on the desk. "You have been chosen as this year's Teacher of the Year."

"Really?" Her gorgeous smile beamed so bright it lit her eyes.

"Yes, really. It is quite an honor, you know."

"Yes, yes I know. I can't believe I won Teacher of the Year."

"Congratulations. As part of the process you have to answer a questionnaire about yourself." Nicholai produced a pen and paper. "Shall we begin?"

"Sure." Julie's eyes widened with excitement.

"First question. What is your name?"

"Julie Saint-John."

"Julie, is that short for something else?"

"Juliette."

"Juliet..." he mused thoughtfully, "...as in Romeo and Juliet?*"*

"Yes. My mother had a thing for the Shakespeare play, except she spelled it with two t's and two e's."

" 'What light through yonder window breaks? It is the east, and Juliette,' with two t's and two e's, 'is the sun,' " Nicholai quipped.

His thoughts trailed. How lucky he was to find the

Juliette to his Romeo. He wondered how she would like being with him, living in his home, being taken care of by him. He couldn't wait to be with her outside of the dream world. Oh, the places he would take her, the things they would do together, the love they would make. Nicholai shook himself out of his reverie and returned to his line of questioning.

"So, on to the next question. How long have you been teaching?"

"Fifteen years," she answered quickly and crossed her legs.

Nicholai's gaze fell to those tempting legs. He imagined the softness of the skin he would find if he ran his hand up her leg. He cleared his throat. "Where do you teach?"

Julie squinted at him questioningly. "Here—" She hesitated. "At Williamton Secondary School."

Nicholai recognized the mistake he'd made and attempted to cover by saying, "I just wanted to see if you were paying attention." He gave her his most dashing smile. "Okay, on to the next question. Family?"

"I have a mother and a father."

"What about any sisters or brothers?" Nicholai leaned forward on the desk in interest. This was working out better than he had planned.

"Only one sister, but I don't understand what my family has to do with being Teacher of the Year." Julie raised a questioning brow, as Nicholai pretended to write down her answers.

His mind whirled, tried to think of a logical question to quell her suspicions.

"And you teach chorus," he said, more a question

then a statement.

"Yes, that's right. I teach chorus."

"And your address?"

"I live at 210 Hamlet Court, here in Williamton."

Nicholai smiled. This line of questioning was getting him somewhere. He pushed away from the desk and moved around to the front. After leaning against it, he crossed his legs at the ankles and braced his hands behind him on the desk. "So tell me, Ms. Saint-John, do you like working at my school?"

"Well, yes," she answered with haste. "Of course, I absolutely adore the children. And some of them are quite talented. They are an absolute joy to work with."

"Do you like working with me?" Nicholai pinned her with a pointed stare.

She looked up from under her long, dark lashes. While she contemplated her answer, a luscious, pink tongue darted out to moisten her lips. The sight almost drove him to his knees. He couldn't wait for the time when he would taste those lips in the real world.

"To be honest, sir, I don't really know the answer to that question."

"You may not know how to answer that question, but I can tell you how I feel. I have to say I am very, very happy to have you in my school." Nicholai stared at her sensual lips, longed for the taste of her kiss. "Not only because you are talented and good with the kids, but also because I find you quite attractive."

"You're just saying that." Julie's gaze dropped to the floor as her cheeks flushed.

When Nicholai realized she still found it hard to believe he'd be attracted to her, he became determined to raise her self-esteem. And he knew exactly how to do it.

He'd kiss her senseless, pour his love and tenderness into the caress until she had no choice but to realize how wanton and desirable she was. When he pushed away from the desk, the force sent the paraphernalia flying. The pencils and pens hit the floor with a curious metallic sound.

"What was that?" asked Julie.

"The stuff hitting the floor," he murmured and cupped her soft her cheeks between his hands.

"No, listen." Julie pulled away as the sound reoccurred.

Nicholai realized it came from outside the dream, something in the real world. "I will go see."

He pulled from the dream abruptly.

Chapter 9

Nicholai's eyes snapped open and immediately scanned the room, coming to rest upon his Juliette as she lay asleep in his arms. Nothing in the room appeared disturbed, but he realized the noise had not been part of the dream.

Julie stirred, as if struggling to rouse from her dream. The sensation of her body moving against his under the covers sent a rush of fire through his blood. How he longed to remain, feel her body next to his, but she could not find him there. Nicholai made his body insubstantial and hovered above when her eyes fluttered open.

Julie heaved a heavy sigh and smiled. He pushed into her mind, curious to know what brought the sweet smile to her beautiful face.

She stretched lazily. The dream had seemed so real. She swore the sensation of his hands against her skin lingered.

Those dreams with my handsome knight are wonderful but too good to be true, she thought as she rolled over and hugged a pillow under her chest.

He ached to lie beside her again. His whole being screamed at him to kiss her for real, now, but that would have to wait. What sweet, painful torture it was waiting for the special moment to happen between the two of them.

The noise sounded again, a loud metallic bang from outside of the inn. Nicholai sent his senses out. They flowed over the environment until he discovered a blank spot near the back of the building. He examined it closely and decided the best way to describe the sensation or lack thereof was to liken it to a black hole in space. *Strange.*

After checking her door to be sure it was locked tight, his essence slipped under, down the stairs and out the front door. Sensing himself alone, he took corporeal form at the bottom of the inn steps. A light snow began to fall, dusting his dark hair and shoulders as his long, graceful strides ate up the pavement.

He crept around the building, seeking the cause of the void. Seeing nothing, his senses flared out once more, pushing further into the night. The warrior discovered two men in a heated argument in an alleyway behind the closest bar and noted the bread shop owner slept above her store. Animals scurried about. A pair of owls hooted in the tree in front of the inn, while a wolf ran away from the edge of town. His senses told him much. All things he would expect to find, except the blank spot...which had disappeared.

Did I imagine it?

He had always been able to sense animals, humans, other vampires, but to have an area where his preternatural senses did not pick up the world was something new. What might have caused it?

In his long life, he did not recall another of his kind having experienced such a thing. Surely, he would have heard of it happening to others. Perhaps it was something unique to him.

Might the dead spot be some side effect from being

in Julie's dreams? He had never been in a dream two nights in a row. Perhaps that played a trick on his mind. The dream had been so real and snapping out might have caused his senses to misfire.

Regardless, his instinct to protect his heartmate forced him to check around the inn. While the snow fell in heavier flakes, he circled the building one more time and ensured everything appeared to be in its rightful place. A Dumpster nestled against the wall of the building, with its pungent aroma wafting in the air. A tabby cat trotted lazily down the alley.

He observed the ground, searched for anything out of the ordinary. Satisfied everything was secure and his heartmate was safe for the night, he dematerialized back to his home to await the next evening just as the first rays of dawn approached.

****

Torches lit the way as Jara traveled quickly through the granite halls. She and Varrick had grown up in this mountain compound. She knew every nook and cranny. Every shortcut.

She used one such shortcut to get to Varrick's throne room. Her guard, Cyrus, followed silently behind as always. Such an unnecessary precaution, but one Varrick insisted upon, since she was next in line for the throne.

As they approached the Receiving Room, Cyrus shuffled around her and opened the massive mahogany door. Jara breezed through, her long gown flowing behind her.

Jara's gaze swept the room. The granite walls curved into floor and ceiling, supported by evenly spaced columns. In the middle of the room, a three-tiered fountain flowed. Fire poured over the tiers and pooled in the large basin, sending yellow and orange light flickering around the room, that illuminated the polished walls.

At the end of the cavernous room, two thrones sat on a rock dais. Though the velvety padding was hidden from view by the demons sitting upon the wooden chairs, Jara knew from experience the thrones were plush and comfortable.

Her brother's red eyes met hers immediately, and he rose. They met halfway through the room. Varrick grasped her hand and smiled, exposing his extra-long canines. "Not that I don't enjoy your visits, but what brings you here today, dear sister?"

Jara noted the sarcasm in his voice. Ever since he'd claimed Elizabeth as his queen, things between them had been strained.

"I have news of Lovazia. I received a phone call from her. She may be in trouble."

Elizabeth rose. Her straight, blonde hair cascaded over her shoulders.

"I'll leave you two to talk," Elizabeth offered, and Jara wondered if she knew how much the king's sister despised her.

"Sit," Varrick ordered. "Jara can say what she needs to, then go. We have things to discuss."

Jara glanced from Varrick to Elizabeth and back again. "Actually, Varrick, my news might be better received in private."

"Is our sister well?" Varrick's voice deepened with concern.

"Yes," Jara said, "but—"

Varrick's furrowed brows rose. "Then whatever

you must say to me, you can say to your queen."

That stung. Elizabeth might be his mate, but Jara would never accept the skinny little twit as queen. Her ire rose. Lovazia's news wasn't for hybrid ears. No half demon needed to know about the existence of vampires. Elizabeth had just learned about the existence of demons, and she wasn't taking that well.

"Your eyes are glowing, Jara. I suggest you calm yourself," Varrick commanded. "Perhaps you need a minute. Leave us. When you are in control, you may come back and share the news of Lovazia."

He was choosing that woman over his own sister. "B-but—" Jara stammered.

"Leave us," Varrick commanded before returning to his throne.

Jara stormed from the room, and Cyrus shut the door behind her. She paused and leaned against the door to catch her breath. The mountain kept the compound at a constant sixty-six degrees. The cool wood felt good against her back.

"I just don't get it, Cyrus. What does he see in that woman?"

"I don't know, miss." Cyrus shifted uncomfortably, running his fingers through his short, blond hair. "She isn't too hard on the eyes."

"But she is so tiny and weak. I don't get it. All these years, I've had to listen to my brother whine about how he wanted to be with her. Ever since she summoned him during a séance, she's consumed him to the point he couldn't even reign properly. If not for me, someone would have used his distraction to dethrone him by now. You know how temperamental our kind can be. If I hadn't kept him focused all these years, someone would have been able to challenge him.

"I mean really! She can't morph into an animal form. She didn't grow up with our customs and rules. She clings to her human life. I just don't understand what he sees in her, other than—"

The sound of shouting coming from the Receiving Room interrupted Jara's sentence.

"Sounds like we should go," offered Cyrus.

Jara hushed him and leaned her ear against the door. "I can just barely make out what they are saying."

"I hate this, Varrick. I really do," Elizabeth proclaimed.

"Hate what?"

"Hate *this*. I hate sitting in the throne room day after day. I hate being stuck in this compound, never seeing my old friends."

"But you know why you must remain here. It isn't safe for you to go back to Mason's Bluff."

"I know, I know. You are worried I'll bring back something that would infect the other demons."

"Elizabeth, my dear. I worry not only for their safety but yours as well."

Bile churned in Jara's stomach. How could her brother care for that twit?

"I miss my friends, my job."

"We've been through this. As my queen, your place is with me. Not in the human world."

"Why do you want me, Varrick?" asked Elizabeth.

Exactly what I'd like to know, thought Jara.

"What can I say? Like calls to like," her brother practically purred.

"What's that supposed to mean?" The pitch of Elizabeth's voice rose. "We are nothing alike. You are large. I am small. You are strong. I am weak. You are male, and I am female. Even our eyes differ. Yours are red, while mine are golden. We are opposites in every way."

"What I mean is under all those little delectable bits of yours, there is a little demon. You, little one, have hot, passionate demon blood in your veins, like myself. We are alike, you and I."

Jara wanted to gag.

"But why me? I don't understand. Why did you pick me?"

Exactly!

"Because, Little Bits, from the moment you summoned me, I have loved your little fingers, little shoulders, your tiny neck, especially your tiny pouty lips."

There was a pause, then Varrick continued, "I love all your little bits."

Jara heard a distinctive smack.

"Don't play grab-ass with me. I'm upset with you."

"You're always upset, Little Bits. But you'll see. You'll care for me more each day." Varrick's voice softened. "And let's not forget that symbol for ruler that is tattooed on your body. How do you explain that?"

"My tribal tramp stamp? It's just a tattoo, Varrick."

"But if our love wasn't ordained by fate, then why would you have chosen the exact demonic symbol for ruler? It's not a coincidence, Elizabeth. Your demon half surfaces from time to time as it did when you were choosing the tattoo."

"Bullshit!" Elizabeth's tone sharpened. "Screw this. I'm outta here. I need some air."

Jara jumped away just in time for Elizabeth to yank

open the door and storm off with Varrick's guard hot on her heels.

Seeing an opportunity to speak to her brother alone, Jara marched back into the room.

"Varrick, can we talk now?"

Varrick held up a thick hand. His high cheekbones and patrician features of his face bespoke of their high breeding. Worry lines creased his eyes. Jara's concern for the emotional toll his mate was having on him was short lived, however.

Varrick shook his head. "I'm not in the mood, Jara. What I need now is a little time in the forest. I need to let my inner beast out, take animal form, and run for miles with the cold wind whipping through my fur."

"Fine, I'll go with you. I haven't taken the form of a mountain lion in weeks. It would feel good to morph."

"No. I want to be by myself. I need to think. Devise a way to win Elizabeth's love and having you there would be a distraction."

A distraction! Well, I...

The sight of her brother morphing into his favorite form, a lion, made Jara lose her train of thought. It was a magnificent sight.

His humanoid form began to shimmer and blur. Varrick's hands contorted, golden fur pushed from his smooth skin. His high cheekbones and full lips shifted. For a second he had a lion's cast to his face, then a full muzzle and whiskers emerged. The king's blond hair grew long and combined with the heavy dusting of blond hair on his chest to form a mane. As his clothes split and fell away, Varrick collapsed to the floor while his body completed the change. With a roar that echoed mightily, he bounded out of the room.

Chapter 10

Julie's feet ached in her fur-lined boots after another day of sightseeing with Penny. The women now stood in front of the most recognizable building in the whole of Russia, St. Basil's Cathedral. With its terra-cotta walls and colorful domes, it appeared truly magnificent. Blues, greens, yellows, and reds swirled around the ornate domes of the church, while teal snaked its way along the building to accent the brown walls. It reminded Julie of the gingerbread house from the fairy tale, *Hansel and Gretel*.

Penny's smile reached her eyes.

"I can't wait to see inside." Penny linked arms with Julie. "Let's go."

The two headed for the cathedral. Apprehension slithered over Julie's skin. She had not been in a church since the funeral. Her stomach twisted in knots. Growing up in the Baptist Church, her faith had been rather strong until the deaths. She found the idea of going into the building a bit disconcerting.

As they approached the ornately carved doors, Julie's unease increased. The nape of her neck tingled. She glanced around quickly, a habit formed from years of being alone and watching out for herself. The sensation grew. The hairs on her arms rose next. A shiver skirted down her spine, but a second glance found nothing amiss.

Julie nearly pulled Penny up the broad stone steps, grabbed the massive wooden door of the church, and made quick time through it.

Inside the vestibule, they removed their coats and draped them over their arms. The interior of the building wasn't what she expected. The extravagant and brightly colored domes of the cathedral's exterior masked a more modest interior. Small, dimly lit chapels and maze-like corridors filled the inside of the church.

Delicate floral designs and images painted in bold colors covered the walls. The paintings, having faded over the years, were in the process of being restored, evidenced by the scaffolding that rose to meet the art painted on the ceiling. Though in need of repair, it still took Julie's breath away. She tore her eyes away from the paintings when Penny approached.

"I wonder where the workers are," Julie mused, noting their absence from the scaffolding.

"Who knows?" Penny gave a quick shrug. "Maybe they are on a break."

"Uh-huh, maybe."

"Come here, Julie. I've got something to show you."

Penny pulled her to the middle of the Chapel of the Intercession. "Look at the amazing blue and gold iconostasis." Her voice sounded breathy with awe. "Isn't it beautiful?"

Julie nodded in agreement. "The people seem to be coming right out of the image, as if it was a gateway from Heaven itself."

Suddenly, a loud crash sounded above them. The women glanced up. One of the scaffolding rigs tipped and a neon yellow object hurtled toward them. Its orange industrial cord thrashed behind it like an angry bullwhip.

"Look out!" cried Penny. She tackled Julie to the floor as the rig careened down with a crash. When Penny landed on top of her, it forced the breath from her body. The nail gun crashed onto the floor of the chapel. The women screamed as the gun bounced along the floor.

Pssst, pssst, pssst. The trigger depressed with each hit and sent long nails hurling through the chapel.

Penny rolled off Julie, and they crouched down then covered their heads with their hands. The gun came to rest on its side, and a deafening silence filled the church. Penny's wide, terrified eyes met Julie's.

"Are you okay, Jules?" Penny wiped her forehead with the back of her wrist. "Man, that was a close call."

"I-I think so," Julie stammered. Her eyes traveled along the wall beside her to where one of the nails jutted out from the plaster. It still vibrated from the force of the impact. Her face paled when she realized it had struck just inches from her head.

"The nail gun almost landed on your head."

"Thank you so much, Penny. You saved my life," Julie gushed, reaching out to grab her friend's hand. She squeezed it tightly.

"Ouch!" Penny pulled out of Julie's grasp.

"I'm sorry. The adrenaline rush must have given me more strength than I realized. I didn't mean to hurt you. I can't believe what just happened." Julie ran a shaky hand through her hair and rose slowly to her knees.

Penny stood, then offered a hand to Jules, which she gladly accepted. Once on her feet, Julie pulled her friend into a warm embrace.

"Thank you so much, Penny. I have no idea what I'd do without you."

"It's okay, Julie." Penny's hand rubbed along Julie's back.

"Are you all right?" Julie's eyes went wide and round. She pulled away and stared at Penny's tummy. "What about the baby? Is the baby okay? I didn't squish you when we fell did I?"

Penny chuckled. "The baby and I are fine. When we fell, I actually landed on you, remember?"

Julie exhaled an audible sigh of relief. "Oh, that's right. Thank goodness it wasn't the other way around. I might have hurt the baby."

Penny shot Julie a reproachful look.

"First, just because your sister is a supermodel, doesn't mean you are overweight." Penny splayed her hand over her tummy. "And second, I'm only in the first trimester. I'm not even showing, for goodness' sake. I don't think any harm could come to the baby. It's too small."

Jules released her bestie from the embrace. She glanced around, her gaze drawn to the scaffolding from which the nomadic gun had toppled. Luckily, it had landed on an empty floor and not done any major damage.

As a priest rushed in to see what all the commotion was about, movement danced in the corner of her vision. Her eyes darted to the spot. Was it her imagination or had that vestibule door just closed?

Chapter 11

Nicholai's eyes popped open, and he stared, unseeing, at the ceiling above his bed. Every nerve ending in his body fired with a prickly heat. Something was wrong with Juliette. He took several deep breaths to calm himself so he could concentrate. The Alpha's consciousness streamed from his body and reached for his beloved. Through the mindlink they shared, he found her easily.

She seemed terrified but alive, and that gave him some hope. He dared not talk to her through their link, for he feared it might scare her more to hear a strange voice in her head, but he needed to know what had scared her so. Being ensnared in his home by the sun, made him impotent. Nicholai roared in frustration.

Anger washed over his body. His fangs lengthened. His heartmate was in trouble, and he could not reach her. Nicholai glanced at the clock. It would be several hours until dark. He balled his fists and beat the mattress.

Jumping from his bed, he paced the room, hands clenched at his side. His mind raced through the possibilities of how to get her help. Could he find a human to send to her? Someone he might trust with her life? Would it be possible to use their mindlink to manipulate the danger? Might he reach her by dematerializing into the shadows?

Nicholai abruptly stopped when the tingling eased from his body. Juliette's fear subsided a bit, and he sensed her calming. Whatever terrified her had passed.

He stayed a quiet shadow in her mind, hoping to find out what had been wrong. He needed to assure the threat did not return. She seemed fine, relaxed. He waited several minutes until confident she was no longer in danger, then slowly withdrew from her mind.

His own heart still raced, and he forced some calming breaths to ease its pace. Whatever had sent such panic through Julie must not have been real to have lasted such a short time.

But what if it had been? Nicholai paced the room.

Had it been a serious threat he would have been helpless to assist her. His kind did not tolerate the sun for more than a few minutes before they succumbed to death. The thought left him utterly vulnerable.

He stomped in exasperation at his own limitations. Emotions warred within him. He felt relieved that Juliette seemed fine and yet furious she'd been in danger when he could not get to her.

Wait. He paused. *Didn't Marcus once call his heartmate to him by compulsion? It is a rare talent but not one unheard of for a vampire. Marcus is younger than I. If Marcus did it, I should be able to do it, especially since Juliette and I share a mindlink. If I can get her to come to me, I can make sure she is safe.*

He lay down on his bed, closed his eyes once again, and willed his body to relax. He inhaled several deep, cleansing breaths and sent out his mental call to his love. *Come to me, Juliette. Come to me.* He paused, stilled his breath, and sent all of his mental concentration behind the command. *Come to me, my beloved. Hear me and come to me now.*

Another breath in and a deep sigh out. He centered his thoughts, letting everything but his desire to see her slip away as he summoned her again.

He continued to call. Every so often, he'd open his eyes and ears and send his senses from the home to see if he detected her near. The minutes turned to hours.

Nothing! He scrubbed a hand down his face. *Time and time again, nothing.*

By the afternoon, mental exhaustion set in, and the day pulled at him. He needed rest. Perhaps when he awoke he would call Marcus for some tips. He must succeed in calling her to him. Determined to see his love again, to see her safe and sound, he'd stop at nothing to make that happen.

****

A shiver of unease wrapped around Julie's spine. Under the pretense of being cold, she shrugged into her trench coat and wrapped it tightly around her body, leaving her arms in place to hug herself. Another wave went through her. She desperately wanted to leave the church and go back to the village.

"Hey, Penny. What do you think about us packing it in for the day and heading back to Yaroslavia? I'm a bit tired after all the excitement."

"Ahhh, Julie. I was really looking forward to going back to the GUM again. I can't believe you of all people don't want to go back. We only got through the first floor yesterday. We still have two more floors of shops to explore. You know a little shopping always makes you feel better. Come on, please?"

Julie's instincts begged her to leave, warned her that to stay would invite only more trouble. She had no logical reason to feel this way, but something pulled her away from Moscow. An overwhelming sense she needed to depart now flowed through her, but she ruthlessly pushed it aside.

Fighting the instinct, she gave her friend a weak grin and reluctantly agreed. "Okay, I guess we can go do a little shopping. It won't kill us." Julie grimaced at her choice of words.

Penny shot her an incredulous look, put her arm around Julie's shoulders, and ushered her from the church. Julie's trepidation increased. With every step, her instincts screamed to go back to the village. It took everything in her power to allow her friend to lead her in the opposite direction.

****

Nicholai's senses pushed through his home and out into the surrounding forest once again. Hope his heartmate might have finally come to him was quickly crushed. A growl pushed from his throat as much from frustration as anger.

He needed to speak to Marcus, learn how to call her to him. Nicholai couldn't believe he was unable to do a task one a century younger than him had managed to accomplish.

With determination, he stood and flared his senses out one final time. Not sensing his love, he reminded himself that might be a good thing. The fact he did not sense her fear or dread was good. She was obviously safe.

Or dead, the little voice in the back of his head nudged at him.

"No," he silenced the voice aloud.

He would not allow his thoughts to go there. She's

alive. She *had* to be. The Fates would not be so cruel as to take her from him when he'd just found her.

He glided to the bedside table and picked up the phone. Nicholai drummed his long fingers on the table as it rang Marcus's number.

"Hello, you have reached the Botticelli residence," said Marcus's voice. "I'm afraid we cannot answer the phone at this time. Please leave a message, and we'll get back to you as soon as possible."

Beeeep!

"Marcus, this is Nicholai. I need to speak with you immediately. Please call me as soon as you get this message. If I am not at home, call my cell."

He slammed down the phone and pounded his thick headboard in frustration. His fist traveled not only through the wood but the plaster wall behind it. He let out a mighty roar, more bestial than human. Helplessness ate at him like a vulture gnawing on entrails of a varmint. He'd always been in control. He was the Alpha who maintained his temper, who kept a calm head and stayed cool, in complete command of his emotions. But having a heartmate had changed all of that for him.

Self-doubt and utter frustration over this situation filled him. He experienced insecurity and vulnerability for the first time in his life. His emotions churned out of control.

Enough! I will no longer put up with my heartmate being out there unprotected. If anything happens to her, it will kill me. She is my anchor, the other half of my soul. I will not risk losing her. I need her…Now!

Chapter 12

Nicholai sat behind the desk in his office at the restaurant. He picked up the phone for the tenth time that evening then put the receiver back down on the cradle yet again. Marcus had not called him back, even with the six messages he'd left. Nicholai replayed the events of the evening in his mind for the umpteenth time.

Having a heartmate made him wishy-washy, uncertain. He'd always been a male who stepped up and took charge of a situation. However, since finding his heartmate, he'd been anything but self-assured.

Tonight it had taken him twenty minutes to decide what clothes to wear. Normally, he would have walked into his closet and picked something immediately, but now he questioned every decision. What if I run into her? Will she approve of what I have on? Those thoughts had given him pause. And those weren't the only questions.

How can I find her? What should I do? Where should I go first? His mind was utter chaos. If this was what it felt like having a heartmate, perhaps his friend Vladimir had been correct in commenting only the unlucky males ever found their mates.

Unable to sleep, he'd come in early to the office, but he found it impossible to concentrate on his work. Payroll was due, but instead of working on the books, he spent his time worrying where she was.

He pushed away from his desk and paced the room. Nervous energy prickled along his skin. When his thoughts turned to Julie, he wrung his hands anxiously, a nervous habit in which he had never indulged before.

He'd gone to Julie's hotel room and found it empty. Not knowing where she was worried him. Concern for her remained in the forefront of his mind.

A sweet, lilac smell wafted to his nose. A deep inhale took the unique scent down into his lungs. He sent his consciousness out into the restaurant and found his Juliette. Relief flooded his body.

A large smile reached his eyes. Nicholai's shoulders relaxed. He breathed easier. He needed to see her, see for himself she was unharmed.

He forced himself to go a human pace as he walked into the dining area and scanned the room. A woman in a red dress stood at the bar. In his usual spot in the corner booth, a couple sat holding hands. A large portly man ate alone. Finally, his roaming eyes rested on his mate.

Dressed in a green, cowl-neck sweater and winter-white pants, she sat with her friend at the same table they'd occupied previously. Her eyes sparkled, drew him in, and her head tossed back when she laughed— the sound straight from Heaven.

What a beautiful sound as sweet as the music she sang in our dream.

He crept behind the bar and busied himself washing a glass, but Nicholai's eyes never left his heartmate. The casual shrug of her shoulders, the way her hair surrounded her round face when she leaned forward. Her every movement called to him.

He would wait no longer. He needed to talk to her, be with her. An idea came to him.

Making his way over to their table, Nicholai's knees weakened when Julie's beautiful eyes rose and locked with his.

Julie sucked in a breath. Desire to know her thoughts warred with his respect for her privacy, but the desire won, and Nicholai pushed into her mind.

She felt in awe of the tall, dark stranger who stood before her dressed entirely in black.

He's so handsome with those alluring eyes and shaggy black hair.

He overwhelmed her. His power flowed over her, around her, through her, as she stared into his amber eyes.

Nicholai smiled, his lips retracting to reveal perfect white teeth.

"Good evening, ladies," he greeted in his thick accent. "I am the owner of the *Kholodnaya Plecha*. Tell me, please, how do you like your meals?"

"We love them," gushed Penny, drawing his gaze briefly.

His attention returned to Julie. "And how about you, ma'am?"

"It's absolutely delicious."

"Good. I am glad you like it. Allow me to introduce myself. I am Nicholai Peterhof." He placed one hand over his heart.

Penny extended her hand first, so Nicholai brought it to his lips and placed a quick kiss on the back of her hand.

"I'm Penny Jones." She giggled nervously at his courtly formality.

Julie extended a hand as if to shake. But Nicholai wasn't about to make their first introduction over a handshake. He gathered her tiny hand in his, turned it over, and bowed from the waist, before laying a slow, gentle kiss on the back of her soft hand.

The kiss sent an electrical wave through Julie's body and back into his. She shook from the contact. The expression on her face indicated she'd felt it all the way to her toes.

Nicholai did not keep the knowing grin from his face as he rose back to his full height. The sensation passed between them because they were heartmates. They had a connection made by the Fates, a bond stronger than anything two human people could ever experience.

He glanced down at her from under the fan of his dark lashes and gave her a stunning smile. In response, Nicholai sensed the desire that swept through her in a sensual wave.

"Tell me your name," he said in a hushed tone.

"Julie."

"Is it short for something?"

"Juliette," she squeaked out and tried to pull her hand from his, but he didn't allow its escape.

"Juliette…As in *Romeo and Juliet*?" He purposely quoted the same question he'd asked her in their shared dream.

"Yes, except my name is spelled with two t's and two e's."

"'What light through yonder window breaks? It is the east and Juliet,' with two t's and two e's, 'is the sun,'" Nicholai quoted with dramatic flair, while he dropped to one knee.

When a puzzled expression narrowed her brows, Nicholai read the cause. A strong sense of *déjà vu* made her recall the dreams they'd shared. She gasped when sinful images filled her mind at Nicholai's slight prompting. She recognized him as her dream man, only he was here in front of her, in all his glorious flesh.

Her cheeks flushed as she remembered the passionate dreams in vivid detail. The scenes flickered in her mind, and heat pooled in her stomach, tying it in knots. Her mind raced. She imagined herself writhing beneath him. If this man was half as good as his dream self, she was in for the vacation of her life.

Wait, what am I thinking? Julie quickly returned from fantasy land. *No way will I be sleeping with this man, no matter how much my body wants to. I'm never going to let him see me naked. Not going to happen. As if he'd want to anyway.*

Her thoughts made his heart sink.

Deliberately retaining possession of her hand, Nicholai stood to his full height of six foot five inches, and gave a wide grin to both women.

"So tell me, Juliette, do you have a last name?"

"Saint-John."

"Well, it's nice to meet you, Juliette Saint-John."

Nicholai's heart leapt for joy when her next thought came.

I love the way my name sounds on his lips, like a tiger's throaty purr.

Penny must have noticed the way Nicholai looked at Julie, for she smiled. "Would you like to join us?"

Julie's eyes widened in disbelief.

"I thought you would never ask," said Nicholai. "I'll go get a chair."

Penny leaned over the small table and whispered, not realizing Nicholai's preternatural hearing picked up the conversation. "I think he likes you."

"Don't be ridiculous."

"I saw the way he looked at you. Trust me, he likes you."

"Shhh, he's coming," hushed Juliette under her breath, as Nicholai returned to their table with a chair in hand and sat down. Within a moment, his wait staff put a place setting before him on the table.

"*Spasibo.* Thank you." He spared a glance at the waitress.

"What can I get you to eat, sir?" she asked him in their native language.

Nicholai continued their conversation in Russian. "Why don't you bring us a tray of canapés? The lobster filo baskets, I think, will do nicely."

"Of course, sir, right away." The waitress scampered off on her mission.

"Did you just order something to eat? *U mina plokha s ruskim,*" stated Julie bashfully.

"Actually, your Russian is not bad," Nicholai replied in English. "I understood you perfectly."

"That's nice of you to say." Julie blushed.

Penny drank her tea. "So what did you order?"

"I hope you don't mind, but I ordered the lobster canapés. I believe you will like them. They are one of Chef's specialties."

"I'm sure we'll love them." Julie took a sip of water.

Nicholai eased back in his chair and placed the napkin in his lap. "So where are you ladies from?"

"England," responded Julie with a smile that lit her

honey-brown eyes.

"Really? By your accent, I would have thought you were from America."

"Well, actually, that is where I grew up, but now I live in England."

"So what brought you to my Yaroslavia?"

"Julie and I are here on holiday." Penny flashed a wry smile when he spared her a glance, clearly aware his attention was on her friend.

"How has it been?" he asked, intent on finding out what had happened that day.

"It's been…Interesting." Julie chose her words mindfully.

"How so?" His interest was piqued.

"Well," she continued. "We've seen a lot of interesting things."

Penny crossed her legs under the table. "We've been to Moscow, seen the Kremlin, and of course we've spent a lot of time at the GUM."

Nicholai nodded. "Anything else?"

"We toured churches today," Julie offered.

Now the conversation headed in the right direction. The Alpha leaned toward Julie, his intent gaze locked with hers. "Tell me how that went."

"It went okay," Julie lied.

Oh, my dear, you will not lie to me.

His eyes dove straight into her soul. "Tell me, was there any trouble?" He lowered his baritone voice an octave, putting a compulsion behind the demand.

"Yes, a little."

"Tell me what happened." Nicholai slipped into her mind once more, so he might watch her memories of the event as she spoke.

"Well, there was a bit of an accident at St. Basil's Cathedral."

He raised one eyebrow when she hesitated. An image flashed in her mind of being thrown to the floor. "Do continue."

"It wasn't a big deal," interrupted Penny, breaking Nicholai's concentration. Julie blinked a couple of times, coming back to an awareness of her surroundings.

"So what happened during this accident?" Nicholai prodded. He rested one ankle on the opposite knee.

Penny shrugged. "Um, not much of anything. Some scaffolding fell."

"What do you mean, 'not much of anything'?" Julie gave her friend a disingenuous look. "She is so modest. She actually saved my life. If she hadn't knocked me out of the way, the rig might have hit me or the nail gun could have crashed down on my head."

"It was nothing." Penny pursed her lips and waved a dismissive hand.

Concern flooded his body, and Nicholai's gaze roamed over Juliette to make sure no harm had come to her. "So, you are all right? You did not get hurt?"

"Oh yes, I'm fine. Thanks to Penny."

Satisfied, he turned his full attention to Julie's friend. "Then I owe you a debt, for I would not have wanted anything to happen to that pretty little head of hers."

A meaningful smile crinkled Penny's eyes. "I agree. We wouldn't want anything to happen to that '*pretty* little head of hers.' "

Penny shot Jules a told-you-so expression, and Julie blushed. Nicholai easily read the silent communication between the two women. He relaxed in the knowledge the affable conversation was going well.

The waitress brought out the tray of canapés and placed it on the table. Nicholai thanked her as Penny popped one of the disks into her mouth and let out an approving sound of pleasure. Nicholai forked a bit of the delicacy and fed it to Julie. Her red lips closed around the lobster, the move so sinuous it stole his breath.

"Do you like it?" His voice sounded rough.

Julie closed her eyes, clearly enjoying the canapé as she chewed and swallowed. "Ummm, yes. It's quite good."

Nicholai's pocket went off with a loud buzz.

Julie glanced down into his lap. "Is that a phone in your pocket, or are you happy to see me?" she quipped.

A sexy smile pulled at one corner of his mouth. "Both, my dear." He raked his hot gaze up and down her body. "Definitely both."

Another blush crept up Julie's face. When he gleaned her thoughts, he found it had been a long time since she had served up a flirt to a man, and she realized he was up to returning her serve with a backspin.

Nicholai stood and retrieved his phone from his pocket, then glanced at it to see who would dare interrupt such an important meal. Recognizing the caller, he needed to answer.

"Excuse me, ladies. I must take this. I will not be but a minute."

He clicked the phone on as he strolled away from the table. "Hello, Demetri," he greeted his friend and cousin in their native Russian. "How are you this evening?"

"I'm fine and you?"

"I am doing well enough."

Grief at having to leave his heartmate pushed in as Nicholai traipsed into the office and closed the door. "You sound bored."

"I am bored. You know how boring reconnaissance can be."

That piqued Nicholai's interest. "Recon? Where are you? Why are you doing recon?"

Demetri sighed. "I am in Wyoming. There may be a situation. I'm not sure, so I called Stephan here to help me discover exactly what is going on.

"There have been a series of possible animal attacks in the mountains. Of course, living in Mason's Bluff as long as I have, I am no stranger to the occasional attack, but these are different. They are more brutal than usual and happening with greater frequency. I hope Stephan will help me discover whether it is an animal or perhaps a rogue vampire that is the cause of such carnage."

"Is Marcus with you? I have been attempting to contact him all day and have yet to reach him."

"No. In fact, Stephan sent Marcus and Christina out to Las Vegas to stay with Katrina."

"Stephan left his heartmate in Vegas while he came to Wyoming? Why didn't he take her with him?"

"He wasn't sure what we would find out here, so it would be safer for her to remain in Vegas under Marcus's protection."

"That explains why I haven't been able to get a hold of Marcus."

"What did you want of Marcus?"

Nicholai knew his cousin didn't have much use for love and believed finding a heartmate made a vampire weak, so he decided not to share the news about Juliette. Besides, he knew what Demetri's advice would be. He'd tell Nicholai to throw Julie over his shoulder and take her to his lair.

"It doesn't matter now," Nicholai said smoothly. "I'll call Stephan's penthouse later and catch up with Marcus."

"Very well. Listen, you should know, depending on what Stephan and I uncover, we may need to call in the Alpha Council so be prepared to come to Wyoming if we need you."

The Alpha Council consisted of six of the biggest, baddest vampires the world had ever known. The Special Forces group of the vampire world, their fighting skills and intelligence were unmatched. Vampires had a policing agency called the Vampire Enforcement Squad or VES, but the Alphas were another entity altogether. They had fought together for centuries, and the Council put an end to any vampire deemed a risk to the breed or to humans.

"Have you contacted the VES? What do they have to say?" Nicholai inquired.

Demetri hesitated. "No. I haven't contacted the Vampire Enforcement Squad yet."

"Would you like me to call Agent Bolovich and try to find out if they have any information about the attacks?"

"No!" Demetri responded a little too quickly.

Nicholai barely contained a chuckle. The last time Demetri had seen Tatiana Bolovich, they had not parted on great terms. They'd all worked together to rescue

Marcus's heartmate, Christina. In the process, Demetri had accidentally knifed Tatiana, and something had happened between them afterward. For when his cousin returned to Marcus's home, he was walking funny, and Nicholai barely caught a glimpse of Tatiana kneeing Demetri in the family jewels before his cousin erected a mental barrier to keep Nicholai from seeing more.

Demetri took a deep breath. "Until we know for sure whether or not it is an animal attack, Stephan and I do not think it is a good idea to involve…"

Demetri stopped mid-sentence. Nicholai knew a second of concern, afraid his cousin might have run into the attacking beast.

Demetri quickly dispelled the alarm when he muttered, "The blonde that just walked by is gorgeous. I could really take a bite out of that. I wouldn't mind having her in my bed. I bet she'd be a tiger."

Nicholai laughed. "Demetri, you do realize you said that out loud."

"Yes, but I said it so quietly no human would hear." Demetri laughed. "I couldn't help it, cousin. Sometimes when they look that good, you have to say something."

A smirk grazed Nicholai's lips. "Sounds like you found something interesting. Tell me about her. What does she look like?"

"She's beautiful. Long blonde hair, tiny little body, curves in all the right places. And with those golden eyes, she looks scrumptious."

"Sounds like your type, Demetri."

"She certainly is," he agreed. "I better go now. Duty might have to wait. I don't have much time. Dawn approaches."

The line went dead, and Nicholai jammed the phone into his pocket. It appeared his cousin might get lucky, and he wouldn't mind doing the same with a certain brown-haired beauty sitting in his restaurant.

Chapter 13

Elizabeth noticed the large muscular man coming her way. How could she not? He was almost as large as Varrick, and men that size were few and far between. His cold, gray eyes raked over her like a predator. She moved to the side, giving him room to pass, when a strange odor assaulted her nose.

Elizabeth forced a breath through her nostrils to clear the aroma. Thankfully, it faded as she approached her car. She climbed into the vehicle and sat for a moment, wrapped tightly in her little blue parka.

She should get back to the compound. She'd snuck out while Varrick was off doing his courtly duties. Her original intention had been to grab a quick bite of breakfast while getting respite from the Demon King, but now that her tummy was full, a day of shopping called to her. Surely, Varrick would be busy for hours and wouldn't miss her. She could hit a box store until the mall opened. Elizabeth noted the time on the console display. Plenty of time to get in some much needed retail therapy and still make it back in time for dinner.

A smile took Elizabeth's face, and she pulled the car from the curb.

****

Nicholai returned from his phone call and chatted companionably with Julie and Penny until long after their table had been cleared of dishes. Now only the three of them remained in the place.

Penny glanced around the room. "Where did everybody go?"

"We closed two hours ago," Nicholai volunteered. "Even the staff went home."

Julie glanced at her watch.

"Wow!" Her eyes widened in disbelief. "I didn't realize how late it had gotten."

Nicholai shot her a wry grin. "It is amazing how fast time runs when you are in the presence of beautiful women."

Julie and Penny giggled.

"I believe you mean how fast time flies," offered Penny.

"Yes. That is it. How fast time flies." A deep chuckle rumbled in his chest. "Forgive me. Sometimes my English gets a little mixed up."

Julie stood. "We should be going."

Nicholai leapt to his feet, grabbed the coat from the back of Julie's chair, and held it for her. After nestling the trench onto her shoulders, he took the liberty of wrapping his hands around her hair and pulled it out from beneath the coat. The brunette locks cascaded down onto her shoulders as the soft strands flowed through his fingers.

After helping Penny on with her coat, as well, Nicholai pulled his own on and grabbed an umbrella from behind the bar. He fished the keys from his jeans pocket then escorted the women outside, pausing long enough to flick off the lights and lock the door behind them.

"Come, ladies. I will escort you to your hotel."

Julie gestured toward the umbrella hanging from his wrist. "Why did you bring an umbrella?"

"You will see," he replied cryptically. "You never know. It might just snow or something."

As if on cue, flakes began to fall from the sky. Heavy, wet, slushy flakes. Nicholai smoothly opened the umbrella and raised it above their heads, then pulled Julie beneath his arm.

"You need to scoot in close, ladies. It is barely big enough for the three of us."

His broad shoulders took up most of the space under the umbrella, and Julie was only too happy to snuggle tightly against him. A thrilled traveled through her at being so close to him, and she wondered if Penny felt the same. His masculinity wrapped her in warmth and protection.

"So tell me," he began. "Where are you staying?"

"We are staying at the inn. At the end of Main Street."

"Very good choice. I know the owner there."

"We've met her, too. She seems nice."

"Absolutely. She is one of the sweetest ladies I know, next to the two of you, of course."

Though Nicholai seemed to have shortened his gait to match the women's, their strides ate up the distance much too quickly for Julie's liking, and all too soon they arrived at the front stairs of the inn.

Nicholai slid his arm from around Juliette's shoulders and ran his fingers down the length of her limb, where he captured her hand in his. When their eyes met, he smiled a warm grin that reached the corners of his amber eyes. "I would very much like to see you again."

Excitement tickled her tummy. Juliette looked up at him from under her thick lashes. "I would like that."

"Would you come to dinner with me tomorrow evening?"

Juliette glanced over his shoulder at her friend, who nodded her head up and down so furiously Juliette thought she might bruise her brain.

"Yes." Julie flashed him a big smile. "I'd be happy to go to dinner with you."

"My dear, you have made my heart sing. I will pick you up here at seven o'clock tomorrow evening if that works for you."

"Yes, that will be fine. I'm looking forward to it," Julie volunteered.

"As am I." Nicholai lifted her hand to his lips. "Until tomorrow, sweet Juliette." His warm breath whispered across her hand as he spoke before his lips brushed the softest kiss on the back of it.

Julie gave him a little wave, then closed the door to the inn.

After greeting the young lady behind the registration counter, the women climbed the stairs. As they reached the top, Penny linked her arm with Julie's.

"You're coming into my room," she commanded, then opened the door and pulled Julie inside. The two women kicked their shoes off and sat down cross-legged on Penny's bed.

Penny spoke first. "He is absolutely *gorgeous*."

"I know. I can't believe he asked me out for dinner."

"Are you kidding me, I can't believe he didn't ask you to snog him, what with the way he looked at you all night."

Julie lightly smacked her friend's arm in jest. "Oh please. I didn't notice him looking at me like that."

"Oh, come on, Julie. He looked like he could eat you up."

Juliette allowed a small smile to grace her face. "He did seem like he was interested. Didn't he?"

"Interested?" Penny scoffed in disbelief. "No. Not interested. I'd say more like enthralled." A blush heated Julie's cheeks before Penny continued. "If you hadn't agreed to go out with him, I would have throttled you right then and there on the sidewalk."

Juliette laughed. "I could tell. Who could have missed you nodding behind his back like that? I thought your head would come off, you nodded so hard."

"Well, how else was I supposed to make sure you said yes?" Penny crossed her arms over her chest. "So, where do you think he will take you for dinner tomorrow night?"

Sympathy brought a concerned expression to Julie's face. "Oh, Penny. I'm so sorry. I didn't think about that."

"Whatever do you mean?"

"I didn't think about you. What are you going to do for dinner?"

"Oh, honey, don't you worry about me. I can take care of myself. I'll find myself some supper. It's not a problem. I want you to go out with him and have the time of your life." Penny patted Julie's leg reassuringly. "Have fun. You deserve it. Perhaps a fling with a sexy Russian is exactly what you need after mourning Steve and the girls these past three years."

Julie's first instinct was to protest, but she had to admit, Penny was right. Her bestie was so kind, encouraging her to go out. She felt thankful to have a friend like her. She couldn't ask for a truer friend.

A horrific thought made her eyes enlarge. "Oh my gosh! What am I going to wear?"

"Don't worry. I'll help you find something. Let's go into your room and look at what you brought. If you can't find anything you like in your closet, we can always go shopping first thing in the morning."

More shopping sounded exhausting. Juliette liked shopping as much as the next girl, but being in the GUM for the past two days had just about equaled her spending quota for the year. Juliette stretched and gave a big yawn. "Can we put off the wardrobe check until tomorrow? It's late, and I'm really tired. I want to brush my teeth and crawl into bed."

Penny mimicked her yawn. "Yeah, might be a good idea. I'm tired, too."

Julie stood, picked up her shoes, and headed to the door adjoining their rooms. "Good night," she called over her shoulder when she opened it.

"Good night, sleep tight. Don't let the handsome, Russian bedbugs bite." Penny giggled when Julie closed the door with a soft click.

Juliette shucked her clothes in record time then piled them in her suitcase. She slipped into her nightgown, brushed her teeth, and washed her face. The cotton sheets on the bed, cool and inviting, welcomed her as she tucked herself in. When she closed her eyes, an image came to mind—a handsome Russian with dark hair and amber eyes whose sensuous smile was so hot Juliette feared it would melt her heart. She couldn't wait to see him again tomorrow. His courtly manners made her feel special. The awareness that her dream man was real and wanted to see her again made a contented sigh pass through her lips. The thought played in her mind while she drifted off to sleep.

Chapter 14

Having just finished some therapeutic shopping in Mason's Bluff, Elizabeth crawled into her car and brought the engine to life. Her gaze scanned the passenger seat where hiking boots sat at the ready.

Normally, she adored hikes. Something about being out in the wild, communing with nature, felt right. The wilderness called to something deep within her soul. Being in the woods brought out her baser instincts. She slept better, lived better after she'd been on a brisk hike.

However, tonight a definite urgency spurred the hike. She'd lost track of time in the mall, and now the sun was setting. Varrick must have discovered she wasn't in the compound. He would be furious with her for not informing anyone where she intended to go.

Elizabeth hit the heater in the Volkswagen, trying to take the chill from her bones, though whether it was from the cold outside or the fear of Varrick's ire, she couldn't be sure. It wasn't far to the hiking trail that would take her back up the mountain to the compound, perhaps twenty minutes. Just enough time for the interior of her car to get toasty warm. She shook off her hood and unzipped her parka.

Elizabeth's car quickly ate up the miles to the trail. After parking, she glanced back at the purchases she'd made.

Better to leave them for another day, she decided. *Varrick will have enough to be upset about without seeing how much I spent today. I'll send a guard down to retrieve them tomorrow.*

She jogged around the car and sat in the passenger seat. With the ease of having done so on a hundred other occasions, she laced up her boots, then zipped her parka, and took off at a brisk pace down the trail.

The frosty mountain air nipped her cheeks as she marched along the uneven ground. Each heavy breath burned her lungs, but the pain made her feel alive. She reveled in the cold on her body. The air smelled fresh, cleaned by the recent rain. With each breath, she took a bit of the forest into her very being, at one with the outdoors.

Elizabeth listened to a bird sing its evening melody in a nest cradled high above in the branches of a maple tree. The pine trees swayed around her in the light breeze, their thick needles a striking contrast to the bare oaks and maples that surrounded them.

As minutes turned to hours and the trail disappeared, the moonlight created changing shadows on the forest floor. The gray and silvery tones cast a wintry glow over the land. The temperature dropped, and Elizabeth cupped her hands in front of her mouth and blew. She should have reached the compound by now. Darkness closed in, and she realized she was lost. A shiver ran through her as much from the cold as from fear.

Elizabeth plunged up the mountainside recklessly with a painful stitch in her side and her body shaking. The pain had hit her sooner than she expected because of the steep elevation. She held her waist and continued up the mountain, her shaky steps faltering with fatigue. She'd lost track of time, but it seemed like she had been hiking forever. Though her body shook from the cold, she was numb.

Her golden eyes searched the forest for a hint of a trail, something that indicated she headed in the correct bearing. She'd always had a natural sense of direction, but here in the freezing temperature, she'd gotten confused, unsure of which way to go. The ground, covered in a fresh snowfall, held no recognizable landmarks.

She slowed her pace, wiping the sweat from her brow, as she turned a circle to take stock of her surroundings. Eerily similar trees, with their attenuated bodies, surrounded her in stark contrast to the lush green pines. The fresh carpet of snow lay pristine in little mounds with only her footprints to mar it. If a path had been there for Elizabeth to discover, it was efficiently covered by the unspoiled snow, leaving Elizabeth to run aimlessly through the forest.

The compound can't be much farther. You can do this. Keep going. Elizabeth encouraged herself as her boots caught on an immovable mound.

The rock, covered completely by the snow, had escaped her notice until her leg twisted. Now it had her full attention as pain travel from her ankle to lodge in her brain.

"Damn it!" she cried, hopping on one foot, grabbing her injured ankle.

Sparing a moment, Elizabeth rolled her foot, testing the ankle's range of motion. It moved; it burned like fire, but it moved.

"Not broken, maybe sprained though," she

observed aloud, gingerly putting her foot down and testing her weight on the injury.

Elizabeth needed to keep going. She needed to keep moving, keep going forward, get to the…get to.

Her thoughts wavered. Where was she heading? What did she need to do? Her mind clouded like the puffs of her breath in the air, pretty puffy clouds that danced in front of her eyes, disappearing in time for her to create another one. One after the other, cloud after cloud. Did that one have a shape? Perhaps she could make a cloud ring.

Her uncle blew smoke rings with his pipe. Pipes smelled good, she liked pipes, but she didn't smoke. Smoking was bad, she learned that in school. School was fun. She liked gym class the best because she liked to run.

Her thoughts ping-ponged around her brain. Elizabeth found it difficult to focus, to concentrate. Automation alone made her step forward. As she did, the pain radiating from her ankle brought her mind into sharper focus. She needed to get up the mountain, find the compound, and find Varrick. Sheer determination kept her moving through each painful step as she struggled to remain on task.

****

Varrick stepped out of the infirmary and ran his fingers through his hair. Demons were highly susceptible to disease, and that more than anything kept their mortality rates high. They were capable of living a long time, much longer than a human, if they remained healthy. However, every exposure to humans brought the possibility of death wrapped in an invisible package called virus. He needed to discover how to protect his people, to save them.

It was a heavy burden on his shoulders, being responsible for an entire race, watching helplessly as young and old died. A burden he'd shouldered alone for decades, but now he had a mate to ease him, help him rule, lift him up when everything bore down on him. It was too good to be true. He needed to hold his mate in his arms, feel she was real.

He'd been neglectful of her today. One duty had led to another without a break, but now he'd reap the reward of a day well worked by spending the night with his sexy Elizabeth.

Varrick went down the hall and into their bedroom but found it empty. He shook his head. *I don't know why I actually thought she would follow my order to stay put. Wonder where she is.*

He lifted his nose in the air and used his bestial sense of smell to track her scent. He followed it down the hallway to one of the entrances of the compound. When he realized it led out the opening, rage consumed him.

Varrick snatched the guard posted there by his neck and threw him on his ass. The male slid across the hall, coming to a stop when he crashed against the granite wall. In an instant, the male scampered to crouch on one knee. One forearm resting on his bent knee, he bowed his head over his arm kowtowing to his liege.

Varrick stalked toward the male. "I can smell her on you. Where is she?" he demanded looking stern and implacable.

"She went out," the guard answered, keeping his head lowered in submission, his eyes on the floor.

"You mean, you let her go alone?"

"She is your queen. She insisted on going alone. It was not my place to deny her."

Varrick paced the floor like a caged animal. "How long ago did she leave?"

The guard glanced up then quickly averted his gaze. "Sixteen, maybe seventeen—"

"Minutes?" Varrick asked hopefully.

"Hours," the guard squeezed out.

"*What!*"

Varrick let out a foul curse. He'd been preoccupied, checking on the sick, taking care of his duties. But he'd never imagined Elizabeth would take off and leave the compound after the warning he'd given her.

Things between them were strained. Perhaps she'd run off. His ire grew. He had to find her.

Now!

Varrick stormed toward the entrance and pushed the button that triggered the mechanism to open the thick, granite door. Within two strides, he let the lion take him, shifting as he ran. The distinct sound of material splitting reached his ears when the clothes ripped from his body with the change. By the time he reached the icy ground, his muscle and sinew distorted into the form of a lion. A thick pelt covered his body, keeping the cold from his bones as he rushed toward his mate.

She'd been gone much too long. He didn't doubt his ability to find her, especially in lion form. Varrick would find her, and when he did, she would never leave him again. The King would make sure of it. She might not have accepted him as her mate yet, but she would at some point.

Varrick ran hard, pushing his muscles faster as thoughts of Elizabeth urged him through the rugged terrain. Following her tracks in the snow, his smooth strides ate up the mountain side. Her familiar scent strengthened on the chilly air burning his nostrils.

The cold kept at bay by his impenetrable lion hide, he didn't worry about the frigid weather nor did he worry about being seen. His only thoughts were of finding his mate.

He had been patient with her, understanding when she wanted some time alone. He had made her laugh. She had responded favorably to him in bed just a short time ago. Why then had she still not accepted they were mates?

It did not make sense.

Hot breath clouded before his eyes in the frosty mountain air, fogging his vision. He heard the pounding of her heart, the snapping of twigs under her feet, before he saw her. Varrick put on a burst of speed, bringing his mate into sight.

His exceptional vision easily made out her shape, her long blonde hair swishing from side to side, her lopsided gate concerning.

He bounded up behind her and placed his front paws atop her shoulders, then gingerly brought her down to the ground beneath his large body, careful not to hurt her with his enormous weight.

Elizabeth struggled weakly. Her limbs flailed when her body sank into the snow. As if playing dead, suddenly she ceased all movement, and Varrick's lion pushed her further into the muddy ground when she relaxed under its weight.

Varrick withdrew his paw from her shoulder. She turned her head just enough for them to make eye contact while he straddled her with his body. The terror on her face pulled at his heart. In his rage, he'd been thoughtless. He was suddenly mindful of how scary it must be to have a large male lion standing over her.

Elizabeth gazed into the lion's eyes, and a look of recognition crept over her rosy face.

"Varrick?" she whispered, fear strangling her voice.

He remained motionless, not wanting to scare her.

"Varrick, that's you, isn't it?" Elizabeth asked, her voice stronger, more confident.

She rolled over and raised a hand at a snail's pace, as if waiting for confirmation the beast standing over her would refrain from hurting her. The reassurance came in the form of a smile. The lion's mouth pulled back into a lopsided grin, and its tongue listed to one side.

Both arms inched up, and Elizabeth buried her shaking hands in his golden mane. He lowered his head so she could run her fingers over his ears and around his head, to cup his muzzle between her hands. Varrick purred his approval when she brought his face to hers and nuzzled his mane.

"You're beautiful," she breathed, then pulled back and stared at him through hooded eyes. "And soft like rich creamy satin."

A long pink tongue licked roughly from her chin to her forehead. The decadent flavor of her tasted like kettle corn, salty and sweet from the combination of perspiration and melted snow. Varrick licked his lips, he couldn't help himself.

Varrick's form shimmered, and the fur shrank back into the skin. The muscle and sinew reshaped. His ears shifted from the top of the head down to the sides. The muzzle shortened into a handsome face held in Elizabeth's hands. Varrick noticed the shiver that went through her body, unsure whether the frigid air or his transformation caused it.

Experienced in frailties, Varrick realized at this temperature Elizabeth would succumb to hypothermia.

"It's too cold to be out here for hours," he admonished her.

"I'm fine. It'sss not cold. Might have made it. D-do you think I have hippo...hypo...hypothermsssia?" Elizabeth slurred.

"Possibly. It is freezing out here, Elizabeth. You might have caught a cold or worse, you might have died." Varrick grabbed her by the arms and gave her a shake. Her head rolled on her shoulders.

"You might have *died*," Varrick repeated, his voice softening with concern, as he held her to him. The perpetual five o'clock shadow on his jaw caught the stray wisps of her hair when he nuzzled his chin atop her head. Her body felt like ice against his bare chest. The body temperature of Demons was naturally a little warmer than humans, but the difference between their bodies startled him.

Her eyes appeared glassy as she looked through him instead of at him. The warning signs were all there: shivering, lack of coordination, difficulty thinking, slurred speech, lack of concern about one's current situation. He needed to get her warm, quickly.

"Elizabeth, look at me." He grabbed her chin roughly in his hand and turned her face up toward his, forcing her attention.

"I'm going to change back into my lion. You need to climb onto my back, Little Bits. Do you understand?"

Elizabeth tried to nod her head, but it appeared too heavy for her neck.

"Answer me. Do you understand?" Varrick's voice brooked no dissension.

"Yessss," she slurred weakly.

He helped her stand, propping her against a nearby tree. If the bark bit into her frozen back, she didn't seem to notice. Holding her to the tree with one arm, he let his lion take him. Beginning with his legs, the transformation moved upward. His muscles contorted, fur pushed through his skin. The arm pinning Elizabeth was the last to alter.

This time she did not shudder at his transformation for she was unconscious. He removed his paw from her chest and quickly threw his body against her knees so her limp form flopped over his strong back.

After letting his concern for his mate tear a roar from his throat, he ran as fast as he dared, careful not to dislodge his listless rider. Varrick headed for his home. *Their home*, he corrected. Concern for her safety spurred him on at a steady clip. He needed to get her back to his chamber. He needed to know she was safe and vowed to do whatever it took to see no harm would ever come to her again.

Chapter 15

Julie tossed her last pair of jeans into the growing pile of clothes strewn across the bed and blew out an exasperated sigh as her hands fisted on her hips.

"Well, that's it, Penny. It's official. That's everything I brought with me. And I don't have a single thing I can wear out tonight. Maybe I shouldn't go at all."

"No. No. No. You're going on the date. Jules, you have to go." Penny sat beside the mound of clothes. "Want to go into my room and see if I have something you can borrow?"

Julie blew a raspberry. "Oh please, like your clothes would fit me."

"Oh, Julie. There has to be something you can wear." Penny pulled a gray skirt from the pile. "What about this? I have a cute cardigan. It would go perfect. Look."

Penny spread the wool skirt out flat on the bed and tucked Julie's white blouse into the waist of the skirt.

"Watch this." Penny sprinted into the adjoining room and returned carrying a pink sweater.

She fit the soft cardigan around the blouse and skirt, then stood back to admire her work. "That is spot on. Sheer perfection," she remarked smugly.

"It's not bad. This might just work," agreed Juliette. A smile took her face as she met Penny's gaze.

"Good eye."

"That ties it. You must go on the date now. We found the perfect outfit. It's meant to be." A grin widened across Penny's face.

In unison, their heads whipped toward the sound of a knock at the door.

Juliette glanced at her watch and panic took her smile. "Oh my gosh! It's already seven. It must be him!"

Penny padded across the room and peeked through the peep hole in the door. Against the door, she whispered, "You're right. It's him."

Penny's gaze remained on the peephole as if she couldn't stop staring at the handsome man who stood on the other side.

Penny turned back toward her friend, a Cheshire cat grin lighting her face. "He's posh in a dark gray suit and matching shirt. With that dark hair and those eyes, he's the picture of sophistication. Oh, how I envy you. If I wasn't married…" she mused wistfully, closing her eyes as she took a deep breath.

"I'm going to tell Frank you said that," joked Juliette.

Penny laughed.

"Somehow I don't imagine Frank would care. He knows he's got me stuck to him now that his baby is in my belly. Besides, a girl can look, can't she? And luv," she continued without taking a breath, "that is one man I'd never get tired of looking at."

Juliette giggled. "Penny, what am I going to do? I'm not dressed."

"I'll go chat him up while you finish getting ready." Penny opened the door just wide enough for her petite figure to fit through.

"Hi," greeted Penny joyfully and pulled the door shut behind her.

Juliette stood before the full-length mirror. After donning the chosen outfit, she smoothed the gray wool skirt and sighed as she noted how the pink cashmere sweater bunched open around the buttons. Julie quickly undid the buttons so the sweater hung loosely about her trunk. It still hugged her body more than she would have liked, but it would have to do.

Scrutinizing the image in the mirror, she had to admit she had her mother's body, and no matter how little she ate or how much she worked out, those curves stayed in place.

Of course, her father had never minded her mother's curves. She envied their relationship. Julie missed having someone she could come home to, someone she knew would be there for her to lean on and confide in, to laugh with and love, even if that person, like Steve, didn't appreciate her curves. Jules shook the thought from her mind and returned her attention to the moment at hand.

She pulled at the sweater hoping to stretch it so it might be a tad looser, then ran her fingers over her hair to smooth down the strays. *There's nothing more I can do. Here goes nothing,* she thought and turned to leave.

****

"I am looking forward to spending some time with our Juliette. When do you think she will be ready?"

"Soon." Her gaze roamed his full height, drinking him in.

When he flashed her a grin, she seemed off balance. "Shall we sit down while we wait for her?"

"Sounds like a grand idea."

Penny hooked her arm into Nicholai's proffered elbow, and the two found a place in the lobby where they could wait for Juliette's appearance.

The pair remained deep in conversation. Nicholai seized on the opportunity to speak to Julie's friend alone and peppered Penny with questions, trying to discern as much information about his heartmate's past and present as possible.

"So you are telling me she is a widow?" Concern drew his lips down into a frown.

"Yes, and she had two daughters. An accident took all three of them."

"That is tragic. I do not know how she can handle such unbearable pain."

Jealousy over the fact she'd once loved another man warred with protectiveness of wanting to shield her from the pain she'd suffered at his loss. Intellectually, he realized he should not be jealous of her dead spouse. If anything, he should be glad she had been able to find love. However, his desire to protect her from anything that would cause her pain made it difficult for him to rejoice in the knowledge she'd once shared her life with another man.

"How old were the gir—"

The sight of Juliette descending the stairs interrupted Nicholai's next question. A vision, her skirt and sweater clung to her in all the right places and showed off her feminine curves. The pink from her sweater brightened her complexion, giving her cheeks a healthy, rosy glow. The light from the sconces on the wall reflected in her shiny, chestnut hair to make highlights as it swayed with each step. She was the most beautiful woman Nicholai had ever seen in all his long years.

With fluidity only one of his kind possessed, he rose from the chair and sauntered toward the stairs, his eyes never leaving Juliette. He extended his hand and captured hers as she maneuvered the final three steps. Raising her hand to his lips, he planted a gentle kiss on the back of it when she reached the bottom of the staircase.

"Good evening," he greeted, retaining possession of her hand.

"I hope I didn't keep you waiting too long." She glanced up, and his hazel eyes caught hers.

"For you, my dear Juliette, I would wait an eternity." *I basically have.*

"Am I dressed okay?" Julie tugged on her sweater. "I wasn't sure what I should wear."

"You are perfect the way you are. You look beautiful, Juliette." She trembled slightly at the sound of her name on his lips.

"So where are you going?" Penny asked, reminding Nicholai she remained in the room.

"I have made reservations for us."

"At The Cold Shoulder?" Penny guessed.

"No. I want to introduce Juliette to some of the other fine establishments my country has to offer. It is a surprise. If that is okay with you, Juliette." He gave her a teasing smirk, then took the coat draped over her arm.

As he helped her into the wrap, she replied, "Of course. That's fine. I like surprises."

"Then shall we go, my dear?" Nicholai offered Julie his arm.

"Absolutely," she agreed, and wove her arm with

his. Julie looked over her shoulder as they headed for the door. "Goodbye, Penny."

"Have fun." Penny waved, then muttered under her breath, "I know you will."

While too low for Julie to hear, Nicholai's preternatural hearing had no trouble discerning the comment. It brought a smile to his face while he and Julie exited the door of the inn.

A blast of chilly, winter air hit them when they emerged into the night. The scent of fresh snow tickled his nose. A shiver went through Julie, and he tucked her under his shoulder. He wished he could transport her instantly to the warmth awaiting them in the restaurant he'd chosen. Unfortunately, while dematerializing might be easy for him, he knew of no vampire who could transport others. They had no choice except to make their way to the restaurant the old-fashioned way, in his car. But at least it would be a comfy ride.

After a short drive, Nicholai led her inside the fancy, old-world restaurant. They sat in soft chairs made of crushed blue velvet around a table covered by white linen. The centerpiece, a single candle floating in a clear round bowl, lit Juliette's features and made her eyes sparkle.

Nicholai found himself with a grin as wide as a schoolboy's. His hot gaze traveled down his heartmate's body to the hand which lay on the round table. His desire to touch her, to caress the smoothness of her skin, seemed too fierce to rein in, so he placed his own large hand on top of hers. It gave him a sense of completion to feel her creamy softness beneath his fingers.

The warmth from the caress sent sparks of

lightning up his arm, and Juliette must have experienced it too for her breath quickened its pace. Nicholai noticed the change, watched her bosom rise and fall with each breath. It was tantalizing, hypnotic. He could observe her body's reaction to his touch all night but reluctantly pulled his gaze higher when he realized he stared at her chest.

Nicholai barely spared their server a glance as she came to the table and removed the empty bowls from the third course. He refused to take his eyes from his mate for more than a second. "How did you enjoy the *silonka*?"

Juliette's gaze met his. "I loved it. You have good taste. Thank you for ordering it. I can't wait to see what else you've chosen for tonight."

"Thank you." He gave Julie a slight nod of acknowledgement.

"You're welcome, sir," the waitress replied.

When the grin slipped from Juliette's face, jealousy lit her eyes.

Nicholai fought the grin. He found her jealousy endearing, if unwarranted. He only had eyes for his Juliette. Knowing she needed a distraction, he asked, "So what do you think of this place? Do you like it?"

Julie glanced around at their surroundings. The restaurant boasted ivory-colored walls which met ornate crown molding. They sat directly across from a stone fireplace, the heat from which blushed Julie's cheeks. He hoped she would love the meal and the setting enough to grant him a second date.

"Oh, yes," she finally stated. "This place is gorgeous, elaborate really."

The waitress gingerly placed the fine china plates

down on top of the gold chargers that lay on their table. The plates made a delicate clinking sound like the plucked strings of an angel's harp. The musical sound drew Julie's attention, and she glanced down at the food placed before her.

"What is this?" she inquired of Nicholai.

"It is Chicken Kiev."

At Juliette's insistence, Nicholai had ordered their entire meal from the *rassolnik* to the *piroshky*. All seven courses had been carefully chosen to give her an authentic taste of Russian cuisine. He wanted to immerse her in his culture, the culture she would be a part of once she agreed to be his.

"And what's that?" she asked with a smile and a slight giggle in her voice.

"It is chicken and herbs wrapped in bread crumbs and fried."

"Chicken? I'm glad it's chicken. I feared it would be some kind of fish. I know Russians love their fish, but the only fish I'll eat is salmon."

"We are renowned for our seafood," Nicholai observed. He gently rubbed his index finger across the back of her hand before reluctantly withdrawing his hand in order to cut his food.

"Speaking of seafood, one thing I've never tried is caviar."

Nicholai's grin widened. "We will fix that tonight, my beloved."

He raised his hand above his head, and their server immediately appeared at his side.

While Nicholai relayed his instructions in Russian, Julie turned her attention to the food and took a bite of the Chicken Kiev.

"Mmmmm," she hummed. "This is scrumptious."

"I am unfamiliar with the term. What is scrumptious?"

"It means very, very good," Julie explained.

"Ahhhhh, like you. I'm glad you like it. So tell me about your family." Nicholai forked another bite into his mouth.

"There's not much to tell."

"Are your mother and father still alive?" he pressed.

"Oh yes, they are very much alive and well. They live in a town called Camdin Falls. It's in Virginia, in the US."

Nicholai grinned. "I know where Camdin Falls is."

"Really? Most people have never heard of it."

"I have a friend who lives there."

"You do?" Shock widened her eyes incredulously. "Seriously?"

"Yes. I've known him for years," he said. "In fact, Alexander and I go way back."

Just how far back, he couldn't tell Julie. Alexander was a member of the Alpha Council. The two of them had been fighting evil together for over a century.

"I have been to Camdin Falls on several occasions."

"You're kidding," Julie commented dubiously.

Nicholai had been there many times, one of which had been to work with Alex to take out a vampire who had set up a human-feeding slave operation on farmland just outside of town. Nicholai thought it best to change the subject before she pressed him on why he had been in her hometown.

"Do you have any brothers or sisters?" he further

inquired.

"Yes, I have one sister, but she doesn't live in Camdin Falls. She lives in New York."

"Ah, New York. I enjoyed my time there."

"You've been a lot of places," Julie observed.

"I get around." Nicholai gave a cryptic shrug of his broad shoulders.

"You are so young to have done so much traveling."

A wryly expression crossed his face. "Oh, I'm older than I look."

His comment gave Juliette pause. "But I thought…"

When she swallowed the comment, he pushed, "You thought what?"

Julie's cheek turned a deeper shade of red, giving her a sheepish appearance. "Oh, nothing."

"Please tell me what you were going to say."

"You look like you are in your early twenties. I am a bit older than that."

"So you believe you are older than me?"

"By at least fifteen years." Julie shifted uncomfortably. "I hope that isn't an issue."

Nicholai leaned over, resting his forearms on each side of his plate. "I have seen a lot in my time. Enough to realize where I want to be, and who I want to be with."

Relief softened her features. She patted her lips with the napkin from her lap and replaced it before she looked at him. His eyes darkened, burrowed into her soul until he captured her with the stark passion in his gaze. She leaned forward. He easily read her intention to kiss him and was all too happy to meet her across the table.

Their waitress chose that most inopportune moment to saunter up to their table, carrying a bucket of champagne in one arm and a glass container in the other. She set the champagne down first, then slipped the glass vessel into the middle of the table between the couple, effectively breaking the magnetic pull between their bodies.

Nicholai let out a disappointed sigh. "The caviar has arrived."

He moved his chair around the table, so he sat beside Julie instead of across from her.

"Are you ready to take your first bite of the food of the gods?"

He took a small piece of blini from the container and placed a portion of Beluga Caviar on the tiny mother-of-pearl spoon. He topped the creation with a dab of *crème fraîche* and fed her the concoction.

"Well, what do you think?" His brows rose with curiosity.

Julie covered her mouth with her hand. "It's salty…but good," she replied hesitantly. "I like it. But it is too much food. With so many courses, I can't possibly eat much more."

"I noticed you haven't been eating too much. Tell me why. Do you not like what I chose?"

Julie shook her head emphatically. "I love what you have chosen. I'm just watching my figure."

"I have been watching your figure all night. I can assure you it looks good to me." Nicholai winked and gave her a mischievous grin. Julie blushed and glanced away.

"I'm glad you liked the caviar. I hoped you would,

especially with the sweet *crème fraîche*."

"You say *crème fraîche* perfectly. Do you speak French?" Julie asked.

"Oui, mademoiselle. Je parle Français. Et tous?"

"I have no idea what you said," Julie admitted.

"I said yes, I speak French. How about you?"

"No. I'm not nearly as good as you at speaking languages. I'm lucky I was able to learn enough Russian to get by on this trip."

Nicholai smiled. He slowly lifted the topped blini to her lips. His stomach clenched when her lips brushed his fingers as they closed around his offering. His inner beast banged its fists against its chest in triumph as he fed her. Providing for his mate was as instinctual as mating itself. Today he would provide, soon he would mate. A satisfied growl threatened to tear from his throat.

"French is but one of the languages I speak."

Julie swallowed the caviar. "Wow! You speak Russian, English, and French. Just how many languages do you speak?"

"I can also speak Spanish and Italian."

"Italian is such a beautiful language. Say something," she commanded dreamily.

Immediately, the perfect phrase came to mind.

"Ti amo, Cara."

"What did you say?"

"Ya tebya lyublyu," he repeated in Russian.

"What does it mean in English?"

He couldn't yet tell her. She wasn't ready to hear his declaration of love though his heart wanted him to say "I love you" yet again.

"One day I will tell you," he promised, and

prepared another blini with the caviar and crème mixture.

"Why not tell me now?"

"Because, my dear Juliette, if you wish to find out what I said, I will require something from you first."

"What is that?"

"I want to see you again. To find out what it means, I require at least one more date with you before I tell you." Nicholai took her hand in his. "I have so enjoyed our time together. Did you enjoy it as well, my dear?"

"Yes," she admitted readily, her eyes down cast on her plate at the half-eaten food.

"Then will you come out with me again tomorrow night? It will be a grand adventure. I promise. Please say yes."

"How can I resist an offer like that? Yes." Julie pushed her uneaten food around her plate. "Where will we be going?"

Nicholai steepled his fingers. "I think it will be a surprise."

Nicholai easily read the thoughts that brought a resplendent grin to brighten Julie's beautiful face.

I love surprises, especially ones that involve spending time with an incredibly handsome man. I have no idea how he knows, but somehow he seems to know things about me, knows exactly what to do and say.

Of course, being in her mind gave him an unfair advantage, but there was no way he would chance doing or saying the wrong thing and driving her away.

"What should I wear?"

A half-smile pulled at one corner of his lips. "Women and clothes. Are you always worried about what to wear?" He chuckled and gave her button nose a gentle bop with his finger. "Something comfortable you can walk around in. Jeans and a sweater should be fine."

"What time should I be ready?"

"I'll arrive at the inn after the sun goes down."

Juliette nodded enthusiastically. Suddenly her face dropped. "Wait. I forgot. I can't go."

Nicholai's heart clenched.

Chapter 16

It's good to be the king. His father's voice boomed in his head. Varrick scrubbed a hand down his face and scoffed at the memory.

Sure being king of the demon race came with perks: his every whim catered to, subjects were loyal, his days were mostly his own. But, as the saying went, with great power came great responsibility. Being responsible for an entire race weighed heavily. His people needed him, and a certain beautiful queen consumed him.

A knock pulled him from his thoughts.

"Enter." His deep voice echoed off the granite walls of the training room.

His sister's guard pushed open the great wooden doors.

"Remain outside," Jara commanded. She tossed her sandy-blonde hair, so much like his own, over her shoulder. Her red eyes glowed above cheekbones which stood out against her hollow cheeks. Pulled into a tight line, Jara's small mouth indicated she wasn't happy.

"To what do I owe the pleasure of your company?" Not that he really wanted to know. Jara always brought bad news.

She gathered energy in the palm of her hand. It coalesced into a reddish orange ball she lobbed into each of the torches on the wall, instantly igniting the tinder. The ambient glow filled the room, and shadows danced in time with the flickering flames.

Jara glanced at the long sword Varrick held in his hand. "Practicing in the dark again?"

"It sharpens my senses."

Jara moved toward him and laid a hand on his thick biceps in a conciliatory gesture. "You needn't tell me. I remember all too well Father's training sessions with you."

Varrick fought the shiver that threatened to creep down his spine at the reminder of his upbringing. Their father enjoyed teaching them lessons. His tutorage typically left Varrick bloody and broken.

"I've come to see how Elizabeth is faring after her outing."

Varrick scoffed. "I'm surprised you care."

Jara had the good sense to look affronted by the comment. "Of course I care. Though I can't see why, you care for her deeply, and that makes me care too.

"I know you don't want to hear this, brother, but having a human—"

"Half human," Varrick corrected.

Jara tipped her head. "A half human in the compound is dangerous."

"I know we are susceptible to human diseases, Jara, but we live in a mountain fortress. The walls are granite. I don't believe Elizabeth is a threat to our health."

Jara moved around the side of the fighting mat. "Perhaps we should find a way to protect us from diseases, just in case."

"Do you think I have not tried?" *Especially after Elizabeth's little stunt could have resulted in her getting a cold or the flu.*

"I think you have been preoccupied by your queen. I, on the other hand, have been in the tomes room. I might have an idea."

A way for him to be with Elizabeth without having to fear catching something that would kill him? "Tell me more."

A sanguine smirk took Jara's face. "I discovered something that may help cure us once and for all."

Hope bloomed in his chest. "Tell me." He motioned for the two of them to sit on the mat.

Jara situated her long, red gossamer robe out of the way and gracefully floated down beside him. "I found a long-buried tome. It described a race of creatures with great strength and speed. They feed on the blood of others—"

"Vampires," Varrick interrupted. "We know of vampires—grew up hearing stories about them as if they were boogie men. Our parents were quick to impress on us to remain hidden from them because they are so violent."

"Yes, but we are just as fast and strong, so why do you suppose we were told to remain hidden from them?" Jara continued as Varrick ruminated on the question. "I might know why. Did you know vampires don't get ill?"

"What? I was never told that. How did you learn that?"

"It's in the tome, dear brother. According to the ancient writing, demons believed vampires carried disease but never became ill themselves. That's why we had to stay away: they could infect us."

Jara's eyes glowed red with excitement. "I believe

if we can harness the vampire healing ability, our people can be saved."

"And how do you propose we do that?"

"I'm no scientist, but I know a damned good one. Lane. I spoke to him to see what his thoughts are on the subject."

Lane's brilliance was well known. "What did he have to say?"

A wicked smile took Jara's face. "He suggested a vampire might be the key to discovering how to boost our immune systems. He'd like to do some experiments."

"Experiments?" Varrick stomach knotted. "What kind of experiments?"

"He wants to kidnap a vampire and see if he can ascertain what in its makeup allows it to heal and remain disease free."

"I can't allow it."

"Why not, Varrick? It's not like we owe anything to a vampire. Have you forgotten about what happened to Alcid?"

"Of course, I have not forgotten what happened to our sister's husband," Varrick snapped. "Authorizing a kidnapping and experimentation, even on a vampire, is not something I do lightly."

"But you'll authorize it? Right, my dear brother?" Jara batted her eyes. "What is the life of one vampire when hundreds of demons might be saved? When your dear Elizabeth might be able to remain healthy?"

A chance for his Elizabeth to live as she wanted, go to town, possibly be around humans and not bring back a disease that could kill them—it was too much to hope for. The thought of experimenting on another being was offensive to him. But if it led to his people having a normal life…Did he dare to imagine a time when demon kind might walk among the humans and not risk their lives? If there was the slightest chance, it would be worth it.

"Fine. I'll allow Lane to experiment on one vampire."

Jara squealed in delight. "I'll go tell him right now." She jumped to her feet.

Varrick rose as well. "But, sister mine, know this. I do this with a heavy heart. Lane is to make his experiment as painless as possible. Understand?"

"Of course. I might even know where to find a vampire."

"How would you know something like that?"

"As I tried to tell you the other day, Lovazia ran into one."

"*WHAT*!" Varrick jumped to his feet.

Jara rested a quelling hand on his forearm. "Don't worry. I told her to leave the bloodsucker alone."

"She better. If Lane needs a vampire, we will either find one or I'll send my guards after the one Lovazia knows of. I don't want her anywhere near the creature. Understand?"

"Of course, dear brother. I'll go tell Lane the news."

"Remember I want him to make the experiments as painless as possible," he reiterated, calling after her as she flung open the chamber doors and left with Cyrus falling in behind her.

A sense of trepidation crept up his spine. What had he done? Giving Jara her way rarely resulted in anything good. However, if Lane could cure their vulnerability so he could be with Elizabeth, then he had to take that chance.

Varrick gathered his energy in the palm of his hand and sent fire down his blade, instantly igniting the fuel. The flames danced in time with each forceful swing and graceful parry as he resumed his training session to work off the impending dread.

Chapter 17

Disappointment pricked along Nicholai's skin. "Why can't you come with me tomorrow?"

"Because I promised to do more sightseeing with Penny." Her eyes flicked up and met his steady gaze from under her long lashes.

Julie took another small bite of her chicken and chewed, allowing herself time to consider the question. "I don't feel right leaving Penny alone for a second night."

Nicholai wanted to belay her worry. "Penny is invited too, if you would like her to join us. The place I have in mind can easily accommodate all three of us."

He intended on taking the women to see the Peterhof Palace. Having once belonged to his family, it now housed a museum located in St. Petersburg.

"Why not bring your friend with us?"

"Do you mind if I call Penny first to be sure she is okay with the idea?" she asked him.

"Of course," Nicholai assured her. "Go ahead. Call her now."

"That's a great idea." Julie stepped away from the table as she drew the phone from her purse. "I'll be only a minute."

She punched in a number and strolled across the restaurant, obviously seeking a place that would afford her a little privacy.

Nicholai spooned a bit of the caviar into his mouth. As he savored the salty delight, he lifted the champagne from the ice bucket and poured himself a glass before doing the same with Julie's flute.

Nicholai leaned back in his plush velvet chair and looked around, noting the people in the room. He watched his heartmate navigate the restaurant, phone to her ear, until a pin-thin, blonde woman obscured his view.

For a reason he could not fathom, his stomach tightened. His protective instincts screamed at him, demanded he go to his mate and ensure her safety. Just as his intuition pushed him forward in his chair and he started to rise, the tall blonde passed by Julie and moved toward the bar.

Juliette walked across the crowded room. The sight of her swaying hips sent a rush of lust coursing through his body, hardening it. She was sheer perfection in his eyes. He loved those curves she lamented about. Nothing enticed him like a woman with an hourglass figure. Modern stick-figure models with their boyish bodies did nothing for him. It thrilled him his heartmate had a fuller womanly body.

He took a sip of champagne and watched her ample bosom jostle slightly with each step in her high heels. The gentle up and down motion mesmerized him and brought a sensuous grin to his lips.

She gracefully slipped into her soft chair.

"So?" he asked. "Are we a go? Do I get to spend another evening basking in your beautiful presence?"

A warm smile reached Julie's honey eyes. "Penny said she wouldn't miss a surprise from you for anything in the world."

"And what of you, would you miss a surprise from me?"

"No, I wouldn't," she responded in a whisper.

Nicholai settled into his chair. "That is want I wanted to hear. You have made my heart sing, *golubchik*."

A sting prickled over his skin as his preternatural senses alerted him to danger. Nicholai sent his awareness flowing through the building, seeking out anything unusual.

Another blank spot.

Concern flooded his mind, and Nicholai took in a deep inhale, trying to scent the cause of the void. His eyes jetted from person to person. He amplified his hearing, tried to discern what caused his inner alarm to sound. But he found nothing unusual, nothing to cause unease…other than the void.

Perhaps I'm overreacting, he reasoned to himself. *Maybe it's another side effect of being so close to my heartmate. My protectiveness is in overdrive.*

Juliette looked concerned. She tugged at her pink sweater, then worried her bottom lip between her teeth. Jarred from his own thoughts by her distress, he shook off his worry and lifted his champagne glass.

"A toast," he proposed, then tilted his glass in her direction and waited for Julie to raise her crystal flute in kind. "To love and the strength it can give to us, *golubchik*."

Nicholai and Juliette mirrored each other as they tipped their flutes forward and touch glasses. The sound of the fine crystal rang in the night.

"Before you ask, *golubchik* means *lovebird*," Nicholai offered.

Nicholai's hand rested possessively on the nape of her neck and drew her to him. He gently brushed his lips over hers.

When her lips parted in licentious invitation willing his tongue entry in her mouth, he deepened the kiss. He tasted her sweetness mixed with the dry champagne. A wonderful combination, one he could drink in forever. Their tongues danced in unison.

His heart took flight. His body responded in kind, soaring to great heights. He reveled in the temptation of her, the taste of her kiss.

A small moan escaped her mouth. The sound drove him wild, tightened the muscles of his hard body. His free hand found the hem of her skirt and slid under the wool to her thigh. His fingers traveled toward her feminine heat in a tantalizingly slow crawl. He sensed her arousal. Heat radiated from her body. The real Juliette was as responsive to his touch as the dream Juliette. More so, in truth.

Her hand found his knee and gripped it tight. He let himself be lost to her touch until he no longer knew where she stopped and he began.

The world melted away for both of them until their server, with the uncanny knack for timing, came to their table. They broke apart at the interruption.

Julie brought her fingers to her kiss-swollen lips, and Nicholai swallowed a moan as he grieved their separation. He noted the way Juliette looked, flushed, ready for more of his touch, and the thought of giving her more, much, much more, made him wish dawn would never come.

Desire burned through his blood. He wanted her, needed her with a desperation like never before, and he knew exactly what would sate it—time alone with her at the inn. He patted his lips with the napkin from his lap and laid it on the table before he signaled the waitress to bring them the check.

Chapter 18

As they drove back to the inn, the car glided along the road with the butter-soft leather cradling the passengers, soothing them into companionable silence. Julie's thoughts turned to the handsome man beside her.

Nicholai was stunning, gorgeous, a perfect example of masculine physique. His courtly old-world manners were something most modern men lacked. He held every door open for her. He'd been exceptionally polite all evening. Julie had never been with a man like him before. He seemed to be the whole package, everything she ever wanted.

But he also seemed too good to be true. And she feared he might be.

Jules had no doubt a man like him would quickly lose interest in someone like her. She'd gone on about herself all night. Of course, his questioning prompted most of what she had said, but she knew better than to talk about herself too much on a date. This was the kind of man who would go for her sister, not someone like her. Not to mention their age difference.

Yep, there are a lot of reasons why this won't last. So this is just a fun holiday fling, and that's okay. She resigned herself it would end soon.

Nicholai reached over and gave her thigh a heartening squeeze as if to reassure her before he eased the car to the curb in front of the inn. After cutting off the engine, he turned toward her, waiting until she returned his gaze before he spoke.

"I want you to know something, Juliette." The velvet timbre of his voice slid over her skin, made her think of rolling around under thick fur blankets in front of a roaring fire on a wintry Russian night. "I had a wonderful time tonight. I enjoyed your company and cannot wait until we get to see each other again."

"I'm looking forward to it, too." Julie glanced at the large hand on her thigh. A burning flame scorched up her leg and heated her inner core. His grip felt firm, yet gentle, commanding, yet giving. She wondered if he'd be the same in bed, gentle, giving, commanding, and firm. What a delicious combination.

Julie reprimanded herself for allowing her train of thought to take her in that direction. Her eyes roamed the chiseled features of his face and memorized the strong lines. Long cheekbones drove a path to his straight nose which led down to those sensual ruby lips and sturdy chin. He was beautiful, in a very manly way.

Nicholai graced her with a warm grin that lit his amber eyes, and another flash of sensual heat coursed through her body.

"You do not realize how glad I am to hear you say such a thing." He exited the car and opened the door for her, then handed her from the vehicle. As she stood, he wrapped an arm about her waist and guided her forward.

Still on cloud nine, Julie floated up the stairs, anchored to the earth only by the strong arm wrapped about her waist. When they reached the door to her room, he wrapped his other arm around her and drew her into his fervent embrace.

His hand trailed up her back, pulling her tightly against his hard muscular form. Her pliant body melted against his, her soft curves a perfect contrast to the firmness of his athletic body. Juliette felt weightless. Her knees weakened, and Nicholai bore most of her weight in his arms. He pinned her against the door with his large frame. Desire coursed through her brain, igniting her fervor.

Nicholai took her lips in a hard, almost punishing kiss. Juliette responded to his passionate aggression by fisting her fingers in his silky hair.

Electricity coursed between them, moved amid their bodies in a circuit. With each pass, the sensual desire grew stronger, sending the couple spiraling in erotic bliss until they both gasped for air.

Nicholai broke the kiss. A rush of cold air cooled her skin when he moved away.

"Wow," Jules told him on a reverent whisper.

"My thoughts exactly," he breathed. "I have no idea how I found the strength to pull away."

Juliette gave a heavy sigh. "You better go before our desire carries us away."

"That's probably for the best," Nicholai conceded with hunger in his eyes that indicated he rather do anything but.

Julie released his ebony strands and slid her hands down his arms. The taut muscles and sinew under the suit jacket flexed beneath her fingers. Nicholai's palms framed her ribcage for a moment before he finally released her from his embrace. He captured both her hands in his as if he were unable to stop touching her. Bringing them to his lips, he placed a light kiss on the back of each.

Julie desperately wanted to invite him in, but before she voiced the invitation, he spoke in that sinuous, husky voice.

"My dear Juliette, 'parting is such sweet sorrow, that I shall say good night till it be morrow.' " He sealed his pact to depart with a brief kiss before turning to take his leave.

Juliette watched him proceed down the stairs, then entered her room. The moment she closed and locked the door, Penny burst through the adjoining door to their rooms.

Jules shrugged off the borrowed sweater and handed it to her friend. "Here, I guess you came for this," she said nonchalantly as if she didn't know why Penny was actually there.

Penny huffed, snatched the sweater from her friend's hand, then crossed her arms under her breasts.

"Yeah, right. Don't be a prat," Penny admonished her. "You know quite well why I'm here, and it's not for my sweater. Now spill it. Dish. How was it? How did it go? What was he like? Where did he take you? What did you do?" She barely contained her enthusiasm as the questions fired from her lips in rapid secession like ammo from a machine gun.

Julie wrapped her arms around her waist. "It was wonderful," she informed her friend, her breath leaving her in a rush. "I've never met anyone like him before."

Penny hugged Julie tight about the shoulders. "I'm so happy for you," she gushed with exuberance. "Tell me all about it. I want all the details."

Julie blushed, remembering all too vividly the details of the times they had kissed. He had made her feel in ways no man had ever before, even her husband, whom she'd loved dearly. Never had her knees weakened simply from a kiss. Nicholai made her body crave his in a way that still had her blood boiling in her veins. But Julie was not a kiss and tell kind of person, and she chose to keep those details to herself.

"He kept me talking about myself most of the night," she admitted awkwardly. "I kind of felt funny. He kept asking questions and turning the conversation to me and my family and my life. Penny, by the end of the night he seemed to know me so well, like he knew what I was thinking. It was unreal."

Penny plunked down cross-legged on the bed and patted the mattress beside her, motioning for Jules to do the same. Julie lay down on her side facing Penny and propped her head on her crooked arm.

"Was he nice?" asked Penny.

"He was more than nice," Jules replied dreamily. "Nicholai was unbelievably polite. He held every door for me, including the car door. The man was kind, friendly, sweet. So much more than nice. It was the best date I've ever had." A pang of guilt made Julie flinch. "I mean, of course, besides the dates with Steve."

Penny gave her hand a sympathetic squeeze. "Jules, it has been three years since the accident, honey. It's okay. You're allowed to move on. It doesn't mean you didn't love Steve. It doesn't mean you have forgotten him or never cared for him.

"You are a great person, and you deserve some happiness in your life. Please allow yourself to enjoy your time with Nicholai. If not for yourself, would you at least do it for me?"

Julie gave her friend a reticent look, and Penny patted her hand. Intellectually, Julie knew her friend spoke the truth. Everyone was entitled to be happy, and she was no exception, but being happy with another man seemed like an injustice to the memory of her dead husband.

The sound of Penny's voice tore her from her thoughts. "This doesn't have to be a serious relationship if you aren't ready yet. Live in the moment. Take it one day at a time."

Juliette rolled her eyes and quipped, "Of course, I'm going to take it one day at a time. This is just a holiday fling. Sheesh! You sound like Dear Abby."

Penny laughed affably. "Well, I've been called worse. Dear Abby gives good advice. She's a smart woman, just like me."

The women laughed together, and Penny collapsed down beside Jules on the bed.

"So where are we going with him tomorrow?"

"I have no idea. He said it was a surprise."

"How should we dress?"

Juliette smiled. "I knew you would ask that. He said it was casual. Jeans and a sweater should be fine."

"I like a man who is considerate enough to tell a woman what to wear. He gets another point in my book. Let's add up the points, shall we?" Penny held up one finger in preparation to count the other points. Adding a finger for each point, she continued, "This man has looks, a body to die for, charm, manners, and judging by the look of you, obvious sex appeal."

Julie blushed as Penny continued, wiggling six fingers in front of Julie's face before they dropped to the bed. "Sounds like he is the perfect man. I'm so happy for you. If you'll simply let yourself enjoy it, you'll have a great time on holiday."

Julie gave a reluctant nod. Penny was right. She should relax and appreciate it for what it was. But if she didn't watch out, she would fall hard for this man. She needed to harden her heart to keep it from being broken. They only had a few more days in Russia. She would have to keep things fun and lighthearted. The relationship would not go the long haul, but she could certainly enjoy the ride while it lasted. And with a man like Nicholai, the ride was sure to be a pleasurable one.

Chapter 19

Nicholai, the deep familiar voice boomed into Nicholai's head, causing the warrior to flinch. *Do you no longer answer your phone?* Demetri demanded.

Calm down. I don't have it on me when I'm in the shower. Nicholai rubbed the last of the soap from his body and turned off the water. He wrapped a towel around his waist as he walked to the vanity.

What do you need of me, Demetri? Nicholai grabbed a second towel and dried his hair.

There is a development here, cousin. Another person has been attacked.

Was it bad? Nicholai ran a comb through his hair.

Yes. According to the local news, the man's mutilated body is beyond repair. These attacks appear to be increasing.

Nicholai crossed his spacious bedroom and grabbed a pair of jeans from his dresser. He thrust his wide legs in and slid them up over his hips. *So what have you and Stephan found?*

Not much, I'm afraid, cousin. With only the two of us here doing reconnaissance, the investigating is slow. We are considering pulling more of the Alphas in.

What about Marcus? Nicholai tugged on his winter-green sweater.

He is still in Vegas with Katrina and his heartmate, Christina.

Is there anything I can do? Nicholai walked to the foyer.

We may have need of you soon.

Nicholai's hunting skills were among the best of the Alphas, second only to Demetri's. No doubt they would have need of those special skills in the coming days.

There has been a development here which needs my attention.

And what is that? Demetri asked.

Here it was. The moment of truth. *I found my heartmate.*

Oh, no. Demetri's exasperation flowed through the link. *Not you, too. First Stephan, then Marcus. Now you? Please tell me she's a vampire and not human.*

Nicholai gave the mental equivalent of a shrug. *Actually, she is a human, and her name is Julie. And I need your help on what I should do to win her.*

Just throw her over your shoulder and bring her to your lair. Explain to her she is your mate, and she will come to love you, as all heartmates must. It's inevitable.

A small grin appeared on Nicholai's face. He'd called that one. *No, Demetri, I'm afraid that won't work, not for a human. Perhaps if she was a vampire and already understood the concept of a heartmate. No, I must win her love.*

Fine. Settle things with your heartmate, and be quick about it in case we need you.

I'm working on it, he assured his cousin, then grabbed his coat and keys.

Demetri's dissatisfaction crossed the mindlink as Nicholai got into his car and brought the engine to life.

Don't take too long with her. Safe travels. With the valediction, the link snapped shut.

On the drive to Julie's hotel, Nicholai's mind replayed the conversation with Demetri. He admired his cousin, always had. And what wasn't to admire since Demetri was not only his cousin and his sire, but also his mentor. Memories of the past pushed in on him. The innocence of childhood morphed into becoming a vampire. The events flickered through his mind like a movie reel.

Demetri had come for a visit at their home and discovered the family had been taken by what was now known as whooping cough. The deadly condition killed his father and spread from person to person until it infected the entire family.

Demetri revealed himself as a vampire to Nicholai's mother and offered to convert her in order to save her life. She begged him to save her two children first, though they were not as ill as she. Demetri reluctantly agreed and after he saved both Nicholai and his sister, Natasha, by converting them, he returned to their mother. But she had passed away as he helped them through the change. It took Nicholai a long time to work through the grief and guilt.

After burying their mother, Nicholai and his sister had stayed with Demetri. He mentored them in the ways of the breed and taught them how to use their special abilities. Tough but fair, Demetri had been their parent and teacher. And friend.

He loved his cousin and would do anything to show his appreciation.

****

Nicholai laid the palm of his hand against the small

of Juliette's back, escorting his heartmate and her friend through the gates toward the magnificent palace built by Peter the Great. Penny's eyes widened when she looked at the brochure in her hands.

"Peterhof Palace," she murmured, glancing up at Nicholai as she tapped the title on the pamphlet. "Isn't your last name Peterhof?"

"Yes, it is," he admitted with a shy grin.

"So this is your place then?" Penny quipped. "I was wondering when we'd finally get to see your house."

The group shared a chuckle and made their way forward.

In reality, Nicholai had, in fact, lived in the grandiose palace at one time. Though his father had not been Czar, he was Russian royalty. It was Demetri's family, the Romanoffs, who built the palace they headed toward. And while he wasn't a direct descendant in line for the throne, Nicholai had summered at this palace in his youth.

When the trio passed through the opulent entry doors, Juliette's breath caught in her throat.

"I have never seen a place so ostentatious." Julie's jaw dropped open in awe.

She glanced around the room, and Nicholai gazed upon the place with a new appreciation through her eyes. Gold flowed like water, covering everything as if Midas himself decorated the place. The walls and mirrors were gilded. The furniture? Gilded too. Even the life-size statues were made of gold.

An audible gasp escaped Penny's lips when she too took in the splendor with admiration. He treasured the time spent in this place. Many happy memories had been made here before it had been converted into a museum during the early nineteen hundreds.

"Shall we, ladies?" he inquired with a grand sweep of his arm forward.

They wandered throughout the palace, walking between the velvet ropes that herded the tourists like cattle through a corral. Nicholai wished to share everything with his heartmate, but barricades sealed many places away from the public. For now, he must be content following the crowd.

They followed the golden rope path to Peter I's study, which was darkly decorated in rich wood tones. A book lay on his desk, opened as if its reader might soon return.

They passed by the formal dining room. Its table set with the ornately patterned royal china. The tablecloth, white to match the walls, displayed the china which was also mostly white accented in gold with a flowered pattern. It was meticulous, pristine. Nicholai gave Julie's hand a gentle squeeze as she looked on with amazement. Pleasure that she enjoyed his childhood residence swelled his chest.

As the tour progressed through the palace's bedrooms, wallpaper with busy designs clung to the walls. "I can't get over how, in every bedroom, the bed covering, furniture upholstery, and wallpaper all match with identical patterns of *fleur-de-lis*, flowers, or landscapes."

Penny nodded her head. "I know. It's almost an assault to the eyes. If the rooms were smaller, it would be overwhelming."

Nicholai took Julie's hand. "Are you enjoying the tour, in spite of the décor in the bedrooms?"

"Oh, yes."

"What's been your favorite room so far?"

Penny spoke first, "The Diamond Room. I loved the collection of exquisite jewelry on display."

"Catherine the Great had good taste. The brooches and crowns were gorgeous. Not to mention the jeweled vases," Julie agreed.

When they entered the throne room, Nicholai shared, "This is my favorite room."

He glanced at the red chair where Peter had rarely sat to hold court and remembered playing on the three stairs that made the riser for the throne. He and his sister would take turns pretending to be rulers when Peter and Catherine were away, for they wouldn't dare such a thing if the true rulers had been there to catch them.

From behind the throne, a portrait of Catherine atop her beloved horse seemed to scrutinize them as they played. In its golden frame, it was a constant reminder, though they were children, they were still royalty and must behave accordingly, with restraint and decorum.

Nicholai stilled, lost in the memories, until Julie pulled him from his reverie with a tug on his arm. His attention turned to his heartmate. She smiled, the warmth of emotions for him showing clearly in the sparkle of her honey-colored eyes.

Nicholai took Julie's hand in his, leading her through the velvet ropes to the Grand Staircase. The fine, white marble stairs rose on either side of the room toward a large landing at the top. Golden, life-size statues stood as sentinels along the gilded iron railing. Penny's eyes widened as they tracked along the walls, looking at the painted cherubs and golden moldings.

"Let's take a picture." Penny shoved the camera into Julie's hand.

"Come on, Nicholai." Penny linked her arm around Nicholai's and pulled him toward the bottom of the immense set of steps.

The two of them situated themselves at the base of the stairs, while Julie crossed to the opposite side of the rounded staircase.

"All right, you two." Julie backed up as far as possible and adjusted the camera. "I think I can get you and those golden statues in the frame. Say cheese. I mean *syr*."

"*Syr*," Nicholai and Penny sang in tandem with big grins on their faces.

Every nerve ending in the warrior's body suddenly lit up like the Vegas strip. Fear crept along his spine, circling it before it wrapped around his heart and squeezed until he could not breathe. His senses searched the palace.

A blank spot registered the exact moment Nicholai's keen eyes noticed movement above Julie's head. Horror gripped him with its icy tentacles when the statue of the golden woman holding a sickle leaned toward his heartmate. Time slowed his vision as it can only do during a time of danger. The heavy sculpture leaned further and further until it hung upside down, its head directly over Juliette's. Suspended ominously in midair, it dangled for a second then fell, making a beeline for Julie.

Instantly, Nicholai stood beside his heartmate. His muscular arm snapped around her waist and pulled her to his side. Cool air flowed over them when the statue cruised by. With a sickening, twangy thud on the marble floor, the figure landed directly in the spot where Julie had stood.

Nicholai's heart stuttered and threatened to stop altogether. He wrapped his other arm around Julie's trembling body, then cradled her head to his chest, over his heart.

Palace employees ran toward them in matching blue coats.

"Is she all right?" the large man asked, his arms flailing as he skidded to a stop on the marble floor in front of Julie.

Nicholai swallowed hard and found his voice. "I believe so."

"Thanks to you," a bystander observed, shaking her head in disbelief as she stared down at the statue where it lay, still rocking slightly from side to side.

Julie's gaze followed the horrified looks of the employees to the golden woman lying on the cracked marble.

"How did that happen?" wondered a second employee, her eyes wide in disbelief. "Those statues are bolted to the marble bases."

Nicholai remembered exactly how the figures were attached. As a child, he'd watched the workmen put them into place. This was no accident.

Penny ran over, a look of terror in her eyes.

"It's a miracle Jules wasn't killed," Penny murmured from behind the hand she held in front of her mouth. The blood drained from her already pale face. The ghostly pallor must have driven home the seriousness of the situation to Julie for her knees gave out when her eyes met Penny's.

Nicholai wrapped her tighter in his embrace, taking the full weight of her body. Julie shook violently.

Nicholai laid his cheek against the top of her head. "It's okay. I've got you," he reassured his mate.

"Are you okay?" Penny's voice quivered as she laid a hand on Julie's shoulder.

Julie did not reply, instead simply nodded her head in assurance, then looked into Nicholai's concerned eyes.

Nicholai's nostrils flared, and a familiar scent drew his brows together in concern. His eyes roamed Julie's face. The heat of his inspection burned its way over her neck and shoulders, then came to rest on her arm where a crimson stain grew on her sweater.

"You are hurt," Nicholai observed, putting her away from him. His hands held her tightly as she tested the strength of her legs. "Can you stand?" Alarm tightened his voice.

The fragrance of her blood flooded his senses, sent his body up in flames, but he tramped down the desire because her well-being was his top concern.

Julie appeared to lock her knees as if willing them to function. Though unsteady, she made them support her. "Yes, I-I can stand," she stammered in a tiny voice.

Nicholai slowly eased his grip and allowed her to support her own weight. He ground his teeth, steadying himself against the delectable scent assaulting him. Keeping one arm around her waist, he peeled the torn sweater away to better see the wound.

Another palace official joined the group. Dressed in a suit, the gentleman's purposeful stride and posture made it evident he was used to being in charge. His gaze swept from the statue to Julie's arm. Realization drew his mouth into a tight line.

"What happened?" he demanded.

Without taking his eyes from the bloody wound Nicholai responded, "The statue fell from the landing. I believe the sickle cut Juliette's arm during the fall."

"Is it bad? Let me see." The man extended his hand toward Julie's arm.

A low growl emanated from Nicholai's throat in warning, stopping the man immediately. He was not about to let another male touch his wounded heartmate.

"Do you need an ambulance?" the manager asked, wisely closing his hand before it dropped uselessly to his side.

"No." Julie looked down at her wound. "It's only a scrape. I am fine." She glanced around at the gawking crowd that had gathered, and a blush colored her cheeks.

Sensing her embarrassment, Nicholai gestured toward the exit. "Come. Let's go get this checked out. I'm sure they have an infirmary."

"No," Julie protested as he led her with a hand on the small of her back. "I'm fine. I don't need a doctor. It's only a scratch."

"At least let me clean the wound for you."

"That would be a good idea, Jules," Penny agreed, taking her friend's uninjured arm.

Nicholai steered the women through the crowd and down to the café located in the gardens. He quickly found them a table, and then helped not only Julie but Penny, as well, to sit before he took his own seat. He kept his body tightly coiled, ready to strike should danger present itself again.

When the waiter approached their table, Nicholai

took charge, and in their native language ordered, "Bring us extra napkins and a glass of water immediately."

Juliette sank into her chair and closed her eyes. "Thank you. I don't think I could have found the right words to order."

"Do not fret. I will see to your every need," Nicholai assured his mate with a gentle squeeze of her hand.

Upon the waiter's quick return, Nicholai instructed him to bring three sodas. Next, he grabbed a napkin and dipped it into the glass of ice water. Julie's heartbeat increased in time with her breathing as he gently circled his fingers around her arm. When the cold rag touched the injury, she flinched.

"I apologize. Does it hurt much?"

"No. It really doesn't hurt." She flinched again.

Nicholai smiled weakly. "Do not lie to me. I can see it hurts. I am being as gentle as I can."

"I know you are." Julie patted his arm. "It's okay. Honestly."

When the waiter returned with their sodas, Nicholai placed their orders. Penny chatted amicably, trying to distract her injured friend, who sat in virtual silence.

Nicholai noticed Julie's demeanor and pushed her drink in front of her. "Here, drink something. You will feel better, trust me." He flashed another feeble grin.

Julie raised her glass and drank obediently. Her pallor appeared much paler than usual, and Nicholai knew the near miss had petrified her. She barely glanced at the waiter when he brought their food.

Concern furrowed Nicholai's brow. He recognized

shock when he saw it. Nicholai stabbed some of the poached salmon. "Here take a bite of this." When Julie didn't respond he continued, "Please, *lastochka*, for me."

Juliette obliged silently, going through the motions of biting and chewing, the actions automatic. She appeared lost in thought, and Nicholai did not need to use their mindlink to know what troubled her mind.

His heart broke. He relived the moment in his mind as he ate a bit of the fish. The image of the golden statue tumbling from the landing above, careening toward his beloved heartmate would forever be etched in his memory.

The images flashed, the smallest details crystal clear. He examined the scene and the people who had been in his peripheral vision. Though his full attention at the time had been on Juliette, upon reexamination, on the landing he clearly saw a man with dark hair beside a woman with a headscarf. The pair had been standing on either side of the figure, but neither appeared malevolent, and he couldn't remember either of them touching the sculpture.

The statues seemed too heavy and well-constructed to fall, but could this have been an accident? This incident, combined with the one in the church a few days ago, made his stomach nauseous. Nicholai looked at the woman he loved. When she glanced up, he reached over and took her hand as much to anchor himself as to reassure her.

"Juliette, I do not want to worry you, but is it possible someone may be trying to hurt you?"

"That's ridiculous," Juliette denied, shaking her head.

Penny laughed. "It's not like she has any enemies. She's a teacher, for goodness sake, not an international spy. Why would anyone want to hurt Jules?"

"Well…" Nicholai searched for exactly the right way to put his thoughts into words. He pinned Penny with his intense stare. "Twice now Julie could have been seriously injured. Think. Is there anyone who might have a reason? You mentioned the other night her husband was a police officer. Is it possible a criminal might be after Juliette because of him?"

"Huh." Penny hesitated. "Her husband and girls *were* run off the road and killed."

"Perhaps the person is out for more revenge and trying to hurt Juliette."

"That's ludicrous. They caught the man responsible for the accident. Didn't they, Julie?"

"Yes," Juliette squeaked out.

"So you see," Penny continued, turning her attention back to Nicholai. "The guy is behind bars. There's no way he is caused the accidents here."

Perhaps I am overreacting, Nicholai thought. But he'd still rather have her under his roof.

"I understand that." Nicholai took a sip of soda. "However, I would still feel better if you would come and stay with me."

"That is unnecessary. What happened at the church was an accident," said Julie, joining the conversation. "Construction work was going on when the scaffolding fell; it wasn't intentional. We were alone at the time. And today was an accident, too. After all, statues come off their bases. It probably wasn't balanced correctly. We have no reason to assume there is some sort of assassination plot." Julie crossed her arms under her breasts.

Penny took a bite of her meal and washed it down. "We only have a few more nights here. Nothing has happened at the inn. Seems like it is perfectly safe for us there. I think you are letting your imagination run away with you, Nicholai."

"I would still prefer if you would come and stay with me for the remainder of your trip. I have plenty of room in my home for both of you."

"I don't think that will be necessary," Julie repeated with finality.

She looked much better. Her color had returned, and she no longer shivered.

Penny quickly added, "Besides, we wouldn't want to be a bother."

"It would not be a bother. In fact, I would like to have the company. It gets lonely—" The ring from Nicholai's phone interrupted his sentence. He let out a curse under his breath and pulled the blasted machine from his jeans. He registered the number on the caller ID immediately.

His loyalty warred within him. It was the leader of the Alpha Council, Stephan. He needed to take the call in case the Alphas needed him. However, he did not want to leave his heartmate alone. Luckily, his preternatural hearing told him a tour group was about to enter the palace. Duty won as he decided Juliette would be safe enough if she were around other people inside.

He shamelessly dropped his voice an octave and put a compulsion behind his words. The deep silken resonance instantly mesmerized the women. "If you ladies will please excuse me, I need to take this call. You would like to continue the tour. There is a group getting ready to go into the Portrait Room. You go with the group, and I will catch up with you in a moment."

"All right," agreed Penny for both of them.

Nicholai tossed enough rubles on the table to cover the bill and a tip as he answered his phone. The Alpha moved away to talk in private, but his eyes never left the women while they moved to join the tour group.

"What is it?" he demanded of their leader through clenched teeth.

"Whoa, Nikko. Take it easy, it's only me." Nicholai was surprised to hear Marcus's voice on the other end of the line.

"What are you doing calling from Stephan's number?"

"I'm staying at Stephan's place in Vegas. I thought Demetri told you."

"He did. I forgot," Nicholai admitted reluctantly, his eyes locked on Julie from a discreet distance. While he spoke, he spread his awareness out into the room in an ever-expanding radius and discovered another blank spot. His muscles and sinew grew taut, ready to attack should the need arise. After a few centuries of training and fighting with the Alphas, his body was the epitome of aggressive instinct. His eyes skimmed the crowded room, searching out the threat. He needed to find the cause of the blank spot, not waste time on the phone. "Marcus, why did you call?"

"I got your messages. I'm returning your phone calls."

"Oh, that. Well, now is not really a good time."

"Why?"

"Because, I'm on a date with my heartmate."

"*What?*"

"Didn't Demetri tell you?"

"No, he didn't. Congrats, old man!" Before Nicholai could thank him, Marcus continued, "I'll help you out, Nicholai, with some advice. What helped me the most was going to Christina's house and looking around. I found out tons about her, like the fact she read vampire romance novels. It helped me figure out how to approach her and tell her we were heartmates."

While Marcus continued, Nicholai moved forward, careful to keep Juliette in sight as the tour group made its way through the Portrait Room and down a hallway toward Czar Peter's bedroom.

"I also found out Christina's favorite perfume and her tastes in clothing and jewelry, which helped me choose what types of gifts she would like and appreciate. Why don't you go to her house and poke around a little?"

"I don't think nosing around Juliette's place is any way to win her trust."

"She wouldn't have to know."

"But I'd know." Nicholai closed his eyes and blew out a frustrated sigh.

As Marcus babbled on, Nicholai sent his awareness out again, but this time he found no blank spot. Perhaps Juliette somehow affected him. It seemed only when she was close did his senses misfire.

"Huh? What did you say?" Nicholai asked.

"Aren't you listening to all my advice? I'm crushed!" Marcus quipped, feigning offense.

"Sorry. Your call pulled me away from Juliette, and I am a little distracted."

"I can tell. I'd better let you go so you can get back to the important things in life, like your Juliette. Call me later if you still need to talk."

Nicholai caught up with the tour group. "I will. Thanks, Marcus. Safe travels."

"Later, Nikko. Good luck."

Nicholai shut off the phone and stuffed the annoying thing back down deep in his pocket. He experienced a moment of panic as he realized Julie and Penny were no longer with the group.

He scented the air, easily filtering out all but her. Nicholai let his nose lead him through the Room of Portraits to a corridor. Palpable relief settled over him when he eyed the two women at the end of the hall.

"Look there." Penny pointed to a portrait hung high in a gilded frame. "Who does that look like to you, Jules?"

"Wow, that looks a lot like Nicholai, same dark hair and amber eyes," observed Julie.

Penny nodded her head in adamant agreement. "I'd say it's spot on."

"It does look like him…but something's not quite right."

"What do you mean, Jules?"

"The man in the portrait looks…younger, carefree…I can't put my finger on it, but there's something—"

"Here," Penny interrupted, lifting her camera. "You took a picture of us earlier, let's compare."

Penny flipped through the saved images, looking for the one taken at the Grand Staircase. "That's funny. Look, Jules."

"That's weird. You're in the picture, but not Nicholai. And there's a blur there. It's like two images got squished together."

"I hope my camera's not broken." Penny turned it over. "I'll be upset if I can't take any more pictures."

Nicholai walked on silent feet up behind the women, wrapped his arms around Juliette's waist, and pulled his heartmate back against the firmness of his body. Obviously, she recognized him at once, for Julie leaned back into his strong embrace and wrapped both her arms around his.

"What are you two looking at?" he asked innocently, his lips brushing sensually against her neck as he snuggled against her.

"The pictures we took earlier," Penny answered. "I think my camera might be broken."

"Why don't we try to take a picture and see." Nicholai extended his hand.

Penny placed the camera in his large palm. The women wrapped their arms around each other and smiled as Nicholai snapped the picture.

"There." He handed the camera back to Penny with the digital screen facing her. "See, it is not broken. That is a great picture of the two of you."

Julie looked down at the screen and mused, "I wonder what happened in the other picture."

"Maybe you moved the camera as you took the picture," suggested Nicholai, lacing his fingers through his heartmate's.

While the trio moved down the hall, Penny stuffed the camera back into her purse. "That must be it."

"So where to next?" Nicholai smoothly changed the subject, anxious to leave the topic of the blur behind. He knew exactly what caused the blur. Him, moving at vampiric speed to pull his heartmate out from under the crushing weight of a statue.

Before taking the picture of Penny and Julie, he deleted the blurry photo from the camera, insuring the evidence of his preternatural ability disappeared. His kind could not have proof of their existence. Vampires tried hard to hide from humans and avoid detection. He couldn't allow the photo to exist.

Nicholai stayed on alert the remainder of the night, continually sending his awareness out and scanning the grounds for any signs of trouble. It took all his years of practice to keep his concern within and present the persona of a relaxed man. He didn't wish to ruin the evening by worrying the women for nothing.

They ended their time at the palace by the canal that stretched from the front of the palace to the gulf. They stood on the expanse of lawn and watched fireworks. The kaleidoscope of colors reflected in the still canal water and off the golden statues that comprised the Grand Cascade.

Julie squealed with delight. "I love the play of lights off the fountain in the middle of the canal. The way the sculpture of Samson and the lion is bathed in the lights from the fireworks, their golden color changes from red to blue to white."

The concussion reverberated in Nicholai's chest with each mortar. Nicholai held Juliette around her waist and brought her against him, her back to his front. He rested his chin on top of her brunette locks. He wanted to lose himself in the moment, in the sensation of her in his arms while her feminine scent surrounded him, but he dared not let down his guard. He remained in a constant state of alert while the women enjoyed themselves, chatting and taking pictures of the spectacular show. Nicholai vowed to the Fates he'd keep his heartmate safe. And the safest place in the world was by his side. He just had to convince her to stay with him. And if earlier was any indication, he had his work cut out for him.

Chapter 20

Nicholai grabbed a bag of blood from the fridge as his pocket vibrated insistently. He pulled the phone from his pants and hit the Talk button.

"Hello."

"Cousin, it's me." Demetri's voice came through loud and clear. "There's been a new development."

"You sound troubled." Nicholai closed the refrigerator.

"I am."

"Tell me what's happened."

"Someone else has died."

"By the Fates above! What is going on there?"

"That is precisely what we are still trying to figure out."

"What happened?" Nicholai ripped the top from the bag and took a sip.

"We still aren't sure. It would seem something eviscerated the victim." Demetri's voice trailed off as Nicholai spit the blood across the transmitter on his phone.

"Eviscerated?"

"Yes, and we aren't sure whether it was animal or vampire. What was that sound?" Demetri asked with a bite in his voice from obvious concern.

"What was what sound?"

"That sound I heard, right before you spoke. Are

you drinking?"

"Yes."

"What are you drinking?" demanded Demetri.

"I'm drinking blood," he reluctantly replied.

"Are you drinking from the vein? Did I interrupt your feeding?"

"No, I'm drinking from a bag." Nicholai's voice sounded thick with contrition.

"Nicholai," his cousin reprimanded. "You need to be at full strength in case we have need of you. You know we are at our best after feeding from a vein."

His words struck a deep wound in Nicholai's heart. Was that why he had not been fast enough this evening? He should have been able to get to Julie before the statue had time to fall. Perhaps she'd been scratched by it because he hadn't been at full strength. Maybe it was his fault she had been injured. The thought twisted Nicholai's stomach.

"Why are you not drinking from the vein?" Demetri demanded, bringing Nicholai's thoughts back to the present.

Nicholai poured the contents of the bag into a glass, then scrubbed a hand down his face pulling it taut. "Because I find I cannot drink from anyone but my heartmate," he grudgingly admitted to his fellow warrior.

"What!" Demetri exclaimed, outraged. "You must be teasing me. You can't drink from anyone other than your heartmate?"

"That's what I said."

"Nicholai, you have to remedy this at once. You are of no use to the Alpha Council if you are weak. And since we no longer have Michael, we need everyone at their best."

Nicholai grimaced. "I understand I need to be at full strength. You don't have to lecture me."

"You obviously need a lecture, someone to talk some sense into you. Go get your mate, bring her to your home tonight, so you can feed from her and be at full strength. You have given her long enough. She'll adjust, she'll have to. Go get her, Nicholai. Enough of this waiting."

"Demetri, I'm working on it."

"You need to work faster. You've known for days she is your mate, and yet she still is not in your home. The sooner you get her to your home, the sooner you make her understand she is your heartmate, the better. What did Marcus say when you spoke to him? Did he not give you some advice on how to speed this up?" Demetri's exasperation sounded across the phone line, despite the long distance separating them.

Nicholai exhaled a deep sigh as he went through his kitchen toward the living room. "Actually, Marcus did have one suggestion," he confessed.

"And what was it?"

"He suggested I go to her home and find out more about her, so it would be easier to win her heart."

Nicholai wondered if a visit to Juliette's home might just settle once and for all whether or not there was someone after her.

"And have you done that yet, cousin?"

As he walked, Nicholai took a long drink before answering. The chilled temperature made him gag. "No."

"Are you going to try that anytime soon?"

Nicholai sank down onto his sofa, balancing the

glass on one knee. "Fine, I will do it tonight," he assured Demetri.

"Very well, then I shall leave you to it. As soon as you are done drinking, go."

He supposed it really might not be the worst idea to check out Julie's place, if only to assure himself there was no threat to her, but being ordered to do so by his cousin irritated him.

"Yes, sir." Nicholai saluted an imaginary Demetri with his glass.

Apparently, the older vampire did not miss the sarcasm dripping from Nicholai's voice. Demetri let an exasperated sigh escape his lips. "Look, Nicholai, I don't mean to be so hard on you. I guess it's an old habit. No matter how old you are you'll always be my little cousin."

That brought a smile to Nicholai's full lips as a memory from long ago passed through his mind of him as a child rushing through the field. He was running alongside a large horse Demetri rode. As the horse clopped along the dirt path, he had run out to greet his cousin in welcome, overly excited, as only a child could be. He had loved his cousin dearly—still did.

"All right, Demetri. Stop acting like a mother hen. I will go tonight to Juliette's home. I will push this relationship as quickly as I can. I know it's for my own good and the good of the Council."

"I'll leave you to it then. If we need backup, we'll call on Alexander first. That should buy you a little time, but get this sorted out quick. I will keep you informed of our progress," Demetri promised. "Safe travels, cousin."

"Yes, same to you. Safe travels."

Nicholai hung up, then took a deep breath and forced it out slowly between clenched teeth. In one gulp, he finished the rest of the blood and slid gracefully from the sofa, heading for the kitchen.

Absorbed in his thoughts, Nicholai absently rinsed the glass. Julie fascinated him. When they were together, he kept her talking about herself because he'd never learn enough about her. The scent of her blood flooded his senses. Understanding her peripherally wasn't enough. He must discern every detail about the woman he loved.

He cherished nearness, feeling the warmth of her body soak into his. He loved her smile, her laugh. She completed him, made him whole. Her voice, like a soothing balm, calmed his restless soul. Being with her felt like being home. He never wanted to be away from her again. To be without her would be like a part of his heart disappeared.

He didn't know how much longer he could remain in this quiet, lonely home without her. He needed her by his side, with him forever.

Be patient, he reminded himself. *We have forever. What is a few more days?*

He'd suffer through until she agreed to be his. Nicholai's self-control had been carefully honed over the years. A warrior, he'd trained to be clever, calculating, calm. He could keep his implacable needs in check until she came to him.

Couldn't he?

Desperation to win Juliette, so he could have her with him and keep her safe, spurred him forward. Julie lived in a little town outside of London, but he had never been to the home, so dematerializing there was impossible, but he'd been to many places in London. He decided to materialize to a familiar place there, then make his way to her home. London was seven hours behind Yaroslavia, so while morning approached here, he would still have many hours of darkness in England.

With a purpose, a strategy, and a destination in mind, Nicholai proceeded to his home office. After bringing up his laptop, he punched in Julie's address to find a place nearby he was familiar with.

With a smile, he dematerialized from his home leaving only a small puff of black smoke behind.

Chapter 21

Nicholai shut the door to the cab and paid his fare, then sent the taxi on its way. He turned toward the tiny cottage. The quaint house reminded him of Juliette—attractive, well kept, old-fashioned in a way, yet current and modern at the same time. It stood proudly with its wooden siding painted a pale shade of yellow and white shutters on the windows. The matching door, also white, welcomed visitors with a pretty wreath.

Nicholai sauntered to the door and unlocked it with a thought. When he stepped into the living room, Julie's scent flooded his nose. He inhaled the delicate aroma and took in the surroundings. From habit, he sent his awareness out into the home and discovered a dog. Gauging by the silence, he reasoned it must be asleep, which would make checking things out easier. He just needed to remain quiet.

His gaze followed the white bead-board paneling halfway up the walls to a fireplace surrounded by a simple white wooden mantel. In front of the fireplace, two sofas, with matching flowered upholstery, sat across from each other. A light blue throw rug lay on the floor, creating a square with two wicker chairs on one side. Tiffany lamps stood on the end tables, and on the coffee table lay magazines and a book.

Nicholai crossed the room and picked up the book. Turning it over in his hand, he whispered the title, "*All-*

Time Greatest Paintings of the 19th Century. I wonder if she likes art or if this is for decoration."

He couldn't imagine Juliette putting on airs, having the book lying about to impress visitors, so perhaps she enjoyed great works of art. He put the book back in place.

His eyes followed a blue wall to a delightful kitchen. Its white cabinets and appliances stood out against the dark Formica countertops. While attractive and functional, Nicholai doubted he would find much of interest there, so he ghosted down the hall to find Julie's bedroom.

Nicholai came to an abrupt stop. At the end of the hall, a large animal leapt to its feet.

So much for being quiet.

The dog's head and tail lowered. It remained motionless, except for the ridge of hair rising along its spine. A low growl rumbled from its thick chest.

The dog charged, its large paws eating up the short distance in a flash. Nicholai dematerialized to the kitchen. He assumed his form in front of the stove and searched for something to distract the animal with. He spied a dog bowl with the name Connor written on it in fancy letters.

The large dog barreled around the corner of the hall, sliding on the wooden floors in his haste. His feet clawed for purchase, but he crashed into the side table sending the Tiffany lamp crashing down onto the sofa.

"Connor," Nicholai called out in his most soothing voice. "It is okay. I am not here to hurt you."

The immense paws landed on the blue rug and gripped it hard, then Connor thrust his body toward the kitchen.

The Alpha dematerialized and reformed in the hall. Nicholai glanced to his left and leapt into the small bathroom, where he landed in the tub. Standing with his feet braced wide, he waited for the animal to come. The telltale clicks of nails on the wooden floor got closer and closer. In warning, the dog's deep bark reverberated off the walls of the cottage.

Nicholai held perfectly still until the dog's girth filled the bathroom doorframe. The brown Irish wolfhound stopped, muscles taut, ready to leap at the threatening intruder.

Nicholai respected the dog. He fiercely protected Julie's home. And no doubt he would protect Juliette every bit as furiously.

Nicholai waited silently for Connor to make his move. The wolfhound stalked forward, ridge bristling. Each step a calculated one, sizing up his enemy. When his long body cleared the doorway, Nicholai dematerialized outside the door and pulled it shut behind the animal.

The door shook when the animal flung himself at the entryway and crashed to the floor. He rammed into it again, but Nicholai's trap worked. The dog scratched against the door. Nicholai watched claws appear under the door as if the canine tried to get his feet.

"Smart dog." Nicholai smiled. "But the door should hold you."

While Connor barked repeatedly, Nicholai found Juliette's bedroom.

"Now, let's see if I can find anything that will tell me whether or not she's in danger."

On the wall beside her bed, a bookcase held a collection of pictures and ice-skating trophies on the top shelf. He ran a finger along the spines of the books. She had a wide array of titles, from college textbooks to romance novels. One in particular caught his attention.

Folklore: From Werewolves to Witches to Vampires, he read to himself. *That's interesting.*

As he hooked the book with his finger and pulled it from the shelf, someone opened the front door and entered the house. His head snapped toward the door to the room. Could it be someone here to threaten Julie?

"Bloody Hell! What happened in here?" asked a deep male voice. "Connor?"

The animal scratched and whined in answer to his name.

Nicholai's breath hitched in his throat. Who was this male comfortable enough with Juliette to let himself into her home and who knew her dog by name? Jealousy tightened his grip on the book.

He remained motionless as he waited to see what the man would do. The bathroom door opened. Surprise furrowed his brows because he'd not heard the man walk through the house. Nails hit the hallway floor and scrambled in his direction. The sound kept him from pondering the observation, kept him from sending out his senses to discover more about the male.

Connor bounded into the bedroom, his eyes locked with Nicholai's. As the dog leapt into the air, the book fell to the floor with a thud, and Nicholai dematerialized to his home.

****

Jara trekked through the forest in her mountain lion form. She licked the blood from her mouth and reveled in the coppery flavor.

One more human gone. One less disease-infested

parasite in the world.

Of course, she knew one or two or ten fewer humans wouldn't make the world safer for demons, but it gave her great satisfaction to lessen the threat to their species. And if enough people died in Mason's Bluff, perhaps she might be able to risk going out occasionally, since there'd be less chance of contracting an illness.

Jara quickened her pace, energized by the kill. Being out with nature called to something deep within her soul. The cool mountain air brought out her baser instinct.

Pine trees swayed around her in the light breeze. A bird sang high above on the bare branch of a maple tree. The aroma of clean air mixed with pine filled her sensitive nostrils, and she took in a deep, cleansing breath.

She wished she could remain longer, but duty called. Not to mention it would be best to be long gone before someone discovered her kill. Jara took off at a full run. By the time she reached the compound, her muscles ached from sprinting on the steep incline of the mountain and her lungs burned from the cold air, but she didn't care. It all felt wonderful to her.

She approached the secret entrance and stopped. Her mind's eye pictured her human form and let the animal go. Her body shook as muscle and sinew contorted out of the animal figure. Long blonde hair sprouted from her scalp while her pointed ears shifted and morphed back into human shape. The soft fur withdrew into her skin, replaced with fine hair. Her claws retracted down to neatly trimmed fingernails and her rough pads changed to fingers. Bones elongated, paws became feet and hands.

Jara stretched. Changing between her animal and human forms was second nature. After all, every demon had an animal form and learned to change as children. The shift was so natural, she barely registered any discomfort now.

Jara grabbed the robe she'd left draped over a tree branch and donned the Grecian-style toga. She looked at the side of the mountain before her, eyes scanning the ivy for the hidden mechanism. Her hand slipped through the thick vine and depressed the rock beneath. A passageway opened in the rock face, and Jara quickly stepped through before it closed behind her. Her bare feet made a distinctive slapping sound on the cool rock floor. Torches held in sconces on both sides of the hall lit her way. The flames flickered and flared from the ventilation. She ran one hand along the rough granite walls, admiring the handiwork. Her people had done an amazing job, tunneling out the mountain, creating room after grand room. For people who didn't have electricity, they had everything else a town needed.

Except freedom. Her hand dropped from the hallway and clenched by her side.

And what was Varrick doing about that? Very little. He spent all his time pining over that little chit, Elizabeth. A human! He really needed to help Jara and Lane find a vampire and hopefully discover immunity from human ailments.

A few turns and she pushed through the double doors to Lane's lab, making a dramatic entrance that caused the scientist's head to snap up.

"Good morning, Jara," he greeted.

"Good day," Jara returned regally as she perused

the male.

The brainy demon's body appeared lean from years of flexing his mental muscles rather than his physical ones. His thick reddish-black hair, slicked back, displayed a good-looking if not effeminate face. His cheekbones stood out in stark contrast against his sunken cheeks, and his thin face made his nose and lips appear large, but not unpleasantly so.

"How are things coming?" Jara glanced around the lab. "Are we ready to capture a vampire?"

"Let me show you," he offered, then took off his white lab coat and draped it over the back of his chair. "As you can see most everything is in place. We have an embalming table, complete with titanium restraints."

Jara pulled on the heavy chains. "Seems secure."

Lane smiled. "Oh, they are. The instruments I ordered are in, for the most part, as well."

Scalpels, forceps, a saw, and other metal instruments lay in a perfect line on a tray. Needles and syringes, sorted by size, filled one cabinet.

Jara ran a hand over one of the syringes. "You'll be needing a lot of these, I suppose."

"Oh, yes. I'll be drawing lots of blood and samples of tissue, not to mention I'll need to inject the vampire with all kinds of substances to see how its body reacts."

"Sounds painful," Jara commented nonchalantly, then crossed the room to a long counter. "I see the microscope arrived."

Lane's eyes lit up, and he joined her. "The best money can buy."

"Varrick's money," Jara reminded him. "Don't forget who is financing this. Do not seem so eager when you talk to my brother. He does not share our exuberance for your experimentations."

Lane appeared shocked. "But he gave his approval."

"Reluctantly."

Her warning couldn't have been better timed, for Varrick pushed through the doors. The immense man filled most of the entryway with his thick neck, biceps as large as her head, and thighs big as trees. His eyes, so much like her own, blazed red on his rugged face. A terrifying sight to behold, his brutish body carried a regal air about it. One look and people knew he was large and in charge, in literally every way.

"Welcome, brother. Lane was just showing me around the lab. Care to join the tour?"

"I'm here to find out if you have come up with a way to capture a vampire yet?"

"No, Sire, I have not, but I am confident I can contain it once it arrives. The tome Jara provided me is quite helpful. It mentions vampires are weakened by titanium and blood loss. I believe if I keep it drained and restrained, we can contain it."

Jara laughed. "Drained and restrained. That can be our motto."

Varrick didn't look amused. "That's all well and good, but we need one first."

"We know where one is," offered Jara.

Varrick shook his head. "It is halfway around the world. Surely there is one closer. One we wouldn't have to figure out how to transport between countries. We need to keep this as simple as possible."

"Perhaps we should ask your subjects," Lane offered.

Varrick shook his head. "I'm disgusted enough

about this little experiment, Lane. The last thing I want is for everyone to find out I authorized it."

"But, brother dear, you are the only one disgusted by it. The rest of us believe what you've done is noble. You are sacrificing a bloodsucker, so demons might have a chance at a better life. You are giving us a chance for freedom. Nothing can be nobler than a ruler who will stop at nothing to improve the lives of his people."

Varrick crossed his arms over his thick chest. "You really see it like that?"

"Oh, yes, sir," Lane gushed. "What you have done might save us all. We could live hundreds of years if not for succumbing to human diseases. You will go down in our books as the greatest ruler of all if your decision saves the race."

"And if it does not? What will the subjects say if we fail, Lane?"

Jara stepped between them. "They will say you did everything possible to try to save us. There is no harm in your subjects finding out about our experiment. Let's tell them about it and see if any of them know of a plausible way to find and capture a vampire."

Varrick blew out an exasperated breath. "Fine. Arrange to have the ideas presented to the three of us. We can add a chair to the throne room and the demons can present their suggestions to us behind closed doors."

Jara gave her brother a kiss on his cheek. "You won't regret this."

"I already do."

Chapter 22

Juliette's awe began as they traveled up the snow-covered drive to Nicholai's home. The front yard boasted a beautiful fountain, dry for the winter, but Julie easily imagined the water flowing from the vase held by the statuesque lady. Her alabaster skin matched the two winged lions, made of marble, sitting guard at the base of the stairs to the home.

Neatly rowed windows surrounded the arched entryway on the plain but capacious brick mansion. Its brick exterior reminded her of her parents' home, same color but many more bricks were needed to complete this grand estate. The plain exterior did not give away the surprises that awaited within.

Though not as opulent as Peterhof's palace, Nicholai's home spoke of wealth and aristocracy. Where the palace had had Midas's touch, this home seemed tastefully decorated with gilded patrician furnishings scattered over priceless Persian carpets. Antiques abounded inside on the gilded mantels and large portraits hung in golden frames. The walls were lined with hand-painted silk upholstery, the ceiling trimmed with thick crown molding inlaid with gold leaf and the chandeliers dripped with crystals.

He'd brought her to the mansion this evening for their date, saying he had a surprise in store. The house alone had been enough of a surprise for Juliette. She could have spent hours roaming the rooms, learning the home's secrets.

But the reading room, with its floor to ceiling bookshelves, became her favorite spot because it contained an attached conservatory. A fountain played soothing trickles of water in the middle. Lush green plants surrounded it on all sides, giving the illusion of summer as she spied a scalped hedge garden through the circular dome of windows. Julie imagined Nicholai in the leather chairs reading a first edition book as the fountain whispered peacefully in the background.

"Let's skip the fourth floor," Nicholai offered. "All the rooms on that floor are bedrooms, and we can save those for another day." He winked.

Julie chuckled, and a blush heated her face at the innuendo.

They made their way to his spacious kitchen. Butterscotch and chestnut marble countertops complemented the maple cabinets that surrounded Julie. A wide island negated the need for the dinette set which sat in the corner.

"So what do you think of the house?" Nicholai glanced at Julie over his shoulder as he pulled the milk from the refrigerator.

"What can I say? It's huge."

"But do you like it?" he pushed, looking as if he needed her approval.

"Oh, yes! What's not to love? It's beautiful."

Nicholai crossed the room, then took her hand and gave it a soft kiss. "Just like you, *lastochka.*"

"What does *lastochka mean?*"

"*Lastochka* means *darling.* Literally translated, it means little swallow. I find it a particularly apt term to express my feelings for you."

"Speaking of translating, I believe you said you would tell me what *ya tebya lyublyu* means, but you never did."

"That translation is for another day, *lastochka*. But I promise that day will come soon."

Nicholai stared into Juliette's eyes when he spoke, and she fell into his deep gaze. She could get lost in him, lost in his strong arms, his sweet words.

Nicholai pulled a pot from the cabinet beside the stainless steel stove, then poured in some milk.

"What are you doing?"

"Making hot chocolate."

"From scratch?" She did not keep the astonished expression from her face.

"Do not look so surprised. Some men can cook you know."

"You can cook, too?" She feigned her surprise this time by widening her honey-colored eyes and placing a hand over her heart. "Why, Mr. Peterhof, you are full of surprises aren't you?"

When Julie giggled, she barely heard Nicholai murmur, "You have no idea."

A sensual smile spread across his lips in response to her teasing. He turned to her with something akin to love sparkling in his eyes. The look of adoration on his handsome face threatened to collapse Julie's knees from under her.

"Would you mind handing me the cocoa? It's in the cabinet behind you." Nicholai gestured toward the cabinet with his head.

Julie spun around. The movement splayed her brunette hair about her shoulders. "This one?" she inquired, touching one of the maple cabinets.

Her date paused his stirring to glance her way. "Un-huh, that is the one."

She pulled the dark cabinet open and scanned the containers inside. She read the Russian word for chocolate, one of the few words she read in the language. The irony she read the word for her arch nemesis in the struggle with her weight did not escape her.

"This it?" Julie produced the metal container with a wry smile on her lips.

"That is it. Thanks." He turned his attention back to the pot of warm milk.

Juliette tried to be helpful by opening the container. Finding the lid on tight, she gave a hard tug. When the lid let go, powdered chocolate arched into the air. It fell to floor coating Julie in the process with the delicious confection. Her eyes went wide with shock when the powdery dust covered her.

Her gasp drew Nicholai's attention from his task. His humorous smile reached his eyes, making them gleam like stars reflecting in the sea. A deep chuckle reverberated from his chest, his muscles rippled beneath his black turtleneck. Her pulse raced, stomach knotted.

Nicholai's eyes intensified as if he realized she appreciated the view. Heat coiled its way through her blood, warmed her. A flame of desire danced throughout her body.

"Let me get that for you," Nicholai said in a husky voice, grabbing a dish towel.

When he brushed the brown powder, the aroma of chocolate surrounded them. He started at the top with her hair, smoothing the towel along her brunette strands softly before moving to caress her face. Each stroke of the towel sent a sensuous sensation rushing over her skin.

His gentle touch caressed like a lover. The butterflies in her stomach became hawks, beating their wings with such force it made her stomach list. Moist heat flooded her feminine core when his caress feathered down each of her cheeks. The pad of his thumb ran across her lower lip through the towel, pulled it down slightly to expose her perfect white teeth. The intimacy closed her eyes. As she sighed, her hot breath escaped over his thumb.

The towel continued down her neck, lingering over the pulse beating strongly at the base for a moment before it continued its way.

When Nicholai brushed the cocoa that had nestled on her bosom, his light touches caused her nipples to tighten into tiny peaks. She hungered for him, the need made her arch into his touch. The slight movement broke the last of his will, and he locked his lips to hers in a crushing kiss.

Chapter 23

As the towel drifted to the floor, Nicholai's hand slid up Julie's arm and rested on the nape of her neck. He brought her mouth to his. His tongue begged entry into the moist cavern. Her lips parted in submission. Seeking every nook as he held her head with a tight grip, his tongue tasted her thoroughly.

His free hand traced its way along her spine and cupped her *derrière*, bringing their bodies together. The length of him pressed hard against her stomach.

Their tongues danced back and forth between their mouths, taking turns tasting each other's sweetness, a sweetness enhanced by the aroma of chocolate in the air. His kisses drove her wild as the flames of their passion licked a trail along her skin, igniting her ardor until it drove all rational thought from her mind. She needed him, wanted him. Wanted this.

His hand fisted in her hair, pulling her head to one side as he pushed again into her mouth. The passion made her blood come to a raging boil, matching the milk on the stove.

He absorbed her soft moan into his open mouth before releasing her lips to feather kisses along her jawline and down her neck. They rested on the hollow spot where her pulse beat strongest. His tongue laved a loving caress over the vulnerable skin. Her pulse quickened at his touch. His soft lips cupped her creamy flesh, sending a shiver down her spine.

Juliette arched her head back into his hand and gave Nicholai better access to her delicate neck. A soft mewling sound escaped her throat as she moved her hips salaciously against his. Nicholai released her hair, then cupped the other side of her rump and lifted her onto her toes, pulling her against him until their bodies seemed to become one. Desire coursed between them. The sensation robbed Julie of her breath. Her hands clutched desperately about his broad shoulders, seeking an anchor to keep her from floating away on a sea of ecstasy.

Nicholai moaned against her neck as her pelvis undulated on his impressive arousal. He laid a trail of kisses from her neck to her lips, which parted in welcome. He deepened the kiss and backed Julie into the counter. The sensation of it against her legs barely registered. With a lift of his arms, he placed Julie on the marble counter and spread her thighs wide enough to accommodate his hips. His heavy shaft against her core produced another surge of wet heat between her legs.

Her hands roamed over his broad shoulders and slid over his pectorals. They flexed under her palms. Her fingers traced the outline of his ribs before they continued the trail downward, searching for his most masculine part.

She found his shaft through his pants, and her fingertips stroked feather-light over the length of him. Her thumb rubbed over the tip where it pressed against the waist band of his pants. She teased it before she molded her hand to him, rubbed up and down his length. She pulled a deep, dark moan of pleasure from his lips, the sound of which sent a ripple through her body.

Suddenly, Nicholai pulled away from her mouth and rested his forehead against hers as he regained both his composure and his breath.

"My sweet Juliette, if we don't stop now, I'm afraid we won't get to our date."

"That's okay, this is working just fine for me," Julie murmured breathlessly as she continued to stroke him.

Nicholai chuckled, causing his shaggy hair to fall about her face, tickling her. "It's working for me, too. Too well. We better stop. You are driving me wild."

"I want you wild." Juliette closed the small space between them and locked her lips to his. Her hands grabbed his bottom. She drew him back against her and wrapped her legs around his waist. Her body ached with need, and this gorgeous man was just the balm to sooth her.

His large hands snaked under her sweater, tracing the lines of her ribs before cupping the full weight of both breasts. One hand kneaded over her bra. The other gently moved the lace fabric aside and rolled her nipple between his thumb and finger. It drew into a tight peak, driving her urgent yearning higher.

Aggressively, Julie fisted both hands in his sable hair and pulled him forward for a bruising kiss. Lips ground against teeth. Ravenous hunger drove her to wanton abandonment. Another rush of creamy heat pooled between her legs as she let her restraint go. She felt wild, free. Sexy.

Julie drew his spicy scent in with a deep inhale. The stimulating aroma sent desire into her core, making her throb with a painful need. Her brain, lost in primal urge, barely registered the mix of smells.

It was not just him invading her senses, taking her control. But something else. What else did she smell? Strong enough to draw her mind back to the present, the astringent odor pulled her from the moment.

The miasma burned her nostrils. Julie realized the caustic fumes emanated from the stove. Breathing hard, she pulled back and looked at the pot. What had once been milk was now a crispy black charred blob.

"Oh, no! We burnt the milk." Julie covered her swollen lips.

Nicholai turned the burner off and removed the pot from the element. "See what happens when you're with me? I can think of nothing other than you."

He always said the right thing, made her feel special. Juliette smiled. His deep penetrating stare, locked with hers, bore into her soul. Juliette squirmed under his watchful gaze.

"I think you need to make some more cocoa," Julie suggested, breaking his uncomfortable regard by jumping off the counter and bending to retrieve a pot from the cabinet beside the stove.

Nicholai took the pot from her hand and let out a regretful sigh. "I believe you are right."

The second attempt at the cocoa cooked successfully under Juliette's watchful eye. It turned out rich and creamy, a hot tasty treat to keep them warm to their bones.

Nicholai tightened the lid on the thermos and turned toward her with his features relaxed.

"Ready to go, *lastochka*?"

"Where are we going?"

"I thought we might go for a little ride." Nicholai

offered his arm to Juliette, and she linked an arm through his.

Julie expected to be led to the front of the house where his car waited. Instead, he tugged her toward the door in the kitchen. As they exited the mansion, her footsteps faltered. A large stable stood on the grounds behind the house.

From her days on the family farm, she was familiar with horses and had grown up riding them. When they approached the stable, the smells rolled to her on the cool breeze. It instantly took her back to childhood. The scents of the leather, hay, and oats mixed with the saddle soap used to clean the tack. They brought an image of her favorite pony to mind that created warmth in her belly and fortified her against the icy winter air. When she entered the stable, the juvenile image pushed from her mind. The majestic animals inside made her heart race.

The couple walked arm in arm through the hay-lined corridor. Juliette stopped in front of a stallion with a satiny dark coat, accented by a white diamond between its eyes. She gave him an affectionate rub on his face. The coat felt soft beneath the pads of her fingers.

A smile lightened Nicholai's features. "That is *Temnaya Ten*, Dark Shadow. He is my favorite stallion."

"That's a perfect name. He's beautiful," Juliette said in a breathy voice.

"I couldn't agree more."

"*Temnaya Ten*," she repeated as she ran her hand down his nose.

"That was quite a good pronunciation. However, I

usually shorten it to *Ten* or Shadow. Come, my sweet."

He laced his fingers with hers and led them through the stable. Julie noted the stalls contained brass nameplates, announcing the horse within. She counted twenty in all. As they walked, each horse, in turn, stuck its head over the stall gates to greet them. The purebreds were a mix of chestnut brown, frosty white, and inky black coats, each standing regally behind their individual gate.

With every horse as magnificent in stature and breeding as Shadow, Nicholai must have a fortune in his stable. She did the calculations in her head and quickly estimated he'd paid well over two hundred thousand dollars for the animals.

Though Julie was not a materialistic woman, she couldn't help but wonder between the stable and the house how much money this man had. Surely, he could not have made so much money by such a young age. Perhaps he had inherited the wealth. She had been taught it was impolite to ask someone about money, so her upbringing left her to ponder that thought as they progressed out of the stable.

The sight greeting Julie's eyes when they exited the stables seemed straight from a Currier and Ives portrait. Light from the home and stable illuminated a sleek steed. Its shiny, raven coat stood out in stark contrast to the virginal snow. Its breath steamed the air in front of the man holding the reins. Attached to the horse, a black sleigh outlined with gold trim contained a red quilt that lay invitingly draped across the leather seat. The stallion pranced impatiently in the snow, sending flakes into the air and making the sleigh bells jingle.

In the background, stood the forest with specks of green pine needles peeking out from their snowy blankets. The aroma of the cool, fresh air took the smells of the stable from Julie's nose. Her breath frosted in the air as they traveled to the sleigh.

Nicholai handed her in, then took the reins from the stable hand with a greeting of thanks. The leather seat creaked when Nicholai sat next to her. His muscular thigh pushed firmly against hers while he fluffed the red blanket across their laps. Nicholai turned to Juliette. A white cloud caressed her cheek as he spoke. "Ready?"

"Absolutely."

Nicholai clicked the reins and sent them off over the snow-covered grounds. With bells tinkling, the stallion moved through the trees at an easy trot, his black tail held high in the air. Nicholai's leg brushed against hers with each jostling bump. A rush of desire coursed through her body. His spicy scent surrounded her, consuming her as it combined with the fragrant night. Each inhale drove the delicious combination deeper within.

She snuggled against Nicholai. This must be the most romantic date anyone had ever been on. Her heart beat a little faster. The snow glistened all around, and a crunch sounded from the sleigh as it glided over the land.

She gazed at Nicholai. His jaw hardened, teeth clenched. Fingers gripped hard on the reins as if he sensed her wanton thoughts. Apparently, the steed sensed Nicholai's tension through the reins for he whinnied, drawing her attention.

Julie broke the companionable silence. "He's a

magnificent animal."

"Thank you."

"What is his name?"

"Kedar, it means *powerful* in Arabic." Nicholai gave a flick of his wrists, urging the horse forward with a snap.

"It's a beautiful name. What breed is he?"

"He is an Arabian stallion."

Julie settled into the leather seat, snuggling under the red quilt. The cool air flushed her cheeks, her vision clouded with unshed tears from the stinging air as it flowed around her face. Her lashes bound, creating a rainbow effect for her vision. It added an ethereal beauty to the winter wonderland.

Nicholai tucked her under his arm and drew her snugly against his side. His warmth surrounded her, taking the chill from her body. He felt heavenly, toasty warm. Juliette wanted to remain like this forever.

"How much longer?" she asked, secretly hoping the answer would be "for eternity."

"Why, my dear woman? Tired of my company already?"

Julie pulled away. Her brows furrowed in consternation. "No! No! I didn't mean it that way."

A smile pulled at the corner of Nicholai's lips. When a deep chuckle pulsated in his chest, Julie realized she had been had. She playfully smacked his shoulder.

Nicholai drew her back to his side. "I know what you meant. We are almost there. It's just over this next rise."

When the sleigh crested the hill, the scene greeting Julie reminded her of a Thomas Kinkaid painting. At the bottom of the hill, a frozen pond sparkled in the moonlight, rainbow prisms dancing on the ice. Bare trees, their branches heavy with snow, lined the pond. Candles hung from the bowing branches, and their dancing flames made the snow glitter with the ambient light. Tiny frozen crystals bid the couple a lustrous welcome.

Nicholai reined the horse to a stop. Kedar pranced in the snow, making his bells jingle. He looked at the couple from over his muscular shoulder as if to say, "We're here."

When the tinkling bells quieted, Nicholai poured a cup of hot chocolate from the thermos and handed it to Julie. She cupped the lid between her hands, then brought it slowly to her mouth. Nicholai watched her pucker her lips and blow.

"Tell me, Julie, do you skate?"

Julie lowered the cup without taking a sip. Child-like glee widened her smile. "Oh yes, I love to ice skate. My sister and I took lessons when we were children."

Julie sipped the smooth cocoa. The chocolaty goodness slid over her tongue, coated her throat as it warmed its way down.

"Yummm. That is exceptional. You must try some." She handed the black thermos cup to the handsome man beside her. Nicholai took the lid from her delicate hands. His large fingers brushed hers in the exchange, sending a wave of heat into her belly. The warmth increased as she watched him turn the cup so he drank from the same place her lips had been.

Julie swallowed the lump in her throat. Her voice sounded small when she spoke. "We make a good cup of cocoa, don't we?"

Nicholai captured her eyes with his intense, hungry gaze. "I think we make a superb team, *lastochka*."

He closed the short distance between them, taking her mouth in a tiny kiss. His soft lips brushed against hers, a feathery touch that made the butterflies in her stomach flutter. Nicholai pulled away and licked his lips.

"You taste like chocolate," he mused, handing the cup to Juliette. "Here, finish it, then we'll go skating."

"But I don't have any skates."

"I have that covered," Nicholai said with a wink. As if by magic, he produced a pair of white ice skates from behind their seat. They hung from his finger by their laces.

Joy spread through her when she reached for the skates and placed them on her feet. With each tug on the laces, she felt lighter, carefree. The weight of adulthood melted away, and she toddled to the pond.

She loved ice skating, loved the air rushing by her face while she glided on the ice, loved the way her lungs burned from pushing her body to do the jumps. When they were kids, both she and her sister had wanted to be professional skaters. Julie usually placed well in the competitions, but her sister, Samantha, had typically won. Samantha had been on her way to accomplishing Julie's dream when she decided to be a model instead.

Though Julie had continued her lessons into her teenage years, her life had taken her away from the rink and into the arms of a nice man who had given her two delightful children. She willingly exchanged her dream of skating for her comfortable reality.

Julie glided out onto the ice, her movements fluid and poised as she tested her skates. A perfect fit, they supported her feet and ankles on the slender blades.

Nicholai glided up beside her gracefully and slipped an arm around her waist. Taking one of her hands in his, the couple waltzed around the pond, with Nicholai twirling and guiding Julie in his strong arms.

"You skate beautifully, Juliette."

"Thank you. So do you."

"Do you want to take it up a notch?" Nicholai raised a questioning brow.

Julie nodded her head eagerly. "If you're up for it."

"When it comes to you, my *lastochka*, I'm always up for it." He gave her a suggestive wag of his dark brows.

The pair chuckled, and Nicholai swept her up, lifting her over his head. Julie wondered for a brief second if she might be too heavy for him. Her concern quickly abated as she floated over her date's head. She arched and her arms moved elegantly behind his back. The cold wind flowed over her neck and chin like silk as she transitioned down to earth.

Nicholai slid her body down the front of his, holding her steady when her skates hit the ice. They turned, their bodies pressed tightly against one another, her back to his front.

"Can you do a throw jump?"

"I can. Can you?" Julie challenged.

She gasped as his powerful legs propelled them forward, gaining speed for the jump. Julie's breath quickened, she struggled to keep up. Faster, faster they whipped around the pond until Nicholai picked her up in the air and pushed her away from him with a robust thrust of his arms.

Like a bird, she flew in a long arc. Midair, she turned her body and landed hard on one foot, gliding backwards away from her partner. She turned her skates and sliced the ice to a stop by a tree. She placed a hand on the trunk for support, trying to catch her breath.

"Are you all right?" Nicholai skated up to her.

"Oh, yes." She breathed. "That was so much fun."

"Ready to go again?" Nicholai held out his hand.

The couple, as perfect a match on the ice as off, played to each other's strengths while they skated. Each Lutz was a perfect spin. Each double camel turn brought their bodies together in a fluid combination.

Acutely aware of his body sliding against hers, Julie felt Nicholai's muscles and sinew flex under her fingers.

Nicholai spun Juliette away from him. Just as she came out of the spin, she thought, *I've never been happier.*

Chapter 24

Varrick tucked the quilt tightly around Elizabeth and wiped a stray curl from her forehead with a sigh. It seemed like forever since he'd carried her unconscious body back to the compound. With the tattered clothes lying in a heap on the floor, he'd washed the mud from her hands, face, and hair using the spring water that cascaded from the rocks in his bathroom, cursing as he did so because there was no way to warm the water above the constant seventy-seven degrees.

While he bandaged her frost-bitten fingers, the red, raw digits glared at him, blaming him for their pain. He cursed himself for not warning her more strongly about going out, cursed her for leaving without knowing how to find her way back to the compound, cursed his sister for distracting him with talk of finding immunity to diseases. But most of all he cursed his handling of his mate.

The Demon King blamed himself for not going slowly, for not taking time to build a relationship, allowing her time to accept him. Instead, he'd forced the situation on her and as a result she was adjusting as best she could but didn't yet understand the demon ways, hence why she'd gone into town and not only risked bringing disease back to the compound but her own life as well when she lost her way home. His worry for Elizabeth's safety and concern for her wellbeing fueled his festering anger.

He'd bundled her in one of his sweatshirts before tucking her under all the blankets he found in his room. When he brushed his hand across her forehead, the coolness of her skin worried him. She still seemed chilled.

He gathered energy in the palm of his hand. It coalesced into a reddish orange ball. Varrick lobbed the thing into the fireplace, instantly igniting the kindling. The ambient glow filled the room, and the flames cast shadows over the furniture within.

It was all he could do for now, keep her warm, safe. He sank onto the bed, the mattress depressed under his weight, drawing Elizabeth against his thigh.

The odor of sulfur stung his nose as Jara appeared at the foot of his bed in a flowing caftan. The sheer fabric swirled around her body as she amalgamated into her solid form.

"Varrick, I have news." Jara's eyes gleamed with excitement.

Varrick raised a quelling hand. "Can you not see I'm tending to Elizabeth? Keep your voice down. She just got to sleep."

"Oh, give me a break. I can't believe I find you doting on that woman again." Jara did not keep the exasperation from her voice.

"Get out!" Varrick hissed as he rose and grabbed Jara's arm in a bruising grip, escorting her toward the door to his chamber. "We will speak in the hall."

Varrick shoved his sister out the door and pulled it quietly closed behind them. "Jara, you are no longer welcome into my bedchamber uninvited," he snapped with sudden acrimony.

"What?" Her light patrician features widened in disbelief.

"You heard me. You may no longer come into my room unannounced. You will learn some manners. I will send for you if I need you."

"Is this because of *her*?"

Varrick's hands curled into fists at his sides, his knuckles white. "Her name is Elizabeth, and she is my mate, your queen. You will show her proper respect."

"But she isn't even a full blooded demon!"

"Her demon blood is strong. Based on what she has shared with me, I believe one parent may have been full demon and the other half, making her three quarters. Unfortunately, both are dead, so we may never know for sure. But even if she is only half demon, I would still take her as my mate."

"Filthy half breeds!" Jara spat, her voice supercilious. "Demons mating with humans, producing offspring. It's disgusting, Brother! How could one of our kind do such a thing? It is one of the reasons we are dying out."

"Do not lecture me on the troubles of our kind," the king admonished her. "I am well aware of what plagues us. It was difficult for me to send our people into the ground to live, taking away most contact with the outside world, but it had to be done."

Jara's face softened. "I understand why. As the human population increased and their technology made traveling between continents fast and easy, they spread illness to our people. With the so called Super Bugs, the viruses resistant to their antibiotics, the problems increased even further until you had no choice but to banish our people from human society, forcing them to live in the ground where they would be safe from human contact and the illnesses that came with it.

"But don't you see, Varrick," the princess pleaded. "Our people need you now more than ever. We need your full attention on matters of the court. You do not need the distraction of troubles with your mate."

"Having Elizabeth does not distract me from my tasks. Every moment the weight of my decisions presses down upon my shoulders.

"Have I not given permission to kidnap the vampire? Did I not bring Lane, our brightest scientist, here to conduct his experiments?"

"You did," she said bowing her head in acquiescence.

"Though it is offensive to me, I am willing to allow a life to be sacrificed in order to save our people. The gravity of that decision is not lost on me, but it is far less than the burden of condemning our entire breed to the bowels of the earth."

"Why would sacrificing one vampire be such a burden? They are blood-sucking monsters. They should all be killed, especially after one of them killed Lovazia's mate."

"You need not remind me of our sister's loss. I watched her grieve for her mate. But I remind you, Jara, we do not know the vampire side of the situation. Alcid's death may have been..."

Jara's eyes glowed red and her blonde hair stood out from her head as her power swirled around her fueled by her outrage. "Don't you dare say his death was deserved. No demon deserves death at the hands of a bloodsucker!"

Varrick pulled his power to him, his eyes glowed

red as his power prickled over the pair. Varrick knew it stung and burned. "Keep your voice down, or I will confine you to your room until you can control your anger."

Varrick waited until her hair settled back into place with each deep breath she took before he eased the level of his powerful energy and continued speaking.

"Jara, you and Lovazia have a deep prejudice against any who are not our kind. Our dear sister, Lovazia, has not been right since her mate died. I didn't understand her delirium until now. If anything happened to Elizabeth, I would go insane. What I don't understand is why you seem to share her deep hatred."

Jara fisted her hands on her hips. "Because the vampires wronged us. You should be declaring war on the entire breed, and yet here you are worried because one might be harmed in Lane's experiments."

Varrick shook his head, looking at his sister with sorrow. "That is why father abdicated to me and not you, even though you are his first born. How can you hate all things not demon?"

"It's easy when those not-demon things are a threat to our existence. Humans threaten us by exposing us to their illnesses; vampires threaten us, too. If we could rid the world of those other breeds, we could live in freedom once more."

Varrick waited until a fellow demon passed them in the hall and disappeared from view before he took his sister's hand. "Have faith, Jara. Lane will find the secret to the vampires' immunities, and then we will develop a way for our own people to have the same immunities. Once human illness no longer affects us, our kind will be able to live for centuries. We will be able to live with humans once more."

Jara snatched her hand away from her brother's hold. "How much time will that take? Years, decades? What will become of us in the meantime?"

Varrick pinched the bridge of his nose. "In the meantime, we will continue to do the best we can to survive. I am done discussing this. My mate requires my attention. Remember, do not enter my chamber again without being summoned."

Varrick turned his back on his sister, effectively shutting down any percolating argument and disappeared behind the door to his room.

****

Julie sat on the closed toilet in the bathroom as Penny ran the brush through her hair and worked at a knot.

"Ouch, that hurt." Julie raised her hand to the back of her head and rubbed her aching scalp.

"Sorry, but this one is a bugger." The knot slipped free, and Penny twisted the brunette locks into a simple chignon. "Hand me a bobby pin."

Julie lifted one to her friend. "Here."

"So tell me more about last night. When you left off, you and Nicholai were walking down Main Street."

"Oh, that reminds me, I saw the cutest set of Russian stacking dolls in one of the little shops."

"Which one?"

"The toy shop across the street from the bakery."

"You going to go back and buy them?"

"I hope to. Don't let me forget to stop in there before we leave Russia."

Penny smoothed an unruly wisp of hair, securing it into place. "I'll try to remember to remind you. Now hand me another pin, please."

Juliette complied. "Thanks for doing my hair tonight."

"You're welcome. I'm happy to do it. I couldn't let you wear that beautiful gown and not have an up-do to go with it."

Penny walked around to face Julie. She took a wisp of hair and curled it around her finger before spritzing it with hairspray. When Penny removed her finger, the lock fell in a loose curl framing Juliette's round face. "Where are you two going tonight?"

"Nicholai said he's taking me to the ballet."

"That sounds like it will be fun." Penny let another loose curl fall on the opposite side of Julie's face. "All done."

"I can't wait." Julie stood and looked at her reflection in the mirror above the sink. A satisfied smile graced her full lips. "It's perfect, Penny! Thank you so much!"

Penny placed a friendly hand on Julie's shoulder and stared into her mirrored eyes. "Nothing but the best for you. You deserve it."

Julie blushed.

"Now let's get you into the gown."

The women crossed Julie's room and retrieved the gown from the bed. The black, floor-length dress, with beading around the bodice, fit her perfectly.

"I didn't see you pack this, Julie."

"That's because I didn't. Nicholai took me window-shopping last night. It was so romantic."

"Not many men would take a woman shopping."

Julie smiled. "I know. When we came to one of the shops, Nicholai opened the door with a silly grin on his face. The sign on the door indicated it was closed, but when we stepped inside the lights came on.

"A dressmaker greeted us, then whisked me away into one of the dressing rooms where five gowns hung."

Penny's eyes widened. "Five? How ever did you choose?"

"I modeled each gown for Nicholai, while he sat on a couch across from three full-length mirrors." Julie remembered how his hungry gaze devoured her as he sipped champagne and watched with crossed legs.

"The green dress was too tight. The yellow one clashed so badly with my skin tone, it made me look sick. The blue one looked nice but not perfect. This black one made everyone smile, so I knew it was the one. When the dressmaker brought me a pair of black sandals with rhinestone accents to complete the outfit, the look on Nicholai's face told me I'd found the perfect ensemble."

In fact, Nicholai's eyes heated as he raked her from toes to head with his scorching gaze. He'd looked at her as if she wore nothing at all. She could have sworn she heard a growl of approval. The memory made Julie's knees go weak and her stomach clench.

Penny held the long-sleeved gown and gingerly slipped it up Julie's body before pulling up the zipper to close her in.

"There, Jules. You're a vision."

Julie spun once.

"Wow, you really are stunning. Just let me take the price tag off."

Penny pulled the tag from the arm of the dress and noted the amount. "Whoa! Eighty-eight thousand rubles! How did you afford that on your teacher's salary?"

Juliette cast her eyes to the floor, looking sheepish. "Nicholai said it wasn't a lot. He bought it."

"You let him?"

"Only because he said it wasn't a lot of money."

Penny chuckled. "It's only about two thousand quid."

Juliette gasped and lifted her hand to her mouth. "Oh my gosh. I had no idea it cost so much. I never would have let him pay for it if I had known."

Her blonde friend smiled reassuringly. "I'm sure he wouldn't have bought it if he couldn't afford it. The restaurant business must be good."

"Actually, he might come from old money. You should see his house."

"Is it big?"

"Huge and very old. It kind of reminded me of the Peterhof Palace."

Penny's blue eyes widened. "Don't tell me his place is as big as the palace!"

"No, no, it's not nearly that big, but it has a lot of rooms. I'm not sure exactly what it was about his home, maybe the furniture or the paintings on the walls, but it did remind me of the palace."

A tender smile graced Penny's face, crinkling her eyes. "I'm so glad you are giving this guy a chance, Jules. You deserve to be spoiled."

Julie absently tucked one of the curls framing her face behind her ear. "He seems so sincere, like he truly cares. I'm just sorry we are leaving in a couple of days."

"Maybe he'll come to see you in England," Penny offered, untucking the brunette curl.

Julie gave an insouciant shrug. "Who knows? I'm trying not to contemplate the future, just live in the here and now."

Juliette meant what she said to her friend. She'd tried not to fall head over heels for Nicholai Peterhof, but he was everything she had ever wanted in a man: good-looking, courtly manners, considerate of her feelings at all times. Nicholai appeared to know her so well, in spite of the fact they had only met a short time ago. He anticipated her desires, appeared to know exactly what she would enjoy. He enjoyed surprising her and his surprises, like everything about Nicholai, had been perfect.

Too perfect.

She kept reminding herself no one could be perfect. There must be something wrong with him, for him to want an older woman with a less than perfect body and personal baggage that weighed her down. It would be so easy to give her heart to him, but if she did, surely it would end in another heartbreak for her. And Julie couldn't handle any more heartache.

Penny cupped Juliette's face between her hands, pulling her from her reverie. "There's nothing wrong with thinking about the future, Jules. You need to be open to the possibilities, be ready to grab an opportunity when it presents itself."

Julie opened her mouth to reply when the sound of her *Mission Impossible* ring tone stopped her mid breath. She raced across the room to answer the cell before it went to voicemail.

"Hello?"

"Hello, Julie. It's DW," greeted the male voice on the other end of the line.

Desmond Wright owned the cottage house Juliette currently rented. The successful British actor, who had diverted into directing and producing, lived in the main house on the estate and allowed Julie to rent his guesthouse.

"Hi, DW. How's everything going?"

"Everything is basically fine."

Julie chewed her thumb nail. "What do you mean, '*basically* fine'?"

"Well, it seems Connor got a bit feisty the other day. He knocked into one of the living room tables and sent a lamp toppling."

"Oh, no, that big brute is always getting into trouble."

"No worries, love," Desmond assured her in his proper British accent that sounded like he'd just stepped from Windsor Castle. "He didn't do too much damage. A new lampshade will fix it right up."

Juliette's stomach knotted. "Shit! Those were Tiffany lamps. A new shade will cost a fortune."

"Don't worry. I've got it covered."

"Oh, no, you won't. You've done more than enough by allowing me to live in the cottage house for such a low rent. It was supposed to be temporary."

"If you recall, I insisted you stay when you tried to give notice, because I like having someone here when I'm away for months at a time filming."

The two had formed a close friendship, and now Julie couldn't imagine living anywhere else. "Well, since you give me a deal on the place, the least I can do is pay to repair anything my dog breaks."

"Nonsense, I won't hear of it. You left Connor in my charge. I am supposed to be looking after him. I should have checked on him more often. He simply has too much energy to be cramped up in that little house all day."

Julie sighed. Once DW made a decision, nothing would change his mind. "Everything else okay?"

Desmond hesitated. "Since you asked, I should mention something. When I came to let Connor out for a potty break, I found more than just the broken lamp. The cottage looked disheveled. I heard your Irish wolfhound scratching at the bathroom door. He'd been closed inside. When I let him out, he ran to your bedroom. I found a book lying in the middle of your bedroom floor." Concerned tightened his voice. "I think a vam…someone might have been in the house."

"Was anything missing from the cottage?" Julie's question made Penny turn her way.

"No, everything is still there as far as I can tell."

Relief made her give Penny a reassuring thumbs-up. "That's good, then there's nothing to worry about. I'm sure Connor just made a mess of the place and accidentally closed himself in the bathroom. He probably went in there to hide in shame."

Desmond cleared his throat. "Perhaps. How are things there?"

"Oh, everything here has been great. I've been having the time of my life. There is so much to see and do."

"I'm glad to hear it. Anything exciting happen?"

Julie's mind flashed to the two accidents. "No, nothing exciting has happened."

Julie waved off the incredulous look Penny shot her with a flick of her hand.

"Nothing to speak of anyway."

"Julie, you wouldn't lie to me, would you?"

"No, of course not. Everything has been just great."

Desmond sighed through the phone, and Julie wondered why he had been holding his breath.

"Listen, love, I need to go. We are doing camera blocking this evening, and I must meet with the crew beforehand. But I want you to be careful for me. Okay?"

"I will. I'm always careful." Penny snorted at the remark, and Julie quickly covered the mouth piece on her cell.

"I hope so. Connor and I want you back here safe and sound."

"Good luck at rehearsal. Break a leg."

DW chuckled, the deep laugh resonated in Julie's ear. "I'm only directing this movie, not acting in it so break a leg isn't apropos, but thanks for the well wishes all the same. Bye, Julie. Take care."

"Bye, DW."

Juliette shut off the phone, then turned and faced her friend who now sat on the bed.

"So, how's everything at home?"

"Fine. Connor's been a pain, but it sounds like DW has it under control."

"I bet he does. He seems like the kind of man who is always in control."

"He is," agreed Julie as a knock sounded on her door.

She sauntered to it and opened it wide to reveal the handsome man that waited on the other side. Nicholai stood dressed in a formal tuxedo, complete with black neck tie and vest. His broad shoulders filled the tailored jacket, and his thick thighs pushed against the black material of his pants when he bowed at the waist. "I have come to escort you to the ballet, milady."

"Which ballet are we seeing tonight?" Unable to take her eyes from him, Julie noted how stunning his profile was with its firm jawline and straight nose that peaked over his full sensual lips. Lips that promised soft kisses and wanton pleasure.

The desire visible in his eyes said what he did not. "*The Nutcracker.*"

Julie's stomach knotted in response to his heated gaze. Her tongue darted out to wet her lips before she spoke. "Sounds perfect. Which company is performing it?"

Nicholai's eyes were aflame as he watched her tongue. "The Peterhof Ballet Company."

Julie's mind worked the possibilities. Was this company named for the royal Peterhofs or for Nicholai? "Do you own the ballet company?"

"Yes."

"You must be a very busy man," Penny chimed in. "Owning a restaurant and a ballet company."

Finally, a strike against him, thought Julie. *He's probably so busy he doesn't have time for a real relationship, just the occasional holiday fling.*

"I manage. Once I get a business up and running, I usually take a hands-off approach if I can find someone trustworthy to manage it for me."

"How many businesses do you own?"

Julie shot Penny a reproachful look for the question.

Nicholai thought for a moment as if trying to remember all the ventures he'd started. "Several," he answered coyly. "But the ballet is one of my favorites.

That's why I called the troop back for this special production."

"What do you mean?" Julie asked.

"They are on holiday for Christmas, but I asked them to return to the city to do a show just for you, Juliette."

"You mean only you and Julie will be in the audience?" Penny did not keep the incredulous tone from her voice.

"That is so." He turned toward Julie. "It will allow us the best seats in the house. It should be quite a show. My musicians play in perfect harmony, and my performers take the stage with flair and poise. They will draw you into the land of the Sugar Plum Fairy."

"That must have cost a fortune!" Penny's brows lifted to her hairline.

Enough was enough. Better go before Penny asked him for his tax documents and bank statements. A broad smile spread across Juliette's face. "I am ready, my good sir."

Nicholai offered his arm and a sexy smile. "Then your chariot awaits, madam."

Chapter 25

Jara stared at the wooden door to Varrick's chamber in disbelief. He dismissed her as if she was a common subject. She was royalty, the first born of the king. If she'd been ruler of the demons when their father stepped down, she would not have put a mate before their people. Nor would she have neglected her duties as she pined over a mixed blood.

Jara stomped off down the hall heading toward Lane's lab, her gown fluttering behind her with each step. If Varrick didn't take his duties to their people seriously, *she*'d see to it Lane discovered a way to save them. She vowed to find a way to keep their breed from going extinct, even if she had to kill every vampire and human to do it.

As the king's sister entered the laboratory, her eyes were immediately drawn to the male sitting at a table in a white lab coat. He sat hunched over a microscope staring into the ocular lens, lost in thought.

Lane raised his head from the microscope long enough to acknowledge Jara's entrance. "Good morning, Jara."

"How are you today, Lane?"

"Never been better. Did you tell Varrick our good news?"

Jara puffed out an exasperated huff. "I tried. But he shuffled me out of his chamber so quickly, I didn't get a chance to tell him we trapped a vampire, thanks to Caden stumbling onto one when an errand for Varrick took him to the next town."

Lane smirked. "I can't believe our good fortune. The Great Spirit must be with us. That reminds me. Speaking of divine intervention, how is the guard doing?"

Jara shrugged. "He's a little worse for wear, but he'll survive. The bloodsucker got in a few good licks. Speaking of which, how goes the experiment?"

"Ahhh," said the man, running a hand across his thickly bearded chin in thought. He straightened his lithe body to its full height and rounded the metal table, making his way over to where the vampire lay.

Jara joined him on the opposite side of the metal embalming table. Titanium restraints bound the vampire's wrists and ankles, keeping her from dematerializing. She lay on her stomach. Her clothing had been cut away as had most of the flesh from her back.

Jara fisted a hand in her black hair and yanked her head up off the table. "Looks like it has seen better days," she commented, dropping the vampire's head down carelessly.

Lane gave an insouciant shrug. His black eyes captured Jara's as he spoke. "If I am to discover the reason behind its ability to heal, certain things must be done. I've already discovered it can heal from stab wounds, burns, and even animal attacks."

"What attacked it?"

"I allowed my wolf to take me, and I did the attacking to inflict the exact type of damage I wanted."

Jara nodded in understanding. "It's much thinner

than I thought it would be."

The vampire moaned when she poked a protruding rib.

"I've been starving it to keep it weak."

Jara leaned her hands against the table. "So you've learned what will not kill it. Have you discovered what keeps it immune to human diseases?"

Lane shook his head, sending his dark auburn hair swirling about his face. "Not yet. I need more time. I have a supposition, but I'll need to do more testing."

Jara's eyes widened when a thought struck her. "Shouldn't you be wearing more protective gear? I thought vampires carried disease."

"Actually, I've discovered the subject seems to be disease free. In fact, I'm willing to bet all vampires are disease free. But be that as it may, I am taking a few precautions until I prove the hypothesis."

After donning a pair of black latex gloves, Lane pulled a syringe from the pocket of his lab coat. He uncapped the twenty-gauge needle and forcefully jammed it into the vampire's excoriated back. As she screamed, he slowly pulled the plunger, collecting yellow spinal fluid into the vial.

"That's interesting," remarked the scientist as he plunged a second needle into a different part of the vampire's spine. "Usually cerebrospinal fluid is clear."

"Like water?" asked Jara as the vampire threw back her head and let out another agonized scream.

"Exactly, but this fluid is yellow, not clear. Perhaps this is the key to their immunity somehow. I'll have to run lots of tests. I'll need more samples, make sure it's the same color in every part of the spine and brain."

Lane walked over and typed into his computer,

absorbed in thought, oblivious to the whimpering cries of pain that filled the room.

"I'll leave you to it then," Jara said, as she crossed the lab. "Let me know if you find anything," she instructed over her shoulder before closing the lab door.

****

Nicholai handed Juliette from the silver sports car and straightened to his full height. His thirsty eyes roamed over her body, drinking in the sight of her in the satin gown. She looked a vision, with stray wisps of her hair falling softly around her face, her neck bare. The dress swayed when she moved to retrieve her coat, flowing over the curves he found so enticing. Nicholai swallowed hard, ruthlessly suppressing the rising desire that threatened to course through his veins to thicken in his most manly part.

"My cheeks hurt," Julie admitted.

Nicholai chuckled. "I imagine they hurt from all the smiling you have done tonight."

"And why shouldn't I be smiling? The ballet performance was stunning. The little girl dancing with her warrior prince to celebrate his victory over the mouse king looked sublime. The musicians played in perfect harmony."

"I knew the way you stood up and yelled bravo, you enjoyed the performance."

"What wasn't to love? The luxuriant lobby with those crystal chandeliers and the plush carpeting, the red velvet seating, the magnificent stage? And now we're here."

Nicholai looked over at his mate, pleased she had found the performance to her liking. He had wanted her to have an especially good time this evening, hoping it might put her in an amiable mood. He intended to broach the subject of her and Penny coming to stay in his home. And with luck, she'd be more malleable to the idea this time.

Things had been quiet these past few days. No so-called accidents as of late. The blank spots had disappeared. But Nicholai knew from his years of training that sometimes a lull in the action only meant the enemy was gathering the troops, readying for a fight. His battle-weary instincts told him trouble might be coming, and he wanted to get his heartmate in the protection of his home before it arrived.

"I thought you would enjoy meeting the cast. I hope you did not mind attending this little after party."

"Mind? Everyone has been very nice and most of them speak enough English that I don't need an interpreter. I'm having a blast."

"It was the least I could do to reward my company for agreeing to do the special performance."

"I can't believe you closed the Cold Shoulder, had it elaborately decorated and hired a gourmet chef to cater the event."

Nicholai glanced around. The decorator had done very well. It looked like Christmas. Red and green dripped from the lights. Each table contained a festive centerpiece. All the musicians, dancers, and crew milled about with large smiles. He'd spared no expense to make sure the wine and champagne flowed like Kivach Falls.

When the music started for the *Prisyadki*, several of his dancers hit the floor. Julie's foot tapped to the beat.

He extended his hand to her. "Care to dance?"

"I don't think I can do that. Look at the way they are kicking out their legs. It's like they are trying to stretch their legs after sitting for too long."

Nicholai's hearty laugh burst forth. "They do look like that, don't they? Come, Juliette. We should dance. It will be fun."

"Oh, all right."

Julie took his hand and allowed him to lead the way to the dance floor.

All around them people squatted with their arms crossed over their chests, kicking out one leg, then the other, in time with the music while onlookers yelled encouragements. With the first kick of her leg, Julie's balance, a bit off from the alcohol, sent her to the floor. Her leg flew up as her bottom hit the hard surface with a dull thud. The black gown pooled around her thighs, and Nicholai put on a burst of preternatural speed. He grabbed the material and pulled her to a stand, keeping her from exposing herself to all those watching.

Everyone laughed, including Julie.

"See, I told you I couldn't do that dance," Juliette said between giggles.

"Perhaps you have had a little too much to drink." Nicholai brushed a wisp of hair from her eyes. "I should take you back to the hotel."

Julie nodded. "Maybe you're right. It's been a great night, but I'm tired."

After bidding the troupe goodnight and making arrangements for the manager to close the restaurant after the party, Nicholai helped Juliette don her coat and escorted her to the car.

They rode in silence. Julie appeared lost in thought on the quiet drive back to the inn, and Nicholai couldn't resist slipping into her thoughts to make sure she had enjoyed the evening.

I can't believe Nicholai arranged a private performance just for me. He must be starting to have some real feelings for me to go to all that trouble and expense.

He barely suppressed the smile. If only she knew the half of it. Real feelings didn't begin to describe how he felt about her. He adored her, loved her like no other. Totally smitten, he'd treasure her until the day they both went into the Great Beyond.

As they drove toward the inn, a thrill warmed his body when Julie imagined the future with him. She believed it would be filled with grand surprises that would take her to exotic places and wonderful people. And through their adventures, she believed they'd come to love each other deeply. She allowed herself to wonder what having children together might be like.

He saw the vision she conjured of their children. He fought the smile that tugged at the corner of his mouth. She imagined a little boy who looked like a younger version of himself and a little girl who had an uncanny resemblance to what his sister, Natasha, looked like in her youth.

The anxiety eased from Nicholai's shoulders. Relief flooded his body. His mind calmed with the realization not only had his heartmate enjoyed the evening, but she also contemplated a future with him and cared for him as he did for her.

She was correct; they would have beautiful children together, but he hoped their little girl would look like her. If she'd only trust him with her heart, he would protect her, love her. Keep her safe.

The thought brought the tension once more into his body, and he white knuckled the steering wheel. Julie still might be in danger. Every instinct within screamed at him to protect his mate. To do so effectively during daylight hours, she needed to be within the walls of his home. And he had yet to convince her to stay with him. He decided to mention the subject once more.

Nicholai cleared his throat, drawing her attention. "Juliette, have you given any more thought to staying with me?"

His mate startled in surprise, then straightened in her seat. "No, I hadn't thought about it."

"I wish you would consider my offer. I have more than enough room for you and Penny at my home."

Julie nodded in acquiescence. "There's no doubt about that. You have plenty of room, but we don't want to put you out."

"It would be safer if you stayed with me." His grip on the steering wheel tightened.

"I don't see any reason for us to move into your home. Nothing else has happened since the Palace. I doubt I'm in any danger."

Nicholai eased the car to the curb in front of the inn and turned to face Juliette, his mouth drawn in a tight line. He took her hand in his before he spoke. "You should seriously consider my offer. I would feel better if the two of you were staying with me."

"Don't be ridiculous. It would be silly to pack up all our stuff to stay with you for just a couple of days. We're leaving Russia soon."

Nicholai's heart seemed to drop to his toes. Only a few more days! He didn't have much time to win the love of his mate before she returned to England. The thought made him want to compel her to stay. However, his honor refused that path. He would not force her to do anything. If she remained with him, moved into his home, it would be because she wanted to, not because he forced the compulsion on her.

"Penny and I discussed it the night we returned from the palace."

"And what did the two of you decide?"

"We decided to stay at the inn until we go home."

Home. Nicholai hoped in a few days the word might mean somewhere entirely different to her. He turned his most charming smile on her. "Very well, I will respect your wishes. Just promise me one thing."

Julie's teeth tugged at her lower lip. "What's that?"

Nicholai brought her hand over his heart. "Promise me you'll be extra careful when I am not with you. I care about you greatly. Keep your eyelids open."

Julie smiled. "I think you mean keep my eyes open."

"Those, too. I don't want any"—his fingers made quotation marks in the air—"accidents to happen."

Nicholai leaned across the seat, stopped his face a handbreadth from hers. "Promise me, *lastochka*."

A warm smile graced her beautiful face. "I promise."

Nicholai closed the scant distance between them and took her creamy lips in a kiss. As he deepened the caress, his hand slid slowly along her arm then rested on the nape of her neck. His tongue pushed between her moist lips to taste her thoroughly. Her lilac scent filled the car, flooded his lungs.

The passion between them rose. Julie's heartrate increased in time with his own. Their breaths mingled, becoming one. He feathered light, maddening kisses along her jaw, then grasped the lobe of her ear between his teeth.

A soft moan escaped from Juliette's lips when Nicholai tugged the lobe. His warm breath blew sensuously in her ear. A shiver shook down her spine. Nicholai's lips moved over her delicate neck, rested over the spot where her pulse beat the strongest.

His tongue darted out to caress the throbbing vein. He lapped at the temptation. It called to him, beat at him. Demanded he take what his body needed. What he craved.

Her blood tasted so sweet, intoxicating. Unlike any other he had experienced in over two centuries. Unique as if it were made only for him. The thought of its flavor heated his blood, driving his need higher. Fangs lengthened in response to the hunger within his body. Hunger for her life-giving sustenance.

Hunger for her that would no longer be denied.

Nicholai pushed into her mind, ready to take control if needed.

Nicholai's breath warmed her neck, and the sensation made her own breath hitch as she realized he opened his mouth. She expected the sensation of his lips suckling at her. Instead, she felt a slight sting, a nip on her neck.

Ready to ease her pain, Nicholai didn't need to.

Quickly the sting abated, replaced by the sensation of Nicholai drawing against her skin. His lips felt silken. Each draw against the flesh made her stomach tighten. She rubbed her thighs together, seeking to ease the ache between them.

Her hands fisted in his supple hair, holding him to

her neck while she bared it to his ministrations. She drifted away, allowing the ecstasy to consume her. His powerful arm coiled around her waist, pulled her against his hard male body. A grunt pushed from her when her hips were drawn against the center console, but she didn't care. She wanted to be closer to his body, and the slight pain only added to the experience.

Julie's groan vibrated against his lips. Licking the small wound on her neck closed, he eased the grip on her waist. He'd taken less than a pint, but when it nourished his cells, it gave him a flow of power unlike he had ever experienced before. He felt alive, agile, potent.

Wicked.

Nicholai pulled away. The desire in her eyes turned them dark. Julie panted and slowly eased against the back of her seat.

He struggled to rein in his lust so he could speak. "I better get you inside before I take you right now in this car where anyone might happen by and see."

He practically purred the threat. A blush colored Julie's cheeks, and she shifted her legs against one another.

Calling on all his years of training, Nicholai forced himself from the car and opened her door. He tucked her under his arm as they journeyed through the doors to the inn and up the stairs.

Julie fumbled with the key to the room, her hand shaking. She narrowed her eyes as if concentrating on finding the keyhole. The key finally slid home and turned, granting them entrance to her room. When Nicholai remained in the hall, she turned a questioning glance on him.

"Do you want me to come in or shall we call it an evening?" Nicholai jammed his hands in his tuxedo pockets to quell the urge to take Julie in his arms and kiss her senseless.

Leaving the light in the room off, Julie stepped against Nicholai. She grabbed the lapels of his jacket and pulled him toward her. His firm body pressed against her soft one. She rose on her tiptoes and gave him a kiss that left no doubt in his mind her answer to his question was "Come on in."

Nicholai kicked the door closed behind them and moved them into the room. The heat of her body made his heart pound and his blood rush to the most significant places. He backed her across the room until her legs pushed against the bed.

Julie slid his jacket over his shoulders and tossed it onto the pillows. His fingers wove in her hair, pulling it from the chignon. It fell about her shoulders as she loosened and removed his tie. Together they tumbled onto the bed. His body blanketed hers. Nicholai braced his weight on one muscular forearm and settled between her legs.

His tongue slid along hers, teasing as she arched her heavy breasts against his chest. His hand cupped one full globe through the beaded material of her gown. He kneaded and caressed the soft mound. Nicholai's passion spun out of control, and his mind hazed with desire.

Her addictive kisses nipped at his lower lip, sending a bolt of lightning sizzling to his shaft. It jumped against her quivering thighs as the tension between them rose.

Nicholai pulled back to give her a long perusal. His

hand left her breast and found her sleek hair. It flowed salaciously over his fingers.

"You are so beautiful," he breathed, then lifted a lock of her hair to his nose. "Everything about you excites me. Your scent." He breathed in deeply before allowing the hair to drop from his grasp. "Your beautiful face." He brushed the back of one hand over her cheek. "Your soft, sinful curves." He ran a palm down her ribs, over her hip, and squeezed her thigh. He pushed his hand further south to the hem of her gown, took the material between his fingers and slowly pushed it up her leg.

Julie's hands worked the buttons on his shirt. They shook as they undid each one, working their way down to reveal the tuft of dark curly hair hiding beneath. Her hands slid as one over the lines of his ribs, up over the dark nipples that pebbled against her palms. They hooked his shirt, slipped it over his broad shoulders.

Suddenly, light bathed the room in a harsh glow.

"Okay, Jules, I heard you come in, give me all the details. I want to hear all about it. We have an early day tomorr—" Penny's voice stopped mid-sentence when her eyes rested on the two bodies intertwined on the bed. Her gaze appreciatively raked Nicholai's muscular back and rested on the twin mounds hiding under his black pants. "Oops. Sorry. It looks like I'm interrupting something."

Penny crossed her arms over her chest and leaned against the doorway between her and Julie's room. "Please continue snogging. Don't let me stop you."

"Penny, get out." Julie peered at her friend from around Nicholai's shoulder.

Nicholai gave Julie a rueful smile. "Early day?"

"We are going to go on one last shopping spree," his beautiful heartmate explained. She smoothed her ruffled hair before tugging her gown over her legs.

"Then perhaps I should go so you can get some sleep." Nicholai pushed off her.

Julie sat up and looked at him from under the dark crescent of her lashes. "You don't need to go."

The mood clearly broken, Nicholai put on his shirt with perfunctory ease and picked up his jacket and tie from the bed. "We better call it a night."

He bent and gave Julie a quick kiss on her sultry lips.

"Don't go, Nicholai. Penny was leaving. Weren't you?"

Penny straightened. "Yeah. You stay. I'll go."

Nicholai shrugged into the jacket, then tucked the tie in one pocket. "I better go. I'll see you tomorrow evening, Julie."

Though he'd have liked nothing better than to remain, he pulled Julie to her feet and wrapped her in his strong arms.

"Don't forget your promise," he said before giving her nose a tiny kiss.

Before she could protest, he turned on his heel and left his Juliette hot and wanting. Though he closed the door behind himself, he waited to be sure Juliette locked it.

The sound of Penny's voice kept him from leaving. "What promise?"

"Nicholai made me promise to be careful. He is still worried what happened at the church and the palace weren't accidents."

Nicholai increased his preternatural hearing. It

sounded to him like someone sat on the bed.

"That's silly, Julie. Nothing else has happened since we've been here."

"I know."

"Now, girl, sit down and tell me all about tonight."

"I can't believe you." Juliette sounded incredulous. "You're acting like you didn't just run Nicholai off. You could have closed the door when you realized what we were doing."

"I'm sorry, Jules. I had no idea. It was dark in here. Were you two going to…You know."

"Probably…Maybe…I don't know."

The Alpha felt quite glad he'd chosen to remain.

"Good for you! It's about time you got some, especially from a handsome beefcake like that."

Nicholai smiled at the compliment.

"Well, who knows if I'll get any now. We go back to England soon. I don't have much time left with him."

That's what you think, my heartmate.

"But if the chance presents itself, you'll take it, right?"

The springs on the bed creaked. "Yes. I've decided you're right, Penny. I deserve a little romance."

"About time you came to your senses. I'm so happy for you."

"Just do me a favor." Julie sounded puckish. "Don't come breaking in on us next time."

I couldn't agree more, he thought, shifting his still engorged cock to a more comfortable position.

A few minutes later, the frigid night air rolled over Nicholai while he stood outside the inn. His body, still heavy with desire, ached with an unsatisfied need. Hoping the air might act like a cold shower to wash away the lust, he walked down the street, but it didn't help. He needed to work off the energy.

Tingles moved over his skin. Nicholai sent his senses flowing out into the night, over the buildings and stores in search of anything requiring his attention. If he was lucky, perhaps a burglar or a car thief might provide a release for his pent-up energy. Alas, all he found was another blank spot.

Curious.

He'd taken Julie's blood this evening. Might her blood somehow be causing these empty spots? He had not heard of Stephan or Marcus experiencing such a thing when they took from their mates, but each vampire was unique. Nicholai wondered if there might be a correlation.

He raked a hand over his scalp, and his slicked hair tumbled around his face. An investigation seemed in order to make sure there wasn't something amiss.

He moved around the inn, twice, to be sure he found no danger. Discovering nothing of note, he slid behind the wheel of his vehicle and brought the engine to life. It purred like the finely tuned sports car it was. He gunned the motor and took off toward his house with all the speed the roads could handle.

The ride home became fast and furious as the warrior tried to work off some of the energy that pulsed through his veins. Hoping to relax, he took several detours, burning off the hours until sunrise, but it did little to calm his body. Only one thing could satisfy this need. Unfortunately, she lay in a bed back at the inn. And didn't that just make him want to turn around.

Chapter 26

Penny flipped her head upside down and tossed her blonde locks back and forth. As she straightened, her hair flung away from her sweet face.

"How much longer?" she asked Julie.

Julie shrugged.

The women waited for the metro in the underground subway station in Red Square. The station, with its high white ceilings, echoed with activity. The marbled walls were decorated with archways containing bronze statues depicting life-size replicas of the Russian people. A construction worker, a mother, a chef, and a military man all watched travelers pass.

While they waited for the train, Julie marveled that even after their third trip to the GUM, they still hadn't made it into every single shop.

"Oh, shoot!" Juliette smacked her forehead with the palm of her hand.

"What is it, Julie?"

"I forgot to get the *matryoshka*."

"The stacking dolls? No worries. We can go to the toy store in Yaroslavia and get some. You really want those things, don't you?"

"I have always thought they were adorable. My grandmother had a set I played with as a child. Grammy and I would set them out and have tea parties, pretending they were a family of identical quintuplets.

"Unfortunately when she passed, we didn't find them. I've always wanted a set of my own."

Julie's eyes went dreamy as she fondly remembered playing on her grandmother's farm. Her memories were sharp. She could almost smell the freshly mowed hay, feel the lush green grass under her toes. It was a welcome change from the stale air of the station and the pain in her feet after hours of walking the GUM.

"Here it is." Penny tugged on Julie's jacket sleeve.

The train's brakes squealed the cars to a stop.

The women pushed into the car against the flow of people exiting and found a plastic seat.

Penny turned toward Jules. "So where are you and Nicholai going tonight?"

"After the ballet and party last night, I want a quiet night. Hopefully, he'll plan something simple."

An amiable smile graced Penny's face. "He likes to surprise you, doesn't he?"

Julie situated her coat closed around her and placed her purse on her lap. "Yeah. It's been fun. I never know what to expect. One night we are ice skating on a pond, and the next we are at the ballet."

"A private showing of the ballet, none the less. I can't believe he did that for you. He must really be smitten with you."

"He said he cared about me last night," Julie admitted as heat crept up her neck to her cheeks.

"I could tell the first night he met you. I saw in his eyes it was love at first sight."

An inelegant snort escaped Julie's mouth. "Yeah, right."

Penny laid her hand on Julie's forearm. "No really.

Don't you remember? I told you he appeared enthralled, and he looked at you with puppy love in his eyes."

Julie shook her head in dissention while she secretly hoped her friend was right. In the short time since she'd met Nicholai Peterhof, she had come to like him a great deal. The way he treated her, as if she was all that mattered to him, made her heart fill with joy. She loved being around him, loved being in his arms. Loved his sense of humor.

She loved *him*.

The realization struck like a hard fist to her solar plexus. She fought to breathe, taking in gulps of air, as she tried to calm her palpitating heart.

"What's wrong?" Penny's eyes widened with concern.

"Can't...breathe...gonna...faint..." wheezed Julie.

"Put your head between your knees," Penny commanded, pushing gently on Julie's back as she assumed the position.

"When it passes, drink this." Julie took the water offered by her friend and worked to calm her breathing.

****

Lovazia slunk silently into the room at the inn. The drapes, drawn against the noonday sun, made the room shadowed. A small crack in the material allowed a sliver of light to beam across the floor. While her vision might be impeded, her sense of smell was not. One inhale and the stench of vampire prickled her nose.

Her lithe figure moved closer to the bed and raised a long sword above its head. The glint of the sun reflected off the shiny blade. Tiny prisms danced along the walls.

Lovazia stalked closer on silent feet toward the mound lying in the bed. She allowed hatred to consume her body, using the strength of the emotion to power the thrust.

The long sword came down in a mighty swoop, whistling through the air from the speed of the arc. Vibrations ran up its length into the hilt as it sliced cleanly through the mound and lodged into the mattress below. The bed shook with the force of the killing blow.

The demon looked down, waiting to see the dark pool of blood form under the weapon. Anticipation brought a smile.

She raised the sword and turned it, carefully checking each side. It appeared clean. *Incomprehensible!* The blade could not have missed its mark.

Her hand reached out, yanked the red and gold spread from the bed. Feathers flew in the air.

"Pillows!"

Cushions lay in the bed in the shape of a body. A female vampire should have been in bed, sleeping the day away. Where was she? The bathroom perhaps?

Lovazia crept to the door of the bath. After placing an ear to the closed door and hearing nothing inside, she cranked the knob. Frustration strengthened her grip, and it buckled under the force. The door opened to reveal an empty room.

Lovazia had waited, planned. The bloodsucker should be in the bed, waiting for her death to come at the hands of the sword-wielding demon.

Rage gave her lithe body renewed strength. The blade slashed through the towels drying over the curtain rod in the shower. Next, the sword crashed into the mirror over the vanity, sending tiny shards of glass raining down over the sink and the tile floor.

Then Lovazia went to work, releasing her anger on the bedroom. She sliced through the pillows, sending tiny white feathers floating through the air. The bedspread was slashed into red and gold ribbons. She tore the drapes from their rods, and the curtains pooled over the shredded bed covering.

Satisfied with the work, Lovazia slunk from the room. She might not have accomplished her goal of death, but she had left a mark. There would be another day, another time. The demon would have her kill.

****

"It has been a long day," Julie said dragging her tired feet up the stairs. Penny followed in tow, pushing her bottom to help her ascend the stairs.

"I know what you mean. Glad it's you going out tonight and not me."

Their feet sounded heavily on the wooden stairs as they climbed. When they reached the landing, Juliette stopped so suddenly Penny ran into her back, causing Julie to stumble forward.

"Look!" Julie gestured toward the door to her room. It was open, the lock obviously broken, entry to the room forced.

The two women inched forward, holding hands as they peered into the open door. Both gasped when their eyes took in the sight within. Though the twilight barely illuminated the room, they plainly saw the disaster.

Penny leaned closer to her friend and whispered, "Do you think whoever did this is still here?"

Julie turned her horrified gaze on her friend. As

one, the women took a step back. Fear crept up Julie's spine and settled deep in her brain. Her eyes grew wide. Nicholai had been right. Someone was after her. Judging by the condition of the room, someone wanted to kill her.

Her knees went weak with the thought, and she fought to remain upright. Penny's grip on her hand tightened painfully.

Penny dared to move forward first. "I don't see or hear anyone in there. Let's go in."

Penny tugged Julie's hand and led her into the room. Piles of cloth lay about the room. Julie tripped when the ribbons of the slashed bedspread caught her foot. She righted herself using the mattress for support, and her hand slid into one of the deep cuts made there.

Julie jerked away. What could have done that? Who would have come into her room? What if she had been in the room at the time?

Juliette's knees gave out, and she hit the floor hard. The blood drained from her face. Her hands went ice-cold.

Penny knelt beside her. "You don't look so good, Jules. I'm going to get you something to drink. It kept you from passing out earlier on the train."

Her friend made her way into the bathroom and glass crackled under Penny's shoes. Unable to find the strength to move, Julie remained on the floor and her eyes once more skirted around the room.

The weight of the situation struck her with such force she had to throw her arms stiffly behind her to brace her weight. Nicholai had been right all along. Why hadn't she listened to him? She could be safe in his home, in his arms right now if she'd only heeded his warnings.

Oh Nicholai, she thought. *Where are you? I need you!*

Chapter 27

Stephan and Demetri sat in the great room of Demetri's home when the sound of the doorbell broke their conversation. Demetri glided across the wooden floors to open the door wide in welcome.

"Come in, Alexander. It is about time you arrived." He clasped his fellow Alpha's forearms in greeting.

"I'd have been here sooner, but you know how those private planes are. Always running on the corporate schedules, never convenient," the blond male joked in his southern drawl. Alex removed the baseball cap from his head as Stephan's long strides brought him to the door.

"I beg your pardon. It's not as if I can control the weather."

Alex's deep chuckle rumbled in his muscular chest. "I realize you're not to blame. A nor'easter blew in just as we were ready to leave. Damn thing kept us stuck at the airport for two days. It isn't comfortable waiting on a plane for the weather to clear."

"Perhaps you might have preferred sleeping in the terminal with all of its windows to allow the sunlight on you during the day. If my jet isn't good enough for you, then you don't have to use it, you know. Maybe you'd prefer to fly back on a commercial airline that only runs during the daylight hours."

Alex raised both hands in surrender. "Hey now, no

reason to get your panties in a wad. I was just kidding. Actually, your plane was very…" He wagged his blond eyebrows. "…accommodating."

A smile broke the seriousness on Stephan's face. "I've never had any complaints."

The three males made their way back to the great room. Alexander brought up the rear. At six feet, he was not only the shortest of the males on the Alpha Council, but also the youngest. However, what he lacked in height and experience, he made up for in knowledge. He was the go-to guy for all things mechanical or technological. A genius with computers, he could hack his way into a government database. And he could turn a wrench like a carnie could turn a phrase.

"Sit." Demetri gestured to one of the plaid chairs that outlined the Navajo throw rug.

Alex complied, laying one ankle on his opposite knee as he took in the large log cabin, tucked away on the middle of the mountainside. The walls, like Demetri, were hard and abrasive. The wood grain, rough and unfinished, gave the home a rustic look. Upon the walls, wool tapestries hung, depicting scenes of the wilderness and hunting. The ceiling was made of thick arched timbers, roughly cut, both functional and decorative. An antler chandelier hung from the ceiling to illuminate the room.

Demetri sat on the leather couch, directly across from the fire roaring under the stone mantel, and stretched his legs out, resting them on the square coffee table that stood in the middle of the large rug. The plain wooden table easily bore the heavy weight of his legs which crossed at the ankles. "So, Stephan, do you want to share what we found with Alexander or should I?"

Stephan grabbed his brandy from the table and leaned back in one of the plaid chairs. Settling his back against the cushion, he raised his glass in salute. "Go ahead, be my guest."

Demetri explained the unusual scene they had come across in the forest and the unique scents. He shared the strange roar they heard as well as the information about the paw prints and how a footprint seemed to disappear under the side of the mountain.

Alex leaned forward with interest as Demetri regaled him with a description of the empty space where neither he nor Stephan could detect anything. "I've never heard of such a thing. You're telling me neither of you could sense anything?"

Stephan swallowed the last drop from his snifter. "That's right. It was empty, blank."

The blond Alpha shook his head.

"We thought perhaps there might be a deposit of titanium running through the mountain," offered Demetri as he rose to refill Stephan's drink. "Do you want anything while I'm up, Alex? A drink or perhaps you'd like something to eat?"

"No, thanks. I'm good." Alex turned his attention back to Stephan. "So what do we do now?"

"Nothing more to do tonight. We'll rest during the day and resume our patrols of the area tomorrow."

"What about that little filly? What was her name?"

Demetri returned to the couch with a decanter of brandy for his friend and a glass of vodka for himself. He poured some brandy into Stephan's snifter and set the bottle down on the table before he answered. "The vampire or the human?"

"Hold up. A vampire has gone missing, too?" Alex

219

asked in disbelief, his azure eyes wide.

"Yes, comrade, that's one of the reasons we called you in." Demetri took a drink of the vodka.

"Maybe you better fill me in from the beginning and bring me up to speed."

Stephan cradled his sifter between his palms. "It began with a series of animal attacks. At least that was what the local papers called them. We believe it may have been something other than an animal that attacked the humans."

"A vampire?"

"We're not sure," continued Stephan. "That's why I came out here. Demetri tried to find what was attacking the population, but he couldn't cover enough ground by himself. I came out to help, but the two of us haven't had much luck.

"We went to the coroner's office and got a look at one victim. The man in his early twenties had his throat ripped out, but according to the autopsy report, his blood loss had been at a minimum, no more was lost than would have pumped out naturally until his heart stopped. There was also a second gash across his stomach. He was practically disemboweled."

Alex ran a hand through his short strands that were swept back on the sides away from his face. "That doesn't sound like a vampire."

"That is what we thought," said Demetri taking up the story. "So Stephan and I pulled the reports of the other victims. Same MO. Each time, stomach was sliced, throat torn, but enough blood remained in the bodies to make a vampire attack seem unlikely.

"Then there is the young human woman who went missing. Wondering if her disappearance might be related to the attacks, Stephan and I walked the trails, but we did not find any sign of the woman or any indication she had been injured."

Stephan pushed from his chair and stood beside the fire. "Then the female vampire vanished."

"Aase," Demetri supplied as Stephan nodded his head in agreement.

"I spoke to Aase's family. Her heartmate told me she had recently found out she was going to have a baby."

Alex gasped. "A natural-born offspring!"

"Exactly," said Demetri. "That is why we must find her before something can happen to her or the baby. A vampiric birth is too rare, a treasure to be protected. We must find the female, make sure she and her baby are safe."

"Do you have any idea where she might be?"

Stephan clasped his hands behind his back and paced the length of the flagstone. "She and her heartmate were visiting family with their daughter in a town not too far from here. We were there last evening, but had no luck locating her. Demetri and I thought perhaps the two missing women were connected somehow, so we focused our search this evening in an area of forest that lies between the location where the human vanished and the town where the vampire was visiting."

"Sounds like a lot of ground to cover."

"Exactly. That's why we brought you in. Three can cover more area than one. We were also hoping you might be able to do some surveillance from the sky."

Alexander's face brightened, a smile caused a dimple to appear in his left cheek. "Hack into a surveillance satellite? Shit yeah! Just show me to your computer."

****

Tears streamed from both eyes to pool on the metal table when the torturer slowly drew the needle from her eye. He removed the metal lid calipers that held open the eye and turned, taking his latest specimen to the table where his microscope sat. He scrubbed his neck as if trying to work out his latest kink.

Aase lay strapped to the table. Her body sore from the numerous wounds it had been subjected to. She knew she bled in several places because she smelled the blood, felt its warmth dripping down her cold, naked body. Her arms lay strapped above her head and her ankles bound.

Her captors had not brought her any food or blood. She'd overheard them talking, saying it was part of the experiment to starve her. Her body needed sustenance, not only to heal but to supply for the babe growing in her belly.

Silent sobs shook her body when she thought of her unborn child. For over two hundred years, she and her heartmate had waited to be blessed by the miracle. As with other women who were converted into vampirism, her uterus had been damaged during the transition. After two centuries, she and her mate had given up hope of ever having a child. Then their tiny miracle happened. They were blessed with a beautiful daughter with raven hair that was the joy of their lives.

Never expecting to receive a second miracle, she'd overlooked the first signs of pregnancy until a few weeks ago when, during a routine trip to a doctor, she discovered she was pregnant again. The night she told her heartmate about the impending birth, he swept her into his arms and twirled her around the room. A smile tried to pull at her swollen lips as the reverie took her.

The pain in her dry lips pulled her back to the present. Her heart clenched as she wondered what her daughter might be doing at that very moment. She hoped she was playing. Or maybe her father was reading a book to her. She loved her child with every cell of her being and hoped to hold her second child one day if she could survive this torture.

Can you hear me, my love? Please hear me. Come save me.

As usual, the connection to her husband, just as all the others she'd tried, didn't work. There was nothing. She didn't sense him or anyone through a mindlink. The monster's female companion had mentioned something about doing a spell of some kind to block communication. But Aase couldn't remember the particulars, because, when the conversation had taken place, she'd just awakened from a drug-induced sleep to discover she'd been kidnapped.

Escape from this madman became priority one. Her daughter and baby needed her. In danger of losing her beloved baby from the wounds being inflicted on her, she must find a means of escape. She'd tell her captor anything, if he'd let her go.

Pain raced to her brain when Aase turned her head toward the man standing across the room. Her neck muscles burned from having spent most of the day lying face down as the skin was taken from her back and needles were pushed into her spine. She opened her chapped lips, the skin pulled taut, cracking open in two places. When she tried to call out, her vocal chords, damaged from days of screaming, allowed only a small rasp to come from her bleeding lips. She closed her eyes against the pain and frustration.

The soft clicking of heels against the rock floor brought her eyes open. The female vampire watched as the male with the dark, reddish-black hair approached. Aase swallowed gingerly, licked her lips, and hoped her saliva would help heal them. She moved her lips forming silent words when the monster looked down on her sunken face.

"You trying to say something?" he asked.

She nodded her head only once, the effort excruciating.

"You can't talk?"

She turned her head from side to side, wincing from the painful movement.

"If I give you a little blood will you be able to speak?"

She nodded again, closing her eyes to the pain.

Aase listened as he walked away, opened a cabinet door and closed it again before walking back to where she lay. She peeked at the monster when he snipped the corner of a bag of blood and held it to her lips. The crimson liquid slid over her teeth and gums. It tasted thick and rich when she swallowed the tiny amount, no more than a tablespoon. When it hit her stomach, all cells cried for more.

"More," she whispered.

He obliged, tipping the bag briefly to her lips. This sip was just large enough to bring her cells some much needed nutrients. They struggled to feed from the tiny amount, each fighting for life. Her baby's heartbeat grew stronger as her body fed it first.

"More," Aase whispered again.

The monster shook his head from side to side. A lock of his slick hair escaped its place to rest on his forehead. He brushed it back with a careless sweep of his hand as he spoke. "First tell me what you mouthed."

Aase took a deep breath. A rush of stale air filled her lungs. When her voice came, it sounded no louder than a hummingbird's wings. "I asked you why you haven't asked me any questions."

The torturer's dark brows furrowed. "What do you mean?"

"You seem to be looking for something. Why don't you just ask me? I'll tell you anything."

He scrubbed a thoughtful hand across his stubbled chin, and Aase tried to push into his mind to glean his thoughts, but like her attempts to use her mindlink to contact her heartmate, it failed. A tear ran down her face. She was too weak to use her power, and the damned titanium restraints kept her from dematerializing.

"Ask me anything," she said, desperate to keep him talking and not hurting her.

"If you are willing to talk, I indeed have questions. But I'll warn you, lie to me, and you'll be sorry."

As if anything could be worse than what she'd already been through.

Their eyes met. "An easy question to start then. How do humans become vampire?"

"We believe it is a mutation of the virus that caused the Bubonic Plague. The first known vampires were made during the plague. Our scientists hypothesized the virus mutated and caused vampirism."

"Plausible theory." The male ran his fingers

through his slicked back hair. "Why do you need blood?"

"The virus changes our hearts, enlarging them. It also enlarges our lungs and muscles. The extra muscle fibers need more blood to fuel our strength. The larger lungs push more oxygen through our bodies. Our bodies can't produce enough blood to supply the need on their own, so we need to drink some to keep our bodies functioning properly. Can I have more blood now?"

Ignoring the request, the maniac continued with his interrogation. "What happens if you don't get blood every day?"

"We can survive for a while without blood, but starvation weakens us. Our bodies conserve energy much the same way human bodies slowly shut down when they go without food."

He nodded his head. "I had already noticed the physical changes in you due to the starvation. Since you seem to be telling me the truth, let's keep going. How does a human become infected with the vampiric virus?"

"To convert someone we must take their blood while they take ours."

"Like a transfusion?"

"Yes, but it takes a while. The vampire and human must form a blood circle. Their blood circulates through their bodies until it mixes thoroughly enough. Once enough of the virus is in the human blood it will change the person."

"So the human is *infected* by the vampire...Interesting."

"In a way, I guess, but we don't think of it in those

terms."

The male leaned his arms on the table, allowing the metal to bear some of his weight. "What about taking the blood? How do you keep the blood from coagulating?"

"Our fangs produce a type of venom. It is injected while we feed, preventing the blood from congealing."

"And how do you get the blood to stop?"

"Our saliva. It has a healing agent in it," Aase answered truthfully.

"Easy enough to test," said the male. "I'll collect a sample of your saliva and test it on an open wound. All right. Answer me this. Why do vampires never get sick?"

Oh course, he would eventually ask a question she didn't know the answer to. Aase's hope fell to the floor like a leaden weight. She needed time to devise a plausible answer. "Will you let me go if I tell you?" she countered.

The monster glared down at her in surprise then a twisted smile curved his lips. "Yes. Tell me, and I'll let you go."

Aase doubted her captor, but desperation to save her unborn child kept hope alive. "What assurances do I have that you will let us go?"

She bit her lip realizing too late her mistake in using the plural.

His eyes widened and traveled from her face down to her belly. He straightened to his full height and reached a hand out to touch the sensitive flesh. Aase jerked, instinctually trying to draw away from his touch. Her restraints prevented her movement. They grated against her skin, chafed her wrists and ankles, and sent a sobering sensation of pain through her body. Tears welled in her eyes as much from fear as from actual pain.

His eyes still riveted on her stomach he simply stated, "You're pregnant."

Though it wasn't a question Aase was desperate to deny the accusation. "No! Vampires can't get pregnant," she lied as her eyes no longer contained the pool of tears.

He turned from the metal examining table. "I think you are lying. I warned you about lying to me."

He wheeled a metal tray full of instruments over to where she lay. "It will be easy enough to ascertain whether or not you are pregnant."

"What are you going to do?" she asked in a weak voice as her body trembled in terror.

Lane snapped on a pair of black latex gloves then picked up a scalpel from the tray, turning it so the numerous torch lights around the room reflected off its shiny surface. He leaned over, placing the scalpel beside her eye, giving her a good view of it as he whispered, "You'll see."

Chapter 28

Nicholai's eyes snapped open. The Alpha sat straight up in his bed, the sheet falling from his bare chest. *Julie's in trouble. She needs me.*

His breaths came in gasps as he tried desperately to calm his nervous system to concentrate.

Think, he commanded himself. *What did she say her plans were today?*

As he remembered her intentions to go to the GUM, he glanced over at the clock sitting on the bedside table. It was dusk. They had arranged to meet within the hour to go out on a date. Surely, she would be in her hotel room getting ready.

Nicholai threw the covers from his body and used his preternatural speed to dress, throwing on the first thing he found. He didn't have time to waste driving to the inn. Instead, he decided to materialize there. Spurred on by urgency, he didn't care if someone saw him. He needed to be with his heartmate. *Now!* Besides, if someone did see him, he'd erase that person's memory.

He took a deep cleansing breath and let it out slowly, focusing his power. He drew into himself, his form shrinking until only a tiny dark dot remained which popped from the room.

A moment later, his strong arms enfolded Julie in a steel embrace that drew her back against his body. "I'm here, *lastochka*."

Julie wrapped her arms around the thick forearms holding her and settled against Nicholai. "I don't know where you came from, but I don't care. You're here."

"You needed me," Nicholai replied simply and squeezed a little tighter. "Am I holding you too tight?"

"Never." She breathed. "It's hard to breathe, but it makes me feel alive, cared for."

Penny's steps faltered when she emerged from the bathroom and discovered Nicholai behind Julie.

"How did you get here?" Penny crossed the room and handed Julie a glass of water.

Nicholai had been fortunate that no one had seen him materialize in the room. He didn't wish to explain how he had gotten there to Penny.

"What happened here? Are either of you hurt?"

He moved beside Julie, so he could assess her for injuries. His gaze raked her body with a demanding intensity until he felt satisfied she was uninjured.

"We're fine," she offered in a small voice.

"What happened?" he repeated, turning his attention to Penny. "Who did this?"

Penny knelt down on the other side of Julie. "That's what we'd like to know. We came back from shopping and found this mess."

Nicholai stabbed her with a glare. Concern for his heartmate furrowed his dark brows. "So someone did this while you were out?"

"Yes," answered Julie.

"And when you got back, you didn't see anyone?"

"That's right," confirmed Penny.

Nicholai pulled his heartmate to his chest in a desperate hug as he realized he might have lost her. The thought of what might have happened if the women had walked in on the person who had done this to Julie's room sickened him. His heart threatened to beat out of his chest.

He put Julie away from him to look down onto her sweet face. "You will come and stay with me now." The decisive tone in Nicholai's voice brooked no argument.

Julie nodded her head insistently, despite it been a statement rather than a question.

"I'll pack our things," offered Penny, standing.

"No," Nicholai said a little more forcefully than he had intended. "I will send someone for your things. I want to get you to my home now. I don't want to wait a second longer in case the person decides to come back."

With the statement, Juliette's face took on the pallor of fresh snow and contorted in anguish. Nicholai's heart broke at the sight. He scooped her into his arms. His bulging biceps barely registered the weight. Julie wrapped her arms about his neck and looked over his broad shoulder, saying good riddance to the room as they strolled to the stairs.

Following them, Penny asked, "What about the police? We need to make a report."

Nicholai nodded. "I will see to that and take care of things with the innkeeper as well before we leave. For now, I want Julie away from this mess."

As the trio exited the room, Nicholai realized he didn't have his car. "After we wrap things up with the police and inn, I'll arrange for a cab to take us to my house."

Penny cast a questioning glance his way. "Didn't you drive here?"

Coming up with no plausible way to deflect the question, Nicholai turned the power of his gaze on both women, then said, "You find it reasonable that I did not drive here. You will not question the need to take a taxi to my home."

Nicholai released them. Guilt pushed in for manipulating their minds, but this wasn't the first time he'd resorted to mind control to keep the existence of vampires a secret, and it wouldn't be the last.

****

Julie sat before the beveled mirror on the Queen Anne style vanity in her bedroom. The room was a winter wonderland of cream, white, and celadon. The colors were used interchangeably in the romantic bedroom, anchored by a custom sleigh bed. Julie had been surprised to find freshly cut white roses placed beside the bed and her toiletries settled comfortably in the bath. Like everything else Nicholai did, he'd thoughtfully arranged to have her things brought to his home and placed in her room.

It felt strange to have someone make her comfort a priority, to have someone who considered her needs and met them before she even considered them herself. She wasn't used to being cared for. Truth be told, she found it a relief after such a stressful night. She brushed her fingers through her hair as she pondered the evening.

When the three of them had arrived at Nicholai's home, he insisted on them staying together so the trio retired to his drawing room. After he lit a fire in the ornately carved stone fireplace, Nicholai poured them all a stiff drink from the bar and told them how he'd contacted an acquaintance at the police station after talking things over with the innkeeper. While he assured them that the matter would be investigated and the police would let them know if they found anything, Penny had chosen one of the wingback chairs for herself while Julie rested on the adjoining couch. After handing the ladies their drinks, Nicholai had, of course, joined her on the couch. Julie rubbed over the spot on her leg where the warmth of his thigh pressing against hers still lingered.

After a few drinks, Julie had relaxed enough to notice the way the fire cast dancing shadows around the room, causing the gold inlay that graced the moldings and wall sconces to gleam. The room, painted a salmon color, matched the upholstery on the chairs. Only someone as confident in his manliness as Nicholai could pull off such decor. In his home, it did not appear girly but, instead, regal and courtly.

Nicholai had kept the women engaged throughout the evening, obviously trying to keep their thoughts in the present and away from the terrifying scene at the inn. It worked. Julie gave her reflection a smile, remembering how relaxed she'd felt sitting there tucked securely under Nicholai's arm. Yes, Nicholai had done his best to keep them occupied all evening, which was probably how he had had time to arrange for her things to be brought to her room unbeknownst to her.

After they'd seen Penny to her room upstairs, Nicholai had escorted her to this beautiful boudoir. As they approached the winter wonderland, he mentioned that his room was next door. He had wanted to be sure she knew he'd be near in case she needed him. Clearly, Nicholai cared a great deal for her.

Julie took the brush from the table and ran it gently

through her hair. She had always found the bristles of the brush pulling through the strands soothing. It gave her a sense of normalcy.

A knock on the door drew her attention. "Come in," she called.

Nicholai stepped through the door, leaving it open behind him. He still wore blue jeans and a gray sweater. The gray brought out the amber in his whiskey eyes, making them glow like the flames that had reflected in her bourbon earlier.

"Before you retired, I wanted to be sure you were finding everything okay."

Julie placed the brush on the vanity. "Everything's perfect. I have no idea how you got all my stuff here."

Nicholai's sexy smile took his face, and a rush of heat surged through her body.

"What can I say, I am full of surprises."

Nicholai took the brush and glided it with care through her silken strands. A contented sigh slipped from between her parted lips. He placed the brush back on the table and massaged her scalp. She melted under his ministrations. Each time his firm fingers pushed against her skin, desire coursed through her body. She leaned on the tiny stool upon which she sat until her back rested against Nicholai's stomach.

His hands traveled down to her neck. The pads of his fingers worked the knots from her nape, easing the tension from her body with each knead until her head lolled on her shoulders and her eyes drooped heavily.

Nicholai met her gaze in the beveled mirror and reluctantly pulled his hands from her shoulders. "You look tired. You should get some rest."

"You don't have to go." Julie straightened. "I'm

not that tired."

She tried to hide the yawn that took her face behind her hand.

"Your body is betraying you, *lastochka*. You better get some rest."

"But I don't want to sleep. I'm afraid I'll have nightmares."

Nicholai squeezed both her shoulders. "It will be all right. I will be right next door should you need me. Call to me, and I'll come running."

By the serious tone of his voice she believed he meant every word. It made her feel safe and protected. "Well, all right then. Good night, Nicholai."

Nicholai gave her a lingering kiss. "Good night, my Juliette. Parting is such sweet sorrow."

****

As still as the night itself, Nicholai listened to the sweet sounds coming from the room next door. The whisper of silk brushing skin indicated Juliette donned her nightgown. The images in his mind made him want to rush through her door and take her into his arms.

While he brushed her hair, she'd looked so sinful, like a sensual goddess waiting for her lover. Her lips half opened, her honey eyes barely visible from under her long, dark lashes. And when he'd scented her arousal, well…only her fatigue had given the protective male within the fortitude to leave for the night.

With a heavy sigh, he crossed the room and laid his hand against the wall. His heartmate lay beyond that wall, the heartmate he'd waited centuries for. Unfortunately, she would need time to accept all that being a heartmate entailed. But what was time to one such as him?

Touching her created a need in him, a longing for both her body and the life-giving essence within. Her heartbeat pounded in his ears, drawing him. Julie's unique lilac scent perfumed the air. He stood motionless, dared not move for the siren call of her blood begged him to take what belonged to him. Nicholai summoned all his self-control and laid his forehead against the wall beside the hand that longed to touch the creamy soft skin of the woman next door.

The time will come soon when she will be entirely mine, he reassured himself. *Body, mind, and soul.* The thought brought a smile to his lips and gave him the courage he needed to move. Pushing away from the wall, he realized he would be able to wait for her, give her as long as she needed. He could allow her to be so close without being in the same room, holding her as she slept, for soon she would be his, forever.

In the meantime, I can always visit her dreams. In sleep, he could hold her, love her as he longed to do. In dreams, she didn't hide from her feelings, did not hold back from him. In the dream world, she was his, eager for his kiss, his touch. Though it might be a little deceitful, he could no more resist diving into her dreams than he could resist the need to quench his bestial thirst. If he could not have her in the flesh, he would settle for having her in the world where all sorts of interesting things were possible.

The thought brought a wicked grin to his face.

Chapter 29

Juliette looked down at the pretty curly-haired brunette who reached her small arms up toward her mother with a sweet smile on her face. She scooped the two-year-old into her arms and placed the girl squarely on her hip. The pair twirled around the living room to the soft music that played on the stereo. They danced to the little girl's giggles, the sound bringing her identical twin into the room to see what caused such pleasure.

"Mommy, Mommy, me, too," the little girl said, holding her arms out to the twirling pair.

Julie put her bundle of joy down beside her sister. The trio joined hands and formed a circle of delight. As they spun in time to the music, the sound of childish giggles rang out in stereo, warming her heart. Her face was not nearly large enough to accommodate the broad smile that spread across her lips at the sight of her girls. The trio twirled around the room again and again until dizziness overtook them and they collapsed, laughing when they fell to the carpeted floor.

The girls crawled on top of their mommy, putting their heads on her belly. Each laugh from their mother sent a ripple through their tiny bodies. They giggled harder. Hearing them laugh made Julie chuckle, and her laugh made the girls chortle. A continuous cycle of blissful amusement flowed as the trio lay together on the plush carpeting. The contented mother closed her eyes and savored the moment.

Suddenly the merry scene morphed in a swirl of colors and sounds until Julie found herself alone. Moisture soaked through her clothes. Cold, damp wetness on her back snapped her eyes open. She patted her stomach, searching for the soft locks of hair. Finding only her own clothing, she patted the floor in search of her lost children. But instead of thick carpet her hands found dew-covered grass.

Her babies were gone! Julie's stomach twisted. The knot brought bile to her throat. She pushed herself onto her hands and knees and turned to discover a double tombstone. Tears burned her eyes and blurred the names. She didn't have to read the names to know who lay buried beneath the double hearts and carved angels.

She knelt on the graves of her daughters.

No, she didn't need to read the tombstone to know what was written there. The etched carvings were forever imprinted into her mind. It contained the names, birth dates, and date of death for each girl. Written across both hearts, a quote from Thomas Campbell read, "To live in the hearts we leave behind is not to die."

Juliette took the quote to heart. The only way she had been able to drag herself out of bed after the death of her family was to believe that they weren't truly gone as long as she held love for them in her heart.

Sobs wrenched from her body, the grief of losing her children taking her as keenly as the day it happened. Her despair weakened her, and she collapsed onto the moist ground. Julie pulled the grass out by its roots with the violence of her grief and anger.

The pain still fresh, sorrow closed in, ripped her heart in two.

They had been taken from her at far too young an age. It wasn't fair. Her girls had not had a chance to live their lives. There would be no proms, no weddings for them. They were wonderful children, so well-behaved and loving. They deserved to know the happiness of having their own daughters one day. But fate had had other plans. No, not fate...evil.

A feral scream escaped her throat.

Pure evil had taken her daughters from her. Evil ripped her precious children from her loving arms. That hideous evil had destroyed all their lives in an instant.

She pounded at the ground. The dampness permeated her clothes, soaked into her skin. It was so cold, deathly cold, and it sent a shiver down her spine, but in her anguish she didn't care. She fisted the grass and tore it from the ground in a vain attempt to get to her children buried beneath.

Julie awoke, sobbing in an empty bed. Tears streamed down her cheeks and soaked the linens. She rolled onto her side and hugged the wet pillow to her body, wishing it was her children.

****

As Nicholai paced his room, Julie's grief called him. He materialized instantly in her bed and gathered her into his strong arms.

The realization that he had suddenly appeared did not seem to penetrate Julie's intense misery. Lost in her sorrow, she did not spare a second to consider how he appeared abruptly there with her. Her arms flew around his waist and her fingers grabbed onto him tight.

He stroked one hand down the back of her brunette mane. The soft strands wove between his fingers. A dreadful keening sound of hurt and despair unlike anything he had ever heard burst through her lips. It tore into him like a hundred knives, disemboweling his soul. He clasped her tighter to his chest, cradling her head in his hand. Hot tears rolled down his bare chest while he gently rocked them back and forth on the bed.

"It's okay, Juliette. Shhhh. I've got you," he whispered against the top of her head.

Julie did not respond.

"Please don't cry, *lastochka*. My heart cannot take it. Please tell me what is wrong," he pleaded softly.

When she tried, grief constricted her throat and took her voice from her. She mustered a weak, hitching sound as she lay boneless in his arms, allowing him to take her weight when sobs continued to rack her body.

The need to protect and sooth overwhelmed Nicholai. He must ease her pain. The Alpha, used to being in control on the field of battle, felt incompetent with his heartmate weeping in his arms. It broke his heart to see her crying. In that moment, he would do anything to ease her torment.

He pushed into her mind and discovered what she could not voice. He easily found her memory of the dream and watched it from beginning to end. Nicholai closed his own eyes against the tears that threatened to spill.

His Juliette had been through so much, and her grief was still as painful this night as it had been that dreadful night so many years ago. The power of it threatened to consume her, consume them both. Being in her mind, connected as they were, her grief was his own. But he'd willingly bear the full force of the anguish if it would ease her suffering.

He fought down the tears that burned his eyes, knowing his strength would see her through this. He must be strong enough for both of them.

Nicholai took her chin in his hand and lifted her face toward his. He waited for her to look into his eyes from under her wet lashes before he spoke. "Shhh. It will be okay, my love. Please do not cry. You are breaking my heart."

In an attempt to kiss away her pain, he gently kissed her tears as they fell on one cheek, then the other. Julie's body responded to its mate instantaneously. Her mind reached for his of its own volition, demanding a distraction, a respite from the grief.

In the next minute, it didn't matter who or where they were. This moment was about chemistry, wanting, spellbinding, ravenous needs that had yearned for this connection for far too long. The moment in which fate insisted they fulfill their destiny.

Chapter 30

Juliette's fingers slid around his neck and into the soft, obsidian hair that framed Nicholai's face. She couldn't help herself. In her dreams, he satisfied her sensual hunger like no other, and that was exactly what she needed tonight. She needed a connection to the real man. She craved him, needed the reality of their bodies joining.

She needed the reality of him.

Julie closed her eyes, savored the touch of his soft lips on her face. She lost herself in the sensation, became only feeling, freeing herself. Her body overtook her mind. The sensuous feel of Nicholai pressed against her blissfully pushed away all thoughts.

Her hands skimmed fast and hot over his muscular chest in search of pure carnal sensation. They traced each rib before rounding to his back as she pressed her mouth hungrily to his. Her kiss was fierce, demanding. She ran her hands down the musculature of his flank.

Nicholai responded to her aggression as if his gentleness and good intentions were pushed aside by tumultuous desire. His large hands cupped her hips, settling her with him down onto the bed. He drew her under his body. The evidence of his arousal lay hard between them. Her legs spread to accommodate his hips, and they settled home in a tight fit.

His hand traveled upward, curling into her waist

before sliding along her ribs. Only his thumbs breached the underside of her breasts before he took their weight in both hands. The heat of a thousand balls of fire rushed through her blood. Her nipples puckered hard against his palms. He lowered his head, kneading one breast while he took the other in his mouth, suckling through the soft fabric of her nightgown.

She arched into his mouth, moaning with need. Her hands fisted in his soft hair and held him against her bosom. His hair was the only soft thing about him. The rest of him? Pure marble, hard and firm, all stony sinew and muscle.

He left a trail of kisses up her body until his tongue rested over the pulse in her throat. It swirled lazily over the throbbing vein before he kissed the delicate spot and continued kissing a path.

She turned her head, needing his lips. His skillful kiss made his tongue dance with hers again and again until it set her ablaze from head to toe.

She needed this. The fire. The wildness. She needed to be lost in the physicality, to be consumed. Needed Nicholai invading every pore, flooding her system with sensations until they consumed her.

She knew this man and the desires he brought out in her were risky. He had the potential to take her heart, make her love again. She'd known it from the first time she'd put herself into his dreamy hands. Dogged hands that now slid down her body with ferocious intent.

His fingers bit into her waist as he jerked her farther up between the bed and his body. Instantly, his lips blazed a trail back down toward her breast as his hands pushed the gown up her sensitive body. The silk glided along her skin like a thousand vibrating fingers.

She held her arms above her head, allowed the nightgown's easy withdrawal. Nicholai wrapped her wrists with the material, then covered her hands with one of his, trapping her hands above her head.

For once in her life, all those real or imaginary imperfections that had previously come to mind when she'd been naked didn't matter. The only thing that mattered in this moment was him.

His thumb stroked across one nipple while his lips continued down the valley between her breasts. A whirlwind of emotions welled up in her. She flung her head from side to side. Julie's hips rose and bucked against his shaft in wanton invitation. An invitation made louder when the heat of her core slid against the length of him.

She didn't know how she had lived without him, his hands on her body, his body pressing against hers. She had to have him. Now!

She pulled at the hand holding her captive, wanting freedom to do as she pleased.

Nicholai obliged, releasing her. Juliette brought both hands to the wall of his chest and pushed him off. He rolled over, allowed her the control she sought.

She stripped him of his boxer shorts in one aggressive move, so she could straddle his hips unbridled. Her wet core rested on his thick maleness. Julie studied him lying beneath her. His smooth skin, soft beneath her hand, warmed against her body. His masculine scent, his very essence surrounded her, filled her senses.

She lowered her lips to his neck. Her tongue ran along his pulse, and his heart skipped a beat.

"I've longed for this, Juliette." Nicholai's voice

sounded thick and gravelly, like it was all he could do to hold himself still and allow her to take the lead.

Julie kissed down his body, mimicking the trail he had forged along hers. She traveled between his pectorals and kissed each one of his six abdominal muscles. When she found the curly hairs that nestled his shaft, her tongue flicked out and touched the tip as her fingers closed around its width. It jerked in her hand, making her smile before she took him into her warm, moist mouth. Her tongue swirled around him while she slowly pulled him in and out of her lips. As she continued her torturous assault, his hands fisted in the sheets. She reveled in the power it gave her over him.

Chapter 31

She would kill him, he knew it. The warmth of her mouth around him, taking all of him within was a sensual tease. If her mouth felt this amazing, how much better would it be when he sank into her feminine core? The thought made him want to spill his seed.

Nicholai caught her head in his hands and dragged her up to his mouth before he lost control. He needed the flavor of her on his tongue and lips. Their kiss blazed with their combined passion. It sent a burning heat throughout his blood that pooled down deep.

When she slid her fiery core along his length, Nicholai gasped at the hot wetness coating him. He grabbed her hips, torn between urging her to stop and urging her to continue her unbearable movements. Her touch, like an inferno, exploded over the entire surface of his skin.

"Don't stop," she demanded as if she had read his warring thoughts.

He let go of one hip and positioned himself at her entrance. With one sure stroke, he slid home, diving deep within her.

Julie arched back, pushed against his chest. A sexy moan escaped her delicate throat.

He lost himself to being inside her. Moving, throbbing, tightening around his length. She wasn't bashful or tentative as he had expected.

She rode him hard as if she were trying to pound something back into the recesses of her mind. The realization made him push into her thoughts to glean what drove her. Fervent need clutched her, vicious and wild.

Nicholai watched his heartmate trap her lower lip between her teeth in singular concentration. He felt her orgasm build quickly. It raced through her blood. Her mind clouded with wanton lust. An appreciative growl pushed from his lips when a climax took her.

Juliette threw her head back and screamed her release. Her velvet folds milked him as she continued the hard ride. With her body still rippling, she leaned down as if to take his lips in a kiss. She licked his lower lip with a slow sensual stroke. Their eyes locked. Stark hunger flooded her eyes just before she captured his lips in a bruising kiss that lasted an eternity.

Desperate for air, Nicholai broke from their kiss. His hands brushed her hair away from her face, then he cupped her cheeks between his hands.

"You feel so damn good," he growled and flipped their entwined bodies over. A subtle tremble vibrated through her body.

He braced his weight on one hand, and his opposite hand found its way down to her most sensitive spot. His finger rubbed small circles over the tiny nub in time to his powerful thrusts. He pistoned in and out of her slick folds with increasing speed, going as deep as possible.

"Come for me," he commanded.

Again she arched her back and let the orgasm take her. The sight sent a rush of lust through him, tightening his balls.

Julie looked into his eyes. Still in her mind, he

understood the look that crossed her face. She'd noticed his eyes had darkened with his passion for her. Saw the need on his face and reveled at how easily she riled his senses. She liked having the power to do that to him.

Julie matched his hunger with an equal appetite of her own. As aggressively as he took her, as brutal as his talent to give her pleasure was, he didn't hurt her. She slid sinuously on the sheets with every delicious thrust into her body. She met each push with a rise of her hips, encouraging him deeper until Nicholai feared she might faint from the pleasure.

Her breaths became shallow and quick, and Nicholai instantly realized her yearning for him was the cause. She wanted him fiercely. She had need that only he was relentless enough to fill.

He drove into her, building her next peak. The more ruthless his pace, the higher she went. And she gave as good as she got. Her touch seemed to be everywhere, nails digging deep into his flesh, setting him off until ecstasy blinded them both.

A dark, predatory noise rasped from Nicholai's throat when she reached the precipice once more. She grabbed his shoulders, dragging him down against her exquisite breasts to capture his lips. The slickness of her sweat-drenched body on his made his surges become frenzied.

Breaking their kiss, he lowered his mouth to the soft spot where her neck met her shoulder. The rush of her blood called to him. He had to taste her. His inner beast demanded a full mating. Still buried in her mind, he ensured she experienced only a small prick when his fangs pierced her delicate skin. Her body tightened with the burst of lust that coursed through her veins.

Juliette's blood, laced with her arousal, tasted tangy and spicy as it flowed down his throat. Her liquid essence flooded his veins, fed his cells. The lascivious combination of her fluids surrounded him inside and out, drove him over the edge.

She appeared completely senseless by the time he succumbed to the explosion of his release. As his liquid fire poured into her, she fell apart. Her body jerked with spasms of pleasure, and she soared to heaven with him. They lay joined while she clenched around him in the aftermath.

He enjoyed her soft curves under the muscular plains of his body. They blended together perfectly. It would be fine with him if they stayed locked together like this for eternity, in the afterglow of their love making.

Juliette ran her hands lightly up and down his back. Each time her fingers lighted over his last rib on the left side, the muscle twitched and he jerked to the side.

"Ticklish?" she asked, running her fingers over the spot.

"Yes." He pushed up onto his forearms. "You better stop that, *lastochka*, or I'll have to retaliate."

Julie giggled. "Oh, yeah? Good luck with that." Mischief gleamed in her eyes as she touched the ticklish spot once more.

Nicholai pushed off, separating their bodies. "That sounded like a challenge."

And he never backed away from a challenge.

He ran his hands over the usual tickle spots on her body. His hand roamed between her waist, hips, thighs, and knees trying to find a place that would send her into a fit of giggles. His efforts were finally rewarded when he found the bottom of her feet.

Nicholai drew back onto his knees and grabbed one foot in a sure grip. With his other hand, he tickled her foot unmercifully. Julie screamed and twisted on the bed, thrashing back and forth in a futile effort to escape. She laughed so hard tears formed in her eyes.

"Uncle," she gasped between giggles. "Please… stop."

He loved her laugh. She didn't do it nearly enough. He wanted to bring joy into her life. She certainly deserved it. He reluctantly released her and lay down beside her on the bed while she struggled to catch her breath.

He found the sheet and comforter in a discarded pile at the foot of the bed and pulled them over their bodies. Juliette stretched gingerly.

The smile faded from Julie's face, and Nicholai instantly realized why. It had been years since her husband had touched her last. When thoughts of her dead husband once again pushed to the forefront of her mind, grief and remorse showed their ugly face. Guilt stabbed at her. Tears spilled from her eyes, running down her flushed cheeks to the pillow as she stared up at the plastered ceiling above.

Self-reproach tore at her heart. She believed she'd betrayed her husband, betrayed his memory and their love by sleeping with another man.

Julie's mind replayed their time together. The sex had been hard and fast. Demanding.

Exactly what you needed, lastochka. *And we did not have sex,* Nicholai corrected, *we made love.*

He purposely sent the thoughts to her along their most intimate form of communication, their mindlink.

He pushed a loving warmth into her mind, trying to soothe her thoughts as he scooped her into his arms and held her to his chest in a loving embrace.

"I'm sorry," she squeaked out, her voice hard from contrition. "I don't know why I'm such a mess tonight. I can't seem to stop crying."

Shhhh, he conveyed, again intentionally using their most intimate means of communication. *Please do not cry, not for what we did tonight. It was a beautiful way for us to show our love to each other, to get closer, more intimate, a way for us to know each other on a deeper level.*

It was what you needed. What you wanted. And you should not feel guilty or sad for that.

He knew she loved her husband and though it broke his heart to admit it, he understood where her thoughts came from. However, she had needed him, wanted him. Being a shadow in her mind, he knew she cared for him and loved him, but she couldn't yet admit it to herself because she believed it would disrespect her marriage.

Every time I touch you, you can tell how much I love you. I am very much in love with you. You have a big heart, he continued, placing his hand atop the beating organ. *There is enough room in there for both the memory of your first husband and me.*

Please let me in. We can have a beautiful life together. All I ask of you is that you allow yourself permission to feel.

I love you so much. Please, he pleaded, *let yourself love me back.*

Nicholai's arms drew her tightly against his chest when the sobs shook her body. She laid her cheek over his heart. The steady beat played a slow rhythm that her own heart began to follow.

"Please, I just need time," she whispered in a breathy voice so low that had he not had preternatural hearing, he would not have heard the admission.

I can give you time. Time is the one thing we have an abundance of, lastochka. *I will give you anything you need.*

He gently cupped the back of her head in one large hand and rested his cheek on top of her soft locks. Nicholai took a deep breath, drawing in her lilac scent combined with the jasmine of her shampoo. Heaven. She smelled like heaven.

All he wanted was to be loved by her, for her to allow herself to love him. It wouldn't be easy. He knew that the love between heartmates could not compare to the love she had experienced with another human, for the connection between heartmates was much deeper. But both heartmates needed to foster the connection, and he sensed she wasn't yet ready to give herself to him fully. Although it pained him to do so, he resigned himself to wait until she was ready to accept the precious gift of his love.

Nicholai ran his fingers through her tangled hair, trying to sooth her needless worries. *If you give me the chance, I promise I will love you forever. Cherish you, protect you. You are my heart and soul. Give me the chance to be those things for you, you will not regret it. You deserve all I can give you and more. Give us a chance.*

Fear gripped his heart, and the beat stuttered. What if she would not allow herself to love him? What if she didn't see their intimate act for what it was, making love, not just hot sex? What if she never acknowledged her true feelings for him? She wanted him, needed him, loved him, for a heartmate could do no other, but until she faced those emotions, he feared she would lock herself away from him. Would put everything on hold, their life, their love.

"Do you not think you deserve love? Someone who will fight for you, protect and love you. Let me love you. I have entrusted you with my heart, Juliette. Hold it safely in your keeping. Do not let it break, my love. You are the light to my darkness. Please let the light of your love shine brightly upon me, let it warm my heart and my soul."

When she didn't respond, he continued, "Each moment we are together, our love for each other grows. You love me, *lastochka*. You might not be ready to admit it to yourself yet, but I am in your mind and there is no doubt."

The deep timbre of his voice reverberated through his chest against her ear. Julie's eyes widened as if she suddenly realized she heard his voice aloud for the first time in many long minutes and the phrase, "I am in your mind" penetrated her self-deprecating thoughts.

She pushed away from his chest and gaped at him with trepidation. "What in the world? You just spoke."

"I've been speaking all night in one way or another," he said, the innuendo clear as his thumbs brushed away the last of her tears.

"No. I mean…What did you mean by 'I am in your mind'?"

Nicholai gave an insouciant shrug. "My sexual prowess is not my only gift." A wry grin spread across his face, bringing an answering smile to Julie's beautiful face.

"But how is that possible? I heard you as clearly as if you had been speaking aloud."

Nicholai pulled her down beside him and gathered her into his steel embrace before answering her. "Speaking to you mind to mind is simply a skill, like any other. You can do it too. The more you practice, it the easier it will become."

"I can't do that." Juliette shook her head back and forth.

"Yes, you can. You can do much more than you think yourself capable of. Try."

He pulled from her mind, so he would know if she used their mindlink to speak.

After a few seconds of silence, she said, "See, you didn't hear me, did you?"

"It takes practice. Try again for me."

More silence. Julie blew out a raspberry. "I can't do this."

Nicholai rubbed her back with small, soothing circles. *Yes, you can. Try again. Listen to my thoughts. Follow them back to my mind.*

Julie closed her eyes and concentrated hard. *Nicholai, this will never work.*

Yes, it did, his deep voice came back to her. Juliette's eyes shot open, wide with incredulity.

"You heard me say that?"

Of course, lastochka.

"Let me try again," she gushed enthusiastically. *I am so excited I won't be able to sleep tonight. I want to stay up all night talking like this,* she sent to him, testing their mental connection.

Nicholai chuckled. *While I would love to hold you*

all night talking, I'm afraid I can't let you do that. You are extremely tired. You need to rest.

But I don't want to sleep. Julie stuck her bottom lip out in a childlike pout that Nicholai found completely charming.

Trust me to know what is best. Your mind and body are tired and need rest. You can practice communicating like this again tomorrow. It is time to sleep, my lastochka, *my darling, little swallow.*

He ran his thumb along her pouty lip and sent a gentle command to her mind, coaxing her into a deep dreamless sleep. Julie's breath slowed, and her body went lax against his. He lay there holding her, wanting, needing her to acknowledge her love for him. She loved him without a doubt; he found it there in her mind.

Nicholai pulled from her thoughts to avoid temptation. It would have been easy to influence her troubled mind, turning the turmoil into feelings for him. He could have bent her will to his, force her to see the love for him she housed in the recesses of her mind, but he would not.

Nicholai wanted her to come to him, give her heart to him, choose him freely. Needed her to realize she loved him of her own volition. For hearing those three little words from her lips would only have meaning for him if they were said by her free will. Yes, he would wait an eternity if necessary to hear her say "I love you."

Chapter 32

Julie awoke and found herself stretched across the empty bed, sated, and deliciously sore in all the right places. She gingerly moved her legs, testing them to see if they had any strength left, and smiled at the memory of the previous night.

Nicholai had been amazing, catering to her every need, body and mind. He'd driven the sadness from her thoughts with their act of love and the guilt from her heart by the way he proclaimed his love for her. She wrapped her arms around her waist in a bracing hug.

It had been a wonderful vacation, full of exciting adventures and holiday romance, but it was time to get back to the real world.

Julie sighed. "Unfortunately, girl, you have a plane to catch this afternoon. No more time for self-delusion. The romance is over."

The theme from *Mission Impossible* interrupted her thoughts. Julie scampered through the chilly room and dug the phone from her purse. "Hello?" She hopped back into bed and snuggled under the warm covers.

"Merry Christmas, honey," her mother greeted cheerfully. "I hope I didn't wake you."

"No, Mama. I'm awake." Julie tucked the blanket up to her chin. "How's Colorado? Are you enjoying the trip Samantha gave you for Christmas?"

"It's beautiful. It snowed two feet yesterday. Hold

on a minute, dear. Here comes your father."

A rustling sounded through the phone. She pictured her father standing beside her mother, their ears on each side of the handset, hands clasped over each other's holding on tight.

"Merry Christmas, Julie Bug." Her father's raspy voice came over the line.

"Merry Christmas, Daddy. Why don't you put me on speaker phone?"

"Hold on," said her mother. Julie heard the phone fumbling around.

"Oh never mind." Her mother's exasperated voice came back on. "We can't figure out how to activate the speaker."

"Have Sam do it," Julie suggested, then laid against the mountain of pillows propped along the velvet headboard.

"Sam's not here. She's off skiing." Her father let out a deep sigh, then continued. "You know how she is. Always on the go. I swear that girl can't stand still long enough for a hen to lay an egg. She said to tell you Merry Christmas."

Julie pictured her beautiful sister in a skintight ski suit, swishing down the slope, her perfectly highlighted hair flowing out behind her as she glided over the snow. She would ski like she did everything else, with style and grace. She had probably picked up some hunky ski instructor already. A pang of jealousy briefly coursed through Juliette's mind until she remembered the hunky man she had picked up on her vacation. A smile crept to her face. Sami would die if she knew about Nicholai. She would need to get Penny to take a picture of her and Nicholai together before they left. She couldn't wait to show it to her sister.

"Tell Sami I said Merry Christmas too. Did you guys get the presents I sent?"

"Yes, we brought them with us. They are under the tree. We'll open them after dinner."

That was their family tradition. Eat a big Christmas Eve meal, then open gifts. It had been that way as long as Julie could remember.

"Did our gifts arrive?"

"Not before I left England. I'm sure they will be waiting for me when I return. DW would have been there to receive them from the postman."

"That Desmond seems like an awful nice man, Julie Bug. Why don't you two date?" her father asked.

"We've been over that, Daddy. Desmond and I are friends. That's all. Nothing more."

"Listen, dear," her mother cut in, saving her from another when-will-you-date-again lecture. "We know this is costing you a fortune in roaming fees, so we will go. We just wanted to call and wish our baby girl Merry Christmas."

Julie's mother's voice hitched as her father continued. "We wish you were here with us."

Tears pushed at the back of Julie's eyes. She missed her parents, missed spending the holidays with family. It was just so hard since the accident.

"I wish that, too. Merry Christmas."

A click indicated her parents hung up. The holidays were always a difficult time for her. She found herself pining over what might have been if fate had different plans for her life. It was one of the reasons she had agreed to come on this trip. She hoped being in a foreign country, experiencing new things, would keep her mind off her loss.

It hadn't.

Instead, she lay in the bed in a house of a man she barely knew. She had made love to him. No, they had sex, hot passionate sex. Nothing more. She was leaving today, and the fling was over. The time had come to get back to her life and leave her Russian behind.

They would go their separate ways. Never to see each other again. The guilt of last night tried to push to the surface, but Julie ruthlessly thrust it down.

What's done is done. You have nothing to feel guilty about, she reminded herself as she pushed up from the bed wondering where Nicholai had gone. Had last night meant more to her than it did to him? Had he left without saying goodbye? Was she the proverbial one-night stand?

Julie shook her head in denial. He wasn't that kind of man. Besides, it didn't matter. She was leaving, so technically it had been a one-night stand.

After slipping on a robe, she pulled her suitcase from the closet and threw it open on the bed. Juliette crossed to the dresser and removed her clothing from the drawers, tossing them in a pile on the bed.

It's a shame, she thought, *that Nicholai went to all that trouble, having someone put away my clothes just so I could get them all back out to pack.*

Nicholai quietly opened the door to the room, a tray of food carefully balanced on one arm.

"Good morning, *lastochka*. I hope you like—" His voice trailed off as he glanced toward the bed. "What are you doing, Juliette?"

"Packing." Julie stilled her hands as she stared at her lover. "Um, that for me?"

Nicholai glanced down at the tray. "I thought you might be hungry," he said absently. "Why are you packing?"

"Penny and I are leaving."

"But I thought you agreed to stay here." He placed the tray on the white, padded bench located at the end of the bed and walked over to her.

"Our vacation is over. Our flight leaves at four."

"Cancel your flight, Juliette. Stay with me, at least until Christmas. Call it a Christmas present."

A confused look crossed Julie's round face. "Today is Christmas Eve. You want me to cancel my flight so I can leave tomorrow?"

"I meant for you to stay until the Russian Christmas—January seventh."

"Oh, I didn't realize you celebrated on a different day. January seventh. That's more than two weeks from now."

The hopeful expression on his face was adorable.

"Say you will stay, and I will be the happiest man in Russia. It will be the best Christmas present I have ever had. Will you stay?"

Julie paused. School didn't resume until January twentieth, so she wouldn't miss work. She didn't have anything needing her attention at home other than Connor. If DW agreed to continue taking care of him, there would be no reason she couldn't stay.

"I need to talk to Penny and make a few calls before I can give you my answer." Julie watched the tension ease from Nicholai's broad shoulders. A smile graced her full lips. He obviously really wanted her to stay a little longer. She had to admit to herself, more time with this handsome sex god wouldn't exactly be difficult to tolerate.

Nicholai plucked a delicate teacup from the tray and offered it to Julie. "Coffee?"

"Oh, yes." Julie held the delicate white-bone china between her hands to warm them. She lifted the cup to her nose and took the rich aroma in before taking a sip. "Nectar of the gods," she commented before she took a swallow of the rich mocha, loving how it ran down her throat to warm her stomach.

"Glad you approve. I worked a long time on that coffee, grinding the beans, percolating the brew until it was perfect," Nicholai teased. A sensual smile tugged at the corner of his mouth as one dark brow rose to hide behind his fallen hair. A rush of heat pooled low in Julie's core. "I believe I deserve a baboon for all my hard work on your behalf."

Julie smiled widely. "A baboon is a monkey. I think you meant boon. What kind of boon did you have in mind?"

Nicholai swept Julie up into his arms, and miraculously, no coffee spilled on her. She'd never met a man so graceful. Everything he did seemed to come effortlessly.

"A kiss, sweet Juliette. A kiss for a cup of... What did you call it? Nectar of the gods?"

He lowered his lips to hers in a gentle caress, brushing his mouth back and forth across hers, teasing her lips apart. He moaned against her mouth, taking in the delicious flavor. Her tongue frolicked with his, moving between them until Julie no longer knew where she stopped and he began.

Nicholai pulled away, leaving her wanting more, much more. Straightening to his full height, he looked down on her and said, "That was a delicious boon."

Julie wiggled in his arms. "If that's the boon for a cup of coffee, what boon do you want for the meal?"

A sensuous grin accompanied his hooded eyes. "I am sure I can think of something," he purred.

****

Penny admired the collection of Fabergé eggs in the curio cabinet. Red, green, blue, and purple jewels adorned each egg. Each detail exquisite, the eye-catching splendor shimmered under the glow of the light from the top of the cabinet. She pulled her eyes from the beautiful sight when Julie walked up behind her. "Hey, Jules, all packed?"

"Actually, Penny, I wanted to talk to you about that. Nicholai asked me to stay, and, after talking to Desmond, I've decided I'd like to say yes. That is if you don't mind going back to England by yourself."

"Mind? Are you kidding?" Penny threw her arms around Julie and squeezed the breath from her body. "I'm so happy for you! I knew it! I knew you two were going to be perfect for each other."

"It's not like I'm marrying the guy. I'm only going to stay a couple more weeks. I'll be back in time for the start of school."

Penny's face dropped. "Oh. A couple of weeks are better than nothing, I guess, and who knows, maybe a couple of weeks will turn into a lifetime."

Julie shook her head and gave her friend a sardonic expression. "Don't put the cart before the horse."

"You're right. I wouldn't want to jinx you."

The women turned as Nicholai strolled into the room with his usual poise and sensuality. They sighed in unison when he bent to stroke the fire back to life, putting his shapely bottom on display.

"You better hang on to that," Penny advised in a whisper.

"I did," Julie admitted in a low voice from behind her hand.

"Julie has some news, Nicholai."

Nicholai turned before he spoke. "Good news, I hope."

"I'm staying."

With a smile that reached his ears, Nicholai swooped Julie up in a big hug and twirled her around twice before placing her back on her feet.

Nicholai let Julie go and glanced at her friend. "Penny, will you be able to stay as well?"

"Unfortunately, I can't." Penny crossed her arms over her chest. "I need to get home. Frank will be furious if I miss Christmas."

Nicholai nodded while he sat down. "It is too bad you cannot stay, but I understand your husband wanting to have you with him for Christmas."

Julie crossed the room and perched on the arm of Nicholai's chair. Right away his hand found its way to her back and gave it loving strokes. "You'll need a ride to the airport then. Unfortunately, I cannot drive you. Julie, would you like to use my car?" Nicholai offered as he absently continued to stroke her.

"Your sports car?" asked Penny, her eyes wide with excitement.

"Yes, unless you would prefer a different vehicle."

"No, no, that silver beauty will do just fine. Thanks."

Julie turned and looked at her lover. "Are you sure? We could always order up a cab."

"I'm quite positive. If I can't take you there myself, the least I can do is make sure you have a safe vehicle to drive. Take my car. It has a full tank of petrol, more than enough to get you to the airport and back."

"Cool. I'm going to the airport in style."

The trio chuckled at Penny's remark.

****

Penny unfolded the map onto her lap. She glanced down at the diagram Nicholai had made. He'd drawn roads, complete with street names and landmarks, using arrows to indicate which ways to go on the confusing streets to get to the airport. The paper jostled as the car bounced along the cobblestone streets of Yaroslavia.

"For an expensive sports car, this thing sure gives a bumpy ride," Penny observed, looking up from the map.

"I don't remember it being so bumpy the last time I rode in it."

"Maybe it's the street." Penny suggested. "Did you drive on this street?"

"No. I don't remember Nicholai ever taking me down here before."

"Hopefully it will smooth out once we reach the highway."

Penny turned on the seat warmer and settled back into the soft leather before continuing. "So tell me all about it. With a body like that, I bet he was great in the sack."

"I don't kiss and tell," Juliette said coyly.

"Oh, come on, Jules. Us old married folk need a little excitement once in a while. Kiss and tell, *pleeeaaassse*." Penny batted her eyes at Julie.

A giggle burst through Julie's lips. "Okay, but

hang onto your panties," she warned. "It was mind blowing, astronomical. The man is insatiable."

"A marathon of shagging. Lucky you. He looks like he'd know how to use that big body of his."

"He does," Julie assured. "But it was more than just sex. Afterward he held me and whispered sweet nothings into my ear."

"Our turn should be coming up." Penny pointed out the windshield. "Sweet nothings, what do you mean?"

Julie turned onto the highway entry ramp and stomped down on the gas pedal to merge. The finely tuned machine took off like a bolt of lightning up the ramp, throwing the women into their seats.

"Whoa, woman. Don't get us killed there, Speedy," Penny admonished.

"Sorry. I guess I didn't know the car's strength. It's like driving a race car."

"It is quite posh. Speaking of things that are posh, you still haven't told me about the sweet nothings your Russian whispered."

Julie took a deep breath before answering. "He said he loves me."

"Wow. That's great, Jules! I'm so happy for you."

"I didn't say it back," Julie confessed, changing lanes, once again sending the pair into the seats when she pushed the pedal too far down.

"Why not?"

"Because it's not right. I can't love him. It would not be right to Steven's memory."

Penny laid a hand on Julie's arm and gave it a supportive squeeze. "Julie, Steve would understand. You have grieved for him and the girls for three years. Wouldn't he want you to find happiness?"

Julie considered what Penny said. "Yes."

"Wouldn't he want you to find someone who could love you, care for you?"

Julie's grip tightened on the steering wheel. She and Steven had never discussed what might happen should one of them die. Neither had wanted to consider the possibility. Now she honestly couldn't say if he would have wanted her to find love with another man. She believed he would have wanted her to have a happy life. But to have that life with someone else? Now that was the million-dollar question.

"I'm not sure."

"From what you told me about Steven, I'm sure he would want you to move on and find someone to be happy with. Take some advice from your old married friend. We never know where life will take us. Sometimes it's best to hang on and go with the ride. See where you end up."

Julie slid her friend a sly glance. "Go along for the ride, huh?"

"Yeah, you might just end up in Happyville. The next exit is the one to the airport," Penny pointed out. "All I'm saying is allow yourself to be open to the possibility of loving Nicholai. You have a handsome, wealthy man saying he loves you. Don't be a fool and throw him away. Don't be afraid to love him."

They spent the rest of the ride in silence as Julie pondered her friend's advice. Perhaps Penny was right. Perhaps she could open herself to the possibility of loving Nicholai. There was a lot about him to love after all.

Julie pulled the expensive car to the curb, and Penny jumped out. After removing her suitcase from the trunk, she leaned into the car. "Remember what I said, Jules. Don't be afraid." A genuine smile reached her eyes. "Happy Christmas."

"Happy Christmas, Penny. Have a safe flight and tell Frank I said hello."

"Will do." Penny shut the door with an auspicious click. Julie felt like her life clicked into place. In that moment of clarity, she decided she would allow herself to love Nicholai. She couldn't wait to get back to him and tell him.

She whipped the car into traffic, humming along to the classical CD that played in the stereo system. Her mind consumed with thoughts of Nicholai, the ride back to her love flew by quickly. She couldn't wait to see the look on his face when she told him she loved him. Julie decided to run into his arms as soon as she got home and declare her love.

It's getting dark, Julie observed, flicking on the headlights. The road was bare, with no streetlights or houses to provide any lighting. She had exited the highway thirty minutes ago, and the shaking in the car had gotten steadily worse.

Julie glanced down at the map in her hand. She thought she had followed it, but perhaps she'd taken a wrong turn. She certainly didn't remember any deserted streets on the way to the airport.

Squinting her eyes, Jules tried to make out her surroundings. The night, black as pitch, kept her from getting her bearing. Nothing appeared familiar about this place, only a long endless road surrounded by a dense forest. Anxiety knotted her stomach.

She hit a button to lower the window and stuck out her head, trying to get a better look. Desperation to find anything familiar drove the bite from the cold air. Only the purr of the car's engine disturbed the eerie quiet of the night.

She did a K-turn and pushed down hard on the accelerator. Fear and unease spurred her on. Suddenly, the car shook violently. Julie instinctively withdrew her foot from the gas when the car pulled hard to the right. The steering wheel came alive in her hand. Jerked from her grasp. Julie fought the car for control and lost. A scream tore from her throat.

The car careened into the forest, one tire running up on a fallen log before the axle dug into a trench and sent the car tumbling. Julie's hair dangled up away from her head briefly before it fell down to her shoulders as the car righted itself. Paper, cell phone, items from her purse flew about the passenger cabin, bumping into her as the car continued flipping through the forest.

It came to rest against a tree, passenger side down.

Julie groaned. Everything hurt, her stomach, her arms and legs, even her eyelashes. Julie moved her sore limbs, testing each to see if they functioned. They did.

The tang of gasoline and oil burned her wounded nose. She sneezed. An intense wave of pain exploded through her body. She moaned in anguish.

Knowing she needed to find help, Julie placed her hands out the open window and pulled with all her might. Her foot caught purchase on the gearshift and helped her ease from the car.

I've got to get back to the road. No one will ever find me here.

She tried to make her way through the small opening, but her arms collapsed, and she fell against the door.

Gotta keep going.

With the self-encouragement, she braced her hands on the crumbled metal and tried to give another push. Her muscles screamed in protest, refused to obey. She lay on the cold door, lightheaded. Her lungs struggled for air, each breath excruciating. Her stomach burned like fire.

She fought through the pain to remain lucid, but her last thought as the icy blackness of unconsciousness closed in on her was of Nicholai.

Chapter 33

Nicholai stoked the fire, then glanced down at his watch. Noting the time, a haunting dread crawled over his skin. "She should have been back an hour ago," he murmured as he returned the poker to its holder and paced the drawing room in agitation.

He had planned a special evening for Juliette, a part of which included the chilled champagne that now awaited her return. The ice bucket, covered with perspiration, sat on the table, reflecting the fire burning heartily in the fireplace.

Nicholai rubbed the palms of his hands against his thighs. Where was she? Why wasn't she home yet?

As the thoughts crossed his mind for the hundredth time that evening, pain overwhelmed him. His knees went weak. When he grabbed the ornately carved mantel for support, his fingers dug into the wood, leaving their marks. Another wave of pain racked his body.

He realized instantly something was very wrong with Juliette. Her agony flowed over their mindlink. Perspiration wet his brow, but he forced the torment aside to think. His heartmate needed help. Every instinct within him demanded he go to her.

Suddenly the suffering stopped. He tried reaching out to her with his mind. *Juliette! Can you hear me,* lastochka? *Answer me!*

He found only blankness. For the first time since he'd created the mindlink, he could not sense his mate. The thought sickened him. Only two things could keep that from happening. She was either unconscious or…

No! He would not allow his thoughts to go there. She must be alive. The Fates would not be so cruel as to take his heartmate from him when he had finally found her. Desperation to find her raced up his spine, and a shiver tore through his body.

Instinct drove his desperate need. He could materialize beside her if only he knew her location. The airport perhaps? No, she would have dropped Penny off long ago. Somewhere on the highway then? Did she stop off for a bite to eat and run into trouble?

A deep growl of frustration escaped his lips. There were too many possibilities. Dematerializing to her was out.

He paced the floor, filtering through the options. He had tried using their mindlink, that hadn't worked. Calling her to him wasn't possible if he could not reach her mind. She might be too injured to respond to the call. The realization ripped another aggravated growl from his throat.

"Wait." He stopped. "The mindlink! She's had my blood. I can track her using that."

He had watched his fellow Alpha, Stephan, do such a thing to locate his female. It must be instinctual. Stephan had known exactly where to find his Katrina. Surely he could do the same.

With hope giving him strength, Nicholai used his preternatural speed and raced through his home, grabbed his car keys, then ran to the car. With a squeal of the tires, the Alpha backed the SUV out of his garage. He tore down the paved drive, the snow arcing behind him.

The SUV turned onto the road with more speed than it could handle. The vehicle's rear wheels flew sideways, throwing Nicholai against the seat. He fought the car for control when it fishtailed along the slippery road.

A string of vile curses spewed until he brought the SUV back under control. The roads were slick, icy this time of year. Why hadn't he thought to warn Juliette?

He pounded his fist on the steering wheel. If something happened to her, it would be his fault.

****

Demetri beat a dozen eggs as the bacon sizzled in the cast-iron frying pan. The aroma of breakfast brought both Stephan and Alexander to the kitchen. Demetri had just poured the eggs into a skillet when it hit. An overwhelming mixture of grief and anger drove him to one knee.

His fellow Alphas rushed to his side and helped him stand.

"What's wrong?" asked Stephan. A look of concern drew his dark brows down over his eyes.

"It's Nicholai. Something is terribly wrong." His cousin's heart-wrenching pain flowed over Demetri, and he quickly tamped it down.

The large Alpha straightened and shook off his friend's hands. "I'm fine. It just hit me before I could put up a mental block."

Nicholai, what is amiss?

It's Juliette. Something is horribly wrong. I can't reach her mind.

Nicholai relayed all he knew of the situation as

Demetri ran a hand through his shoulder-length black hair and pulled it away from his face.

"What is it?" Alex moved around Demetri and turned off the stove.

"It's Juliette. Something has happened. She didn't return after taking her friend to the airport. Nicholai can't reach her mind through their mindlink. He believes she may have been in an accident, but he can't find her."

Stephan placed his large hand on Demetri's thick forearm. "Tell him to use his blood. If they have formed a mindlink, she will have had enough of his blood to permeate her cells. His blood is a part of her now, forevermore. Tell him to use the call of his blood to find her."

Nicholai, your mate has your blood coursing through her veins. Sense its call. Use it to find her.

Don't you think I have thought of that, Demetri? It isn't working.

You are too upset. Demetri closed his eyes in concentration and sent his cousin waves of calm reassurance through their link. *Now, try again. You can do this, cousin. Still your mind, feel the draw. Your blood calls to you, hear it.*

****

Faith and hope flowed through Nicholai's body. It lessened the tension in his muscles. His rapid heartbeat slowed. Nicholai's breathing eased in time to his heart.

A vibration, a hum nudged his brain. It was slight but enough to let him know he needed to turn the car to the right. The vibration increased moving into his body with each meter of road he crossed. Instinct told him he headed in the correct direction.

He drove on, following the hum, turning left, then right, then right again. The vibration increased until at last he thought his body would shake like a nine point two on the Richter scale.

He slammed the SUV into park and jumped from the car. Leaving the deserted road behind, he ran into the woods. His vision took in the sights of the forest though no moon lit his way. He leapt over a fallen tree and landed in a trench. A dark object near his foot drew his stare.

He stopped to fetch the red plastic from the forest floor. Flipping it over in his hand, his heart seemed to sink to his stomach as he realized it belonged on a car.

A tail light cover!

Throwing the cover aside with careless abandonment, Nicholai's only thought was getting to the woman he loved. With a burst of preternatural speed, he jumped from the trench and ran through the trees until he came upon a car.

It no longer resembled his vehicle. It appeared smaller, shaped like a "U" because it hugged the tree. The stench of oily gas and transmission fluid mixed with the woodsy scent of the forest, turning his stomach with each breath. His eyes traveled up the undercarriage of the car and rested on the limp form lying on top.

"Juliette! Juliette, my love."

He ran to her unresponsive body. His feet crunched on the broken glass that lay scattered over the ground.

Nicholai carefully pulled her from the wreckage. Cradling her in his arms, he scanned her over. Bruises darkened her face, and she had a laceration. Contusions covered her arms. Her stomach appeared distended, firm to the touch, so unlike her usual supple form. He used his free hand to raise her pant legs above her knees until they could go no further. More welts, one of which looked especially bad.

Nicholai placed his hand reverently over her weak heartbeat. It stuttered under the pads of his fingers. She lay dying in his arms. He threw back his head, his hair flung behind his shoulders as a mighty bellow ripped from his throat. His animalistic roar echoed throughout the surrounding land, the sound of which sent animals scurrying through the forest in fear.

Unshed tears blurred his vision as he cradled his heartmate in his arms. He covered one of her wounds with his hand, trying to stanch the bleeding. Her rich blood flowed between his fingers as it dripped to the ground.

Too much blood. The tears ran down Nicholai's cheeks.

She would die, here in the cold—in his arms.

****

Nicholai, we are coming to help, offered Demetri. *We will be there in minutes.*

Stephan and Demetri were the first to materialize on the lawn of Nicholai's estate. Stephan turned toward Demetri as Alex coalesced next to him. "How do you propose we find them?"

"Using my mindlink. Nicholai can feed me the directions." After a brief pause, during which he contacted his cousin, he continued. "He said they are close. This way."

The three Alphas took off at blurring speed while Nicholai and Demetri communicated the directions.

The sight greeting the three males when they came upon the wreckage was heartrending. Nicholai sat on the cold hard ground, his mate clutched to his chest. Her head lulled back over his arm. Juliette's hair swung in time to the rocking motion of their bodies. Dark stains coated the white shirt Nicholai wore, no doubt her blood. Her arms hung limply away from her body, dangling toward the snowy forest floor. Demetri sent his senses out, hoping to discover they had made it in time, hoping she wasn't dead.

Chapter 34

Cold sweat dampened Nicholai's brow. He stared down at Julie, willed her to move. The withdrawal of her from his mind, being unable to reach her, felt so painfully wrong to him.

Movement in front of them brought a snarl to his lips. A feral sound rumbled from deep within his throat. His mate lay injured, dying. No one should be near. He must protect what was his. Protect *her* at all costs.

Nicholai bared his fangs and hissed as the males approached. A growl of warning followed when his protective instincts took rational thought from his mind.

Demetri approached first. His arms up in surrender, head bowed in submission. "We are not here to hurt her, Nicholai. We are here to help. Let Stephan heal her."

Another fierce growl escaped Nicholai's lips as Demetri continued. "Do you want your woman to live, cousin?"

Nicholai's head snapped up. He stabbed Demetri with his fiery eyes. "Of course, I want her to live. How dare you ask me that!"

"Then put your fangs back in your gums, and allow Stephan to heal her."

Nicholai's body slumped over Julie's limp form in capitulation. Stephan approached cautiously, his hands behind his back. The movement drew Nicholai's attention. He repressed the reflex to attack, his rational mind finally winning the war with his instinct.

Stephan presented no threat. He had a heartmate to whom he would always be faithful. Nicholai realized he could trust his longtime friend and compatriot to heal his female.

A heavy sigh clouded before his face as he spoke. "I would be eternally grateful to you, Stephan, if you would help her."

Stephan knelt before the couple on one knee. "I'll need to touch her to assess her injuries. Will you permit that?"

Their eyes met over her lifeless body. "Yes. Do what you must to save her."

"Very well, please place her on the ground."

"It's too cold," Nicholai protested, tilting his head in the direction of the road. "My SUV is not far. I'll put her in the backseat."

Stephan nodded and rose to his full height. He backed away from the couple, giving Nicholai room to stand.

"Hurry," the Alpha leader said softly.

The three Alphas followed behind the pair as Nicholai ran to the SUV with Juliette in his arms. Alex held open the back door so the distraught warrior could climb in and lay Juliette on the leather seat. He smoothed a lock of her hair away from her face, then folded her hands over her stomach. His mate looked like a sleeping angel. In stark contrast to the dark upholstery of the car, her skin appeared ghostly pale.

Unshed tears clouded his vision again as Nicholai found Stephan waiting in the open door. "May I assess her now?" he asked patiently, giving Nicholai time to process what he said.

Nicholai could only nod, afraid to speak for fear it would cause the tears to flow. He spun around as the opposite door opened behind him.

Alex held one hand on the open door, the other raised in deference. "Whoa there, big fella. I'm simply wondering if you want to come take a walk with me while Stephan examines your mate. You know, get some fresh air?"

Demetri stepped up behind Alexander. "That would be a good idea, Nicholai."

"Absolutely not. I can't leave her."

Stephan crawled into the back of the SUV, taking up what little room was left. "It's a tight fit back here, Nicholai. If you get out, I'll have more room to work."

"But—" Nicholai started to protest, however, Stephan cut him off.

"Plus, I need to concentrate when I'm healing, and having an overprotective male breathing on my neck won't help."

Nicholai's shoulders slumped. The thought of relinquishing Juliette's care to another male seemed abhorrent to him, but the concern for her safety defeated everything else. He unfolded from the vehicle without further protest and took one last look at the woman he loved.

Alex hooked an arm over his tired shoulders. "Come on, let's you and me take a stroll. The night air will do you good."

****

Demetri watched his cousin be led down the road and silently thanked Alex for sufficiently distracting Nicholai. He peered into the open door. His massive frame filled the doorway. "How is she?"

Stephan met his gaze, and concern etched lines across his forehead. "It's bad, Demetri. She has a bruised brain and is bleeding internally."

"Can you heal her?"

"Yes, but it will take a lot of energy, and I did not feed yet today."

Without hesitation, Demetri pulled his coat and shirt sleeve up to his elbow and thrust his arm toward Stephan. "Take from me. My blood is powerful. It should give you what you need."

Stephan bowed his head reverently. "Thank you, my old friend."

When Stephan took Demetri's wrist with a firm hand, his fangs lengthened and sank into the flesh. Demetri waited patiently as Stephan drank his fill, knowing his power would flow through the healer, nourish his cells with each draw.

"Thank you." Stephan turned his attention back to the woman who lay motionless on the seat before him. He rubbed his hands together briskly above her still body until a faint yellow glow appeared. Its intensity increased until it illuminated the entire passenger cabin, bathing Stephan and Juliette in its warmth.

The brightness too powerful for his eyes, Demetri took a step back and averted his gaze. Nicholai and Alex turned in unison when the night brightened. The SUV looked like a nuclear bomb exploded within.

Nicholai took a step toward the vehicle when Alex caught his arm. "Don't. Let Stephan do his thing. She's safe."

Demetri shielded his eyes and observed the healer lay his hands across Juliette's stomach. They rose and fell with each shallow breath she took, then slowly rose higher as her breaths deepened. Her internal bleeding impeded, her stomach shrank, no longer distended with blood as Stephan encouraged her body to absorb the fluid.

Stephan's hands moved up her body and rested on each side of her face. The yellow light's intensity flared once more as he cradled her head between his palms. Stephan closed his eyes and sent his healing energy over her brain to heal the tissue.

Juliette's heart beats stronger, steadier with each passing moment. Demetri sent the update to Nicholai over their mindlink.

Nicholai's relief flooded his mind.

Obviously satisfied that the most severe of her injuries were healed, Stephan moved his hands over her arms and sent his healing heat over her bruises, then did the same over the fractures in both legs.

The yellow light faded as Nicholai and Alex approached the SUV. Stephan exited the cabin, and Demetri once again extended his wrist. Stephan waved off the offer, swaying slightly from the exhaustion.

His features softened when he examined Nicholai's grief-stricken face. Only a short time ago, he had sported a similar look when his heartmate had been gravely injured.

"Nicholai, she will be fine. She's asking for you. Go to her. Reassure her that all will be well. But she needs rest. Do not speak too long before sending her to sleep. She needs a deep, restful sleep to heal."

Nicholai nodded and grasped the Alpha leader's forearms in both his hands. "Thank you for saving my heartmate, Stephan. We are forever in your debt. You have but to ask, and I will do."

"All I ask is that you find as much happiness with Juliette as I have with Katrina." Stephan managed a tired grin which did not quite reach his eyes. "Now go to her. See for yourself that she is better. It will ease your worry."

The trio of males watched Nicholai climb into the car, then Alex broke the silence. "You look drained, Stephan. You should feed. I freely offer my blood to you." The blond Alpha thrust his arm toward the tired male.

"I thank you for your offer and will gladly accept when we get back to Demetri's house. For now, we need to leave the couple in peace."

"Is it wise to leave so soon?" Demetri raised a dark brow.

"Nicholai needs time alone with his mate. He'll watch over her. She's in good hands."

Nicholai, if you have no further need of us we will take our leave.

Go, cousin. We will be fine. I thank you for all you did this night. Safe travels.

"Come, we go back to my home," instructed Demetri before his form coalesced into a pinpoint.

The large Alpha watched his two friends reform in his kitchen simultaneously. Demetri leaned against the counter, his arms folded over his chest as Stephan and Alex sat down at the kitchen table.

Alexander shrugged out of his coat and hooked it over a dinette chair before turning to Stephan. He cuffed his flannel shirt away from his wrist, then thrust his arm toward his leader. "You said you would feed once we returned."

"I did. Thank you, Alex."

As Stephan took from the younger Alpha, a concerned expression crossed Alex's face. "You know, Demetri, something wasn't right about that car accident tonight. Did you notice the wheels?"

"I have no idea what you mean."

"There were only three tires still attached to the car."

Demetri sat at the table. "It was a violent crash. Perhaps the wheel came off during the accident."

"I considered that, but the tire was not in the forest. I found it when Nicholai and I were walking down the road. And that's not all. I also found a lug nut."

Demetri scrubbed a tired hand down his face. "And that's important because…" he prompted.

"Because when I picked up the lug nut, I noticed something. There were gouges in the metal, like someone used the wrong tool on it."

"Okay, so Nicholai takes his car to a bad mechanic. What of it?"

"No one would take that car to a bad mechanic. And no mechanic worth his salt would use the wrong tool to either tighten or remove lug nuts from a high-class sports car like that. I don't believe for one minute that the nut I found was removed by a mechanic."

Demetri considered the statement. Alex was a car guy guru, a fine connoisseur of all things automotive. If he said no mechanic made those marks, then no mechanic did.

"So who did that to the car?"

"If someone other than a mechanic loosened the lug nuts, that begs the question who and why. What if someone wanted to cause an accident? And what if that someone knew that driving with loose lug nuts would cause the lug nuts to fall off? And what if that someone also knew that with the lug nuts gone, the tire would fall off?"

Stephan licked the tiny wounds on Alex's arm closed and leaned back in his chair. "Are you suggesting that someone sabotaged Nicholai's car?"

Alex shrugged. "Seems like a possibility."

"To what end?"

"To the end that happened. Losing a wheel at high speeds would send the car crashing out of control."

Demetri pounded his fist on the table. "So someone is out to hurt Nicholai?"

"Or his heartmate," suggested Stephan.

Alex pursed his lips and rubbed his chin thoughtfully. "Appears that way to me."

Chapter 35

Nicholai sat gingerly on the bed and ran his fingers through Juliette's hair. He remained securely in her mind after he gave the command for her to wake. Awareness slowly crept into Julie's consciousness. As if swimming through molasses—thick, black, sticky molasses—she struggled her way out of the dark abyss. Her eyes fluttered open. She blinked as if trying to bring the world into focus.

Nicholai lifted her hand to his cheek, and she turned to look up at him. He knew she registered the concern etched deep in his features. The expression in his eyes pained her—his worry and guilt.

"You look worse than I feel." Julie's hand cupped his cheek, and the joy of her touch comforted him. "Your face looks sunken and pale. And those dark shadows under your beautiful, amber eyes make my heart hurt."

Tears fell from her eyes to the pillow that cradled her head. A sob came from her chest; it ripped through her rib cage and lungs. Nicholai's cool fingers slid over her cheeks, so the pad of his thumbs brushed the tears away.

"Shhh." His voice sounded soft, filled with emotions. "I wouldn't advise crying, *lastochka*. You are still recovering from the accident."

Juliette brought a hand to her face and rubbed her

eyes as if trying to clear the cobwebs from her mind. She worked to stop the tears. *An accident*? The thought coalesced in her mind.

She dug in the muddy recesses of her memory trying to recall the accident. Nicholai observed as she worked backward through the images. She recalled driving Penny to the airport, moving in with Nicholai, her room at the inn being tossed. Maybe that was the accident he'd referred to.

"Recovering? You mean from someone trashing my room?" Her voice sounded raspy, dry. She swallowed, trying to wet her parched throat.

"Here, drink this." Nicholai lifted a glass to her lips. Like a rain on a desert oasis, the cool water brought her to life, reviving her. After only a few sips, Nicholai took the cup away. Her mouth instinctively tried to follow.

"A little at a time. I'll give you more in a minute. How do you feel?"

Julie attempted to sit, but her head screamed in pain at the slight movement. Her lungs burned, her stomach rolled its protest. Nicholai slid his arms around her back and helped her up.

"Easy. Take it slow. Your body needs a little more time to recover. You're mostly healed, but you'll be sore for another day or two from the accident."

"There you go again. What accident?" she asked, her voice a little stronger, giving Nicholai hope for the first time in days.

"You had a car accident."

Her seated position afforded her a look around the room. It was a large room, the walls of which were covered in a red velvet paisley design. Across from the immense bed, with its golden comforter, stood a large fireplace. Dark wood framed the hearth making an ornately carved mantel. The golden inlay glowed with the last embers of the dying fire. Several pieces of matching furniture embellished the room—romantic but masculine in design. *Perfect for Nicholai*, Julie decided.

Her thoughts made him smile.

"Where am I?"

"My chamber." His chest swelled in pride that she approved of the room.

"If there was an accident, why am I not in the hospital?"

"I had my personal doctor come and tend to you." Nicholai needed to change the subject before she could ask any more questions about her medical care. He didn't want to lie to his heartmate, but he wasn't ready to explain all about the breed or Stephan's ability to heal. Not yet. As Nicholai looked down into her curious eyes, guilt reared its ugly head and snapped at him.

Demetri had informed him about Alex's supposition regarding the car being sabotaged. He couldn't imagine how anyone got on his property without him knowing. But obviously someone had. The car had been parked in his garage for days before the accident. Someone must have snuck onto his estate and loosened the lug nuts.

It didn't take Nicholai long to assume the person who had trashed Juliette's room must have learned where she now stayed. Though how that person could have known which car she would drive was anyone's guess. Perhaps the person had loosened the tires on all the cars. Not wanting to leave Julie's side, Nicholai made a mental note to check them at a later time.

"Here, try another drink." He brought the glass to her mouth. "Do you remember anything about the accident?"

A pensive look crossed her face as she contemplated his question. "I remember dropping Penny off at the airport." Her eyes squinted in concern. "I can't remember anything after that."

Nicholai gave her hand a reassuring squeeze. "That is okay, Juliette. It is not uncommon to forget what has happened a few moments before a head injury occurs. Do not strain too hard. I am sure the memory will come to you, eventually."

He touched her face, which still appeared paler than usual. She nestled into his touch, reminding him of a lost puppy when she looked up at him with her big brown eyes.

"I need to go to the bathroom."

"Of course. Here, let me help you."

Nicholai produced a soft pink robe and helped Julie slip her arms into the silky fabric.

"It's toasty. Did you heat this?"

Nicholai smiled. "I might have put it in the dryer for a while to warm it up. I thought you would be cold, getting out of bed for the first time in two days."

Hoping his gesture made her feel loved and cherished, Nicholai pulled back the sheets while simultaneously wrapping the robe around her body. He realized the moment his statement had registered.

She stopped moving, half in and half out of the bed. "Two days!"

****

Stephan padded silently up behind Alexander who sat hunched over Demetri's computer. "Find anything?"

Alex straightened in his chair, rubbing a hand against his neck in a futile effort to work the tight knot there. "Maybe. I found a hot spot on the thermal. Here."

The blond Alpha pointed at an infrared image on the computer monitor.

"Where is that?" asked Stephan leaning on the desk, bracing his weight on one hand.

"It's about ten klicks from here. Inside the mountain."

"That's about where Demetri and I found those bizarre animal tracks."

Alex brought the cup of coffee to his lips for a deep drink. The warm liquid soothed him as it trickled down the back of his throat, warming his chest. "Think there is a connection?"

"Probably not," said the deep bass voice from across the room.

The two Alphas turned together to see Demetri's large frame leaning against the doorjamb, arms crossed over his broad chest. "Don't forget Yellowstone is nearby. This whole area has a lot of geothermal activity. What you are seeing there is probably an underground lava aquifer or a hot spring."

Alex nodded in acquiesce. "I thought as much, but because it was near where you saw the tracks I wanted to mention it."

"Have there been any more reports of people going missing?" asked Stephan, straightening to his impressive height as he scrubbed his hand down his face. He pulled his dark hair back into a queue, securing it with a leather cord.

"I know of none. It would appear all is quiet." Demetri shrugged. "We've found nothing on our patrols. No mutilated bodies. No reports of anyone, vampire or human going missing."

"It's as if whatever had been here has moved on," offered Alex, shutting down the computer.

"I agree," concurred Stephan. "I don't see what more we can do here. Do you have any suggestions, Demetri?"

Demetri straightened, allowing his arms to rest against his sides, his fist balled in frustration. "I can think of nowhere else to look for the pregnant female. If Alex did not find anything of note using his skills on the computer, I have no idea what more we could do." Demetri's brows drew together in anger, fire flashed through his gray eyes. "I am sickened by the thought we will give up without finding the female."

Stephan moved to place a supportive hand on Demetri's shoulder. "I too wish we could have found her. We must take solace in that we gave the search a valiant effort. What more could we have done?"

The three males ambled in silence into the kitchen. Demetri pulled three bags of blood from the fridge. After pouring the contents into glasses, he handed one to each of his friends.

As the life-sustaining substance slid down his throat to nourish his cells, Demetri's mind raced through all they had done to try to locate the missing women. "I suppose there is nothing more to do. I will contact the female's heartmate and inform him we are halting the search."

"Are you sure? I could do it," offered Stephan.

Demetri pulled a chair away from the kitchen table and sat heavily. "No, I'll do it. You go home and spend time with your mate."

Stephan could not keep the smile that reached his blue eyes from his face. "It will be good to get home to my Katrina."

Alex wagged his eyebrows up and down several times suggestively. "I bet it will. I'm surprised you were able to go this long without, um…seeing her."

The males shared a chuckle as they finished their drinks.

"Do you want my plane to take you back to Virginia, Alex?"

"As much as I enjoy your version of the Friendly Skies, I believe I'll just pop on home. I'll have my clothes shipped to me."

"Then, since you won't be needing it, I'll have my plane go to Las Vegas to take Marcus and Christina home, since Christina cannot dematerialize yet. And I'm sure Marcus will find a way to keep her entertained on the long flight."

The warriors shared another round of laughter before Demetri spoke. "I think I will continue to patrol the town and surrounding territory. If I stumble upon anything, I will tell you."

Demetri removed the empty glasses from the table, taking them to the sink. He could not stop his thoughts from going to the pregnant female. He desperately wanted to find her, to discover she and the baby were safe. His chivalry demanded he maintain his search if only to give the family some closure. Though it may be futile, he could do no less.

Stephan stood. "I doubt you will find anything, my old friend."

"I realize that, comrade," the Russian conceded. "But this tragedy has occurred in my territory, and I need to continue to do something about it. I will contact Nicholai and update him."

"Very well, then it is time for Alex and I to take our leave. Safe travels, my friends."

"Safe travels," Demetri and Alex replied in unison as Stephan coalesced into a small cloud of black smoke.

"I could stay, patrol with you," offered Alex, turning to grasp his fellow Alpha's forearms.

"Not necessary. We both know I probably won't find anything. I just cannot sit at home doing nothing, even if the threat has passed. I will not rest until I find out what happened here."

Alex nodded in understanding. "I would do the same if it had happened in Camdin Falls. Safe travels."

Demetri Romanoff returned the valediction, then his young friend dematerialized. He paced the room, chastising himself for not discovering the threat in his territory. It was the first time the team had not completed an objective. Failure was not an option for one such as him. His face contorted with self-recrimination, his brows furrowed over his gray eyes, the corners of his lips drew down. He punched his fist hard into the opposite hand, the sting bolstering his resolve.

The Alpha would not fail. He would persist in the search until he found what was responsible for the strange occurrences on his mountain.

Stephan might be right, maybe there was nothing for him to find, but he had to try. At least for a little while longer. He would call Nicholai and inform him of the latest developments. He would also inform his cousin of the plan to continue searching, just in case. Determination quickened his steps to the phone.

****

The sound of mating filtering through the wooden door stopped Jara's fisted hand midair. She listened to the pounding sound of flesh on flesh combined with the low male growls.

Her hand dropped silently to her side. Now was not the time to disturb her brother. She turned and made her way to the laboratory, deciding to check on the progress Lane was making with his subject.

She pushed into the double door, making a dramatic entrance that caused Lane's head to snap up.

"Have you made any progress?" Jara crossed the room.

Lane snapped off his latex gloves and threw them into the trash. "Not since it died."

The female demon's brows furrowed. "What do you mean it died?"

"Her body couldn't take anymore. Her heart stopped, and I couldn't bring her back this time."

Anger twisted the features of Jara's face, her red eyes pierced Lane's as she spoke between clenched teeth. "Tell me you discovered why they live so long."

"I cannot." Lane put both hands up in surrender. "This fortress is inadequate. I need electricity, not torches and candles to run my experiments. I need proper lab equipment, the kind that runs on current. And I need a proper place to work, Jara. Working here is like trying to be a rocket scientist in the dark ages. I might have been able to keep her alive, if I had had the proper equipment."

Jara paced the room. Her brother had barely authorized taking the vampire. He would never condone taking another one. "What am I to tell Varrick?"

"Tell him I need another subject and an appropriate place to work. A male this time."

"A male?" Jara asked, turning to face the scientist.

"A male will last longer," explained Lane. "It will also give me a chance to see if male vampires respond the same way physically as the female."

"And you believe a male subject and electricity will make a difference?"

"I have no doubt with the proper equipment and a proper subject for my experiment, I'll be able to discover the reason for the vampire immunity."

Jara clasped her hands behind her back and blew out an exasperated breath. If she approached the subject carefully, perhaps she might manipulate Varrick into approving a male subject. Lane had a point about needing electricity, after all, and she knew just the building that would meet his need.

A smile graced her face taking the furrow from her light brows. "I might know of a place that would work. My father had a compound made. It is in the middle of nowhere. There is an industrial generator to power the building. It would be private and allow you to conduct your experiments without interruption."

A hopeful look took Lane's effeminate face.

"I'll go see Varrick. You stay low. I don't think you'll want to run into him for a while. He won't be happy that we need to get a second bloodsucker."

****

The sound of knuckles rasping on his chamber door drew Varrick's attention. The shadow on his jaw caught at the stray wisps of Elizabeth's golden hair when he turned his head toward the sound. His arms slid from around her exhausted body, and he rolled out of the bed. After tucking the sheets around her sleeping form, he wrapped a robe about his body. Cinching the belt, he opened the door to their room and discovered his sister awaited on the other side.

"Can I speak with you, brother?"

"Of course."

He slipped out into the hallway, closing the door behind him so as not to disturb his sleeping mate.

Jara backed away, giving him room.

"The vampire is dead," Jara bluntly announced.

Varrick's eyes narrowed. "What do you mean the vampire is dead? I thought Lane was keeping her alive until he discovered what causes vampiric immunity. Can I assume that since she is dead, he discovered the key to immortality?"

Jara lowered her eyes to the floor and shook her head, sending her wavy locks swaying from side to side.

"I'm afraid Lane didn't discern the secret to their immortality. He needs another subject and better working conditions."

Varrick scrubbed a tired hand over his jaw, the sound of rough beard scraped under his fingers. "I do not like that the vampire lost her life, and yet we do not have the answers we seek."

Jara had the good sense to look somewhat contrite. "I know, brother, but what is the life of one vampire in our noble quest? Given the right working conditions, I'm sure Lane will be able to discover how we can achieve immortality.

"I suggest you allow him to use father's compound up north. It will afford the needed privacy and has the electricity needed for Lane to do his experiments properly. I can go there with him to supervise his experiments, make sure he does not fail again."

Varrick noted the hopeful look in his sister's eyes. "I can see you are more than willing to supervise Lane." Varrick's nostrils flared as he breathed in deeply.

Red flooded Jara's cheeks, matching the color of her eyes. "I will admit, the idea of going with Lane to the compound is not entirely repulsive."

Varrick crossed his arms against his chest. Jara had been a pain as of late, always interrupting him with his mate. Her jealousy was palpable. It would not be a bad thing to have her some distance away while he continued to work on his relationship with Elizabeth.

"Very well. Take what you need to get Lane set up in the compound. I trust you can find a way to secure another vampire?"

"Leave everything to me. You needn't do a thing. Lane and I will take care of everything."

"Very well. When will you leave?"

"Soon. Lane has some things to clean up in the lab first."

"And getting another vampire?" Varrick prompted.

"I've got a lead on that as well. It shouldn't take long to acquire one."

"Jara," Varrick said in a low warning tone, crossing his arms over his thick chest. "Make sure this is the last vampire you need. I will not permit a third to be taken."

Chapter 36

"Are you positive you do not want Alex to come back and help you?" Nicholai's voice came from deep in his chest cavity, sonorously.

"Yes. I am positive there will be no threat. I just want one last look around to be absolutely sure we did not miss anything."

"Stephan is very thorough. If he felt comfortable going home, then I am sure there is nothing out there to find."

"Exactly my point. There is no reason for anyone to come searching with me. I can handle myself."

Nicholai chuckled. "I know you can, cousin. Thank you for the update."

"Anytime. How is everything there? Has there been any more trouble?"

"No more accidents, if that is what you mean. But I checked my other vehicles and found some of the lug nuts loosened. I'm afraid Alex was correct. It would appear someone sabotaged my cars. I believe someone may be targeting me."

"Any idea who would do such a thing or why?"

"I have no idea."

"How are things with your heartmate?"

"Going well. She is upstairs as we speak baking cookies."

"How very domestic of her," Demetri said, the

smile evident in his voice.

Nicholai took a deep inhale, taking the scent of chocolate walnut meringue cookies into his lungs. "They smell delicious."

"I'm sure they will taste as good as they smell. Perhaps I should come over and try some."

"Sorry, cousin, but they are all for me, an early Christmas present she called them."

"How very selfish of you. I thought I taught you and Natasha how to share and respect your elders," Demetri quipped.

"There are some things we males do not share. Heartmates and cookies being two of them." A wry grin played across Nicholai's features. "If there is nothing else, I need to go."

"To be sure. No doubt you can't wait to sample your heartmate's…cookies."

"Goodbye, Demetri."

"Keep vigilant, cousin. Safe travels."

Nicholai promptly hung up the phone and took the stairs three at a time, bounding into the kitchen.

Chapter 37

The next day, Julie stared out the beveled panes of the window, watching the snow fall. She dug her fingers into her neck and pressed at the tension there.

Nicholai silently padded up behind her. His strong fingers brushed her hand aside and went to work on the knot. "Allow me."

"That feels so good." Juliette rested her forehead on the cool glass.

Quickly conquering the knot, he encircled her waist with both arms and drew her back against him. Juliette rested her head against his muscular chest and gave a contented sigh. She wrapped her own arms around his as they watched the snowflakes twirl in the wind.

"It is beautiful, yes? The way the flakes dance?" Nicholai rested his chin on top of Julie's head.

"Yes. I've always loved the snow. It's so pristine and pure."

"Like you. Pure, beautiful."

Juliette gave an inelegant snort. "I'm hardly either of those things."

"Do not say that. To me you are the most beautiful woman in all the world."

Nicholai sensed the subtle shift in her body. She suddenly stiffened as if defensive. He gently pushed into her mind, discerning the reason for the change.

Juliette's chest tightened. She wanted desperately to believe him, but she was afraid to, afraid to allow herself to care, to give him her heart. Afraid to admit her love to either him or herself.

"You are perfect to me. I can never believe otherwise, because you are my heartmate, *lastochka.*"

Juliette appeared confused. "You mean soul mate?" She believed his translation was incorrect. *How cute.*

"No, I mean heartmate. A heartmate is much more than a soul mate, so much more. You are the other half of me, you complete me. You are the light to my darkness. You are my reason for living. I have spent my life looking for you, waited an eternity to find you. And now that I have you, I cannot live without you."

Julie turned in his arms. "I have never heard the term heartmate. Is it Russian?"

Nicholai considered telling her what he was and how his people believed in the concept of heartmates, but decided now was not the time to confess. Julie had just recovered from her life-threatening injuries. Like a new bud of a rose, she appeared fragile and delicate. Soon he would inform her about the breed, but he wanted her to accept her love for him before he shared a revelation that might drive her away. He hoped their love would be strong enough to survive the disclosure.

"It is not exactly Russian," he confessed.

"Then what?"

"I will tell you another time."

"Please," she begged, sticking out her bottom lip in a pout.

"You are too cute, you know that?" He gave the pouty lip a tug between his teeth.

Nicholai had everything he could want right there in that moment. His heartmate in his arms, snow falling softly outside the window, and a fire crackling in the background, warming the room. Whatever would come later, they had their moment right now. Right here.

"What did I ever do to deserve you?" Nicholai pulled her close, tucking her against his thick chest.

His hand cupped her chin and gently tilted her head up to face him. He looked deep into her soul as he spoke. "My love, if I live another thousand years, I will spend every day thanking the heavens for you. You are the most beautiful thing in my life. I wish you could see yourself through my eyes."

He sent his emotions into her mind, projecting his love and acceptance into her thoughts. "You are truly stunning. I love every curve." He brushed his hand along the side of her body as he spoke. It rested on her hip and his fingers caressed her as he continued, "I love your hips and your stomach."

Nicholai slid his hand, splaying it out over her stomach. "I cannot wait until one day your beautiful stomach grows round with our child. As long as you will have me, I will spend every moment of our lives trying to make you happy. Trying to be worthy of your love."

Juliette covered his hand with her own, giving it a squeeze. Her belief in him flooded his mind. She chose to accept his wanting, no needing, to be a part of something special this holiday.

She moved slightly. Rather than allowing her to leave his embrace, Nicholai shifted with her.

"Normally, the Christmas holidays aren't something I celebrate. It's painful trying to rejoice without the ones I love. But this year everything is different because I have you."

Tears of happiness welled in her eyes, eyes that were alive with the blaze of the fire dancing in the irises.

"Come," he requested, hoping to take the tears from her eyes.

Nicholai led Juliette by the hand through his home. They proceeded down the hall in companionable silence to the music room where he pushed the door open with a grand sweep of his arm to bid her entrance. The room looked beautiful with its tan walls and decorative molding painted white. The carpet, intricately patterned with reds and beige, crushed beneath their bare feet as they entered. Several chairs in various styles were scattered around the room, each padded with tan velvet fabric. In one corner, stood a baby grand piano with a large flower arrangement on the top.

And in the opposite corner, a huge Scotch pine stood majestically, its pristine branches twinkling with tiny white lights and colorful glass balls, the largest of which were almost the size of her head. The white lights sparkled off the vibrant ornaments, causing a beautiful twinkle effect.

Her emotion struck him. As he gazed down onto her round face, the soft lights of the tree reflected brightly in the depths of her honey eyes.

"Do you like it?" He gave her hand a squeeze.

"It's gorgeous. When did you have time to do this?" she asked in awe, swallowing thickly. "You've been taking care of me for two days."

Nicholai gave a nonchalant shrug. "It was

nothing."

"Don't say that. This is amazing." Julie cradled one of the large orbs on the tree in her hand.

"I am glad you approve. I realize it's a day late. I hope you don't mind."

"It's perfect. Oh, Nicholai!"

Julie turned and wrapped her arms around his neck in a tight hug. His arms snaked around her back, lifting her to her toes as he took her mouth in a soft kiss.

"It is not quite perfect, Juliette. Something is missing. It needs a star. Would you like to put the star on, *lastochka*?"

Nicholai released his mate and strolled behind the tree. He emerged with a stepladder in one hand and a burgundy star in the other. Outlined in gold glitter, it sparkled, reflecting the lights from the tree.

Setting the ladder in front of the tree, he handed Julie up the rungs. After assuring her foothold, he gave her the star to place on the tree.

Leaning forward against the ladder, Julie reached high and slipped the fragile star into place.

"Beautiful!" Nicholai's warm hand traced its way up her calf, caressed the outside of her thigh. "And I am not talking about the tree.

"Be careful," his whiskey voice called from below. "We don't want you to get distracted and fall into my waiting arms."

The sinuous hand found her inner thigh and rose slowly. His fingers slipped beneath her skirt and discovered silk panties. Her breath quickened. The digits slid beneath the soft material and over her most delicate folds. She didn't suppress the moan that rose from her throat when he slipped a finger between to find her moist with need.

He needed to taste her honey on his tongue. Reaching up, he took her waist in both hands and helped her from the ladder. He found her lips as she descended and thrust his tongue between them. Without breaking their kiss, Nicholai swung Julie into his arms and carried her through the home to his bedchamber.

Nicholai kicked open the door and crossed the room with quick strides. He pulled away from their kiss and placed her gently on the bed. He contemplated her beauty, her lips swollen from his kiss, her cheeks flushed with desire for him. Never had he seen a more beautiful sight.

With sure fingers, he deftly undid the button on the waist of her skirt. After sliding the zipper down the side, he pulled the fabric over her legs. Next, he hooked her sweater with both hands and removed it from her delectable body.

Her hair pooled on the bed as she lay before him, clothed only in her bra and matching panties. Their deep red color reminded him of a Christmas present. One he wanted to open and play with evermore.

He knelt on the floor before her, taking the panties down her thighs as he lowered to his knees. Julie shuddered in anticipation when the cool air touched her heated core. She closed her eyes awaiting what would come.

Nicholai stood and removed his clothes. As they pooled on the floor, he leaned over her, blanketing her mostly naked body with his. Flesh against flesh, Julie's temperature rose. Her breath quickened when she opened her eyes and found him staring down lovingly into her face. She ran her hand along his cheek and temple to capture the shaggy bangs over his forehead. Taking the bangs away from his eyes, her hand continued its way over the top of his head and fisted in his hair.

She lifted her head and captured his lips in a searing kiss. Her fingers slid through his strands as she clasped his neck, holding his lips to hers.

When he made his way down her body to her delectable breasts, his thick, raven bangs tickled her. He tucked the satin material of the bra under one globe and took the creamy flesh in hand. He kneaded the large mound while he exposed the other one with his free hand. Both nipples puckered against the cool air.

His lips kissed the valley between her breasts and trailed over to attend to the other mound. His tongue circled her nipple, the sensation arching her back. A low rumble of approval vibrated against her sensitive flesh. Next his quick fingers snapped the clasp of her bra, and the material pulled sensuously across her breasts as Nicholai bared her satin skin to his appreciative gaze.

Nicholai's mouth scorched a trail of kisses down her stomach, his mouth hot and demanding. She relaxed under his attention. Her heart fluttered like a hummingbird's wings. Nicholai groaned, the sound boiling up from the deepest regions of his body.

He cupped Julie's rounded bottom in both hands, then pulled her to the edge of the bed. He knelt before her, brought both legs over his shoulders. His tongue found her velvet folds and licked a long path to her most sensitive nub. Nicholai's teeth scraped the spot, alternating with his tongue. Each pass made her body clench. His heartmate arched in pleasure.

He sucked the tiny nub into the heat of his mouth. The pressure sent her over the precipice. Her fingers fisted in the covers when her climax took her. She flung her head from side to side, as if attempting to relieve the pressure building once more, while Nicholai's mouth moved lower.

His tongue thrust between her folds to sample her. Her sweet flavor fueled his hunger, drove his need higher. His body painfully tight, he forced himself to remain on his knees, determined to bring her to another orgasm before filling her for his own pleasure.

His sinuous mouth worked at her core, lapping her honey. He built more pressure, sent her higher with each talented lick.

His fangs grazed her inner thigh, and a shiver took her body. He slid two fingers into her folds as his teeth latched onto her without warning. He couldn't help himself. She was his heartmate, he had to taste her in every way.

Julie fell over the precipice once more, this time screaming the climax that rolled through her body. She convulsed around his fingers. She tried to move her legs, but they were pinned, one by Nicholai's mouth, the other by the hand not inside her. A possessive bestial growl rolled out from his chest, and she gasped loudly. He knew exactly how he wanted his mate and he held her open for his perusal.

He licked the tiny wounds closed and laved his way up her body to find her full lips once again. Nicholai's mouth scorched against hers with a natural talent that made her senseless. He kissed her aggressively, the flick of his tongue touching her lips, demanding entry.

When she opened her lips, he positioned himself at her lower entrance. With one sure thrust, he slid into the heat inch by decadent inch until she pushed her hips against his urging him in.

They danced the waltz as old as time, varying their speed to match their need. Julie raised her hips and met him thrust for thrust. Nicholai made the dance last, drawing her pleasure from her, making her call his name as she came for him again and again. Each orgasm made her body convulse tightly around his, milking him until his own release became imminent.

Nicholai kissed down to where her neck and shoulder met. He jerked her forward against himself and latched his teeth into her soft flesh. Juliette gasped when his teeth pierced her skin. Nicholai ensured Julie did not register the bite as anything more than a hickey. His hand wrapped around her neck and held her still while he drew her crimson life-force into his mouth.

He lost himself to the sensation of her velvet heat. His own climax built. He fell over the edge with the flavor of her coating the back of his throat. Julie crossed her ankles behind his back, locking him to her. The pleasure of the sensations he created sent her into a rolling climax that milked his seed from him. As she flowed onto him, he flowed into her, pumping his hips until they both lay spent.

He licked the tiny puncture wounds closed as the last of their climax gripped their bodies, then lifted his head to gaze at her. He shifted, taking the brunt of his weight on his forearms.

Juliette gave a satisfied grin and ran her fingers lightly over his back. "Merry Christmas to me."

"Consider me the gift that keeps on giving,"

Nicholai said, a smug grin of male satisfaction on his face.

"You can say that again." Julie's legs fell limply to the bed. "You can give me that gift any time you want."

A deep chuckle rolled from Nicholai's chest as he gingerly separated from her body then stood at the side of the bed. "Speaking of gifts…"

He reached under the bed and withdrew a decorative bag. Julie pushed up and leaned her back against the headboard.

"What's this?"

Nicholai handed his mate the bag. "Open it."

Julie withdrew the green tissue paper from the bag and reached inside. When she pulled out a set of wooden stacking dolls, amazement widened her eyes. "How did you know I wanted these?"

"A little butterfly told me," he quipped.

"You mean a little bird told you?" she corrected, opening the dolls one by one to reveal the next in the stack.

"Is that how the saying goes? A bird?" Nicholai paused until Julie nodded in agreement. "Huh, bird it is then."

Julie held the smallest doll in the palm of her hand.

"That's unusual." She examined the doll. "Typically the last doll is solid. This one seems to be cut around the middle."

"Perhaps there is something within. Why don't you open it and see?"

Julie opened the tiny doll and peered inside the body. Seeing something shiny, she turned the doll upside down. A platinum chain fell onto the bed.

Nicholai reached for the necklace and held it

before Julie's eyes. A heart-shaped diamond pendant spun from the length of chain, sending a rainbow prism arching along Juliette's creamy skin.

"I thought you celebrated Christmas on January seventh." Julie turned her back on Nicholai and pulled her hair up into a loose pony tail.

He circled her neck with the chain, adeptly fastening the clasp. The backs of his fingers brushed her neck while he worked. "I do, but your Christmas has already passed, and I wanted to get you a little something. Do you like it?"

His love turned and faced him, fingering the heart pendant. "It's beautiful. I love it."

Nicholai's stomach knotted at her choice of words. How he longed to hear her say she loved him. He deliberately used the most personal form of communication they had when next he spoke.

I am glad. I wanted to give you something that would symbolize my love.

Julie's eyebrows shot up in surprise. *I don't think I'll ever get used to this way of talking with you.*

It is most natural between heartmates. You will adjust in time. Nicholai brushed the back of his hand down her cheek, then laid his palm on the pendant which rested over her heart.

I have given my heart to you, lastochka. *Please do not break it.*

****

"We are still no closer to capturing another vampire," Lane pointed out to Jara and jammed his hands into the pockets of his lab coat.

"You don't need to tell me." Jara fisted her hands on her hips in pique.

"How can I save our race without a test subject?" Anger lit Lane's eyes. "You must do something."

How dare he show anger toward her! She was royalty. Just when she decided he needed a lesson in manners, Jara's phone rang. She pulled it from the pocket of her white pantsuit and noted the number displayed.

"This might just be the answer to our prayers. Excuse me," she said and seized on the excuse to quickly exit the lab before her temper got the better of her.

Her heart beat faster. Interest straightened Jara's spine. "Is your vampire a male or female, Lovazia?"

"Well, hello to you too, sister dear."

Jara ambled down the hall. "Yes, yes, hello. Now answer the question, is the vampire you bumped into male or female?"

"I told you before, female."

Jara's hope crashed to the floor. "We need a vampire, Lovazia. A male."

"Sorry, can't help you. The bloodsucker I've been hunting has a companion..." Jara's hope rose. "...but she is female too."

Annnnnnnnd just like that her optimism was once again dashed.

"Besides, I have plans for the bitch." Wickedness permeated Lovazia's voice.

"What do you plan on doing?"

Jara reached her room and went inside.

"Killing her, of course."

"Yes, but we need a vampire, and since we are having trouble finding a male, perhaps your female one might do. Capture it or wait until we can get there, and we'll help you capture it."

"Capture it? I want to kill it! They are all blood-thirsty monsters who deserve to die for what they did to Alcid."

Jara laid on the bed. She understood her sister's need for revenge. "If you help us capture it, there will be lots of pain and torture for it, then death. Wouldn't that be a better punishment?"

"Hmmmm." Lovazia seemed interested.

"We need a vampire, Lovazia. Varrick hopes to be able to find a cure for our susceptibility to human ailments. Do you understand what that would mean? We could mingle with humans. Live outside of the cave. We could have a real life, not spend it skulking about, hiding our existence."

"Some of us already do that, Jara. Just because you and Varrick choose to live life sequestered, doesn't mean the rest of us do."

"Aren't you scared of dying?"

"At some point, we all die. I'd rather go out fighting personally, like trying to kill a vampire."

Perhaps another tactic might help her sister see reason.

"Vampires are difficult to kill, little sister. They can take a lot of physical abuse. How do you plan on getting rid of the beast?"

"You needn't tell me. I've already tried and failed a couple of times."

Thank goodness. There might be a chance. An idea occurred to Jara.

"Well then, why not wait until we can get there? We can help you kill it," Jara lied.

"Not necessary. I've decided to do it the old-fashioned way. With my bare hands, or paws, as it were." Lovazia laughed before continuing, her voice low with deadly intent. "I'm going to find it and let my wolf rip its heart from its chest."

Jara knew her sister well. Almost nothing could change her mind once she'd made it up. She decided to play along with killing the beast for a minute, hoping to steer the conversation back to capturing it instead.

"You are a strong fighter, especially in wolf form. But don't waste time playing with your kill. Get in low and fast. Take the heart without allowing time for the thing to fight back. It will come after you with all it's got."

"I know how to fight, Jara. Father made sure all of us were trained properly."

The older demon's mind slid back to the time of their youth when she had been forced to stand by and watch as her sister was routinely beaten in the training ring by much larger and stronger opponents. Their father had said it was the only way to develop their skills, but Jara and her siblings always believed their father had a sadistic streak and liked to see his children beaten down.

"I remember exactly how you were trained. Still, be careful. I don't want anything to happen to you. I wish you'd reconsider taking on the beast, Lovazia. We could have someone there in a day or two to help you."

That person would be there to capture the bloodsucker, not kill it, but Lovazia didn't need to know that.

"I'll consider it," Lovazia promised. "I need to go, Jara. Bye."

"Lovazia, wait."

The phone went dead.

Jara chucked the thing across the room. Her anger grew until her hair stood away from the scalp with her energy.

Knowing Lovazia, she'd probably hunt the vampire tonight. Of course, there was also the smallest chance Lovazia might see reason and choose to capture the bloodsucker instead.

"Yeah, right." Jara rolled her eyes.

Chapter 38

Julie awoke and discovered the tiny hairs on Nicholai's chest pillowed her cheek, her body still replete. She thought back over their night together.

They'd spent long hours making glorious love. He had driven her to dizzying heights, wound her body tighter until it ached with a need so great only he could satisfy it.

I love you, lastochka. Her mind replayed words he'd said to her as her dreams tried to claim her the previous evening.

She believed him, convinced by the way he'd looked at her, the way he held her with his quiet strength. He truly loved her. He loved her with his body and soul many ways each day, always seeing to her needs before his own.

She had to admit, Nicholai was everything and more she could want. Her heart raced every time he neared. When they were apart, she longed to see him, felt desperate to touch him. She heard him in her mind, sensed him near when she could not see him in the flesh. Julie still wasn't exactly sure how he did that, but it made her feel safe, loved, and she was content not to examine it too closely. Feeling closer to him than she ever had to another person, she did not want anything to ruin this special relationship.

Somehow, he had become a part of her, and lying

in his bed, she realized her heart had known him from the first moment they met. One look in his amber eyes and she'd fallen deeply in love, though she would never have admitted it. She had been too scared.

Well, she wasn't scared any more. She loved him, and it was damn time she summoned the courage to tell him so.

She pushed off his chest and contemplated his sleeping form. The features of his face were at ease. He looked like a child, innocent in sleep, with his dark hair falling back away from the handsome lines of his face. She stroked a finger lightly down his straight nose. It glided over his full sensual lips. His lower lip tugged slightly under her digit.

In fascination, she watched the lip bounce back into place, perfecting the picture of his regal face. Now that she really studied him, he bore a striking resemblance to the portrait that hung in the Peterhof Castle. Seeing him so relaxed, so unburdened. He appeared young, carefree, like the young man in the portrait.

Nicholai's lids flew open. His loving gaze captured her, and she fell into his amber eyes.

"Like what you see?" His deep voice reverberated in his chest under her fingers.

A wicked grin spread across her face. "I do. Very much!"

Nicholai wrapped a muscular arm around her middle and pulled her cheek to his chest. "Glad to hear that, my dear." Gentle amusement sounded in his satiny voice. His soft laughter stroked over her like velvet heat.

Julie trailed her fingers through the fine hairs on

his chest. They were soft under the pads of her fingers. She listened to him breathe, her head rising with each gentle inhale. His heart sounded strong behind his ribs. The rhythm beat steady, slow. Her own heart skipped a beat when he tenderly rubbed her back with one warm hand. Up and down, it massaged her sore muscles from neck to buttocks.

He spent extra time on her neck, working the muscles and sinew until she went boneless. His talented fingers took the slight ache that always accompanied their lovemaking. His hickeys seemed to have a bit of a sting, even though he never left a mark.

"Is there anything you would like to do tonight?" Nicholai asked.

Julie snuggled closer against his warmth and pulled the blanket under her chin. "No. Why? Was there something you wanted to do?"

"I thought we might take Kedar out for a moonlight ride through the woods."

"That sounds lovely," Julie said, the wistfulness lowering her voice.

"Good. After we eat, we can go for a ride."

Her lover reluctantly pulled himself from the bed and stood before her in his full glory, blissfully unencumbered by his nudity. The muscles played under his smooth skin as he crossed the room to the bath. Her body responded to each ripple, every flex. When he closed the bathroom door behind him, a small sigh, as much from sated contentment as disappointment from the gorgeous view leaving her sight, escaped.

The shower turned on. She stretched, lifting her arms above her head before wiggling off the enormous bed. In stark contrast to the warmth of being in bed with

Nicholai, a blast of chilled air hit her skin. Her muscles tensed as her arms circled her middle. Julie considered joining him in the shower but decided her body needed a little recovery time before they made love again. For while Nicholai never hurt her, her muscles were always a little sore from working hard to keep up with his boundless appetite for sex.

She unwrapped her arms around her waist and quickly retrieved some clothes from the top drawer in the dresser. Julie donned her jeans and sweater as fast as she could and strolled upstairs to the kitchen. If Nicholai was taking her riding, the least she could do was make them a meal before they went.

****

Lovazia stalked through the woods. The half-moon cast gray and black shadows over the new fallen snow. She turned her angular face toward the moon. No doubt its silvery reflection glowed in her red eyes. Her skeletal frame, so light her feet barely made impressions in the snow, plunged through the trees recklessly. Loose stones rolled under her feet as she clambered through the barren forest.

The demon breathed in the crisp winter air. It burned her nose, made her eyes tear. She hated the cold, and if that damned vampire bitch would just die, she could go home right now to her warm bed. Instead, she traipsed through a forest, heading toward a fight to avenge her dead husband.

It mattered not that it might not be the one that killed Alcid or that her brother wanted it captured. All that mattered was that honor dictated she kill it.

Stupid bloodsucker! It had to be my luck to run into her. I don't know how she'd been able to be out during the day, but there is no doubt what she is.

The stench of vampire on her had been too strong, and Lovazia would never forget that scent.

Tonight she would kill it. No more accidents that failed. No more missed opportunities. Tonight, she would kill the blood-hungry beast with her bare hands, or paws, as it were. One of them would not live to see the dawn, she vowed, sure she knew who that would be.

An evil grin spread across the demon's drawn face as she stalked along on silent feet. She had done research, tracked the vampire to its lair. The thing stayed in a large home, an isolated home that served Lovazia's purposes well. They could fight to the death, and no one would notice. She could leave the body to rot without its being discovered. She would be able to shift at will, and no one would see. Yes, this home seemed like the perfect place to carry out her plans.

Alcid, she sent the message up to her deceased husband. *Tonight I will avenge you, my love. I will continue to murder every vampire I encounter until I am sure I have killed the one that murdered you. And once my revenge is complete, I will join you in the afterlife. Wait for me just a little while longer, my love, for one day we will be together again.*

****

Nicholai shortened his gait so Juliette's petite strides kept pace. The bitter cold kissed her cheeks, leaving its ruby marks. She put a hand on her faux fur pillbox hat and pushed it down over the tops of her ears. Julie pulled her matching coat tightly around her body and held the collar closed with one gloved hand. Nicholai gathered a bridle from a hook in the tack room.

With the expertise of a man who'd ridden horses for many years, Nicholai took the bridle in one hand and lightly cradled Kedar's raven nose with his other arm. He stroked the stallion's face coaxing him to remain in place as he brought the bridle over Kedar's muzzle. The horse opened his mouth and took the bit. With deft fingers, Nicholai secured the throatlatch strap, making sure it was not too snug, checked the keepers, then took the reins in his hands. He opened the stall and led the magnificent stallion out into the stable.

Julie approached the pair from the front and carefully rubbed the horse's satiny coat while Nicholai threw a blanket on its back.

"Ready to go?" Nicholai ran a hand down the horse's side.

"Didn't you forget the saddle?"

Nicholai flashed Julie a mischievous smile. "I thought we'd ride bareback."

"Bareback?" Julie's eyes went wide. "I haven't ridden bareback since I was a young girl helping Daddy break in his mares."

Nicholai vaulted effortlessly onto the horse and extended a hand down to Julie. "Then it is about time you did it again."

Juliette's stomach did a flip as he pulled her easily up onto the large animal. She settled onto its back, leaning against Nicholai's chest. His powerful arms encircled her with their strong protection.

"Hold on tight," he warned and dug his heels into Kedar's flanks.

The stallion shot forward, swift and surefooted. The stable faded from view as he dashed through. Nicholai's body bounced behind hers in tandem with each powerful gallop of the steed beneath them. They leaned over his neck, racing along the property toward the woods.

The wind whipped about her face, making tears well in Julie's eyes. The scenery blurred as much from the speed at which they ran as from the tears. Nicholai reined in the mighty horse when they neared the tree line and slowed to an easy trot.

The powerful arm around Julie's waist drew her back against the firmness of Nicholai's body. Her heart pounded hard in her chest.

"That was amazing," she breathed. "For a minute I thought you were going to keep him at a gallop through the trees."

"They are too thick. I would never take such a risk with you, *lastochka*." Nicholai gave her a slight squeeze. "Is not the forest beautiful?"

Julie's gaze swept the landscape. The moon's rays glittered on the snowy bows. The birch trees stood with their trunks painted white to match their limbs. Thick pine branches held fast under the weight of the new-fallen snow, making them appear as if they wore white blankets made of virginal cotton about each limb. Sparkling mounds cluttered the ground between the trees, hiding the forest's treasures beneath.

Save the sound of the hooves pounding on the ground, they journeyed through the silent night to a clearing in the trees. Nicholai clicked to his stallion, and with a flick of the reins, the steed increased into a rolling canter up a steep incline. Julie's thighs pushed against the sides of the horse as she tried to match the new rhythm.

Nicholai's breath warmed her ear when he spoke.

"Not too much farther. It's right up ahead."

"What's up ahead?" Just as the words left Julie's mouth, they crested over the ridge.

The frozen valley below took her breath away. A glaciate waterfall stood still as a statue against the rocky terrain. The cascading water, stopped as if by magic, reflected the moon's soft rays and cast tiny prisms on the snow below.

Julie's breath hitched in her throat. She took in the serene beauty of the land as they cruised at a slow trot. Debris rolled under Kedar's hoofs. It created a hollow rattle in the night, barely audible to Juliette.

When they reached the valley, Nicholai pulled up the stallion and handed the reins to Julie. She patted the horse's steaming neck as her lover dismounted with a fluid grace. He turned, grabbed Kedar's reins, then reached up for Julie. Her thick coat seemed to melt as his strong hands clasped around her waist. She put her hands on his shoulders, and the bulge of muscle under his coat played under her fingers when he helped her down. A thrill went through her body.

Her breath frosted the air in a white plume. The lovers held each other, his hands about her waist, hers resting on his shoulders. Quiet as the moon above, they stared deeply into each other's eyes. Nicholai captured her lips in a gentle caress that welcomed her to this special place.

When they came up for air, Nicholai spoke first, "Tell me what you are thinking."

"I'm not sure I can think after a kiss like that," Julie quipped, her smile tugging at the corners of her lips.

"Come, let's walk. There is much beauty still to

see." Nicholai took her gloved hand in his.

Their boots crunched through the unspoiled snow. Nicholai led her behind the frozen water. With only enough room for them to walk single file behind the falls, Julie ran her free hand against the smooth ice. The frozen water, translucent enough to let light through, allowed her to make her way. She stopped to admire a peculiar feature.

"Look," she said. "It looks like someone made a heart in the ice."

She tugged her hand free from his and ran it over the heart-shaped ice. "Are those initials?"

Julie stood on her tiptoes and leaned closer to the ice. She took off her glove and ran her finger along the cold surface. She traced the indentations. The letters N, P, a plus sign, and the letters J, S.

"Did you do this?" When she turned, love sparkled in Nicholai's eyes.

"Yes," he admitted. "Do you like it?"

"It's beautiful."

"It can't compare to you."

Julie turned again toward the carving. It must have taken him some time, for the letters were deep within the ice. She could not imagine how he had accomplished such a feat. When did he sneak out of the house to do this? It would have taken a while; the ride alone had taken several minutes.

An enraptured sigh left Juliette's lips, frosting the air. Her Nicholai always surprised her, always did something sweet and romantic. It was one of the things she found endearing, one of the many things she loved about him.

He always made everything seem perfect, just like

this place. Beautiful, romantic, a perfect place for her to profess her love to him. The thought gave her the courage she needed to finally say those three little words.

"I love you, Nicholai," she breathed, turning to find him gone.

Julie whipped her head from side to side. He was nowhere to be seen.

"Nicholai!" she called out, her voice shakier than she would have liked.

"Out here, *lastochka*."

As Julie emerged from behind the veil of ice, a snowball landed on her faux fur hat and covered her brunette strands with flakes. Nicholai stood across from her tossing another snowball ominously from hand to hand.

"Got you," he called, amusement lifting his voice.

"Oh you! I'll have you know I used to pitch for a softball team. You're in big trouble, buddy." Julie bent and scooped a handful of snow. While she shaped it into a ball, Nicholai sprinted away, then turned to lob his ball. It hit with deadly accuracy right in the middle of her chest. Julie gasped and went after him, packing and throwing with precision honed on the ball field.

Nicholai dodged, looking over his shoulder at her, laughing, then he turned on her. Quick strides brought him her way, and he hurled one last ball that hit its mark. His eyes narrowed, and a look of intense passion took his handsome face. He dropped his shoulder and caught her waist, taking them both to the snow in one effortless move.

They sank into the powder. Nicholai caught her wrist as she tried to stuff a handful of the icy slush down his coat. She laughed up at him and pushed up with her heels, rolling them over so she rested on top. They wrestled in the snow, their laughter flowing through the trees, carried by the wind that whipped around them. The snow swirled about their bodies.

"You are so beautiful." Nicholai gazed down on her with sparkling eyes and ran a finger across her cheek. "Your cheeks are rosy from the cold. The crystal flakes dance on your lashes as you bat them to get off the snow." His finger moved over her lips. "Your lips are parted from your heavy breaths. The gesture is sexy beyond measure."

He lowered his head and kissed her senseless.

Minutes passed with Kedar watching from his place tethered to a nearby tree. They made two snow people, one of which was a well-endowed woman and the other a portly man. Then they circled each other for another battle royale with the snowballs. The time passed quickly, and a slight shiver flowed through Julie's body when the cold soaked into her bones.

"Your lips are turning blue. Let's go home," Nicholai suggested, tucking her under his arm. "I will start a fire, and we can drink hot chocolate to get warm."

Julie wrapped an arm around his waist and nodded. "Sounds like a good idea to me."

Nicholai untethered Kedar's reins and mounted with an easy leap. After handing Julie up in front of him, he clicked to the horse, and with a snap of the reins they were off.

They rode in companionable silence, enjoying the night. Julie's body naturally bounced in time with the steed beneath them. Nicholai's muscular thighs pressed against hers as they worked to balance his weight on the horse.

Her mind replayed the night's events. A smile crept on her face when she remembered the heart Nicholai had carved into the frozen ice of the waterfall. NP + JS. It was so romantic. She wanted to be with him forever, like this, loved and cherished, riding with him through the night.

How she loved his arms protectively around her. Loved the way he treated her as if she was the only woman in the world for him, the one woman he could love. How she loved...him.

Loved him with all her heart, and she could finally admit it to herself. She loved everything about him, his smile, his sense of humor, the way he cared for her. She loved him.

Julie gathered herself, taking a deep breath as courage straightened her spine. "Nicholai, I—"

A sudden, terrified whinny from Kedar interrupted the declaration of love. The steed reared. Slashed the air with his forelegs. Julie grabbed for the stallion's mane as Nicholai pulled hard on the reins and dug his powerful thighs into the horse for purchase. The arm around Julie's waist tightened, and he bent her forward over the horse's neck with the force of his body. They managed to stay astride the mighty steed when Kedar dropped back down onto all four legs.

"What the hell?" Nicholai asked as the horse once again reared, cutting through the cold air with its flailing forelegs.

This time the pull of gravity won, and Nicholai tumbled backward off the horse with Julie still clutched to his front. They hit the ground, Nicholai taking the brunt of the fall. Snow puffed out around them from the impact. Snorting in terror, the steed charged off into the trees, leapt over a fallen trunk, and disappeared into the night.

Juliette rolled off Nicholai and got to her feet. "You okay?"

Nicholai leapt to his feet and brushed off his backside. "Don't worry about me. I'm fine. Are you all right? Were you hurt?"

Juliette shook her head. "I'm fine." She scanned the woods. "Where's Kedar?"

"I'm not sure, but when I find him I'm going to turn him into glue," Nicholai threatened, wiggling two fingers through a hole in his coat that resulted from the fall.

Julie laid a hand on the man's forearm. "You don't mean that. Something spooked him. It wasn't his fault."

Nicholai looked into her eyes, and the anger melted from his face. "I would no sooner harm the horse than I would harm you. I need to go find Kedar. Will you be all right to wait here while I go find him?"

"Of course."

"I will have your word you will stay here on the path. Do not move. I do not want to have to go find you tonight as well."

"I promise. I'll wait right here until you get back."

He ran the back of his hand down her cheek, caught her under the chin, and tilted her head back for a searing kiss that pulled her breath from her lungs.

Nicholai disappeared into the darkness of the forest. Around her, the night fell still and dark as if something had scared off all the animals. She noticed behind her the trunk of a tree rested in the snow. Her eyes roamed over the landscape, noting every shadow, every shape.

From behind the fallen tree, something caught her eye. Was that movement? One of the shadows changed, separated, became two. She squinted, trying to bring the shapes of the night into better focus. Was something creeping through the night? Moving closer?

Chapter 39

When Nicholai walked away from his beloved, he flared his senses throughout the trees to check for any danger. The stallion's fear came to him while it ran through the forest. But the blank spot worried him most. Of course, he had drunk from Juliette the prior evening, so perhaps there really was a correlation between feeding from his mate and the blank spot.

The way the horse took off at a full gallop, he would be long gone by now, but using his preternatural speed and senses Nicholai knew he would easily find the animal. After a glance over his shoulder to assure Julie could not see him, he took off at a full run through the trees.

Sensing the stallion on the other side, Nicholai slowed his pace as he reached the top of the hill so as not to scare it. Approaching cautiously from the front, he murmured soothing words in Russian. He ran a steady hand down the horse's neck. Kedar pranced but held his ground as Nicholai rubbed his side. It gleamed with sweat from the hard run. Nicholai faced the animal and stared into its intelligent eyes while he rubbed its nose. In the onyx stare, he saw the fear, the uneasiness. Nicholai sent his emotions over the beast, trying to wrap the animal in comfort, hoping it would calm the horse so he could ride him back to Julie.

Kedar shifted uneasily from hoof to hoof. Nicholai

waited for the animal to calm. It happened first in the neck muscles that relaxed under his hand, then he witnessed the change in the stallion's dark eyes.

Once he believed it safe, Nicholai mounted his steed and took him firmly by the reins. With a flick of his wrists and an easy kick of his heels, he headed back toward the woman he loved.

****

A cold wind hissed through the trunks, rattling the bare branches. The sound made Juliette shiver. She'd been watching the shadow for a while. It moved closer, stalking her low to the ground. She could not make out exactly what it was, but it definitely headed her way. Its predatory movements sent another involuntary shiver down her spine as she strained to figure out what it might be.

It appeared too small to be a bear, too big to be a fox. Her eyes fought to adjust in the sparse light, struggling to see what pushed toward her.

Every instinct screamed to run, but she held her body still, not wanting to trigger the predator. Julie forced the breath into her lungs, tried in vain to calm her racing heart. Julie examined the ground, searching for anything she might use as a weapon in case the animal attacked.

She spied a rock. Not particularly large, but Julie decided it was better than nothing. With the beast continuing closer, she forced her leaden feet to take two slow steps to the side and bent to pick up the stone.

****

Astride the great horse, Nicholai enjoyed the whip of the wind through his hair when a cold terror flooded his body. *Juliette is in terrible danger!*

Needing to get to his mate, his heels dug deep into Kedar's flank and spurred the horse into a gallop.

It seemed as if they rode forever until finally Kedar broke through the tree line. Relief flooded Nicholai's system. They were close, almost to Juliette. He should be able to see her any minute.

As they bound up the trail, Nicholai's heart jumped into his throat. He clearly saw the wolf, its fur silver in the dim moonlight. His pulse pounded a furious rhythm as it slinked along the ground toward his mate.

Julie took two steps. "No," he yelled. "Don't move!"

Fuck! He was too far away for her human hearing to detect what he said. He kicked the horse into a full run, sending snow into the air behind them. In horror, he watched Juliette bend and retrieve a rock, giving the wolf the opportunity it had been waiting for. Panic seized him when the beast growled and leapt at his mate.

The snowflakes stilled before his eyes as time slowed to a pace only possible in a time of life or death.

Chapter 40

Nicholai watched in horror as the next few seconds played out in slow motion. The wolf leapt. With fluid movement, his heartmate scooped a rock from the ground. Wolf and woman collided, pushing Julie backward. The wolf's powerful jaws clamped around her forearm. The hat flew from her head when her bottom hit the frozen ground with a hard crunch. Her breath puffed from her lips from the force of the wolf landing on top of her, driving her back into the detritus. Nicholai dove for the animal, intent on saving the woman he loved.

Its powerful jaws easily bit through her coat and sweater to the delicate skin beneath. The sharp fangs penetrated her sinew and muscle, then lodged in the bone, and Julie let out a scream. The vice-like grip tightened. The bone in her arm snapped under the pressure. It ripped another scream from her throat.

The wolf shook its head, trying to tear the arm from her body. She lost control of the muscles in her hand, and the rock fell to the ground. Its lips pulled back from its teeth as it growled a deep rumbling sound that shook her arm. Her face distorted in pain. A dark stain spread along her coat. The coppery scent of her blood drove the animal into a frenzy.

The wolf released her arm and snapped at her face, its wide jaws aiming for her neck. Julie tried to bring her uninjured arm up to block the killing blow, but her arm barely lifted an inch before it was blocked by Nicholai's leg as he sailed through the air and took the wolf from her body.

Nicholai wrapped the wolf in his arms and tucked his body around the beast while they tumbled to the ground. They rolled end over end, each looking for a purchase that would allow them to land on top.

When they came to rest, Nicholai lay on his back, his arms tight around the wolf. Its ribs flexed under the pressure. The wolf raised its head and bit into Nicholai's shoulder. His muscles weakened somewhat in response, the exact opening the wolf needed. As his shout of pain tore through the night, the animal pulled its legs tightly to its body and used its thick muscles to push off Nicholai's chest. Its claws dug deep, leaving long rips in his flesh when it shoved away.

It landed lightly on its paws with preternatural grace that did not go unnoticed by Nicholai. The warrior rolled to his feet, rotating his injured shoulder to test it. The wolf limped slightly, took shallow breaths that puffed in the air in front of its long muzzle.

Julie sat on the forest floor watching, with wide, frightened eyes. Wanting to spare her from witnessing what no doubt would be a brutal battle, Nicholai pushed into her mind.

You will not see blood. Wounds will appear as mere scratches until I command otherwise.

Nicholai spared her one last glance before the wolf drew his gaze. Nicholai and the wolf circled each other like two mighty predators dancing a macabre death dance. Each studying the other for weakness.

The silver wolf, larger than most, seemed well over

a hundred pounds. Muscles rippled under its thick fur. A snarling growl showed long sharp teeth.

Careful to keep the wolf in front of him as it tried to circle, Nicholai noted intelligence in its eyes. On one loop, shock narrowed Nicholai's brows when it turned its back, and he discovered the wolf was female. It was unusual to see any wolf this size, let alone a female. Females were not known for their aggression. If it were spring, he might believe she had some cubs nearby which she defended. He could not fathom what had triggered such an attack this time of year.

Perhaps it was rabid.

The thought sent a wave of fear mixed with rage through his blood when he remembered it bit both of them. Rabies didn't concern him, his vampiric immune system would destroy the virus, but Julie's human system could be ravaged by the disease. At the very least, it would take a series of painful shots to heal her. Nicholai's quick mind sent him an image of Julie lying on a gurney suffering. It was all the incentive needed to spur him into action.

Nicholai launched at the wolf, but the animal anticipated the attack and dodged. The vampire feigned right, hoping to lure the wolf so it would turn and expose its side. The move took Nicholai off balance in a way that exposed the side of his body, but he chanced it. The wolf was not fooled. Instead of going for the ruse, it snapped at the Alpha's exposed ribs, cutting through the cloth and flesh. Pushing the pain from his mind, he spun his body, flinging the wolf from him. It hit the ground with a huff and landed on its paws in a squat.

Snow and debris flew from under her feet when the

wolf charged. Nicholai straightened to his full height, shifted into a fighting stance, and braced for the coming attack. He had underestimated the wolf, but he would not make that same mistake again.

The wolf slammed into Nicholai with the full force of her weight. The two rolled in the snow. Nicholai pounded the wolf in the muzzle with his fist, landing a direct hit that sent the wolf's head spinning in the opposite direction. Its body had no choice but to follow, and it rolled off Nicholai.

Before the wolf could get its paws beneath her, Nicholai pounced on her and pinned her to the ground. The wolf yelped in fear.

The duo struggled. Teeth gnashed, limbs flailed, until the wolf gathered its legs beneath it and gave a mighty push, sending Nicholai backward. Both predators scrambled to their feet and faced one another. A burst of silver fury scattered the snow between them as the wolf charged again. The snarls of the wolf, carried on the wind, whipped around Nicholai.

The two forms blurred into one mass. Round and round they moved. Dark spots splattered on the snow. The unmistakable stench of animal heat and blood permeated the air. It sickened his stomach.

Nicholai doubled over when the wolf's claws struck home and sliced deep furrows across his stomach. Blood pooled at his feet and turned the snow a dark red as an unbearable pain burned across his midsection. Nicholai wrapped an arm around his waist, stumbled backward against a tree, and let it support him.

The wolf sniffed at the scent of his blood in the air once before turning toward Julie. The wolf became an explosion of silvery speed. A growl rumbled from its snarled lips. Julie threw up her uninjured arm just as it launched for her face, mouth open, sharp teeth exposed.

Fear closed Julie's eyes. She opened her mouth to scream, but no sound escaped from her throat. Nicholai summoned the last of his energy and reached the wolf in three long strides.

The yelp that sounded inches from her face brought open Julie's eyes. He spun the wolf by its tail and flung the animal aside. Its body made a satisfying smack when it hit against a thick tree trunk and slid to the ground. Nicholai staggered from the effort, one arm held tightly against his middle.

The wolf scrambled to her feet. Her breath coalesced in thick, white plumes in front of her muzzle as she dragged air into her lungs. She swayed a touch. The ribs must be broken, but the pain, rather than deterring her efforts, seemed to give her incentive to continue the attack. She stood her ground as he stalked toward her.

Nicholai moved forward on silent feet. With luck, he could finish this fight in one more move. Nicholai knew this battle needed to end fast before he lost the last of his strength due to the blood seeping from his flesh.

The beast leapt at him, feigning a strike at his thigh with her mouth. As Nicholai's hand reached down to intercept the muzzle, she pivoted in midair, sending her sharp claws out to rake his stomach. Her claws found the furrows in his flesh and followed their paths again, first with one mighty paw, then the other. Each swipe dug deeper. The final blow pierced through the last of his muscles.

The Alpha staggered backward and eyed the pink intestine spilling from his gut. Sweat beaded on his brow from the intense pain. This was the end. The wolf had managed a killing blow. Without blood to replenish him, his body would not recover from this injury. And his death would give the wolf the opportunity to kill Juliette. He must kill the beast before he succumbed to death.

Nicholai lunged at the wolf and caught it about the neck. Teeth nipped in his face as the animal struggled. He tightened his hold, one muscular forearm pinning its body against his, the other pinning its neck against his chest. Like castanets, the large teeth snapped, looking for skin.

The snarls and growls ceased. Its tongue lulled at the side of its mouth. It struggled for breath and shook viciously, trying to break free from Nicholai's hold. Its legs kicked madly in the air.

Nicholai struggled to keep the wolf against his frame until it went limp. He rose with the animal in his arms and slammed the wolf's body over his knee. An audible crack echoed in the night air. Nicholai threw the wolf away from him. It hit a snow-covered tree with such force that flakes from the branches rained down over the limp body.

Burning sweat rolled into his eyes. As he took a step toward the body, the agony of his stomach made his knees week. Julie stumbled toward Nicholai, and he quickly held his intestines in place with both hands.

"Nicholai, are you all right?"

He draped an arm about her shoulders. "I will admit, I've been better, but I'll live."

Wanting to distract her, he motioned toward the

animal with a nod of his head. "Look."

The snowy wolf blurred and rippled, warped into something else. Silvery fur turned into pale skin, hard muscles contorted into soft feminine curves.

"It's a woman," Julie gasped, looking down at the snow-covered form on the ground.

"That was no woman," Nicholai corrected. Pain made his voice raspy. "It was something else entirely. I'm just not sure what."

Nicholai's legs gave. The frozen ground bit into his knees when he went down, taking Julie with him. His heart beat throbbed in the wounds on his body.

"Nicholai!"

Pain stabbed at him, twisted his body until he lay flat on his back in the snow, looking up at Julie. His only concern, though, was for her. The beast might be dead, but she had wounds that needed tending. She needed to get to safety, but he would not be the one who got her there.

The shocked expression on her face twisted into concern for him. He wanted to comfort her, reach out to her, but his muscles would not obey. His vision blurred, the world went silent. He struggled to talk. The coming darkness swallowed the words. He floated away on the blackness, allowing it to take his pain with his consciousness.

Chapter 41

Julie knelt beside Nicholai. The instant his eyes closed, her mind registered his grave injuries. Her stomach twisted in knots, threatened to purge her dinner. Her throat constricted tight and tears clouded her eyes, making Nicholai a blurry mess of red. Panic rose, choked her breath. She hadn't realized how badly he'd been hurt.

Nicholai needed help desperately. The tears fell, allowing her to see the miles of bloody intestines that pushed from the gaping wound across his stomach. He didn't have much time. Julie looked around, not knowing what to do in the middle of the woods. Not even an animal occupied the space, their horse having long ago run off again in fear.

A phone, the thought came to her. *I can call for help.*

Out of habit, she scanned frantically for her purse, knowing her cell phone would be inside. When she remembered that she'd left the purse at the house, she chastised herself for the futile search.

Maybe Nicholai brought a phone.

She folded open the remains of his coat and anxiously patted the pocket of his jeans.

She found nothing in the first pocket. "Damn it!"

She patted her way across his legs until she discovered what she needed. Relief pulsed through her, giving her a ray of hope. Julie lifted her face toward the heavens. "Oh, thank you. Thank you!"

She worked the phone from the pocket soaked in blood. Her fingers turned red as she held it.

It was 9-1-1 in the States, 9-9-9 in England. What the hell was the emergency number in Russia? Had she bothered to learn that before getting on the plane to come here?

I didn't, she realized in terror.

Surely, Nicholai would have some numbers programmed into his phone. Perhaps one of them would be the emergency number.

Shit! She stared down at the Russian alphabet on the phone's display. *I can't read that.*

She pushed random buttons feverishly, hoping she might get lucky and hear it connect. A list appeared on the screen. She watched the highlight bar move south.

A contact list? Julie wondered.

Julie hit the green button, hoping that the tiny phone on the button meant that it was the Call Button. Her heart nearly beat from her chest with anticipation when it rang.

"*Privet*, Nicholai," a male voice greeted.

Juliette's hand clamped down on the phone. "*Vweetye*. Do you speak English?" she asked, her voice as shaky as the hand that held the phone.

"Who is this? Why do you have Nicholai's phone?" the deep voice demanded with a suspicious growl.

"Nicholai has been injured. He needs help. Can you help us?" Julie gushed.

A vile curse bellowed in her ear. "What has happened to Nicholai? Why did he not call me himself?"

"He's passed out. Hurry, he's injured, there's been an attack! He's dying!"

"Where are you?"

Julie glanced down on her lover, tears spilled onto Nicholai's face. "We are in the forest behind Nicholai's estate. Please, can you send help?"

"I'll be there in minutes. Do not leave him." The voice brooked no argument before the line went eerily silent.

****

Vladimir Starikovich scrubbed a rough hand over his stubbled head and stood. He quickly laced his biker boots, pulled on his leather jacket, and dematerialized to Nicholai's estate.

His form coalesced by the stables. He'd hunted in the forest with his fellow Alpha and knew the estate well. Vlad sent his awareness throughout the surrounding area until he sensed the fading energy of his friend next to the strong aura of a female. He homed in on their direction. The realization that his friend lay injured and unconscious in the woods with only a female to protect him spurred him to put on a burst of vampiric speed, and he took off for the forest with a curse.

****

A rustle in the trees caused Julie's heart to seem to leap into her throat. Was it another wolf? How could she protect Nicholai with a broken arm? It didn't matter. She'd die to protect him.

A dark figure emerged from the tree line. He advanced with purposeful strides. His long steps ate up the ground as he crossed the terrain toward her. He was tall, at least as tall as Nicholai. His sturdy face sported a dark goatee around a mouth set in a taut line. His black eyes held an intensity that made Julie cringe, but she didn't cower from him. Instead, her shoulders slumped with exhaustion as she realized assistance had finally arrived. Someone came to help, and by the looks of him, he'd have no problem getting Nicholai the help he needed.

Just in time too, she thought as Nicholai's body chilled beneath her hands where she kept them in a futile attempt to stay the rushing blood.

Julie pulled her hands from the bleeding wounds, waved her good arm and called, "Over here!"

She moved aside and knelt behind Nicholai's head. "He needs an ambulance."

The man knelt beside Nicholai's still form, assessing his injuries. His eyes lingered over the gravest injury. The intestines, now a gray color, didn't look good to Julie.

"No ambulance." His gruff voice grated on her. "He needs blood."

Julie nodded her head. "Yes, he needs a transfusion. He needs to get to a hospital."

The man's gaze pinned her, holding her eyes in his. "What is your name?"

Julie let out an exasperated sigh. They didn't have time for this. Nicholai needed a doctor now. His breath grew shallow. She was losing him.

"What is your name?" the man repeated.

"J-Julie."

"Ahhh. Nicholai's heartmate. Demetri mentioned you. So you are the woman who has taken Nicholai's good sense. No doubt he has you to thank for this."

"Can you help him?" she asked, not caring in this moment of life or death to examine his rudeness.

The man glanced down at the man she loved, concern furrowing his dark brows. "I can, but I'll need your help."

"Anything. I'd do anything for him. Just help him," Julie pleaded as she ran her fingers tenderly through Nicholai's hair.

"He needs blood."

The man grabbed her wrist and brought it to his mouth. He opened his lips, exposing his teeth.

Fangs! The guy has fangs! Is he another shape shifter? Julie gasped and tried in vain to pull her arm from his sturdy grasp.

He startled at her reaction. "He needs your blood to strengthen him. Why do you hesitate?"

The set of fangs that shown white in the moonlight against the man's lips riveted Julie. He was about to bite her...with his fangs! Juliette's voice eluded her.

"*Chyort voz'mi,*" Vlad cursed. "Do you want to help him or not?"

Help. Yes, they needed help. If this man was like the beast that had attacked them, he wouldn't be trying to help, Julie reasoned. She summoned her courage and nodded slowly.

"Then he needs your blood. Let me open your vein so you can feed him."

The threat snapped Julie's voice back into place. "You want to feed him my blood! Are you mad?"

"Of course, I want to feed him your blood. It will heal him. Do you have a problem with that?"

Julie tried again to pull her arm from his fingers. The effort was futile. "What are you talking about? He needs a transfusion. You can't absorb blood by drinking it."

The stranger lifted a questioning brow. "Do you not know what Nicholai is?"

"Again, what are you talking about?"

"Nicholai is a vampire."

Julie flinched at the word. *I am in the middle of nowhere with the man I love dying, and the one person who I called to help is insane and obviously has no intention of helping Nicholai. What am I going to do now?* Her thoughts flew through her head. Should she run for help, leaving her dying lover behind with a madman? Should she play along with this man's insane fantasy hoping at some point he'd leave? Perhaps she could talk him into seeing reason. *Not likely*, her inner voice admonished.

"Listen to me, Julie." The man's voice dropped an octave.

Julie's full attention snapped from her chaotic thoughts to the man kneeling beside her. Her mind went blank, and she sat motionless awaiting his next command.

"Nicholai is a vampire, as am I. I am sure he would have preferred to break the news to you himself, but he didn't, and I don't have time to wait for you to grow accustomed to the idea. You will allow me to open your vein, and you will allow Nicholai to feed from you."

Juliette nodded her head in earnest, sending her tousled locks flowing around her face. She pushed her arm toward the man.

He bent over her wrist and scored it with his fangs, then placed it over Nicholai's parted lips and stroked his throat, triggering his swallowing reflex. Julie's blood dripped into Nicholai's mouth.

Nicholai's eyes fluttered. His hand grabbed Julie's arm and held it to his mouth. He took long draws from her wrist. Each one brought him back to life.

Julie swayed, her energy waning. Her heart ached with its struggle to beat.

"You can't give him any more," Julie vaguely heard the stranger say just before the fog cleared from her mind.

"Sleep now, Nicholai. You need to heal."

Julie immediately came back to herself. *Nicholai is a vampire.* The stranger's dark voice replayed in her thoughts.

Images flickered through her mind like old moving pictures through a Kinetoscope. Their first date where he made the comment about being older; the portrait in the palace that looked so much like Nicholai; Nicholai somehow crossing the room at the palace to save her; Nicholai appearing in her bed after her nightmare; his use of the term heartmate; the way he fought with the wolf at inhuman speed; the way he had been drinking from her arm as she came back to herself just now. Her eyes focused on the slashes across his stomach. The intestines pinked up and the filleted skin knitted together before her astonished eyes.

It all coalesced in Julie's mind, fitting together like a 3D jigsaw puzzle, creating a handsome vampire with black hair and amber eyes.

A vampire known as Nicholai.

Chapter 42

Jara sashayed into the bedroom, floating on cloud nine. Everything was coming together. Lane had recently completed his lab in the new compound, and it was ready to receive a vampire when they caught one. Now if they just found a vampire, they would be all set.

Perhaps Lovazia would be able to help. She had found a female vampire after all. And where there was one, there was bound to be others. Not to mention, she supposed she should check in with her sister.

She grabbed the phone from the table and dialed her sister's number. The call went straight to voicemail.

Odd, thought Jara, *it's not like Lovazia to have her phone off.*

Jara left her sister a message, asking her to call her as soon as possible. As she clicked off the phone, a knock sounded at the door. When she opened it, Caden stood on the other side, his face downfallen.

"What's wrong?" she asked.

"I have some news. Perhaps you should sit down." The guard pushed into the room and closed the door behind him.

"I don't want to sit. Tell me what's wrong," Jara demanded, then crossed her arms around her waist in a reassuring hug.

Caden had never looked so grim. "I…uh…"

"Well, come out with it. What do you need to tell

me?"

"I have two things, actually."

Jara threw her hands up in the air. "I don't have all night. Spit it out."

Caden shifted his weight to the other foot. "The Queen and I were talking the other day about her excursion into town."

That little twit. "I heard about the outing. She probably brought some disease back into the compound."

"I don't know about that." Caden shrugged. "But she said something that got my attention."

"Go on."

"Well, she happened to mention that she ran into a big man. A real monster. Tall guy, lots of muscles."

Too bad he didn't eat her like a good monster would.

"Why should I care?" asked Jara.

"Because she said that he reeked. She almost gagged."

Now that piqued her interest. "He reeked, you said?"

Caden's blond hair swayed when he nodded his head. "That's what she said. I'm thinking we should check it out. There might be a vampire right here in Mason's Bluff?"

Hope blossomed in her chest. If this was his first bit of news, she couldn't wait to hear the rest. "You said you had two things to tell me, what is the other?"

The guard looked like he wanted to vomit.

"You should sit down." Caden escorted her toward the bed. "I received a call from Shira. She had been touring Russia with Lovazia. There was a fight."

"I know," Jara interrupted. "Lovazia told me she found a vampire. I just tried to call her to see if there might be a male nearby. We need to find one for Lane."

"Jara," Caden's voice dropped low, interrupting her ramble. "Lovazia is dead."

"What? Impossible!" The female demon's voice resonated with disbelief. "She can't be dead. A female vampire shouldn't have been much of a match for her."

Jara's stomach knotted, and she worried dinner might reappear.

"Apparently it was. Shira found her body lying naked in a forest. It would seem the vampire killed her."

Shock took Jara's legs, and she sat down hard on the bed. Caden sat beside her and drew her under his arm. Tears fell from her eyes, wetting his shirt as he held her.

"I don't understand. How did this happen?"

"I don't know."

Pain ripped through her. The loss weighed heavy on her shoulders. Another loved one gone. How many must she bear? How much grief could one demon endure?

"Damn vampires!" Jara shouted. "First they take her mate, then they take her. I make a vow here and now that there will be no more demons lost at the hands of the vampires. I will do everything I can to see they are wiped from the earth."

Caden rubbed his hand up and down her arm in a comforting gesture. "What can you do, Jara? You are but one demon."

Jara pushed away from his strong embrace and wiped the tears from her cheeks, determination straightening her spine. "Oh, there's plenty I can do, especially with Lane's help. The vampire race will regret the day they waged war on demon kind by killing one of the ruling family."

****

Julie's eyes followed the white bead-board paneling on the walls to the simple wooden mantel over the fireplace. From the white wicker chair, Julie stared absently across the room as she ran a hand through her dog's fur. Murmuring something Julie did not catch, Penny reclined across from her on one of the flowered upholstery couches. Connor sat at her feet on the blue rug, acknowledging her affection with the thumping of his tail. She turned on the Tiffany lamp, then propped her feet on the coffee table between the magazines and a book.

The blood-soaked images of the past twenty-four hours played through Julie's mind. The scary vampire that had emerged from the forest and forced her to give her blood—taking her free will as easily as taking candy from the proverbial baby. Her lover lay dying before her eyes. His body chilled beneath her fingers as she worked to stop the flow of the blood. The memory of awakening from a trance to find Nicholai feeding on her had all been too much.

She rubbed her hand over the cast on her arm and noted the bruises on her wrist left by Vlad's fingers. They had clamped around her arm as he dragged her back to the estate with Nicholai hanging limply over one shoulder. Scared, unsure what was real or safe, Julie had tried to run from the brutish man only to have him catch her. He commanded her to sit by Nicholai's bed, forced her to watch his wounds knit together

348

unnaturally before her eyes.

A virus causes the vampiric change...You're safe...you must be converted...no choice because you are his heartmate. Memories of Vlad's words sounded in her mind. Perspiration had dotted her forehead when she balked at the conversion. Vladimir had made it clear she would have no choice in the matter.

That had been her tipping point.

When Vlad went to sleep, Julie snuck from the mansion, stole one of Nicholai's cars, and hopped on the first flight out of Russia. Apparently, the lore about vampires not being able to go out in the daylight must be true, because no one had followed her or tried to stop her as she made her escape in broad daylight.

With the evening settling in now, her panic rose. Would Vlad come for her? Did he know where she lived? She'd told Nicholai where she lived. Were vampires psychic? Could Vladimir pull the information from Nicholai's mind?

She had discovered their secret. They were vampires. Surely, Vlad would come for her if he could find her.

Julie blinked and focused on the bottle hovering in front of her face.

"Here, you look like you need this." Penny thrust the pint of beer into Julie's hand before turning to retake her seat on the couch.

Connor jumped up beside the pregnant blonde and rooted on the cushions, then curled into a tight ball.

Penny absently rubbed the top of his head as she spoke. "You've barely said two words since you got back. What happened, Jules?"

"I don't want to talk about it." Julie took a swig

from the green bottle.

Penny kicked off her shoes and tucked her bare feet underneath her. "Come on, I'm your best friend. You can tell me. Did Nicholai break your heart? Did he cheat on you?"

Hmmm, break her heart. *In a way*, Juliette thought. Her dream man, the man she'd given her heart to, had turned into a nightmare, a blood-sucking and soulless monster of a nightmare right before her eyes. A monster that had monstrous friends, who would make her like him. Yes. Her heart was broken.

The person she had thought Nicholai was died in the woods last night, and her heart grieved the loss. She couldn't stand losing another man she loved. Served her right though. She had known he was too good to be true. It had been right to fight her attraction to him. She had soiled the memory of her husband. And for what?

For an abomination of nature.

Her stomach churned at the thought, and the beer threatened reappearance.

If she were honest, she still cared for the man she thought she knew. Seeing him lying on the frozen ground, bleeding into the snow, had been more than she could bear.

"He didn't cheat on me, but we're done."

Penny gave her a pitiful look. "I'm so sorry, Jules. I really thought you'd found love."

"I did, too." She had felt so fortunate to find love a second time. To watch it slip from her grasp had been unbearable.

With the revelations from that creature, Vlad, her mind steeled against a future with Nicholai. How could they be together? She'd be lucky if he let her live. Then again, what did she really have to live for now?

"You'll find someone," Penny assured her.

"Twice fate has taken love from me. I don't want to ever go through that kind of loss again."

She would never allow herself to love again. Never! It hurt too much. Perhaps it would be a blessing if Vlad showed up to take her life or at least her memories. Could vampires erase memories?

The sound of her doorbell whipped her from the melancholy thoughts. Her heart raced. Was it Vlad? Nicholai?

Before she found the words to stop her friend, Penny opened the door wide. A grateful breath hissed from between Julie's lips when she discovered Desmond in the doorway. He looked dapper in his tailored suit, his white-collared shirt unbuttoned low enough to expose his muscular chest, giving him a dressy-casual look of a model.

"How was your vacation?" Her neighbor shut the door behind him.

Suddenly Desmond froze mid stride, his eyes and nostrils widening in unison. A pang of remorse stabbed Juliette's heart when his expression eerily reminded her of the two vampires she'd left behind in Russia.

Great. Now I'm seeing vampires everywhere. I must be losing my mind, she decided as Desmond gave Connor a pet on his head.

"Don't ask," Penny muttered and plopped back down on the couch.

Desmond sat in the wicker chair beside Julie, eyeing her warily. "That bad?"

His tone sounded casual, but his observant gaze raked her face as if searching for the answer she was

351

reluctant to give.

Julie nodded and downed the rest of her beer in one long gulp. The handsome actor stood and sauntered to the kitchen. He plucked three bottles from the fridge. They clinked together as he strolled back, then handed one of the bottles to Julie.

"None for me." Penny patted her stomach. "I'm pregnant."

Desmond sat. "Julie mentioned that. Congratulations."

"Thanks." Penny flashed him a smile that quickly faded as she watched Juliette tip the bottle to her lips and drink the contents in a single, long drawl.

"You could say it was a bad trip." Julie set the empty bottle down a little too forcefully on the coffee table. The loud clunk made Connor jump.

"I guess so, judging by how you downed that pint. Want to talk about it?" Desmond balanced his own bottle on his knee.

"Not really. Sufficed to say, I won't be going back to Russia soon."

Penny's brows lifted questioningly. "I'm sure it can't be as bad as all that. A few days might give you a new perspective."

Julie snorted rudely at the suggestion. "I doubt that. An entire lifetime could not give me a new perspective."

"Come on. Talking it out might help. Tell us what happened." Penny reached for Julie's hand.

Julie shook her head. If she told Penny what happened, the vampires might come after her. Hurt her and the baby. Julie would not be responsible for something like that. She couldn't have any more death in her life.

"Look, I'll say this. Nicholai isn't what I thought he was."

Desmond's brow furrowed with concern. The corners of his mouth turned down before he looked at Penny.

"Penny," he said, his voice dropping low. He waited until she made eye contact before he continued. "I think you should leave. I'd like to talk to our friend in private."

Penny's eyes went hazy. Without a word, she obediently rose, donned her shoes and coat, and left. Desmond waited until the car left the drive before he turned to Julie.

Julie's eyes widened when he turned the force of his gaze on her. She recognized that look, had seen the same one on Vlad before her world went blank. She screamed, making Connor jump to her defense. When she rose, the dog moved between her and Desmond.

Julie backed away. Desmond put his hands up in the air as if he was unarmed. However, she knew better. He might not have a weapon, but if he was anything like Vlad, his powers were weapons enough.

"Julie," he spoke softly, his voice deep and soothing. "Come back and sit down. I'll not hurt you."

Her mind went fuzzy, and her feet moved of their own volition, taking her back to the wicker chair. Her senses returned when her bottom lowered onto the cushioned seat. She pushed out of the chair and turned on her longtime confidant.

"Don't do that."

"Do what?" He shrugged innocently.

"Do that thing with your voice." She gave herself a

bracing hug. "You're one of them."

"What do you mean?" The puzzled look on his face made her take stock. Was she wrong about Desmond being a vampire? Maybe her mind was playing tricks.

No. He had all the signs. Too good-looking, too graceful, that nose thing they all seemed to do as if they were taking in the world by smell, that hypnotic voice. No doubt about it. Desmond was one of them.

"I mean, you are a vampire," she whispered, wishing her voice sounded stronger.

Desmond eyed her for a long moment as if sizing her up. His brows narrowed. "A vampire?"

"Come off it. I know all about the existence of vampires."

"Exactly what do you think you know?" His voice sounded calm, but Julie got the sense that underneath the exterior he presented lay a vicious predator.

"I-I just know about them," Julie stammered, backing away to stand by the fireplace. Her hand found its way down to the poker. She grabbed it tight and held it down by her side.

Desmond's observant gaze took in the weapon. "Now, Julie, if I am a vampire, do you honestly think the poker would do you any good?"

Julie's heart raced, and fear flooded her body. He was right. She had seen the strength Vlad showed. If all vampires were that strong, then she had no hope of getting a hit on Desmond. She leaned the poker back against the fireplace.

"That's better, love. Come back and sit down," he purred, patting the cushion of the chair next to him. "We have much to discuss."

Chapter 43

Desmond and Julie had been talking through the night. He'd confessed he was indeed a vampire, then explained vampires were not undead creatures of the night. They were not soulless. Instead, most were products of an infection, a virus that changed their DNA in such a way their bodies required they drink blood. To hear him explain it, vampires were little more than victims of a plague.

When her dog rolled over languidly with a toothy yawn, Julie obligingly scratched his belly. "So basically, you are plague victims."

"Not exactly. Vampires are far from sickly, feeble mortals. In fact, just the opposite. A vampire can snap a human in two without trying, and we live very healthy, long lives. In fact, we are immune to disease."

When Julie didn't reply, he continued, "Tell me what happened in Russia, Julie."

She stiffened. Each time he pressed her about her holiday, she had said as little as possible.

"Someone tried to kill me," she finally admitted.

"A vampire attacked you?" His statement came out more like a question.

"I really need some time, Des. I need to process what happened before I talk about it," she said, too tired to examine the events of the past few weeks.

"I'll let it be for tonight. But one thing before we

drop this—are you frightened of me?"

She had known Desmond for years. To discover he was a vampire, put the breed into some perspective. Desmond wasn't evil. He was a good friend. He cared about her. If he was a vampire, then perhaps being a vampire was not as awful as the movies made it seem.

She smiled for the first time since returning to England. "No. I'm not scared of you."

Juliette did a quick comparison of Desmond and Nicholai. Both had good lives, both seemed respectable, both appeared to care for her, one as a friend and the other as a lover. Perhaps vampires weren't all so bad.

Before Julie completed her train of thought, Desmond leaned over and patted her thigh. "Good. Come on, love, let's get you pissed. You'll forget all about that nasty business in Russia."

"Getting drunk won't help."

"But it can't hurt either." Desmond handed her another beer. "Now first things first. Let's fix that arm of yours."

****

Nicholai's eyes fluttered. His lashes batted the long wisps of bangs hanging over his eyelids. His vision cleared on Vlad who sat beside him. Memories flashed through his mind: blood, screams, jaws filled with razor-sharp teeth. Claws ripping into his flesh, fangs sinking into his sinew. The chill of death spreading as his life drained away. And through all the pain, a soft frightened voice, begging him not to leave. *Juliette!*

Nicholai bound from the bed and swayed on his feet. Vlad moved beside him instantly and placed a steadying hand on his elbow. "Hold on, my friend. Take it slow. You've been out a long time."

Nicholai turned, desperation narrowing his eyes. "How is my Juliette? Is she all right? She was injured. I must go to her."

"You must sit down." Vladimir gave him a gentle push toward the bed.

Nicholai spun out from under Vlad's large hand and marched to the door of the bedroom. He flung it wide. It creaked on its hinges from the force as his strides took him down the hall toward the guestroom his mate used.

He pushed the door open and his brows furrowed. The room remained perfect, pristine white, everything in its place. Only one thing missing…*Juliette*. His gaze fell to the table by the bed. There sat the heart-shaped pendant draped around the *matryoshka* he'd given her.

His heart seemed to sink to his toes when he lifted the Russian dolls from the table.

His senses flowed throughout the home, in search of his mate. Down the stairs, into every room. Finding no sign of her, he pushed farther still, out onto the grounds, past the stables, into the woods. He pushed until he swayed from exhaustion.

"You need to sit down," Vlad repeated.

Nicholai rounded on him, fists clenched. "Where is she?"

"I have no idea, my friend."

Nicholai traversed the room in three angry strides. His face heated with ire. "What do you mean, you don't know?"

"When I awoke, she was gone."

Nicholai paced the snowy carpet. "Did someone grab her? She's been under attack."

Vlad shook his head. "That is unlikely. Her clothes

and belongings are missing."

Nicholai crossed to the closet and ripped the door from its hinges in his haste. Sure enough her clothing was gone along with her suitcase. He crashed into the bathroom. Her personal items were absent as well.

Vladimir's gaze followed him when Nicholai emerged from the bath and sat on the bed in utter defeat.

"Why? Why did she leave me?" Nicholai lay on the bed, burying his face in the pillows that held the scent of his heartmate. He breathed deeply, took in the delicate lilac scent.

Had he not provided for her? Had he not proven his love to her? He'd fought for her, saved her not once but twice. How could she leave him, knowing he'd been injured? He refused to believe she would be so cold. To leave without saying goodbye, to leave without knowing if he would live or die. Those were not the actions of a heartmate.

A heartmate should remain by his side forever loving and caring for him. He was supposed to be the most important thing in his heartmate's life. A heartmate put their other half above all else. Yet his mate had done exactly the opposite. Run from him when he had needed her most.

Vladimir sat beside him on the bed and laid a hand on his shoulder. "Do not despair, friend. She will return to you. She must, for she is your mate."

Nicholai glanced up. Agony tore at his heart. "Do you know why she left?"

"We should go to the kitchen to talk. This will be a long story, and you need to feed."

Reluctantly, Nicholai nodded his agreement as

hunger pangs burned his stomach.

When the two males settled themselves in the kitchen, Nicholai forced down three bags of blood while Vlad shared the events of the past days. Nicholai learned Julie had called for help and stayed over him, protecting him as he lay dying in her arms.

Those were the actions of a heartmate. "So why did she leave?" Nicholai inquired around the top of a bag.

"You needed blood. After I told her what we are, she panicked. She was reluctant to feed you. I had no choice but to force her compliance, or you would have died."

Rage boiled within his veins. Knowing Vladimir, he'd manhandled Julie and scared the shit out of her. He pushed the emotion down, realizing getting mad would not make anything better.

Needing some fresh air, Nicholai pushed through the back door. He stared blankly over the white landscape. His home felt empty. Never had he been so alone. His heart was broken, ripped from his chest. It remained with the woman he loved, wherever that was.

"Do you have any idea where she went?" he asked Vlad when the Alpha joined him outside.

"I'm not sure. As I said, when I awoke, she'd left."

"Perhaps she went back to England."

"That would be a logical assumption."

"I should go to her. See if I can persuade her to return."

"I would give her a little while. Nothing makes a female crave her mate like being separated from him."

"But she needs my protection."

"Did you not kill the thing that came after her?"

Nicholai contemplated the question. He had fought

the wolf that turned into a woman and killed it. What had that thing been?

He had lived many centuries and seen much in his long life, but he had never run into a shape-shifter before. He thought werewolves were things of folklore. Perhaps they *were* real.

Nicholai's shoulders stiffened when he noticed a shadow slinking across the property along the tree line. The animal's black pelt glistened with flakes of snow. A dusting of the stuff coated its muzzle.

"It's another shifter," he whispered. His muscles tensed to pounce.

Vlad's hand rested heavily on his shoulder. "No, you are wrong. It is only a wolf. Do not hurt it."

"How do you know it is not a shifter?"

"I can tell," he replied cryptically. Noting Nicholai's doubtful look, he continued, "I touched its mind. It is a wolf."

Nicholai sent his senses out for anything unusual. He found nothing, no blank spots. No Juliette. Her absence left him bereft.

"I cannot believe she is gone. Why were you so highhanded with my mate?" Nicholai demanded, turning on Vladimir.

"I simply told her the truth. I did not know you had not yet told her about our kind."

Nicholai paced to work off some of his pent-up rage. "I was waiting until she had admitted she loved me. I wanted to hear her say the words, admit to herself as much as to me she cared. Then I would have sat her down and explained everything. It would have been perfect. I would have been gentle, careful not to frighten her." Anger heated his ears, and he pinned

Vlad with an intense stare. "But instead, you had to ruin everything. What am I going to do?"

Under Vladimir's watchful gaze, Nicholai blinked away unshed tears.

"She is afraid, Nicholai. Once she has time to think things through, she will return. I am sure of it."

Nicholai's gaze remained unfocused as he stared once more out into the distance. "I hope you are right, because without her, I don't want to go on."

Chapter 44

A scream tore from her throat, jarring Juliette awake. Without delay, Desmond Wright's strong arms drew her to his side. Though the confinement initially sent a shiver of fear through her, she fought the feeling and wrapped an arm around his lean waist.

"It's okay, Julie. You are safe with me." The sound of Desmond's voice sent a calming sensation through her mind.

He'd spent every evening with Julie since her return from Russia. Mostly they sat, as they did now, in the living room with a movie playing. It mattered not what they did; only that he was there.

"You haven't been sleeping well. Those dark circles under your eyes, the way your face looks drawn, all say you need more sleep." Desmond held her head to his shoulder.

"I wish I could. I'm due back at work tomorrow. Since I returned home, I haven't slept more than two hours a night. Every time I fall asleep, I see—"

Dread fell over her as memories of Nicholai's injured body, lying broken and bloody, filled her mind.

"I know, love."

It had been almost a week since she had left Russia, but her experiences there remained. Her mind, fretting over the trauma she had been through, would not let her rest peacefully.

"I don't want to talk about it."

"I could protect you better if you gave me more details. You've hardly shared much other than you were attacked multiple times in Russia. I don't want to push you, but I'm afraid a vampire might be after you. That would explain the scent on your clothes your first night home. It would also explain an incident that occurred while you were gone when I came to check on Connor and found him locked in the bathroom. Someone had obviously been in the house. Not to scare you, but as I entered your bedroom, I spied a black wisp of smoke wafting in the air."

"The thing that attacked me is dead," Julie offered.

"But there might be others working with him. I'd feel better with more information."

"Desmond, I realize you are trying to help, but reliving it won't help me. I'm trying to put this whole thing behind me and forget about it. I'm sure the thing is dead."

"I consider you under my care and protection, and I take the responsibility quite seriously. I'll not push you, but know this, I'll be keeping watch, ready for an attack should one come. I'll defend you with my last breath for I love you like a sister."

He hugged her tight, and she cuddled against him, believing every word. He'd never let anything happen to her. It reassured Julie, even if she believed the danger had been managed.

Julie pushed her hair away from her face and took a deep breath. The luscious scent of roses filled her lungs, bringing with it thoughts of love lost.

Two dozen roses had arrived almost every day since she'd left Russia. She'd delivered most of the bouquets from Nicholai to the local hospital, but one she kept, unable to share it with anyone else. The bouquet contained a poem. The endearing words and striking alliterations had expressed the depth of Nicholai's love for her in a way nothing else could.

Tears burned her eyes as the rosy perfume filled her nose. She believed his declaration of love, did not doubt the depth of his feelings for her, but the love for her husband, coupled with a fear of being thrown again into the icy depths of grief and despair by losing another man she loved, kept her from reaching out to him.

Julie looked up at Desmond. His face blurred with her tears when he spoke.

"I can sense your sorrow. It might help if you talk about it."

"Not now," she whispered.

Desmond nodded as if he had expected the answer, and Julie burrowed into his shoulder.

Connor leapt onto the flowery couch beside them. The large dog turned several circles before he settled and took up most of the couch as he laid his muzzle on his crossed paws. Julie absently stroked his fur, seeking the comfort that came from a canine friend who would love her no matter what.

Love. Unconditional love.

Nicholai had offered her that. He had been understanding, never pushed her. He'd allowed her time to accept her love for him. He had been gentle, always loving her with his words and actions, in addition to his body.

Tears fell from her eyes, wetting Desmond's shirt, and she remembered Nicholai's romantic words, heartfelt words she didn't doubt he meant. He loved her with all his heart, and her consternation had thrown it all away.

Thanks to Desmond, she now understood like humans, some vampires were good and others evil. They were not soulless, undead monsters. Desmond convinced her not all of them needed to be feared. But could she love one?

Being with Nicholai felt like being home. With him all things seemed possible. He'd made her believe she was sexy, beautiful, like she was the only woman in the world. With him, she felt desirable and cherished.

And she had thrown it all away. She could never face him again. He deserved much better than she could ever give him. She was a broken soul, damaged goods, and he should have someone every bit as perfect as him. Surely he would eventually tire of her, move on, and find the perfect woman. She only needed the strength to hold out a little longer against the overwhelming urge to go to him.

Pulled from her contemplation, Julie jumped when the phone rang.

"Don't answer that," she commanded.

Desmond settled back against the couch. "Why not? It might be important."

"I know who it is. I don't want to talk."

"No kidding. I could take a message."

The ringing came to a halt. "See, Des. It stopped."

She knew exactly who had been on the other end of the line. It was the person who had called most every day since she'd left.

If she could just stay away, life would go on without him. Eventually the roses would stop coming, her phone would no longer have messages from him.

Seeing him lying on the frozen ground, his paleness matching the snow around them, had been too much. Better to cut him out of her life now than to have him ripped violently from her after years of loving him.

And really, it was best for him too. The logic sounded feeble, even to her, but she'd go with it.

He would be better off without her. And she would do what was best for Nicholai. He had almost *died* because of her.

They were total opposites. He was wealthy, she was a teacher. He was strong, powerful, overwhelming, and she was...not. Even if they got past all that, how long could a relationship with him possibly last?

No. A future wasn't possible, and if she held out a little longer, Nicholai would eventually realize that.

****

Nicholai slammed the phone down, then stalked across the room and stared out the window of his office. His gaze roamed over the grounds. The wind whipped through the bare trees, and their spindly branches sent shadows dancing over the snowy land.

It had been a series of torturous days since Juliette left his home. Days that left him empty and alone. He'd been seeking contact with her, touched her mind now and then to assure himself she lived. However, it was not enough. He needed to be with her, feel her there next to him.

His body needed her as much as his mind did. His heart, his very bones, ached from her loss. The other half of his soul was gone. It made him nearly mad with need for her.

Juliette. Her name sent a stab of pain into his gut.

Desperate to hear the soft sweet sound in his ears once more, he called her several times a day, hoping just once she might pick up the phone. He'd been tempted to communicate through their mindlink, but for now she obviously wanted no communication from him or she would have returned his calls. Therefore, he would stay a quiet shadow in her mind.

He let the windowsill take his weight as he rested both palms on the marble. He needed to find a way to win her back. Every day he sent her flowers, each time professing his love for her on a card. Nicholai did not want to push, but he was not sure how much longer he could stand not being near her.

Surely she felt the same way. How could she not when she was his mate? In the recesses of her mind, she admitted her love for him. He had seen her concern for his safety, her fear for him the night he had fought the shape-shifter for her. But he also saw her self-doubt, her fear of allowing herself to love yet another man who might be taken from her one day. Those fears had kept him at bay these past days.

He needed a new plan, a way to win her. His mind raced through the possibilities, discarding each idea as it came until finally he decided on an option. It might be risky, but then being with Juliette was worth any risk.

A smile spread across his face for the first time since he had awakened to find his heartmate gone. He knew exactly what to do.

Chapter 45

A knock at the door drew everyone's attention. Connor bounded off the couch with a loud series of warning barks.

"Expecting someone?" Desmond rose to his feet.

Juliette stood and placed a hand on the vampire's forearm. "It's probably another flower delivery. I'll get it."

Julie went to the door. After threading one hand through Connor's collar to restrain him, she reached for the knob.

As she opened it, Desmond yelled, "Get back, Julie! I recognized that scent. That is the vampire who attacked you."

She had only a second to realize Nicholai stood in the doorway before Desmond's powerful thighs brought him to the door in a single bound.

He grabbed Nicholai's shirt with one hand, his other made a fist that landed squarely on Nicholai's jaw.

Nicholai's head snapped back. Shock took his face. With a mighty push, Nicholai threw Desmond backward across the room into one of the flowery couches. It moved under his weight, crashed into the end table, and the Tiffany lamp tumbled to the floor.

Julie's eyes went wide. The two men became a blur of motion, bodies flying apart, then back together. She had to concentrate to make out the shapes of hard forms in the powerful whirlwind.

Connor pulled, lunging at the whirling mass. His deep growls and barks added to the chaos as the two males swirled around the living room. They spun around the room like a tornado, moving so fast Juliette's eyes did not register their kicks and punches. However, she heard bones crunch and the slap of skin while the two exchanged blows.

The furniture that exploded when the blurry mass neared evidenced the fierceness of their battle. Julie watched one piece of furniture after the next burst into pieces. First her delicate coffee table, next the end table where the Tiffany lamp had been, then the rocking chair. When the mass moved toward the antique credenza, Juliette screamed.

Her beautiful roses sprayed about the room. Red petals floated slowly to the floor in surreal contrast to the fast and furious movements of the fighters.

The activity drove Connor to a fevered pitch. She barely kept him out of harm's way. Wanting to be a part of the action, the dog strained against the hold on his collar.

A body flew toward her, and she jumped sideways to avoid it. As she leapt, something caught her foot and knocked her off balance. She landed on one knee. Unfortunately, the rug provided little padding.

Before she registered who had flown toward her, the two men were a blur again. When Julie stood, she lost her grip on Connor's collar. To her surprise, the dog did not move. A ridge rose along his back as if he sensed something, something that kept him away from the action.

Power built in the room. It prickled over her skin, making the hairs stand on end. Suddenly a powerful blast sent the two males flying in opposite directions. Desmond came to rest in a crumpled heap inside the fireplace. The bricks deteriorated over his slumped form while Nicholai slammed into the wall and the plaster cocooned around him.

A quick glance between the two assured Julie both were stunned but conscious. She took advantage of the momentary cease-fire and stepped in front of Nicholai.

"Stop!" she commanded and held up a hand toward Des. "I love him! Don't hurt him!"

In surround sound, the two vampires asked, "What did you say?"

"I said don't hurt him," Julie repeated, looking down at Desmond where he lay slumped and bloody on the floor.

Nicholai peeled himself free from the wall and turned Juliette by the shoulders. "No, before that. What did you say?" he softly asked, his eyes searching hers.

Julie cupped a hand to his bruised cheek and carefully wiped a trickle of blood from the corner of his mouth with her thumb. "I said, I love you."

Nicholai pulled her into his strong embrace. "How I have longed to hear those words from your lips. You make my heart sing with a joy I have never experienced in all my long centuries of life."

Julie wrapped her arms around Nicholai's narrow waist and held him tight. In that moment, she knew she belonged with him. It had been wrong to fight their relationship. This felt right, being in his arms again, professing her love for him. She wanted to stay like this forever. Be with him forever.

Nicholai ran his hand down her hair. "My heartmate, you honored me with your proclamation."

Desmond rolled onto his hands and knees and Connor licked the wounds on his face. He gave the dog a gentle nudge, then stood stiffly, brushing the pulverized brick dust off his jeans. "Did you say heartmate?"

Nicholai threw a stabbing glare in his direction and maneuvered Julie behind him. "Juliette is mine. She is my heartmate. Who the hell are you?"

Desmond straightened his shoulders, ignoring the question. "If she is your heartmate, why did you attack her?"

Julie stepped out from behind her love and noticed their wounds healed before her eyes.

Nicholai's brow furrowed in confusion. "What do you mean *attacked her*? I never assaulted her. I would never hurt Juliette."

"But I thought…Perhaps I jumped to the wrong conclusion." Desmond had the decency to look contrite. "I thought he was here to harm you, Julie."

"Why in the world would you think that?" Julie asked.

"In all fairness, it's not like you gave me all the important information. You'd been attacked. I believed you were still in danger. When he showed up, I realized he was the vampire I'd found evidence of in your home while you were gone."

Julie raised her hand. "Hold up. What? Nicholai came here while I was in Russia?"

Nicholai nodded. "I admit I came here, but I had a good reason that I'll share later once we're alone, if you'll permit me." As if wanting to change the subject and fast, Nicholai continued, "You have impressive skills, Desmond. Where did you learn to fight like that?"

A wide smile took Desmond's handsome face as he ran a hand through his brown hair. "I honed my skills during the decades I spent studying martial arts in Asia. But what about you? Where did you learn moves like that?"

Nicholai stood in contemplative silence. His eyes narrowed slightly as if he were sizing up Desmond. "The Alpha Council."

"The what?" Julie asked.

Desmond, on the other hand, must have known exactly what the Alpha Council meant for his eyes widened, and he straightened a little like he'd just been informed he stood in the presence of royalty. "You are a member?"

Nicholai nodded. "I am. Perhaps we should sit down so I can explain."

Nicholai released his mate to upright two of the unbroken chairs in the room. He placed them across from one another. While Desmond sat in one, Nicholai sat with Julie on his lap in the other and proceeded to explain that the Council was an elite group of vampires who protected the world from evil.

Julie took the information in stride. It all made sense. Nicholai was the man, no vampire, she corrected herself, that she knew him to be. Kind, loving, regal. A protector. A perfect lover. "So that makes you my Alpha Lover," she quipped, making both men laugh.

Desmond stroked his chin. "But if you aren't the one who attacked Jules, then who did?"

"Nicholai didn't attack me, DW," Juliette informed

her friend. "Nicholai saved me."

Julie pushed away from her lover and situated herself between the two males as she explained. "It was a woman who hurt me. A woman who turned into a wolf."

"A werewolf?" Desmond's dark brow rose. "I was not aware of the existence of such a thing."

Nicholai wrapped his arms around Julie's waist and drew her back against his hard chest. "She may not have been a werewolf. She may have been a shape-shifter of some kind. We are not exactly sure what she was."

Juliette turned her head to look at Nicholai. "So a shape-shifter came after me?" It was more of a question than a statement.

"The Alpha Council believes it is possible, *lastochka*."

"Is Julie still in danger then?"

Nicholai gave her waist a squeeze. "I would like to think not, but I am not sure."

Desmond leaned forward. "With the possible threat out there, I assume you'll be converting as soon as possible, Julie."

"Converting? You mean become a vampire?"

"That is what it means, Juliette." Nicholai's hand moved to the nape of her neck and gave it a comforting massage.

It was a one-way deal. There would be no going back, and she didn't want to rush the decision. "I need some time to consider becoming a vampire."

"Of course you do, *lastochka*. Take all the time you need. I will not put any pressure on you. There are many benefits to the conversion such as long life, strength, and speed, but the process is painful. I want you to be sure you are unwavering in the decision before I convert you."

Julie gave him a tight hug. "I appreciate your patience. I'll tell you when I'm ready."

"I wouldn't wait too long, Jules," Desmond suggested.

"I took care of the shape-shifter, so we can wait a little while. For now, the threat is gone." Nicholai's hand ran over her thigh in a loving gesture that sent heat spiraling through her belly. Obviously sensing her response, hunger leapt into his eyes.

"Well, it's time I take my leave," Desmond offered. "I'm entrusting my friend to you, Nicholai. Take care of her."

The couple stood to see him out.

"I could do no other. I'd protect my heartmate with my life."

Desmond crossed the threshold, and Nicholai reached out a stilling hand. "Before you go, I have something I need to say. Thank you for protecting Julie. You sensed a threat and jumped into action without delay. Even though your assessment was wrong, I understand why you made it and attacked me. The Council has an opening. If you are interested, I'd like to speak to the team about you. I think you would make a good addition to the group."

"I'd be honored." Desmond bowed.

"I'll be in touch." Nicholai grasped Desmond's forearms. "Safe travels."

"And to you," Desmond replied, before waving goodbye to Julie and dematerializing.

Julie closed the door to the cottage and flicked the

lock. She turned and discovered Nicholai holding a *matryoshka* set in his hand. She instantly recognized the set of dolls as the ones she left behind when she fled from his home.

"You left these," he said softly. "I thought you might like them back."

Julie heard a soft rattle when she took them from his hand. She glanced at him, puzzled. "Did you put the necklace back inside?"

A sexy smile spread across Nicholai's face. Mischief lit those beautiful, amber eyes. "Why don't you open them and find out?"

Juliette deftly opened each doll in the series until she arrived at the smallest one. She pulled off the top and dumped the contents into her hand. Her eyes widened at the ring she held. The antique, filigree-style ring had a large white sapphire set securely in a beaded setting. She turned the ring and noted the intricate detail on the sides. The beauty of the ring struck her silent.

Nicholai went down on one knee, taking the ring from her hand. In traditional Russian custom, he slipped it on the ring finger of her right hand.

"My Juliette," he began the proposal. "I have waited centuries to find you. You are the light in my heart, my reason for breathing. Without you, my life has no meaning. You have become the purpose of my existence. Please say you will marry me. Be mine forever."

Julie splayed the fingers of her right hand, noting the way the unique stone sent prisms dancing in the night. Her eyes searched Nicholai's and found sincerity and love. No man had ever looked at her with such stark emotion before. Her heart fluttered.

She could definitely spend eternity with this man. This was the love of her life. She had thought she'd found love with Steven, but she now realized that was only superficial compared to what was between her and the man kneeling before her.

"I'm waiting for your answer," Nicholai prompted, and stood to his full height. He cupped her face between his hands.

Juliette flushed. "Oh, yes! Yes, Nicholai! I'll marry you."

She flung herself into his waiting arms. He bent his head to hers and took her full lips in a searing kiss that left her toes curling into the carpet. She belonged with him, would be his forever. Neither of them would ever experience another day of loneliness. From now on, they would be together, inseparable.

He secured her to his body. His firm hand pressed into the small of her back, fitting her to every detail of his muscular form. Nicholai broke their kiss, taking her breath from her lungs when she looked into his eyes.

His love and sincerity showed there. But most of all, she sensed it. Felt his certainty of it, knew it was the truth. He would never hurt her, never betray her, never tire of her.

Life and death were absolutes, and no one could change what would be. But she would take what came, as long as they could be together. He was worth the risk.

She could trust him to protect them both from all the dangers in the world that would threaten them. He would do anything to stay with her, keep her in his protection. She was his life, and he was hers. Their love for one another could overcome any obstacle. It had to, for Julie would allow nothing less. They would be together, now and always.

Epilogue

Six weeks later

Julie checked her hair and makeup a final time in the mirror above the dresser. Giving her curls a bounce with her hand, she bounded out the door and up the stairs.

She ran into a hard body. A set of thick arms snapped around her like steel bands, taking her from her feet. She gazed into the face of the man, appreciating the strong line of his jaw, the square cut of his handsome face. The way his chestnut hair feathered softly away from his eyes. His chocolate eyes looked on her with a glint of humor.

Julie flushed, aware of all the muscle lurking beneath his tailored suit. She could not help but appreciate the physique.

"Whoa, there. You almost took me out." Marcus's deep voice reverberated against her chest as a smile took his full lips.

The sound of a throat clearing brought her head around before she replied.

"I suggest you put my heartmate down, Marcus."

The second Juliette's feet touched the floor, Nicholai's arm wrapped around her waist and pulled her back against his front in a possessive embrace.

Marcus's hands rose in surrender. "Hey, man, I

was just making sure she didn't hurt herself. She came up those stairs so fast, she almost knocked me over."

Julie turned and placed an arm about Nicholai's waist.

"Uh-huh." A genuine smile took the seriousness from Nicholai's voice. "I just bet she did. I've known you a long time, Marcus. You never let an opportunity to take a beautiful woman in your arms pass you by."

"That was the old me. I have Christina now. She's the only woman for me."

"It is precisely for that reason you are still standing." The warriors shared a chuckle as the three of them ambled into the ballroom.

Juliette's gaze swept the room, taking in all the gorgeous male eye candy. She appreciated the finely sculpted bodies. But they were as lethal as they were beautiful. A chill went down her spine, but she couldn't be sure whether it came from being surrounded by deadly vampires or the low growl that emanated from Nicholai's throat as he stood beside her, obviously reading her thoughts. Perhaps both she admitted to herself as he placed a possessive hand on the base of her delicate neck.

"You know, only an old romantic like you would find your Juliette, literally. Congratulations, man. I'm glad you found your Juliette...Romeo," Marcus quipped with a smirk.

"Down, boy," Christina drawled, coming up behind the couple to lay a delicate hand on Nicholai's shoulder. "You know your heartmate only has eyes for you."

"It is precisely her eyes I am worried about. She seems to be too appreciative of the sights around her."

"Now, now. We girls can always look. We just

can't touch." Christina squealed the final word of her sentence when Marcus goosed her behind.

"Is that so, *cara*?" Marcus planted a kiss on Christina's lips.

"I don't think Juliette should look or touch," growled Nicholai, while his fingers massaged Julie's neck.

"I promise. You are the only man for me." Juliette flashed Nicholai a broad smile that defused the situation instantly.

"Juliette, I think this party needs a little music. I'll play, if you'll sing. How 'bout a couple of songs to lighten the mood?" Christina asked, her southern drawl as smooth as homemade ice cream on a hot summer's day. "This is your engagement party after all."

"I'd love to." Julie gave Nicholai a quick kiss before she sauntered to the grand piano as Christina's introduction echoed in the massive room.

When Juliette started the first verse, the room quieted. The only sound audible was ice rattling in the glasses. All the guests turned to face the duo at the piano. Their rendition of "Swan Song" sounded haunting and beautiful.

Everyone appeared spellbound by the women's performance. After five songs and three encores, the women begged off, needing refreshments.

They crossed to the bar, and the bartender handed them each a drink.

Julie took a sip. "You play amazingly, Christina. How do your fingers move so fast over the keys? They were a blur."

A mischievous smile graced her pale face, lighting her emerald eyes. "I have to be honest. It's the vampire powers. I have unbelievable speed now. It's great. I can play anything. I love being a vampire."

Marcus joined them and laid a hand on his mate's shoulder. "She was made for it. Born to be a vampire. Christina has learned to master her powers quickly. She can even dematerialize, which is unheard of for one who turned so recently."

Julie paused. While she downed the last of her drink, she pondered the pride in Marcus's voice when he spoke of Christina's conversion. Though Nicholai had not pressured her to become a vampire, she realized he believed it would be safer if she did so. To his credit, he seemed willing to give her the time she needed to consider the decision. She appreciated his patience.

"Have you met Kat yet?" Christina took another sip.

Julie shook her head and placed the empty glass on the bar. "Nicholai mentioned her. She is Stephan's heartmate, correct?"

"Yep. She's the beautiful blonde cheerleader-type sitting over there, next to Vlad."

Julie's eyes tracked the area to where a woman sat talking amicably with the scariest vampire in the room. Her blue-gray eyes sparkled on her pretty face. She showed no sign of fear or contempt for the man to whom she spoke. Julie admired her courage.

She leaned closer to Christina and whispered, "She doesn't seem the least bit scared with Vladimir. Is that because she has converted too? Is she a vampire?"

After putting her glass down, Christina laid a friendly hand on Julie's forearm. "Yes. Stephan converted her. But it's not because she's a vampire that she isn't worried about Vlad. She knows if one person so much as implied a threat against her, Stephan would be right there to rip his throat out.

"Being a heartmate has its advantages, sweetie. One of which is you'll never again have to worry about your safety. Our mates put our safety above their own. They would lay down their lives for us. So don't you be intimidated by Vlad or anyone here. Nicholai would never allow anything to happen to you."

Warmth and love flooded Juliette's mind. *She is correct,* lastochka. *I would never let anything happen to you. You will always be safe.*

I believe you, Nicholai. I'm just a little insecure with all these vampires around.

There is nothing to be of concern. They are all my friends…or yours. Every one of them would protect you with their life.

Julie glanced at Desmond who sat talking to Nicholai's sister, Natasha, in the sitting area. Nicholai had invited her friend to the party for two reasons. First, he had known she was a little homesick and could use a familiar face at this party. And second, he had mentioned the man to his fellow Alphas as a possible addition to the team and the men wanted to meet him.

I love you, Nicholai.

And I love you, my little lastochka.

Juliette crossed the beautifully decorated room and joined her sweetheart. The planner had really outdone herself. From the golden couches and matching chairs that made an intimate seating area, to the rich mahogany bar which stood in one corner manned by a gentleman in a black-vested uniform, every detail of the room had been staged to highlight the paintings that encased images of springtime and golden sunsets in gilded frames.

Nicholai took her hand and placed a soft kiss on the back of it then turned his attention onto the two Alphas standing before him.

"It doesn't feel right." Alex raked a hand through his short, blond strands.

Stephan nodded in acquiescence. "I agree. We had all that activity for weeks. People killed or disappearing daily then, bam, nothing."

Alex's brows furrowed over his aquamarine eyes. "Interesting how everything stopped as soon as we began investigating. Kind of makes you wonder, don't it?"

Nicholai popped a bite of caviar in his mouth and considered Alex's observation. "Demetri said he planned on patrolling, even though the activity has stopped. Perhaps he discovered something."

Stephan turned his penetrating, sapphire stare on Nicholai. "I assumed Demetri would be here this evening."

"He said he would be here," offered Julie.

"Where is he?" Alex asked.

"Your guess is as good as mine." Nicholai shrugged.

Stephan's eyes narrowed. "You're worried."

"It is not like my cousin. He said he would come to our party. He should be here."

Alex shifted his stance. "I have an uneasy feeling. Maybe you should try to contact him, Nicholai."

"Already did, both by phone and through our mindlink. I can't reach him."

Julie noticed a tic in Stephan's jaw before he spoke. "That is troubling. If you cannot reach him through your mindlink, something must be wrong."

"Either that or he is ignoring me."

Stephan stood in quiet speculation. "How many places does Demetri have?"

"Three," Nicholai replied.

Julie noted the concern etched in her heartmate's eyes.

"Vlad?" Stephan called.

As Vlad approached the group, he gave Julie a nod of acknowledgment.

Stephan laid a hand on his shoulder. "Vlad, Demetri is unaccounted for. I want you to pop over to Demetri's home here in Russia and see what you can find. Alex, you go to his place in Wyoming, and I'll go to his home in Savannah. Check around, see if you can find any clues as to his whereabouts and report back here within two hours. Marcus, Nicholai, and Desmond will stay with the women."

"I hope Demetri is all right." Julie wrapped an arm around Nicholai's waist.

"If anyone can take care of themselves, it is my cousin." Nicholai gave her shoulders a squeeze. "Let's not let the unknown spoil our special night. Until we find out otherwise, we will assume everything is fine."

Julie watched Kat saunter over on long dancer's legs. She moved gracefully and lithely, like a supple feline. "Let's take our minds off the what ifs. Tell me all about the wedding plans."

"Did someone mention weddings?" Christina called from across the room, then made her way over on quick feet.

"Where did you and Stephan marry?" asked Julie.

"In Vegas. We did a quickie wedding with Marcus

as our witness. Quick, easy. No fuss, no muss. I highly recommend it."

"Oh, no." Christina shook her head and made her auburn curls brush over her shoulders. "I'm looking forward to a big wedding. I want it all: flowers, a catered reception, a large, tiered cake. The whole shebang."

"Me, too." Julie pictured the scene. Nicholai looking dapper in a tux with tails, her in a long flowing gown. "I want a big reception afterward with all our family and friends in attendance."

"Me, too," announced Christina as Marcus came up behind her and circled her waist with his arms. He rested his chin on her shoulder when she continued. "I want everyone there. All the Alphas, their families, heartmates, our friends."

"Sounds like you and Julie will be inviting the same people. Maybe you should share the guest list." Marcus nibbled on his heartmate's ear.

"Sounds like we'll be coming to two weddings back to back. Why not just have them on the same day and get it over with? That way we only have to dress up once," quipped Natasha, joining the group with Desmond on her heels.

"Or better yet, why not have a double wedding," suggested Desmond.

Christina and Juliette's eyes widened simultaneously.

"That's a great idea," the women said in unison.

Each of the women turned to face their mates, but it was Christina who spoke first. "What do you think, Marcus? Can we? Do a double wedding?"

"If it will make you happy, *cara*, then it would

make me happy." Christina jumped into her mate's arms, giving him a hug.

"How do you feel about it, Nicholai?" Julie glanced up at him, excitement tingling over her skin.

"When you look at me like that, I can do no other but say yes." Nicholai placed a kiss on her lips to seal the deal.

The time passed with the group huddled together discussing wedding plans. Julie, concentrating on the plans, almost missed Alex, Vlad, and Stephan materialize one by one into the room.

"Did anyone find something?" Nicholai asked.

Vladimir and Stephan shook their heads.

"There was a half-eaten sandwich and a spilt glass of blood on the kitchen counter in Demetri's house." Alex dropped the volume of his voice. "There were also signs of a struggle not too far from the house. When I remembered Nicholai saying Demetri was patrolling the surrounding forest, I decided to take a walk. Up the trail, I came across a patch of snow that appeared packed down. It looked like someone had been pulled through the snow. I followed the drag marks. They led into the side of the mountain."

"Like the footprints Demetri and I found." Stephan shifted his weight. "Did you notice anything else unusual?"

"No." Alex shook his head. "I sensed nothing, other than several blank spots in the mountain."

"Blank spots?" Nicholai straightened. "I've been sensing voids as well. They happened every time Julie was attacked. Could there be a connection?"

"Perhaps." Stephan rubbed a thoughtful hand over his chin. "Demetri and I sensed voids as well. We definitely should investigate further, but locating Demetri is the priority."

"That doesn't sound good," Desmond observed. "Any idea who would attack Demetri?"

"Knowing him, it might be anyone," a female voice called from the door.

Everyone turned toward the entryway. The woman with short hair sauntered across the room. Her leather duster flared behind her with each step.

She turned her yellow eyes on Alex. "Even his own mother could find a reason to attack a male chauvinist like him."

"Tatiana, you made it." Alex flashed a boyish smile. "I hope you don't mind, Stephan, but I called Tatiana in on this once I discovered the foul play. The VES helped the last time we had a problem. I thought she might be of some help with this."

Nicholai whispered in Julie's ear, "Tatiana Bolovich is an agent for the Vampire Enforcement Squad. She worked with the Alphas on our last case when a fellow Alpha, Michael, went rogue and kidnapped Christina. She gave us intel that helped us close the case."

Dressed in a leather bodysuit and shit-kicker boots, Tatiana looked every bit the femme fatale. Her hair matched her leather, gleaming blue-black as a raven's wing, the ends bluntly cut, stopping just above her shoulders. Her feline-like eyes glared at the males as if daring them to take her on.

"So what's this about Demetri going missing?" she asked.

"I found something suspicious on the property around his place in Wyoming," explained Alex.

"Then you're with me." Her tone allowed no argument. "Tell me how to get to his house. You and I are going there, so you can fill me in and I can have a look around."

"Yes, ma'am." Alex snapped to attention with a smile on his face, appearing all too happy to have a reason to spend time with the sexy woman.

Tatiana rolled her eyes and led him from the room by the crook of his arm without so much as a see-you-later to the rest of the guests.

"All business that one," Desmond remarked, with a tilt of his head.

"You have no idea," Marcus murmured.

The festive mood now broken, the guests left one by one after saying their farewells.

Nicholai led Juliette to their bedroom.

"I'm so sorry about your cousin." Julie wrapped her arms around his neck.

Nicholai's arms encircled her waist. "He is a strong male, a great warrior. I'm sure Tatiana and Alex will uncover what has happened."

"We will hear some good news soon," Julie offered.

"I hope you are correct." His dark brows furrowed. "I worry for my cousin."

"I know you do. Didn't you tell me Demetri is prone to solitude? Perhaps he went somewhere to be alone and think."

"I will be glad when we know something for sure."

"With the Alphas on the case, we are bound to find out something before long." Julie stood on her tiptoes and gave him a peck on the lips. "In the meantime, let's not worry. I'm sure soon we will hear he is safe and sound."

Nicholai smiled. "I love your optimism. In fact, that's not all I love."

He ran the fingers of one hand through her hair. "I love your soft hair."

The fingers traced down her throat. "I love your creamy skin."

"I love your button nose...your rosy cheeks...your sexy lips." He accentuated each named part with a kiss, lastly taking her lips in a searing caress that left Juliette breathless.

When they broke apart, the heat in his amber eyes burned over her. He wanted her, needed her to ease his worry. It was there in his mind for her to see.

Julie's arms tightened around his middle. She leaned in for another taste of him. Her tongue pushed through his lips, explored his mouth. Like chocolate with a hint of brandy, his warm kiss melted her until their bodies became one. Needing a breath, Julie separated their lips and stared up at him. Passion had replaced the concern on his face, like she'd kissed away all his troubles.

"I love you, beloved." Her warrior gazed at her with stars in his eyes.

She found it amazing to have a man regard her as if she were his entire world. He was certainly hers, and she couldn't wait to make their lives together official.

"I love you too, Nicholai."

The smile on his face lit his eyes and lightened her heart. "I'll never tire of hearing you say that.

A word about the author...

Born in Virginia, Brenda Sparks now resides in the Sunshine State. Balancing her writing and personal life is challenging at times, but writing suspenseful paranormal romances is a passion that won't be denied. Her idea of a perfect day is one spent in front of a computer with a hot cup of coffee, her fingers flying over the keys to send her characters off on their latest adventure.

Brenda loves to connect with readers. Please visit her at www.brenda-sparks.com.